A Calm and Gentle Rain

New Hope Falls: Book #10

By

KIMBERLY RAE
JORDAN

THREE**STRAND**
P R E S S

A CORD OF THREE STRANDS IS NOT EASILY BROKEN.

A man, a woman & their God.
Three Strand Press publishes Christian Romance stories
that intertwine love, faith and family. Always clean.
Always heartwarming. Always uplifting.

A CALM AND GENTLE RAIN/ Kimberly Rae Jordan. -- 1st ed.
ISBN-13: 978-1-988409-62-7

When my father and my mother forsake me,
then the LORD will take me up.

Psalm 27:10

CHAPTER ONE

Cecelia Albrecht stared out the front windshield of the car, gripping the steering wheel tightly as she witnessed her suspicions being confirmed. He may have denied it time and again, but she'd been certain he'd lied. It wasn't like he was a paragon of virtue. Geof Stewart had a lot of things going for him, but his character wasn't one of them.

She glanced at her phone in the holder on the dashboard to make sure that it was zoomed in and recording. It was a clear, sunny day, which worked well for what she needed. She hadn't dared park closer, so not having rain to obscure what she needed to capture was definitely a good thing.

Trying to keep her emotions under control, Cece closed her eyes, not needing to see what played out since her phone would capture it all. She should be relieved that she finally had a reason to escape the wretched relationship she'd had with Geof. Instead, all she felt was a sense of failure that, yet again, she hadn't managed to have a successful relationship.

She wondered how long she could keep this latest development from her dad. Probably not long, since Geof would likely call him as soon as everything went down. In her case, it wasn't a good thing that her dad got along so well with the man she'd been dating and now intended to break up with.

Breathing in and out, Cece tried to calm the anxiety that crawled up and down her spine like ants. How had she ended up in this situation? How was this her life?

Asking questions like that was useless. It would change nothing. Breaking up with Geof would change one thing, but everything else would stay the same.

Opening her eyes, she saw that the tableau she'd hoped to capture had ended. She leaned forward to tap the screen of her phone and stop the recording. Not bothering to watch it, Cece tapped out of the camera app and used another one to call for a ride.

It was going to cost a fortune to get back to New Hope, but she had no other options. Her dad would certainly not come get her, and if her dad wouldn't, neither would her mom. Andy might... but she didn't want him mixed up in her break-up with Geof. Even though he'd probably be happy it had finally happened.

With the ride called, she looked into the passenger seat and all the things she'd piled there earlier. Everything Geof had ever bought her. Maybe he could give the stuff to one of his other women friends. He'd been generous with gifts, but they couldn't offset the rest of his horrible behavior towards her.

Cece started the car up and drove it the short distance to his driveway, where she parked it beside the car of the woman who'd arrived a short time ago. Of all the gifts she was returning, the car was the hardest to part with. She wasn't sure how she was going to afford another one, but at least her house was within walking distance of the bakery where she worked.

Resolutely, she got out of the car and made her way to the front door. After a moment's hesitation, she pressed the doorbell and waited, the car keys gripped tightly in her hand.

"Cecelia." When Geof finally opened the door, he glared at her. "What are you doing here? I told you I was busy."

Normally, the hard, angry edge to his voice would have had her retreating. But not that day.

"Yes. I know exactly what you're busy with. I've got it on video for posterity."

Geof's handsome face darkened with anger, and it took everything within Cece to not step back from him.

"What exactly are you playing at?"

Wearily, Cece sighed. "I'm not playing at anything. I'm here to end things, like I should have done long ago."

" *You're* breaking up with *me*?" Geof scoffed. "I don't think so."

"I don't know why you care. You've clearly found my replacement already. Maybe you can give her the car." Cece lifted her hand and dangled the key ring from her finger. "She might also be interested in all the other things you've bought me. Everything is in the car."

Geof snatched the key ring from her, jerking her finger painfully. His eyes narrowed as he stepped closer to her, looming and aggressive. "You're never going to find a man better than me. You're lucky that I put up with your whiny attitude."

Cece fisted her hands at her sides. "Then you'll be happy to see me go."

An alert sounded from her phone, letting her know her ride was there. She glanced over her shoulder and saw a vehicle pull to a stop at the curb.

As she turned to leave, Geof grabbed her upper arm in a bruising hold, forcing her back around. Glaring down at her, he said, "You walk away, don't bother coming back."

"Don't worry." Cece jerked her arm from his grip, trying not to wince at the pain that shot up to her shoulder. "That will never happen."

The fierce anger in his gaze made Cece scared to turn her back on him. But she did, determined not to show him any weakness in that moment. With measured steps, she walked away from him and down the steps to the sidewalk.

A weight lifted from her shoulders with each step she took away from Geof, filling her with the certainty that she'd made the right decision. One she should have made ages ago.

When she reached the waiting car, she confirmed it was her ride, then slid into the back seat. It felt like things were well and truly over between them as the car pulled away from the curb, leaving Geof's house behind.

Though she shouldn't have, Cece couldn't help but glance back. Geof still stood on the porch, his hands on his hips as he stared after the car.

She wished she could have warned the woman who'd gone inside his house that she needed to leave him. Sooner rather than later.

However, trying to push her way into his home would definitely have resulted in more bruises than just to her arm. Thankfully, the one thing that definitely wasn't bruised by this decision was her heart. She'd protected that almost from the start of her relationship with Geof. Love, whatever that was, had not been part of their relationship.

Cece could only hope that the raging storm her life had been over the past year or so would finally calm and allow her to just... rest.

~ * ~

Andy Hale stared at the woman seated across the table from him, trying to focus on what she was saying. This was the third time they'd met for dinner, but he didn't think that anything was going to develop between them. Lynne was one of the nicer women he'd interacted with from the dating app, which was why he'd asked her out again.

Though he'd finally decided that he needed to be more proactive in finding a girlfriend, it wasn't going like he'd hoped. Cece was never far from his thoughts lately, even when he was on a date with another woman. He'd already spent too much of his life focused on someone who would only ever see him as a friend, and sometimes, not even that. Unfortunately, he just couldn't seem to get her out of his mind.

"I used to think I'd like to have a lot of children, but since I started working in the daycare, I've changed my mind."

"Another fun day with the kids, huh?" Andy asked as he cut into the steak he'd ordered.

"That's one word for it. I would use frustrating. I swear they must've all had a Zoom call last night to organize their plan of attack. It was like tag-team tantrums."

Andy managed a smile at that. Tag-teaming toddlers. He hadn't spent much time around kids, although there were a few babies popping up in the Bible study group recently. That wasn't a surprise, however, since there had been several weddings in the past few years.

"Someone needs to take those plastic phones away from them."

Lynne laughed. "The manager needs to send a memo asking the parents to confiscate them."

Andy appreciated her sense of humor, which was one of the reasons he'd asked her out again. Now if he could just find himself attracted to her in other ways. Would that come in time? He had so little experience dating that he didn't know.

Lynne was easy to talk to, so their time together went by quickly. Still, a piece of Andy's heart wished that he could have been what Cece wanted in a boyfriend. They'd known each other for over a decade, however, and nothing had ever changed between them. Since she was currently in a long-term relationship, he'd finally accepted that it never would. Hence, the dating apps.

Once they'd finished their coffee and dessert, Andy was ready to go home. Lynne had insisted on meeting him at the restaurant, so they said their goodbyes on the sidewalk before going their separate ways.

As Andy drove back to New Hope Falls, he tried to keep from thinking about Cece. She wasn't entitled to occupy more of his thoughts than any other friend he had, but that was never the case because of his feelings for her.

If only he could figure out how to relegate Cece to the friend zone and leave her there. But just when he thought he was doing better at that, she'd show up at the bookstore wanting to talk or she'd text him about something. It had been even more common over the past year, for some reason.

When he got home, he let himself into the house he shared with his mom and younger sister. The lingering scent of their dinner hung in the air. Some sort of casserole, no doubt. He was pretty sure his mom had enough recipes that she could make a different casserole for every day of the month. However, she wasn't cooking as much as she used to.

He found his mom in her recliner in the corner of the living room. Some sort of documentary was playing on the television, which she paused on the laptop that sat on the end table beside her when she saw him.

As her world had slowly shrunk to the four walls of their home, Andy had set things up so that her laptop was connected to their television. It had taken her awhile, but she'd eventually figured out how to maneuver between the cable shows she watched and the online streaming services she had on her laptop. She even liked to watch YouTube videos.

"Hi, Ma," he said as he bent to brush a kiss against her cheek, getting a familiar whiff of her perfume. "Enjoy your evening?"

"So far, so good," she told him with a small smile. "How was yours?"

"It was good."

"Do you think there's potential for this one?"

Andy sank down on the ottoman that she kept near her recliner for just that purpose. "I don't know. She's very nice, and we had plenty to talk about."

"That's good."

It was, Andy agreed. But would that grow into something more? Or would she just be someone he could have fun conversations with? Only time would tell.

"Where's Phoebe?"

"She left after supper to spend the night at Aubrey's."

Andy nodded, not too surprised. He knew that Phoebe wished that she could move into an apartment with her best friend. But because of their mom's health deteriorating like it had, it was necessary for them both to be around to help her.

Still, they'd come to an agreement that she could spend a night or two with her friend. He never spent the night away from home, so he was usually around to help his mom in the late evenings. She wasn't totally incapacitated, so most of the time, he and Phoebe's plans depended on how their mom was feeling on any given day.

When his dad had passed away unexpectedly while Andy was still in high school, he'd accepted that it would be his role to support his mom and sister in a way he would not have had to had his dad lived. He knew that his mom felt like she was a burden on him, and that she hated needing his help.

Of course, none of them had foreseen the health issues that would plague her. Those hadn't started until after he'd graduated, and thankfully, he'd still been living at home and able to help her.

"Let me get you some tea." He got to his feet. "I'll be right back."

He didn't bother to ask her what type of tea she wanted, as it was always the same at that time of night. It didn't take long to prepare it in the special travel mug he'd found for her. In the past year, she'd been struggling with weakness in her arms and legs, which would come on without warning. The only way it was safe for her to drink beverages anymore—especially hot ones—was to have them in a travel mug, just in case the weakness manifested itself unexpectedly.

He carried the chamomile blend back to her. "Here you go."

"Thanks, darling."

Sitting back down on the ottoman, he said, "How's the pain?"

Nerve pain had plagued her off and on for years without rhyme or reason, which was highly frustrating for her. She hated not knowing why her body was acting the way it was. The doctors had tossed out possibilities over the years, but none of her symptoms fell neatly into any one box.

So far, he still felt okay leaving her while he worked because he could get home quickly, if need be. His boss understood his situation and had given him permission to close up the bookstore if he needed to help his mom. It hadn't happened yet, and Andy prayed that it never would because it wouldn't bode well for his mom's health if it did.

"About a three," she said, using the zero to ten ranking they'd set up to help him gauge how bad her pain was.

"No extra meds then?"

She shook her head. He knew that she tried not to take anything more than the prescription that the doctor had given her for daily use. It was something else that seemed to be hit or miss on whether it worked.

That was what frustrated them the most, especially his mom. The pain seemed to show up without any cause, requiring her to take extra meds if it got out of control. They'd tried adjusting so many things in her life from her diet to environmental things, but nothing ever made a consistent difference.

"Did you ask her out on another date?" his mom asked, diverting the conversation from a topic she hated, to one she liked: his dating life.

"Not yet. I'll give it a day or two, then maybe see if she'd like to go out again."

His mom frowned at his words. "That doesn't sound good."

"What do you mean?"

"You should be excited about seeing her again. So eager to spend more time with her that you'd text or call her before you go to bed."

That definitely wasn't the case for Andy. "Does it always have to be that way?"

"It was that way with me and your dad."

"That doesn't mean that's the only way to fall in love."

"I suppose, but I'd like to see you a little more excited to spend time with a woman. Hopefully that will come."

Andy hoped that too, because he needed to find a way to move past his feelings for Cece. In the past, Cece had jumped from boy-friend to boyfriend, leading Andy to think she didn't actually love any of them.

Her latest meathead boyfriend, however, had been around for awhile, which made Andy think that perhaps their relationship might actually end in marriage. The idea made him feel a little sick because as far as Andy was concerned, Geof was a horrible man, and Cece deserved better.

"If this one doesn't light a spark in you, I'm sure you could find another one. I just wish there was a nice young lady at church that you were interested in. I'm not keen on you meeting women on your phone."

They'd had plenty of conversations about how he was meeting women to date. The concept of dating apps was completely foreign to his mom, though, so it was likely going to be something they never agreed on. Although, if he found a woman that made him happy and that she liked, she probably wouldn't complain about the apps anymore.

When his mom's phone rang, Andy got to his feet. "I'm gonna head downstairs. I'll be back up to say goodnight a bit later."

He didn't say he'd be back to check on her for bed, but they both knew that was what he'd be doing. In the meantime, he'd go read for a while. He should spend some time working on the book he was writing, but he was stuck at the moment and didn't feel like dealing with it right then. Instead, he'd read the newest release from his favorite suspense author and escape everything in his own life for awhile.

A lack of interest in books had been a definite con about Lynne. Books were sort of his life. They were his job, but they were also his main form of entertainment. He liked TV shows and movies too, but if he had a choice between them or a good book, he'd choose the book every time.

Strangely enough, Cece also liked books. It wasn't something she shared with many people, but since he worked in a bookstore, she'd begun to talk to him about the books she'd read. They'd had some great conversations about them. He'd even read some of her recommendations and vice versa.

As Andy settled into his favorite recliner that was tucked in the corner of his room, his fingers itched to pick up his phone and text Cece. Curling his hands into fists, he counted to twenty, then grabbed his book from the end table and opened it to where he'd left off the previous night.

CHAPTER TWO

Cece didn't have to deal with the full ramifications of her decision until Sunday evening. It was longer than she'd expected, and stupidly, she'd hoped that life would just go on. The pounding on her bedroom door brought her back to reality with a spike of anxiety.

"What were you thinking?" her dad demanded when she opened the door, his bulk filling the space. Not answering his question wasn't an option.

"He has other girlfriends," she said, already knowing that no excuse for the break-up would be valid in her dad's eyes.

He narrowed his gaze at her. "And?"

"And I didn't like it." She always started out standing her ground, even though it would be much easier if she just backed down right away.

"Well, if he had to turn to other women, then I would say the problem is with you."

Cece hated having her dad put into words the thought that had crossed her mind when she'd first realized *why* Geof walked away from her to take calls or answer texts and why he'd told her not to stop by his place without permission.

"You should be glad he was nice enough to give you expensive gifts, even if you were lacking in some areas."

She crossed her arms. "I gave it all back."

"You are just determined to prove how dumb you are. Not that it matters. Geof said he'd take you back, so call him and set up a time to see him so you can apologize."

"I'm not getting back with him."

Her dad's expression darkened. "Yes. You are."

"He hurts me."

If she thought that would change her dad's mind—which really, she hadn't—she would have been disappointed.

"Well, I can hurt you, too. I *need* you to go back to him. I have a business deal that will fall through if I don't have his support."

"Why would he even want me if I'm so terrible?" she asked.

"I didn't care enough to ask. All I care about is that you get back together with him." He lifted a clenched fist and rested it on the doorframe. "Or else."

The trapped feeling that always simmered inside Cece flared up, engulfing her and filling her with despair. She seemed to constantly live her life in that spot between a rock and a hard place. With her dad being the rock and whatever jerk of a boyfriend her dad wanted her to date as the hard place. It was a cycle she couldn't seem to break.

He pointed a finger at her. "Call him."

Cece gave a single nod, just to get him off her back. She'd figure out how to avoid doing that once he wasn't in her face anymore.

Giving her a final glare, he turned and tromped toward the stairs that led back to the main floor. With a shaking hand, Cece closed the door, grateful that the confrontation with her dad hadn't been any worse. There had been plenty of times when she hadn't gotten off so easily.

After leaning against the door and breathing deeply for a moment, Cece locked the door and headed for her bed. She needed a plan of action. More than ever before, she *had* to find a way to break free of her parents.

Her gaze was drawn to her cell phone. She desperately wanted to call Andy, but she knew she didn't dare. Being in such a vulnerable state, she would be tempted to spill everything. She knew that

Andy would listen and sympathize, but she didn't want him to know just how bad things had gotten for her.

Her friendship with Andy and her job were the two good things in her life, and she didn't want to jeopardize either one by spilling the ugliness of her life all over them. So instead of calling or texting Andy, she pulled her journal out of her bag.

Rather than spewing her feelings all over the pages like she'd done every other time she'd written it that week, Cece tried to focus her thoughts on making a plan. It wasn't the first time she'd tried it—and it might not be the last—but she felt a more intense desperation to do so than she ever had before.

The question was, what could she do about her situation?

If she still had a car, she might have considered living in it, just to get away from her dad. Unfortunately, that option was out of the question because Geof now had the vehicle.

She had no friends that would help her. If she hadn't ticked Sarah off, she might have been able to stay at the lodge for a bit. Although she wouldn't have had a way to get to work from there.

As she settled down at the small table in the corner of her room, Cece fought the urge to cry. A part of her wanted to let the tears flow, just to spite her dad, who always told her that only weaklings cried. The problem was that she really did feel weak right then, like all the strength she'd had when confronting Geof had been used up.

Staring at the blank page of her notebook, she gripped her pen and tried to gather her scattered thoughts. A place to live was top of her list. But there was no way she could manage what was needed to secure even the cheapest of apartments.

Her dad charged her board and room, which didn't leave her enough to save for a place of her own. She enjoyed her job at the bakery, but it didn't pay super well. And she didn't have any education beyond her high school diploma, since her dad had constantly told her that she wasn't smart enough to go to college.

There had been no way that he would ever help her pay for college, either.

Place to live.

She wrote it down even though it seemed an unreachable goal. But without that, any other plans she made would be useless.

Car. Yet another impossibility.

How did people do this?

They probably had parents who were willing to help them, as well as friends. Unfortunately, she'd alienated what few friends she'd had. Except for Andy. For some reason, from the moment he'd found her crying under the bleachers in high school, he'd remained her friend. Nothing she did or said seemed to chase him off.

However, their friendship hadn't included sharing much about their living situations. She knew he lived with his mom and sister, and that his mom had been struggling physically, but she didn't know the details. Just like she'd never shared the details of her messed up home life.

Shoving her notebook away, Cece gave up. She was just too stupid to figure out a plan. Though she knew what she needed to do, she couldn't see a way to make any of it happen. She was trapped, just how her dad liked the women in his life.

She didn't want to be like her mom, kowtowed by an overbearing and abusive man. As far as she could see, there was no happiness in her mom's life. But what did she know? It wasn't like they had a close mother-daughter relationship. Certainly not the type of relationship that Sarah McNamara had with her mom, Nadine.

Jealousy burned inside her as she thought of the women who'd once been her friends. They all had happy lives, with men who loved them. Even Jillian had landed a hot firefighter who clearly adored her despite her having gained a ton of weight. She didn't even look like the cheerleader she'd once been alongside Cece and Sarah.

And there Cece was... trapped in a home with the only possibility of escape being another jail with another controlling man.

It wasn't fair.

It just wasn't fair.

The next morning, Cece let herself out of the house, stepping into the cold darkness. Her shifts didn't usually start so early, but Brooke, the owner of the bakery, had asked her to come in and do the early morning baking since she had an appointment. Though it wasn't a long walk, on such a chilly morning, it felt like it took forever, and she really missed the car.

Once inside the bakery, she let go of all the worries and focused on her job. It was one thing that was hers and hers alone. Her dad had no sway over her work there, aside from taking a large chunk of her paycheck.

By the time she opened the bakery at eight, Cece was feeling a little more settled. She was safe within the walls of the shop. Her dad had never stepped foot in the bakery, and she'd be happy if that remained the case.

The bell above the door jingled not long after she'd opened, drawing her from the kitchen in the back. She recognized one of the regulars, Mr. Overmeier, who owned the grocery store down the street.

"Good morning, Cecelia," he said, his voice gruff and loud. Unlike her dad, however, the man was always polite. "How are you doing?"

"I'm fine, thank you." She began to prepare his usual order. "How are you?"

"I'm doing just fine," he said. "Looking forward to the coffee this morning."

"Welcome to early spring in New Hope, right?"

He chuckled. "That's for sure. Can you make a mocha for Julian? I'm sure he'll appreciate a warm drink when he comes in. And throw in a couple of those cinnamon buns as well."

Cece did as he requested, appreciating how good the man was to his employees. He frequently bought drinks or goodies for his staff. His kindness was probably why he didn't have a high turnover of employees. Her dad might have had more luck with his businesses if he treated people better.

"Thank you so much, my dear," the man said as he added some bills to the tip jar. "Have yourself a nice day."

Cece gave him a smile. "You too."

She watched him leave, but before she could return to the kitchen, the door opened again. This time, it was Kieran Sutherland, the police chief.

"Hey, Cece," he said with a nod of his head. "Gonna need an extra-large black coffee this morning."

"Baby keeping you up?" she asked as she grabbed a takeout cup, then moved to where the coffee carafes were located.

"He's actually a pretty good sleeper," he said. "But every once in a while, he reminds us that he *is* a baby. Last night was one of those nights."

"But why are you up with him?" Cece asked. "Doesn't Cara stay home with him still? Or did she go back to work?"

Kieran gave her a curious look, then said, "Well, even though she only has a couple of classes at the studio right now, Cara takes care of him during the day. There's no reason she has to shoulder all his care when I'm around to help her out. So I got up with him once last night, while she got up with him the other time."

The man's willingness to help his wife out like that was a foreign concept to Cece. She would be willing to bet her nearly empty bank account on her dad never having gotten up with her as a baby. Not only that, she was pretty sure her dad had made her mom sleep in a different room so that he wasn't bothered by her getting up with Cece at night.

"I'm sure Cara appreciates that," Cece said. She sure would, if she had a baby.

If her dad had his way, she'd be having children with Geof, and Cece doubted Geof would have any more interest in getting up with a baby than her dad had. He would make sure that Cece knew it was *her* job to take care of the children. She was the woman, after all.

"Thanks," Kieran said as he took the coffee after paying for it. "Have a good day."

Just as she was returning to the front with more pastries for the glass bakery case, another familiar face walked through the door. A welcome one.

"Morning, Cece." Andy's greeting lifted her spirits like none of her other customers had.

His lanky build and slightly mussed appearance hadn't changed a lot since high school. He was taller and broader, but he'd never bulked up like the football players had. He also had a beard that was a bit longer than scruffy length.

"Hi, Andy."

"How's it going this morning?"

"It's been pretty steady," she said. "You know how it is with people and their morning coffees."

"I wouldn't know a thing about that intense desperation first thing in the morning for a coffee." He shook his head. "Not me."

"So you're here for a cup of green tea to start your day?" she asked, feeling like smiling for the first time in days.

"Uh... Are there any other color options?"

She gave a huff of laughter. "Not a green fan, huh?"

"Makes me think of grass. I don't want to eat grass or drink it."

"Milk or water then?" Cece hoped that no one else came in for a couple of minutes, just so that she could have this brief interlude of lightness in her day.

Andy wrinkled his nose, then lifted his hands in surrender. "Fine. Count me in as one of those desperate people."

"Large coffee with one cream and one sugar coming right up."

"Thank you. Thank you."

"If you're that desperate, you should make yourself a cup at home."

The corners of Andy's eyes crinkled as he grinned. "Are you saying that your coffee is the same as what the single cup maker at home makes?"

"Definitely not," Cece said. "But if you're desperate..."

"I can handle that coffee the rest of the day, but I like to start my day with a cup from here."

Cece didn't tell him how glad she was that he did. A comment like that might make things awkward, and she really didn't want that.

After she made him his coffee just the way he liked it, she rang it up, giving him her employee discount. Brooke didn't mind that she used her employee discount for Andy since Cece had no one else besides herself that she ever used it for. And she rarely bought anything for herself either, because she had little money to spare for baked goods.

"Thanks so much," Andy said after taking a sip of the coffee. "Guess I'd better head to work. I'll see you later."

"Yep. Have a good day."

"I will certainly try my best. Hope you do as well."

She watched through the large windows at the front of the shop as he made his way down the sidewalk to the bookstore. With the first customer wave of the day done, Cece took the time to get another round of coffee going and filled any gaps in the items in the bakery case.

Brooke showed up just after ten, smiling as she walked in. The woman wasn't a New Hope Falls native, having moved there when her husband got transferred to the area.

"Good morning, Cece."

"Good morning."

"How's it been so far?" she asked as she unbuttoned her coat and slipped it off.

"Pretty steady."

Brooke glanced over the case as she headed to the back where the kitchen and her small office were located. "No problems with the baking?"

"Nope. Didn't burn anything."

Brooke laughed. "I didn't expect that you would have. You haven't burned anything in ages."

When she'd first begun working at the bakery, Brooke had tried having her bake almost right away. That hadn't gone very well. But in the years since then, Cece had begun to gradually do more of it until she felt comfortable coming in early on occasion and doing all the baking without any sort of supervision.

One thing that Cece had never been able to do as well as Brooke, however, was cake decorating. She could make the cakes, no problem, but Brooke was a pro at the decorating. People came from surrounding towns to order cakes from her.

The next wave of customers that showed up was smaller and included a couple who didn't just grab and go. They usually bought a drink and one of the baked goods before settling at a table with their tablets or laptops. One woman who came in and lingered at a table spent much of her time reading a book that looked like a Bible and making notes.

Cece wasn't sure who she was, but the woman always gave her a warm and friendly smile. She'd only started to come into the bakery in the past few weeks, so Cece suspected she was new to New Hope Falls.

Though she looked to be close to Cece's age, she had less style than Cece. Much of the money Cece had left after paying her dad for board and room went to clothes, makeup, and hair care. She had an image to uphold, after all. As long as she looked good, hopefully no one would care about what else was going on in her life.

This woman, however, didn't appear to care a whole lot about her appearance. She had a much more casual style, and she wore little to no makeup.

Cece knew she was focusing on the woman in order to avoid thinking about her own life, but she couldn't help it. Thinking too much about the mess she was dealing with while she was at work was just asking for trouble. She had to smile at customers, and if she thought too much about what was going on in her own life, she'd scowl at them all.

The last thing she needed was to lose her job because Brooke got complaints from customers about Cece not being friendly.

With that in mind, she picked up the coffee carafe and visited the two women who were currently hanging out in the bakery, offering them a free refill since they'd both ordered plain coffee and not a specialty drink.

For the next couple of hours, she didn't have to deal with her mess of a life, and Cece was determined to enjoy the reprieve.

CHAPTER THREE

Andy finished writing an email to Drake Swanson, the owner of the bookstore. The man was rarely around anymore, and his apartment above the bookstore was empty more often than not. Andy took his absence as a compliment, since it meant that Drake trusted him to run the bookstore well enough without his supervision.

He'd been working for the man since high school, and Drake had also paid for him to take some business admin and finance courses over the years. Now, Drake deferred to him on most decisions regarding the store, which made Andy really happy.

Still, he made it a practice to keep Drake in the loop with regular reports. Andy figured it was better to just send the emails. Drake could choose not to read them if he didn't want to.

The bell over the door jingled, drawing his attention from the laptop. He smiled when he spotted Cece coming in. She stopped by on her break sometimes, but this was a little later than usual.

"Hey there," he said. "Taking a late break?"

She shook her head. "I'm done for the day. I was in early to do the baking since Brooke had an appointment."

"Do you do any baking at home? Or is it just at the bakery?"

"I don't do any baking or cooking at home." Cece glanced away from him, her gaze traveling around the store. "Mom does it all."

In all the years they'd known each other, he'd never met her parents. They hadn't even shown up at Cece's graduation from high school. She'd said that they'd been on a business trip or something. Andy wasn't sure he believed her, but questioning her on that hadn't been worth risking their friendship over.

Andy crossed his arms and leaned a hip against the counter. "I've gotten pretty good at making toast, grilled cheese, and fried eggs."

Cece gave a huff of laughter. "Spoken by someone who doesn't have to watch their weight."

He knew that was a hot topic for her, so he just let it go. "Did you have a good day, even though it started a lot earlier?"

"Yep. Pretty much the same old, same old. I do enjoy coming in early since it's quiet. I like working on my own like that."

Yet something else he'd learned about her over the years. Given she'd been a cheerleader in high school and had constantly been in the presence of the other cheerleaders, he had assumed she liked to be around people all the time. In fact, the opposite was true. She seemed to much prefer being on her own.

"Did you come in for anything specific today? Or just to hang out with me for a bit?"

She rolled her eyes at him, then said, "Do you have anything new and interesting?"

"Nope. I've only ordered in old and boring stuff."

"Well, then I guess there's nothing to interest me," she said with a laugh. "But maybe I'll just wander around to make sure."

Andy watched her head for the section of the store where he displayed the stationery products. He had a few customers who came in regularly and bought notebooks, planners, and pens, even though they weren't interested in the books. He'd discovered that certain people appeared to have an addiction to stationery products. The fancier, the better.

Cece was one of those people, though she didn't buy the most expensive of the items he stocked. Josie Thompson was one of his customers who did, however. She'd asked him to let her know whenever he got new stock in.

Josie would probably be stopping by in the next week or so because her boss ordered books from Andy on a fairly regular basis. He had a couple of titles coming in soon for the man.

Andy attached the file he'd prepared for Drake, then sent the email off. After that, he looked over the list he'd been making for his next book order while he waited for Cece to reappear. Though he would have liked to wander the store with her, just chatting about life in general, he knew he had to treat her like a wild animal. One wrong move, and she'd bolt away.

He knew that many people didn't understand his friendship with Cece, and how he tended to protect her. Some of those people were also people he considered friends—like Jillian Ward and Sarah McNamara Allerton. But he'd seen Cece in a situation that no one else had. While they assumed she was mean or difficult all the time, Andy had seen behind the hard façade she presented to the world.

"You got some new pens in," Cece said as she wandered back toward the desk.

"Yep. Did you find one you liked?"

Her gaze didn't meet his, going instead to the windows of the store. "Not today. The one I've got still works."

"Not writing much lately?"

Her gaze darted to his then, and she frowned. "Oh, I've been doing plenty. Just haven't run out of ink yet."

"If you see one you'd like, I can set it aside for you until you need it."

She seemed to consider that for a moment before going back to the stationery section. When she returned, she set a fancy black gel pen down on the counter.

"So you'll keep this one for me?" Cece asked.

"Yep. I will." He had no idea why she wasn't just buying it. She wasn't usually known for restraining herself when she wanted to buy something in the store. It made him wonder if something was wrong. He took the pen and opened a drawer in the counter to lay it inside. "Whenever you want it, just let me know."

Though she nodded, she seemed a bit distracted, making Andy want to ask her if something was wrong. She had shared personal things with him in the past, but it was definitely hit and miss. Too often, she'd clam up and go on to avoid him if he pressed her when she seemed upset about something. In a few instances, she'd eventually let him know what was bothering her.

"I broke up with Geof."

Well, that hadn't taken too long. He wanted to tell her how glad he was that she'd taken that step, but instead, he just said, "I'm sure that was a difficult thing to do."

"Yeah. He didn't want me to end it."

Andy frowned. "Did he threaten you?"

Cece wrapped her arms around herself and shrugged. "I'm fine."

That didn't reassure Andy at all. None of the boyfriends that Cece had had over the years had been great, in Andy's opinion, but Geof was definitely the worst. He was convinced that the guy had gotten physically aggressive with Cece, though she'd never confirmed that.

The first time Andy had seen bruises on Cece's wrist, he'd asked her about them. She'd gotten mad at him and told him to mind his own business. It had been hard, but he had done as she'd asked.

People probably would say that he catered too much to her, and that he should stand up to her when she got testy and irritable with him. There were days when even he didn't understand why he didn't just walk away from her. If someone asked him *why* he stuck with Cece, Andy wasn't sure what he'd tell them.

"I had to give the car back."

"Wait." Andy held up his hand. "Your car was actually his?"

"He gave it to me, so I felt like I had to give it back when I broke up with him."

"What are you going to do without a car?"

"Get more exercise?" she said, her tone deceptively light.

"Be serious."

"I am." She shrugged again. "It's not like I go anywhere that I'm not able to walk to."

Andy knew that wasn't true. She liked to go to movies and to watch musical theater in Everett or Seattle, but in order to do that, she needed a car. The closest thing New Hope had to theater was the high school drama presentations.

"Well, if you need to go somewhere that requires a car, give me a call. If I'm available, I'll give you a ride."

"Thanks," she said. "But I think I'll just be sticking close to home for the time being."

"Has Geof been in contact with you since the break-up?"

"Not with me, no."

"Not with *you*?" Andy narrowed his eyes at her. "Who *has* he been in contact with?"

"No one important. You know how it goes."

Unfortunately... or maybe fortunately... he didn't know how it went because he hadn't been in a relationship serious enough to warrant a break-up. He didn't say that, though. His dating life, or lack thereof, had rarely been the subject of their conversations.

"Well, if he goes stalkerish on you, let the police know."

"Yeah. Sure."

Cece's cavalier attitude toward the type of man Geof had shown himself to be made Andy want to give her a shake. But unlike Geof, he would keep his hands to himself.

"I'd better go," Cece said, her gaze meeting his again.

Andy was used to her abrupt conversation shifts, so he just nodded. But then, for some reason, he felt the need to remind her that he was there for her. "Remember to call me if you need a ride."

She flashed him a smile that might have made his heart skip a beat if not for the deadness in her eyes. "I will."

Andy let out a sigh as the door closed behind her. He shifted to watch her walk down the sidewalk in the direction of her house. It was a good thing it wasn't raining, or he might have been tempted to close the store for ten minutes and drive her home.

This woman... She brought out the protective side of him, even when she pushed him away. And now, just when he was starting to date, she was available again. Except... even when she was *available*, she'd never been available to him.

He seriously doubted that this time would be any different. She'd never gone for a guy like him, and there was no reason to think that she'd change now. Still, there was a flicker of hope. But honestly, it was an insane hope, and one that he shouldn't even harbor considering the differences in their lives.

In truth, he wondered if he should even pursue a relationship with *anyone* at this point in his life. It wasn't like he could get married and leave his mom on her own. Any woman he got serious with would have to be super special because she'd need to understand that, at least for the time being, he and his mom were a package deal.

While there was a part of him that had kept that spark of hope alive since high school that Cece would one day wake up and fall in love with him, a larger part knew that wasn't ever going to happen. And it was more than just him not being the type of guy she usually dated. She wasn't a Christian, and if there was something his dad had impressed upon him before his death it had been that any woman Andy was considering a serious relationship with should be someone whose heart was in tune with God.

That was definitely *not* Cece. So he'd carry on with their unique friendship and pray that at some point, she'd come to understand that she had in value in God's eyes and that she was worthy of a guy who would treat her well.

He pulled open the drawer and took the pen out. Though he was sure he wouldn't forget it was there for her, Andy wrote her name on the front of an envelope, then slipped the pen inside. After putting it back in the drawer, Andy turned his attention to the next item on his to-do list.

He had a very consistent schedule for the hours at the store. Because the hours weren't extensive, he was the only employee. From Tuesday to Friday, he was in the store from ten until six, and on Saturday he was in from nine until five. Drake had given him permission to hire a part-time employee, but he hadn't felt the need to yet. Everyone knew the store was closed on Sunday and Monday, so they planned accordingly.

A short time later, the bell above the door jangled again, drawing Andy from the small storeroom where he'd been prepping some books for return. A young woman lingered near the counter, and when she spotted him, a smile lifted the corners of her mouth.

"Hey there," Andy said with a smile in return. "Can I help you with something, or are you just looking around?"

She gripped the strap of the bag that was slung across her body. "I... uh... was wondering if you were hiring."

"No, I'm sorry, we're not. This is pretty much a one-person business."

"Aw. That's too bad. I've always loved bookstores, and I thought it'd be cool to work in one."

"Well, I have to say that it's been my dream job." Andy moved to stand behind the counter. "I don't think I've seen you in here before. Are you new to New Hope? Or just new to the bookstore?"

"I'm new to New Hope. My husband and I have just moved to town. My in-laws live here, and we're staying with them."

"Welcome to New Hope. I hope you're enjoying it here."

She nodded. "I am. Very much so. I'm still hoping to find a job, though. Do you know of anywhere else that might be hiring?"

"I can't say for certain, but I'm sure that most businesses around here would be open to you inquiring. If they aren't hiring, they might be able to point you in the direction of someone who is. Have you asked anywhere else?"

"Not yet. I've been into most of the businesses on this street, just to get a feel for things. You're the first person I've gotten the nerve up to ask about a job."

"Well, I'm sorry I wasn't able to give you a better answer."

Her smile came easily. "No worries. I guess it just wasn't God's will for me to work here. Perhaps He has something better for me."

Andy's brows rose at her reference to God. "Have you visited any of the churches here yet?"

She shook her head. "My in-laws attend a church in another town, so we've just been going with them."

"Well, if you're looking for a local church, the one I attend is great. I can give you the information for it if you'd like."

"That would be great," she said, her smile growing. "We'd like to find a church of our own."

Andy picked up one of the business cards he kept on the counter and held it out to her. "This is all the information about the church. Pastor Evans is wonderful, and he'd be happy to answer any questions you might have about the church."

"Thank you so much." She beamed at him. "I'm glad that I came in here."

"Well, if you like books, be sure to come back. I try to stock a good selection of Christian fiction and non-fiction, but I can order anything you might want. Just let me know."

"I will definitely be back," she said. "But I'd better be going now."

"I'm Andy Hale, by the way."

"Mia Walker."

She shook his hand when he held it out, then said goodbye and left, turning in the opposite direction from what Cece had taken.

It had been awhile since anyone had asked for a job at the store. Most people who moved into New Hope these days seemed to commute to one of the nearby cities or towns for work. It was kind of nice that New Hope hadn't died out, even though each year, it seemed that the majority of its youth left when they graduated from high school.

He could see that urge in Phoebe now. If she had the option, she'd probably be living in Seattle. Andy was glad that he'd never wanted to leave New Hope. If he had, he probably would have struggled a lot when it became clear that he'd need to stay with his mom.

But he was basically content with his life, though admittedly he wasn't completely content with his single status. Since he wasn't confident that would ever change, he knew he needed to not let it become a seed of discontent in his heart, making him upset with God because he didn't have any prospect of a romantic relationship.

CHAPTER FOUR

Even though she really wanted to, Cece managed not to stomp her way down the sidewalk to the bakery. That was a good thing, though, since the water in the puddles would have splashed up on her jeans. It was those puddles, and the rain that had created them, that made her mad.

It was a stupid thing to be angry over because rain was frequent occurrence in New Hope Falls. Still, she would have been much happier if it had been a clear day like the previous one. Now that she was without wheels, the rain was particularly annoying.

She glanced in the large front window of the bookstore as she passed it, but its interior was dark since Andy wouldn't open it for a couple more hours. Her visit to the store the day before hadn't been planned, and she should really try to avoid it in the future because the temptation to spend money there was high. If the stationery products didn't tempt her, the books would.

That was probably the only good thing about not having a car anymore. It would keep her from going to most of the places where she liked to spend money. The bookstore, however, was an accessible temptation that she probably wouldn't be able to avoid as much as she should.

When she got to the bakery, she closed her umbrella, grateful that the store had a small overhang above the door. She gave the umbrella a shake, then let herself inside. There was light spilling out from the kitchen in the back of the shop, and the aroma of baked goods filled the air.

"Morning, Brooke," Cece said when she spotted the woman icing cinnamon buns on the large stainless steel work surface in the kitchen.

"Good morning." She flashed Cece a smile that looked a little weary.

Cece went into the small room Brooke had set up for them to leave their bags and jackets in. She stuck her things in her small locker, then went back to join the woman.

"Do you need me to do anything before I start to prep the front?"

"Actually, I wanted to talk to you for a minute before we get busy."

Cece felt a bolt of alarm shoot through her. Was this one more thing that was going to go wrong in her life? She couldn't afford to lose her job, but she didn't think she'd done anything to warrant that. Maybe she could have been friendlier to customers. Would Brooke give her a second chance if she promised to do better?

"I hired someone yesterday," Brooke said as she sat down on one of the stools she kept around the table.

"You hired someone?" That sounded even worse. "I wasn't aware that you were looking."

"I wasn't, to be honest, but something has come up that is going to change things for me."

"Is everything okay?"

"Everything is great," Brooke said, a smile wreathing her tired features. "After many years of trying to conceive, John and I had accepted that it would just be the two of us. Lately, I have been really tired and not feeling great. When I went to the doctor a couple of weeks ago, I found out that I was pregnant."

"That's great."

"It is," Brooke agreed with a beaming smile. "And after much discussion with John, we've decided that I'm going to step back from my active role here at the bakery."

"So you hired someone to manage it?"

Brooke shook her head. "Actually, I hired someone to do your job so that you could step into mine."

"Really?" Relief flooded Cece, along with some excitement. "You want me to do the baking?"

"I'll still take care of the bookkeeping side of things, and I'll continue to do the specialty cake orders we get. However, I'd like you to take over the day-to-day baking side of things, so you'd have to come in early."

"I can do that," Cece said, not even needing to think about it.

"Wonderful! You've proven yourself capable of doing the baking, so I'm sure you'll be just fine."

"I haven't burned anything recently," Cece agreed. "But if you want to introduce any other baked goods, you might have to help me at first."

"That's definitely not a problem. I don't mind coming in sporadically. I just want to make sure that I'm getting plenty of rest and am able to enjoy this pregnancy. This might be the only one I experience."

"How have you been feeling?" Cece hadn't been close to anyone who was pregnant, so she didn't know how things were supposed to go.

"Really, really tired," she said. "And I've had a lot of nausea. Though thankfully, I haven't thrown up at all yet."

"That's good."

"It is," Brooke said with a nod. "Poor John would probably lose his mind if I started throwing up. He already wants to bundle me up in bubble wrap for the next seven months."

Cece felt envious of Brooke and her relationship with her husband. John stopped by all the time, and he was always friendly towards Cece and the other staff. It was also clear that he absolutely adored Brooke.

For no apparent reason, the man would show up with flowers or candy. One time, he'd even shown up with a necklace for Brooke that he said he'd bought when he saw it because it reminded him of her. They had been married a long time, but they still seemed really close.

"But he's happy, right?"

A smile softened Brooke's features. "Yeah. He's over the moon. I know that he's going to make a great dad."

Unlike hers, Cece thought. Brooke and John's baby would be very lucky.

"Anyway, I will give you a raise to go with the job," Brooke said. "Because this will be more responsibility for you."

"I really appreciate that," Cece told her. Already her mind was spinning with how helpful the extra money would be. She just wished there was a way to keep her dad from finding out she had extra money coming in.

"You've been a great employee," Brooke said. "I feel completely comfortable handing over this responsibility to you."

Cece didn't know what to do with the rush of warmth that flooded through her. It was so rare that anyone expressed any appreciation for her or her efforts. To have this conversation go from worrying that she was going to lose her job to her getting a raise and additional responsibilities was shocking.

She couldn't wait to tell Andy. Given her situation at home, she had no one there to share the good news with. She certainly wasn't going to tell her dad, and telling her mom was just like telling her dad, so she wasn't going to say anything to her either.

It had been something she'd learned very young. Anything she told her mom, her mom told her dad. While other girls might confide things in their moms, Cece learned that she couldn't have that sort of relationship with her mom.

The only person who would probably care about this news was Andy. She could hardly wait until he came to get his coffee that morning so she could tell him about her conversation with Brooke. Maybe everything was going to work out after all.

A short time later, the new employee showed up. Cece frowned for a moment, realizing that she was the woman who had been coming into the shop each day to sit at one of the tables.

"Cece, this is Mia." Brooke laid a light hand on Cece's arm. "Mia, this is Cece. She's going to train you for the job."

Mia gave Cece a friendly smile. "I'm really looking forward to working here."

Cece was a little leery of the woman, but she smiled in return, knowing that it was important that she make this work. "It is a great place to work."

"I've seen how nice it is from spending some time here."

"I thought I recognized you."

Mia smiled. "Yep. That was me."

"Well, come on back to the office so I can get all the paperwork sorted out and share a bit more about your position here. When we're done, Cece will show you how things work here."

After Mia had gone into the back with Brooke, Cece stood for a moment, wondering if she should start her usual morning prep, or if she should wait for Mia so that she could show her. She glanced at the clock, then decided she needed to do her usual things because people were going to be coming in, expecting their coffee and baked goods to be ready.

Over the next half an hour, Cece got the coffee going and stocked the bakery cases. When Mia and Brooke reappeared, Cece was in the middle of serving two customers. They stood to the side, waiting until Cece was finished.

"We don't tend to get large rushes of customers," Brooke said. "But first thing in the morning, we do have a steady stream of people wanting their morning coffees. Cece does a great job of keeping it all running smoothly."

Cece hoped that she'd be able to train Mia well. She wasn't known for her patience, and after how challenging she'd found her role when she'd headed up the reunion planning, she wasn't sure she was supervisor material.

When Andy walked in, Cece was surprised to see Mia give him a smile and a little wave.

"I got a job here," she said as he approached the bakery case.

"That's wonderful. I'm glad you found something."

"This was the next place I asked after you said you didn't have any openings, and Brooke said that it was perfect timing because she'd just decided she needed to hire someone."

"A real answer to prayer for you, huh?"

"Definitely." Mia nodded, her smile sparkling. "Most definitely."

Cece wasn't sure how she felt about Mia's and Andy's interaction. She couldn't share her own news now because he was already excited for someone else, and hers would feel rather anticlimactic.

Actually, she did know how she felt. She was a little angry. Andy was her one friend. The one person she looked forward to seeing when he came into the bakery to get his coffee each morning. Now he'd be smiling and chatting with Mia.

"Hey, Cece," he said, *finally* turning his attention toward her. "How are you doing today?"

"I'm fine." She knew her tone was a little snippy, but she couldn't seem to help herself. "Here for your usual?"

"Yep."

As Cece moved to make it, Mia said, "Maybe I should make it, so I start to learn what the regulars like."

When Cece hesitated, Brooke stepped in. "I think that's an excellent idea. Why don't you tell Mia what you usually get, Andy?"

"Sure," Andy agreed, though he looked at Cece with a frown.

She busied herself with other things while Andy recited his order to Mia. It was a simple enough order, so there wasn't much

Mia could mess up. When Mia rang the coffee up, Brooke said, "Andy is a good friend of Cece's, so she usually gives him her employee discount."

"Okay," Mia said with a nod.

"We don't indiscriminately give out a discount, but since Cece doesn't use it for anyone else, I gave her permission to use it for Andy."

"Thanks, Brooke," Andy said with a grin. "Although your coffee is so good I wouldn't have a problem paying full price."

"Well, in that case..." Brooke laughed, and Mia and Andy joined in.

Cece didn't feel like laughing. Why she was reacting so badly to Mia and Andy being friendly with each other, she didn't know. She'd never had a problem with him interacting with Sarah and Jillian. Well, not much of one anyway.

Andy picked up his coffee and took a sip. "Tastes good."

Mia beamed. "I can't take credit for the coffee yet, since Cece still made it this morning. Hopefully I'll be the one making it soon."

Where Cece had initially felt only happiness at the new responsibilities that Brooke had offered her, she now was feeling a bit of unease at giving up the things she had been doing. She didn't want to not be able to make Andy his coffee each morning. No doubt Mia would win over their regulars and have them smiling and chatting with her in no time.

"Hope the rest of your day goes well, Cece," Andy said as he moved closer to where she stood.

"Thanks." She gave him a small smile. "Hope yours does as well."

Andy returned her smile, then he said goodbye to Brooke and Mia before leaving the store. Cece watched him go, but then turned her attention back to the sleeve of takeout cups she was adding to their dwindling stock.

"Do you feel comfortable on your own out here for a bit?" Brooke asked. "I'd like to have Cece spend a little time in the kitchen with me."

"Yep," Mia said, excitement clear in her voice. "And if I need help, you're not far away."

"That's true." Brooke turned to Cece. "Come on back when you're done with that."

After Brooke had gone back to the kitchen, Cece finished transferring the sleeve of cups.

"So what should I do while there are no customers?" Mia asked.

Cece glanced around, looking for things that the last shift of the previous day might not have gotten around to doing. "You can wipe down the glass on the cases. I usually do it a couple of times during my shift, as people like to touch it when they're looking at the baked goods."

She showed Mia where they kept the cleaning supplies. "The last shift is supposed to wipe down all the tables, but I tend to do it again in the morning, just in case they didn't get around to it. Basically, we want the shop to be as spotless as possible since we're selling food."

"That makes sense," Mia said with a nod. "I noticed how clean it was when I came in."

"That's what we want all customers to think. The last thing we want is a complaint about cleanliness."

"So, is Andy your boyfriend?" Mia asked.

Cece froze, then frowned at her. "My boyfriend?"

"Yeah. I thought maybe since you gave him a discount that he was your boyfriend or something."

"No. He's not my boyfriend. Just a... good friend." It felt weird to call him that because there were times it didn't feel like they had a friendship, and yet at other times, they had something that felt like so much more than just friends. But most people wouldn't understand what she and Andy had... and some days, that included her. "I've known him for a long time. We went to school together."

"He seems like a really nice guy. I talked to him at the bookstore, and he also gave me information on the church he attends."

Cece didn't know what to say to that, so she just nodded. "I'd better see what Brooke wants."

As she walked into the kitchen, she found Brooke sitting at the worktable, a large binder in front of her. Cece recognized it as the one she used to keep the recipes they used in the bakery.

Trying to push aside her irritation from earlier, she approached the table. She needed this change to work because it might be a way for her to save up money so she could get a place of her own sooner rather than later.

"I really think Mia is going to work out great," Brooke said when she looked up. "Though I'm sure our regulars are going to miss seeing your lovely smiling face each morning."

"I'm certain Mia will charm them all soon enough." Cece was proud that she managed to keep the sarcasm out of her voice.

"She's still on probation, though," Brooke said. "I want to make sure that she's a good fit over the next month. If she's not, then we'll find someone else."

Cece nodded her agreement. Though she didn't have particularly positive feelings toward Mia at the moment, she didn't really know anything about her. It was possible she needed this job as much as Cece needed her new position. As long as she actually did the work and was nice to the customers, Cece wouldn't say anything to Brooke that would jeopardize Mia's job in the bakery.

She could be testy and maybe even mean at times, but she wasn't completely heartless.

CHAPTER FIVE

Just after noon, Andy caught a glimpse of Cece as she walked by the bookstore. She held an umbrella as she hurried along the sidewalk. He waited to see if she'd even look in the window, but she just kept walking, head bent down.

He hadn't seen her when he'd gone into the bakery that morning. For the second day in a row, Mia had taken care of his order, giving him the discount that he hadn't been aware Cece was giving him.

He had enjoyed his little interaction with Mia, but he'd wished Cece had been around too. He was concerned about what was happening with her at the bakery, given that Mia was working her shift.

And now she'd just marched past his store like she'd forgotten it was even there. It was almost like she was mad at him, but Andy had no idea why she would be. He wanted to stop her to find out what was going on in her mind.

If she'd tell him... Unfortunately, he had enough experience with her to know that she'd likely brush him off.

Glancing at the time on his phone, Andy frowned as he realized that she was also leaving the bakery earlier than she normally would. Was she doing the baking again? He knew she did it once in a while, but since she'd just done it a few days ago, he didn't think she'd be doing it again so soon.

Had she lost her job? Or quit? He doubted that she'd quit without good reason, because she enjoyed her position in the bakery.

As he focused on his work, Andy debated on texting her, even knowing that she probably wouldn't discuss anything over text.

Finally, his own need to make sure she was okay overrode his common sense where she was concerned. With phone in hand, he settled down on the stool he kept behind the counter.

Hey! Missed seeing you at the bakery this morning. Everything okay?

Though she didn't answer right away—which wasn't a surprise— Andy felt better for having reached out. He set his phone down and turned his attention back to his work.

It was almost half an hour before his text alert chirped. Even from where he stood at a shelf near the back of the store, he heard it. Hurrying back to the counter, he snatched up his phone.

Lynne: *Hi Andy! Hope your day is going well. Just wondering if you were available this weekend. I won some tickets to a newly released movie.*

Andy knew he shouldn't feel disappointed that the text wasn't from Cece, but he did. He still wasn't sure that he could see a future with Lynne, so he wasn't sure how to respond.

With a sigh, Andy sank down on the stool. What was a good length of time to wait to see if something could work with someone? It wasn't that Lynne wasn't nice. She was sweet and funny and a Christian. But for some reason, Andy didn't feel a connection with her the way he hoped he would with a potential life partner.

He wasn't interested in dating just for the sake of dating. He wanted a relationship that would hopefully lead to marriage. So, if he didn't feel like there was hope for more than just a friendship, he didn't see the sense of wasting his time, or hers, by continuing to date.

Andy sat staring at the phone screen for a minute, trying to formulate a response. It felt like he needed some guidance to know what to do when it came to stuff like this. But guidance from whom?

Looking up, he considered his options. Did he want advice from a man or a woman? He and Tanner Mikkelson had forged a friendship of sorts, starting when they'd served on the reunion committee together. The man clearly knew about relationships, since he was in one with Emma Clarke. He could also call Sarah, who he was pretty sure would be more than happy to give him relationship advice.

It was kind of embarrassing, though. Other people seemed to know how to navigate relationships and everything that came with them, while he was stumbling around in the dark.

The door to the bookstore opened, and Andy frowned when he saw Geof walk in. He wore a navy suit that looked like elves had sewed the pieces of it together while it was on his body. It fit him like a glove.

Feeling like he needed to meet him standing up, Andy got to his feet as the muscular man made his way to the counter.

"Looking for something to read?" Andy asked, though he wasn't sure Geof ever cracked a book. At least not the kind that Andy carried in the store.

"Nothing you'd have," Geof scoffed.

So they agreed that Andy wouldn't stock the type of books that Geof read. It wasn't an insult, as far as Andy was concerned.

"Well, the sign outside says *Bookstore* and not *Gym* or *Steroid Dispenser,* so feel free to move along."

Geof growled. Honest to goodness growled. "You're pretty mouthy for such a scrawny guy."

"Compared to you, most of the world would be considered scrawny, so I'm in good company."

"And yet, you're alone in here," Geof said as he glanced around the store.

Andy glared at him. "Are you *threatening* me?"

Geof's smile was slimy and mocking. "You're no threat to me."

"So, what are you doing here?" Andy said with a sigh.

"I'm here to have a conversation."

"I can't believe that we have anything to talk about."

"Oh, you're not going to talk," Geof said. "You're going to listen."

"Hate to tell you this, but that's not the definition of a conversation. That's more in line with a lecture, and since you're not my parent or my teacher, I don't have to listen to you."

Geof narrowed his beady eyes. Okay, his eyes weren't exactly beady, but since Andy thought of the man as a snake, the description fit.

"If you know what's good for you—and for Cece—I would advise you to listen to my *lecture.*"

Andy sighed and picked up his phone, tapping the contacts to find Kieran. He brought the screen up, then set his phone on the counter, out of reach of Geof.

Geof glared at him. "What are you doing?"

"Oh, I've just brought up the number for the police chief. If you get out of line, I won't hesitate to call him."

The man's expression darkened. "You're such a wimp that you have to stand behind the police chief."

"I might be a wimp, but I'm a smart wimp."

"Whatever," Geof scoffed. "You need to tell Cece that she'd better reconsider this breakup."

"Why on earth would I tell her that?" Andy asked. "As far as I'm concerned, her breaking up with you was the smartest thing she's done in a long time."

Andy wouldn't have thought that the man's glower could get any more intense, but apparently it could. His reaction was a bit frightening, if Andy was going to be honest. He knew that if their encounter turned physical, he would definitely come out on the losing end.

Still, for Cece's sake, he would stand his ground with this brute of a man.

"Cece will suffer if she chooses not to come back to me."

Andy stared at the man, trying to push his own anger into his expression. He knew he was playing a dangerous game with a man who was much stronger than he was, but the last thing he'd ever do was tell Cece she should get back together with him.

"From what I saw, she was suffering *with* you. No one should ever put their hands on someone else the way you put your hands on her."

Geof smirked. "That's between Cece and me."

"Not anymore, it's not. She kicked you to the curb, so you need to just keep walking."

"Ah, but if I do that, she's going to be the one on the street."

"What are you talking about?" Andy asked, not afraid to express his confusion because he needed to understand what was going on with Cece. He was pretty sure she wasn't going to be the one to tell him what was happening with Geof.

"Let's just say that Cece's dad needed some money and business help, and I offered to give him a hand."

"Then your issue is with him, not Cece."

"Oh, but Cece is part of the deal we struck."

Andy felt a little sick. What on earth was going on in Cece's life? His phone text alert sounded, but he didn't check to see who it was.

"What does that even mean?" Andy demanded.

"It means that Robert Albrecht needed some help, and I offered it to him."

"Out of the goodness of your heart, right?"

Geof laughed. "I didn't get to where I am in the world doing things out of the goodness of my heart."

"So Robert owes you what?"

"If Mr. Albrecht wants to continue to receive my help, which is allowing him to keep control of his business and his home, he will uphold his end of our bargain."

"You're crazy," Andy said. "Who would agree to a deal that included their daughter the way you're saying Cece's dad did?"

"A desperate man." Geof's expression was scary in its glee. "Robert Albrecht is a desperate man."

Andy wanted to punch Geof in the face. He couldn't even come close to comprehending the sort of person Geof was. To take advantage of a desperate man that way was just wrong on so many levels. So, so wrong.

"You must be a desperate man yourself."

"Why would you say that?" Geof said with a scoff.

"Well, apparently you can't get a girlfriend without blackmailing her into being with you. That smacks of desperation, bro." Andy shook his head. "Real desperation. Not a good look on a man."

"Almost as desperate as a wimpy man who loves a woman who will never give him a second look."

Andy clenched his teeth, trying not to let Geof see how his words gutted him. "You need to leave. I'm not going to pass on your message, so you might as well go."

Geof made a show of slowly glancing around the store. "Maybe you should worry about your own business."

"I'm not worried about the bookstore," Andy said. He was quite sure that Drake could out muscle this guy. Not physically perhaps, but Drake was not a pushover when it came to business and money.

"Talk to Cece. If you care about her, you'll tell her to get back together with me."

Andy didn't respond, just stared at the man. Finally, Geof gave him one last smirk, then turned and sauntered from the store.

Alone again in the store, Andy tried to figure out what he should do. Finally, he decided to give Kieran a call. What was the use of knowing the police chief if you couldn't ask him for advice?

"Hi, Kieran. This is Andy," he said when the man answered his phone.

"Hey there, Andy. How's it going?"

"Well, at the moment, I'm a bit annoyed and confused." At the prompting of the man, Andy shared what had happened with Geof. "I realize he didn't actually assault me, but the whole encounter has left me feeling a little uneasy. Not just for me, but for Cece as well."

"That's completely understandable," Kieran said. "No one enjoys being threatened. Do you think Cece would speak to me about what's gone on?"

Andy sighed. "I'm almost certain she's not going to talk to *me* about this, so the likelihood she'll talk to you is non-existent."

"I think you should talk to her about it, and maybe try to impress on her the importance of protecting herself from this guy."

"I realize that you probably don't know Cece at all, but she has got to be one of *the* most stubborn women around. I'll try, but I make no promises."

"Maybe when she finds out that Geof paid you a visit, she'll be more likely to listen to what you have to say. But regardless, if this guy persists in harassing you or Cece, let me know, and I'll see what we can do about it."

"Thanks," Andy said. "Appreciate you listening to me."

"Well, I'm glad you called. I like to be apprised of situations of this nature before they escalate, even if I can't legally do anything about it yet."

After the call had ended, Andy checked the text he'd received while dealing with Geof. Sure enough, it was from Cece.

Cece: *I'm fine. Why?*

Just worried that you might have been sick since you weren't at the bakery this morning.

Cece: *I was there. I'm just in the kitchen now, doing the baking. Mia is taking my morning shift out front.*

You got a promotion?

Cece: *Yep. Brooke is pregnant, so she wants to cut back on her time at the bakery.*

Cece: *I'll be doing the daily baking. She'll still be doing the specialty stuff like birthday and wedding cakes.*

That's great! Congrats!!!

Cece: *Thanks.*

Andy tried to figure out how to broach the subject of Geof's visit, needing to make sure that she was safe. *Any chance you'd meet me for dinner? Maybe at Norma's?*

Cece: *Why?*

Trust Cece to be blunt and to the point. *To celebrate your promotion?*

Cece: *hmmmm I suppose. What time?*

It wasn't the most enthusiastic of responses, but he'd take it.

I close at six, so shortly after? You could meet me here and we could walk over, if you'd like. Or I can come pick you up.

Cece: *I'll come to the bookstore.*

Andy wasn't sure he about broaching the subject of Geof in a public place like *Norma's,* so he should probably talk to her about it at the bookstore before they went to eat. She might call off the dinner as a result. But if it meant that she'd be safer, then he was willing to sacrifice a meal together.

Okay. See you then.

He found it hard to focus on bookstore stuff for the rest of the afternoon, rehearsing all the different ways he could tell Cece about Geof's visit. He really wanted her to also confide in him about what all was going on. Perhaps if he approached it right, he could show her once again that he was trustworthy.

Although, if, after all the years they'd known each other, she didn't realize she could trust him, perhaps nothing would ever convince her. It hurt his heart to think that she might not trust him, but he'd never give her a reason to think she couldn't.

He figured he'd better give Drake a head's up on Geof's threat, just in case the guy actually had more clout than Andy thought he did. Drake was several years older than him, and he'd come from a wealthy family, but the man had never made Andy feel like he was just his boss.

The two of them had talked a lot over the years, so Andy knew that Drake wouldn't lose his mind and curse Andy out for jeopardizing the business. If anything, Drake might decide to send a fleet of lawyers to put the fear of God in Geof.

Andy wished that he had the ability to do that. But since he didn't, he'd have to just settle for praying for Cece and trying his best to be a support for her. Even when she seemed to not want that from him.

Geof might have felt like Andy's love for Cece was something to be mocked, but Andy knew differently. It might never amount to anything, but he still loved her. Part of him thought that, for whatever reason, God had put this love in his heart for her. It didn't mean it would lead to anything, but it did mean that Andy felt strongly about protecting her. Which might have been why God had placed him in her life.

Perhaps that was why Andy struggled with dating other women. He hadn't yet found one that he felt he could love the way he loved Cece. With what he'd learned from Geof, Andy thought that maybe he needed to set aside his plans to date for the time being.

It wouldn't be fair to a woman for Andy to give so much of his time and attention to Cece as he helped her through whatever was going on with Geof. He also didn't want to not be able to help Cece because he was tied up with another woman.

Andy resigned himself to staying off the dating apps until things with Cece seemed to have settled down, and he was surprisingly okay with that.

CHAPTER SIX

Cece paused near the door when she heard her dad call her name. She'd hoped to get out of the house without talking to him. The tension in the house over the past several days had been high, and she hated it. Absolutely hated it. She'd tried walking on egg-shells around her dad, but that was something that was hard for her to do.

"Where are you going?" he demanded as he approached where she stood near the side door that she always used to enter or leave the house, since it opened onto the landing at the stairs that led down to her basement bedroom.

"I'm meeting a friend for dinner."

"A friend?" he asked, his frown deepening. "What friend?"

"A work friend." She couldn't tell him it was Andy because if he got wind that she was meeting a guy, he'd probably physically prevent her from leaving the house.

"What's their name?"

"Mia." Cece wasn't a big fan of lying, but she made an exception when it came to her parents. Their actions had forced her into it in order for her to be able to live her life.

"Where are you going with her?"

"*Norma's.*"

He stared at her intently, as if trying to read her mind. "You need to contact Geof. He let me know today that he still hasn't heard from you."

"I'm not going to talk to him, Dad." Cece gripped the strap of her purse where it lay across her chest. "And I'm not getting back into a relationship with him."

When her dad's hands fisted and his face flushed with anger, she took a step closer to the door. She could see her mom hovering in the background, but Cece knew that she wouldn't be stepping in to help her.

Before her dad had a chance to say anything more, Cece spun and jerked open the door. She bolted out, slamming the door behind her, then fled down the sidewalk to the front of the house. Thankfully, her dad seemed to care what his neighbors thought, or else he'd be chasing her down, yelling at her.

Cece didn't slow to a walk until she was at the end of the block. Her chest lifted and fell with rapid breaths as she stood at the corner, waiting for a couple of cars to clear the intersection before hurrying across to the next block. A quick glance back showed that neither of her parents had followed her out of the house.

Unfortunately, she was probably going to pay a price later for leaving the way she had. But right then, all she wanted was to get to Andy. Once she reached him, Cece knew she'd be safe. He was the one person in her life who had never hurt her. He'd even gone so far as trying to protect her.

When the bookstore came into sight, Cece slowed her steps and began to take measured breaths, trying to calm herself down so that Andy wouldn't suspect that something was wrong. Although, it might all be for naught, since the man seemed to be able to read her emotional state better than anyone else.

Cece pulled the scrunchy out of her hair, then reworked it into a ponytail. She'd changed into a pair of thick leggings and a long sweatshirt after work, so she was looking a little more casual than she normally would have for going out.

When she reached the bookstore, she pulled open the door and stepped inside. Andy stood at the counter, working with the cash register. He glanced up, and when he saw her, his expression lit up with a smile.

"Hey there," he said. "I'm just cashing out."

"I know I'm a little early, but I figured I could wander the store while you finished up."

He gave a low laugh as he punched some keys on the POS machine. "I know what a hardship that is for you."

A chunk of the panic that had hit her when she'd heard her dad's voice eased now that she was with Andy. The bookstore and the bakery were the two places that she enjoyed being in the most. One day, she hoped to have a cozy little apartment that could be her oasis from the world, too.

"You doing okay?" Andy asked.

Cece realized that she'd spaced out, standing just inside the door hugging herself. "I'm fine."

Andy focused on his task as he said, "Are you sure about that?"

"What do you mean?" Cece demanded, stepping closer to the counter.

"I had a visitor today," he said without looking away from his work.

"A visitor? Who are you talking about?"

Andy glanced up at her. "Geof came by."

"Geof?" Fear spiked through her. "Why did he come here?"

Setting aside his work, Andy gave her his full attention, his blue-gray eyes showing concern. "He wanted me to convince you to get back together with him."

Cece was speechless. She had no idea how to even respond to that. Why would Geof drag Andy into things? Even as she questioned that, she knew the answer. Geof hated Andy. Had seemed to see him as a threat of sorts.

"I told him that wasn't going to happen. That never in a million years would I encourage you to get back together with him."

That also didn't surprise Cece. Andy hadn't hidden his dislike for Geof. The two definitely couldn't stand each other. Geof had insisted that Andy didn't like him because he'd wanted Cece for himself. Andy had said that Geof wasn't good enough for her and that she deserved better.

Geof's belief that Andy wanted her for himself had given Cece pause. She had a hard time believing that, after seeing her at her worst, he'd want anything to do with her romantically. However, it might explain why he'd stuck with her all these years. Still, she hadn't totally bought that observation from Geof.

Geof might be wrong about Andy, but Andy had also been wrong about her. She didn't deserve better, though her heart longed to believe she did.

"He threatened you, Cece," Andy said, his brow furrowing.

"Did he threaten *you*?" The idea made her feel sick.

Andy gave a huff of laughter. "Not in any way that mattered."

"He could beat you up," Cece said. "He's done it to others."

"Like you?"

She looked away from him. It wasn't like she could deny it. Andy had guessed it one day when he'd seen her with bruises on one wrist and the other one wrapped.

"He threatened your dad, too," Andy said. "Is your dad in some sort of financial trouble?"

Cece sighed as she shrugged. "I'm not sure what's going on. Even though I initially met Geof through my dad, and my dad encouraged me to date him, I didn't realize that they were doing business together. That information only came out recently."

"So, your dad is trying to get you back with him, too?"

She didn't want to have to admit that. What did it say about her that her dad was willing to use her that way? And that her mom just let him? She was simply a pawn for him to use to better his own life. He didn't care about her at all.

The only person who seemed to care about her was Andy.

Why did her life have to be so horrible? Why couldn't she have been born into a family like Sarah's? But even when she'd had a crush on Eli, she'd known that she'd never fit in with the McNamara family.

Were Andy's and Sarah's lives better than hers because they went to church? Because they believed in God? Even Eli was married with a baby now. And where was Cece? Stuck in her parents' basement, being forced to date a man she hated.

"My dad doesn't think he's a bad guy."

Andy scoffed. "No offense to your dad, but he's wrong."

"Is this why you invited me out for dinner?"

Andy frowned. "I did want to talk to you about it, but that's not the only reason."

"I don't really feel like going to *Norma's* right now," Cece said. She felt beaten up by Geof's continued presence in her life, especially since he was threatening the people around her.

"Let me order pizza or something. We can eat it here."

"Why do you want to hang around with me after Geof's threatened you?"

"You were my friend before Geof was ever on the scene," Andy said, his expression serious. "That means something to me."

Cece felt tears prick her eyes, but she refused to cry.

"So what do you say? Pizza?"

"Sure," she said with a shrug. There was no way she was going home, not when her dad was acting the way he was. Hopefully, he'd be cooled down by the time she got home later.

Andy grabbed his phone and placed an order with the local pizza place. The fact that he remembered what she liked on her pizza when Geof couldn't remember anything she liked—let alone her food preferences—just added to her jumbled emotions.

"Why don't you take a wander around the store while I finish this up?" Andy said. "Then we'll go eat in the break room."

Cece nodded, then headed for the stationery area. Not that there was likely to be anything new since she'd last looked, but she found it strangely soothing to flip through journals or planners. She still needed to pay for that pen she'd had Andy set aside. Maybe it would be a gift to herself when she got the first paycheck that included her raise.

"Ready?"

She looked up from the book she'd been reading the back cover of after she'd finished looking over the stationery products. Though she enjoyed fiction, she usually read eBooks, so she rarely bought books from the bookstore.

"Yep." She slipped the book back onto the shelf.

Andy carried two flat boxes and had a bottle of soda tucked under his arm. "Let's go eat."

She followed him to the break room at the back of the store. It wasn't super big, but then Andy didn't need a big room, since he was the only one using it. There were no windows, but there were pot lights in the ceiling that cast plenty of light. The light gray walls had white trim, and there were large landscape pictures that made it seem like the room had windows, even though it didn't.

Andy set the pizza boxes down on the table along with the bottle of soda. "Have a seat."

Cece slumped into one of the chairs at the table, watching as Andy got a couple of plates and glasses from the cupboard. Music drifted through speakers in the room, the same music that Andy played out in the store. She didn't know what the songs were because it was Christian music, and she knew nothing about that.

After he set the plates on the table, Andy sat down across from her. A chunk of his hair fell across his forehead, making Cece want to reach across and brush it aside. His casual style wasn't something that she usually appreciated on a man, but it suited him.

She'd never seen him in a suit. At work, he seemed to mostly wear dark slacks with a button-down shirt. Outside of work, he wore jeans and T-shirts.

Though it didn't paint her in a great light, she could admit that one of the reasons she'd stayed with Geof for so long, even after he treated her so poorly, was because of his appearance and wealth. He was muscular, and everything he wore fit him perfectly. He prided himself on his appearance, going to the gym daily and paying extra to have his clothes fitted for him.

Heads always turned when they were out together. Women looked at her with envy, and she'd enjoyed that attention. Until she'd realized that there were women who didn't have to envy her because they were on his arm too.

The perfection he sought for his own appearance had carried over into his expectations for her. He'd often nitpicked her outfits and criticized the food she ate. He would have had plenty to say about the pizza she was about to eat, which made her want to eat every single piece of it. And she knew that if she did that, Andy wouldn't blink an eye.

Since Andy always said a prayer before his meals, she waited to start eating until he lifted his head. He'd ordered her pizza with bacon, tomato, and extra cheese on it. He tended to go for just a plain pepperoni, with extra pepperoni. Whenever they had pizza, they always got the same thing.

"Pizza okay?" Andy asked after she'd taken a couple of bites.

"You know it is."

A corner of his mouth tipped up, and the corners of his eyes crinkled as he smiled. "They never get it wrong."

"Your mom isn't expecting you home for dinner?" she asked.

"Phoebe is with her tonight."

"Is she doing okay?" Though they didn't talk about it much, she knew that his mom was struggling with her health.

"She's had a couple of better days recently, so that's good."

Cece wanted to ask more details about his mom, but she didn't want her curiosity about Andy's family to open the door for him to ask her more about her family. She'd always kept any friends she'd had away from her parents once she'd realized that her family was far from the norm.

Even Leah and Sarah, whose parents had ended up divorced, had seemed to have a close relationship with both parents. Before their dad had left the family, he'd show up at school to bring them to stuff, and he'd always volunteered to go on field trips with their class. She'd watched him tease and joke with the twins, hugging them frequently. Her dad had never been that way with her.

And there was no way to explain her robot of a mom. She was often spaced out on alcohol or some kind of pills. Cece had eventually come to realize that it was likely the only way she could endure being married to her dad. Neither she nor her mom seemed capable of escaping the hold he had on them.

"And how's the writing?" she asked, steering the conversation away from the subject of families.

Andy grimaced. "I haven't had much time for it recently. I need to get back to it if I hope to publish the book by the deadline I've set for myself."

"If it's a deadline you set yourself, why does it matter if you meet it or not?"

"Just the principle of it, I suppose. I like to set goals and, if at all possible, follow through with them."

Cece had never had goals for herself. She hadn't even really been trying for a promotion or raise at the bakery. Her life was lived on a day-to-day basis. If she made it through the day without a confrontation with her dad, she considered that a win.

Unfortunately, she doubted she'd have many of those days in the near future. As it was, she was pretty sure he'd be waiting for her to come home later. Her stomach cramped at the thought. If he got angry enough at her, the confrontation that followed would be fierce.

"People are waiting for the next book, right?"

Andy chuckled. "I don't exactly have a huge audience for my books. But I'm hoping that if I keep publishing them, that audience will grow."

"I like what I've read so far," Cece told him.

He gave her a lopsided grin. "I've always appreciated your support."

She'd helped him brainstorm when he'd started his current book, and he'd even taken her suggestion of names for a couple of the characters. Helping him had helped her feel like she was contributing in some way to his life.

"I can't wait to read this one, so you better get it finished soon."

"I'm trying my best. I think things have kind of stalled because I need to figure out how to get the group out of their current predicament and have it be realistic."

Cece swallowed the bite of pizza she'd taken, then said, "Well, this is YA dystopian fiction, so I would assume that as long as it's not too gory, you could do most anything. It's not like you're basing it on facts. You destroyed the world, Andy."

He gave a snort of laughter. "You helped me. And I think it still needs to at least be grounded in the plausible."

For the next little while, Cece was able to relax and escape her reality and head into the one that Andy had created. It might have taken place in a ruined world, but the main characters were honorable and loyal, sticking together through thick and thin. It was ridiculous to think that she'd rather live in Andy's made-up world than her own real one.

They finished eating their fill of the pizza, then Andy went out to the front to grab his plotting binder. While he was gone, Cece cleared the table, then poured herself another glass of soda.

When he came back, he put the binder on the table, then sat in the chair kitty-corner to hers rather than across from her. He bent over the binder as he flipped it open. Gripping the pen in his right hand, he jotted down notes about what they'd discussed.

She leaned closer, reading what he was writing, her shoulder brushing against his arm. He glanced over at her, lifting his hand to shove back the chunk of hair that had fallen over his forehead. This close, she noticed that his blue-gray eyes had a dark circle around the outside of the irises, along with darker flecks of gray. Long dark lashes that any girl would probably kill for framed his eyes.

"So, where do you think it would be plausible for them to find some extra food and weapons?"

"What if they stumble across a homestead that belonged to a prepper?"

"A prepper? Those people who stockpile stuff?" His brow furrowed for a moment, then he smiled as he nodded and added that to the page that was already nearly filled with what they'd discussed. "That's an excellent idea."

Cece flushed with pleasure at his words. Helping him like this was always so satisfying. "Maybe they could build their own home base, instead of constantly wandering. Then they could send groups out to scavenge as necessary. It would mean that at some point, they'd also have to defend it, right?"

"Yep. Yep." He furiously scribbled more notes in the binder before glancing over at her again. "Can you go grab my tablet off the counter?" But then he paused. "Do you need to go? I didn't mean for this to turn into a brainstorming session."

Cece waved her hand. "It's fine. I don't have anywhere to be."

She left him with his binder and went out to the main part of the store. The lights had all been dimmed so no one would think the store was open, but there was enough light for her to see the tablet on the counter. She grabbed it, then went back to the break room.

"Let's see if we can find a spot for this homestead," Andy said as he took the tablet from her, their fingers brushing as he did so. "Then I can visualize it better."

"Thank you," she said.

Andy turned his attention more fully to her, his brows drawn together. "For what?"

She felt a little embarrassed and wished that she hadn't said anything. Shrugging, she said, "For letting me help you with this."

"I'm *lucky* that you want to help me. You've come up with some great ideas, especially for this book. I'm definitely going to dedicate it to you."

Emotion clogged her throat, making Cece swallow hard. "Really?"

"Really." He grinned at her. "Maybe you should be my co-author. We'd make a pretty good team."

The idea was way too appealing. "I don't think that's fair. You're still doing the majority of the work. I'm just having fun with the brainstorming."

"I'm glad."

The smile that followed his words was gentle, making her want to lean against him. How she wished that she was good enough for him. But Andy deserved an amazing woman who could bring light and laughter to his life. Those were definitely not things she'd ever brought him.

But until that amazing woman came along and took him away from her, Cece was going to enjoy being his friend.

CHAPTER SEVEN

Andy's fingers itched to type, but he knew that would have to wait. The unexpected brainstorming session with Cece had been just what he needed to re-ignite his excitement for his story. While he wasn't able to make a living writing books, he enjoyed being able to write and share his stories with people who liked to read in the genre.

They'd been at it for almost an hour, their heads bent together over the tablet as they'd perused areas on the map where they could put the homestead/base. He'd printed off the map once they'd decided on a location, then they'd begun to research prepper homesteads. It was the most fun he'd had in a while.

"I need more pizza," he said as he got up from the table. "That was quite a workout."

Cece laughed, her eyes sparkling. "For your brain."

"Well, that's the most important thing to work out, I think." He brought both pizza boxes over to the table and set them down. "I should have bought some ice cream or brownies."

"I could have brought something from the bakery."

"Yeah. With the change of plans, we kind of deprived ourselves of dessert."

"I probably wouldn't eat it anyway," Cece said with a frown.

"Why not?" Andy knew the answer, but he wanted her to say it. He needed to be able to reassure her that it didn't matter.

She shot him a blistering look. "You know why."

"One dessert wouldn't be an issue."

"Probably not for you. Somehow, you seem to be able to eat anything you want without gaining weight. That's not the case with me." She eyed the pizza. "I probably shouldn't even eat more of that."

"Do you *want* to?" Andy asked as he picked up a piece from his box.

For the whole time he'd known her, she'd been obsessed with her weight, and it was something she often mentioned about other people. People like Jillian Ward. He wished that she'd stop focusing on it with regards to herself and others.

"Of course, I want to eat another piece."

"Then eat one. You don't have to eat all of it. Have one more piece, then take the rest home for tomorrow."

She shook her head. "I'm not taking it home."

"Why not?"

As usual, she didn't respond. Just shook her head again.

Andy hated to end their evening on a bad note, but he had to make sure that she was going to be safe. "You're not getting back together with Geof, are you?"

Her hesitation lasted just long enough to make his gut clench with fear. And when she shook her head, it wasn't exactly convincing.

"Cece, please. Don't let him back into your life."

Her gaze flicked to him for a moment before she stared at the table again. "I'm not sure I'll have a choice."

"You're an adult," Andy reminded her. "You have a choice."

"I still live with my parents. I don't have enough money to get a place of my own."

"You pay your folks for rent?"

She nodded. "My dad takes money for room and board."

"Is it a lot?" It surprised Andy that she was volunteering that much information, so he wanted to take advantage of her unexpected openness to find out what was truly going on in her life.

"Yeah. He takes about seventy-five percent of what I make for rent and the food I eat."

Andy stared at her, quickly doing some math in his head. He didn't know exactly what she made, but he knew what minimum wage was and had dealt with income tax rates when doing his own payroll. The amount her dad was likely charging her was horrendous.

A fair amount of his own money went to the expenses of the house, but his mom also got disability, and Phoebe contributed as well. It sounded like Cece's dad was placing a big chunk of the financial responsibility for their household expenses on her.

"Brooke gave me a raise with this promotion," she said. "I don't want my dad to know because he'll just up my rent. I want to try to save up enough to move out."

"I think that's a good idea." It was a terrific idea, as far as Andy was concerned.

She hesitated for a moment. "Do you think you could help me figure out how much I need to save?"

"Sure," Andy said without a moment's hesitation. He would love to help her take some steps toward freeing herself. "I'd be happy to do that."

"Thanks. I should know about this kind of stuff, but my folks have never been helpful in teaching me. Plus, I guess I kinda figured whoever I married would take care of the finances like my dad does."

"That might still end up being the case, but there is no harm in educating yourself." He thought of the apartment above the bookstore. It was Drake's, but the man was hardly ever there anymore. It had been almost a year since he'd last visited. Would he be willing to let Cece stay there?

Andy was a little reluctant to ask because he had no idea how much personal stuff Drake had left there. He'd only gone into the apartment when Drake was there for meetings with him. When the man was gone from New Hope, Andy didn't go inside the apartment.

"When you get your first paycheck with your raise on it, we'll sit down and crunch some numbers, okay?"

Cece nodded, but she was frowning. "I feel so dumb."

"You're not dumb at all," Andy assured her. "Not knowing about stuff like this doesn't make you dumb."

Her gaze dropped to her hands. "My dad has always said I didn't need to know how to deal with money. I just needed to look pretty. That that was all I'd ever be good for. Geof seemed to agree."

Anger flared inside Andy. "Nope. That is *all* lies. You are so much more than just a pretty face."

Cece rubbed a hand over her mouth. "I don't know why I'm telling you this stuff."

"I don't know why either, but I'm sure glad you are." He reached over and touched her hand. "God made you to be more than someone who just looks pretty. You're a good employee, a good baker. Brooke wouldn't have given you that responsibility if you weren't. You know how to organize things. The reunion was great."

"Ha. I don't think so. I should've vetoed that comedy trio."

"So there was one bad thing, but that was more the fault of those guys than it was yours."

"I shouldn't have taken on that responsibility." Cece sighed, her shoulders slumping. "All it did was make people hate me more."

Andy couldn't deny that she'd made things more difficult for herself with people like Emma and Jillian. However, he also knew that if she showed that she was willing to be more understanding of people, friendship might be an option again.

The new glimpses he'd had into her life that evening made him understand her a bit more. Being raised to think her only worth was in her looks, which probably also included a lot of critical comments from her parents, had no doubt made her feel defensive.

"I don't think anyone hates you," Andy said. And he was confident that was actually true. Even though Jillian, Sarah, and the others didn't like her behavior much, he'd never gotten the feeling that they hated her.

She gave him a skeptical look. "Doesn't matter, regardless. It's not like I'm hanging around with them."

"You could if you wanted to."

"I doubt that," she said with a scoff.

She drew one of her legs up and wrapped her arm around it. Wisps of hair framed her face, escaping from the messy bun on the top of her head. It gave her a soft, approachable look. As usual, she wore a full face of makeup. He wasn't sure he'd ever seen her so casually dressed, and he liked it. Somehow it made him feel like she was getting more comfortable with him.

Knowing what he did now about her dad and how he'd raised her, it made sense that she always made sure she looked well put together. Her dad had reduced her to nothing more than her appearance, so obviously she'd feel it was important to always look good.

"Why don't you come to church with me?" he suggested.

She frowned. "Why would I do that?"

Andy shrugged, not put off by her tone. "Maybe you'd be able to reconnect with people like Sarah and Jillian."

Her hesitation before brushing his suggestion off told Andy that perhaps she wasn't as opposed to the idea as he'd thought she'd be.

"I haven't been to a church in... forever."

"Not even for Christmas?"

"Christmas isn't a big thing for my family," Cece said. "I'm not sure about going to church. I think it would be kind of weird."

Andy wished they were having something special at church that he could invite her to. If he didn't think she'd find the more intimate setting of the Bible study overwhelming, he would have considered inviting her to that. She'd been to the study before, but it had been a long time ago, and she'd stopped coming at some point.

"I guess it might seem weird to people who haven't attended before," Andy admitted. "But it's all pretty normal to me. If you ever want to go, just let me know, and I'll pick you up."

"Does your mom attend?"

"Sometimes. It really depends on how she's feeling. Thankfully, they stream the services, so if she can't attend, she can watch them."

"Church services are streamed?"

"Yep. I mean, maybe not every church does, but ours has been doing it for the last couple of years." Andy paused, then said, "You could watch a service to see what it's like."

She seemed to consider it, but unsurprisingly, she didn't commit one way or another. "I should probably head for home. I gotta get used to early mornings now that I'm getting up to do the baking."

"Let me take you home," Andy said, closing the lids on the pizza boxes.

"I can walk. It's not that far."

"It's getting late. Let me give you a ride."

"If you're sure."

"I'm absolutely positive."

They cleaned up their dishes, then Andy gathered up his things and they went out the back door. It was chilly and drizzly, so he was glad that she'd taken him up on the offer to drop her off. They climbed into his car, then he took a minute to lock the building and arm the alarm before backing out of his spot behind the building.

His car wasn't anything fancy, but it was reliable, and more importantly, it was easy for his mom to get in and out of when he had to take her places. It was also clean for a change. He was glad he'd taken the time to do that the day before.

The drive didn't take long at all, and soon he pulled to a stop at the curb in front of the moderately sized home on one of the older streets of the town. He climbed out and went around to open Cece's door, a bit surprised she hadn't already gotten out. But even after he'd opened the door, she hesitated, staring toward the house.

"Are you going to be okay going in there?" he asked.

"Yeah. Yeah, I'll be fine." She got out of the car and lingered close to him, making him wish he could wrap his arms around her. Looking up at him, she smiled briefly before stepping away. "Thank you so much for the ride home. I appreciate it."

"You're welcome. Anytime." He closed the door. "And now that I know you're in the back of the bakery, I'll give you a shout out when I grab my morning coffee."

Her smile lingered a bit longer that time. "Okay."

"Also, let me know when you get your paycheck, and we'll set up another pizza night to talk about how to maximize your raise."

She nodded, then said goodnight before heading toward the house. Andy turned to watch her as she walked around the side of the house, then disappeared into the darkness. He frowned when no light came on, not happy that she had to let herself into the house in the dark.

He got back into the car, but didn't leave right away, just in case. When it seemed likely that she'd had enough time to get inside, he put the car into gear and pulled away from the curb.

Though he hadn't been able to extract a promise from her not to go back to Geof, Andy was so glad for all the new insights he'd gained into Cece and her life. He wasn't sure what had changed for Cece, that she was being so vulnerable with him, but he was grateful for it.

The things she'd revealed had given him a much clearer understanding of her life. He already prayed for her daily, but now he had specifics to pray for.

Unfortunately, getting to know even more about Cece would not help him get over his feelings for her. In fact, it was probably going to make him care for her even more. His protectiveness had kicked into overdrive with the things she'd revealed.

It showed him more than anything that she was feeling stressed and perhaps scared. He hoped that for the few hours she'd spent with him, the weight of what she was dealing with had lifted, even just a bit. Andy wished she'd let him do more for her. Hopefully, helping her learn more about her finances would be a step toward her gaining her freedom from her dad.

The house was quiet with most of the lights off when he arrived. He made his way through the kitchen to the hallway that led to his mom's bedroom.

There was light coming through the crack in the door, so he rapped lightly, waiting for her to reply before pushing the door open. She was sitting up in her bed, her tablet propped up on a pillow in front of her.

"Hello, darling," she said, smiling at him as she removed her reading glasses. "How was your evening?"

He sank down on the chair beside her bed, relaxing back into its cushions. "It was... good, I think. Cece talked more about herself than she usually does. Man, her life has not been easy. Her dad is a real piece of work."

"Why do you say that?"

"He's basically raised her to believe that all she's good for is getting married, preferably to a rich man. She seems to feel her only value in life is to be pretty."

His mom sighed. "That's terrible. It must have been a challenge to live in that type of environment. No wonder she struggles to relate to people if she thinks they'll only like her if she's pretty."

"I really hope that she knows that in my eyes, she's more than just a pretty face," Andy said.

"I think she does know that," his mom said gently. "You've certainly stood by her when others haven't."

Andy nodded. "I would never walk away from our friendship unless she flat-out told me that she didn't want to be friends anymore. Sometimes her actions seem to be designed to push me away, but until she says the words, I'm going to stay."

"You're a good man," his mom said with a smile. "Your dad would be so proud of you. I know that I am."

"Thanks, Momma. I already knew I was blessed to have you and Dad as parents," Andy said. "But after hearing about Cece's life, I know I'm doubly blessed. I'm grateful that you both were such good people, raising me and Phoebe to see value in people beyond just the surface."

"It was definitely a lesson you learned well."

"How are you feeling?" Andy asked. "Did you have a good evening?"

"I'm tired, but I was able to walk using just the cane for most of the day."

"That's good. Did Phoebe make you a decent dinner?"

A corner of his mom's mouth tipped up. "We had spaghetti with butter and parmesan."

Andy chuckled. "No sauce, huh?"

"You know that we only have sauce when you're around."

"Well, I'm glad you enjoyed your supper."

"Yep. We ate it in the living room while we watched reality shows."

"Sounds like you had fun. Maybe I should stay out more often."

"If it makes you happy, I'd say you definitely should."

Andy thought of the woman he'd gone on a few dates with and realized that he'd had more fun eating pizza and brainstorming with Cece than he'd had on any of those dates. It looked like it was time to let Lynne know that he didn't see any future for them.

He knew that he wanted a relationship like the one his parents had had. They'd set a great example of how to strive to make each other happy. His dad's thing had been to bring his mom little gifts that he knew his wife would like. Everything from flowers to fuzzy socks had found their way from the store to Andy's mom, courtesy of her husband.

Andy had tried to do what he could to step into his dad's shoes so that his mom was still spoiled with little gifts, especially since she was struggling so much with her health. He knew his dad would have been devastated to see his wife suffering as she now did.

"Well, I'll leave you to your book," he said, gesturing to her tablet. "If you need anything..."

"I'll be fine, darling," she assured him with a smile. "I'll see you tomorrow."

As Andy walked down the stairs to his room a short time later, his thoughts went to Cece again, and he hoped that she was safe. She hadn't exactly come out and said that her dad got physical with her, but he wouldn't be surprised if he did. If her dad approved of Geof... well, that told Andy that the man didn't have a problem with a man laying hands on a woman.

He didn't know how to help Cece, and he felt particularly helpless in his inability to be able to do anything to keep her safe. He would have to just keep taking his cues from Cece and pray that God would keep her safe when she was with those in her life who should want to protect her, but who failed to even try.

CHAPTER EIGHT

Cece stood in the dark outside the side door, gripping her keys tightly. The metal edges bit into her fingers, and it took her a minute to work up the courage to find the key to the door and push it into the lock.

First hurdle was seeing if her dad had changed the locks on her. He'd threatened it over the years, but so far, he hadn't done it. She kind of doubted he'd done it this time either, because it would cost him money. The only reason he might have called a locksmith in the past few hours was if he and Geof decided banning her from her home would send her into Geof's arms once again.

She'd like to say that wouldn't happen, but if it did, where would she go? Would she be strong enough to swallow her pride and call Andy?

Relief spiraled through her when the key turned. She grabbed the doorknob and slowly twisted it, hoping that her parents had gone to bed already. Unfortunately, she'd seen lights on in the kitchen, so it was possible her dad was waiting for her.

She pushed the door in and stepped inside. The small landing was dark, but she didn't turn on a light, just quietly shut the door, then turned the dead bolt. Keeping her steps light, she moved down the stairs to the basement.

When she finally reached her room, she closed the door behind her and locked it. Relief swamped her as she leaned back against the smooth wood surface of the door. She wasn't naïve enough to think a confrontation with her dad wasn't still in the offing, but at least she didn't have to deal with it that night.

She'd enjoyed her evening with Andy, and she didn't want a fight with her dad to spoil it. Especially since she had to get up early in the morning.

Pushing away from the door, she went to her attached bathroom to get ready for bed. She removed her makeup, then brushed out her hair before twisting it on top of her head so it wouldn't get wet when she took a quick shower. After brushing her teeth and applying all of her skincare, she changed into her pajamas, finding comfort in her nightly routine.

When she slid into bed, Cece hoped she'd fall asleep quickly. But instead, she lay curled on her side, thoughts tumbling through her mind.

For as long as she could remember, her dad had held his archaic views on women. She'd heard many times how he wished she'd been a boy since her mom hadn't been able to have any more kids. Cece wasn't sure what her life would have been like if she'd had a sibling or two. One thing she was quite certain of was if she'd had a brother who held the same beliefs about women as her dad, her life would have been even worse.

It wasn't too likely that a guy being raised by someone like her dad would turn out like Andy. Phoebe was fortunate that she'd had a great dad and brother. Not everyone in life was so lucky.

It took Cece far too long to fall asleep, so when her alarm went off the next morning at three o'clock, she regretted having accepted Brooke's promotion. She had to adjust her bedtime, and she also needed to figure out how to apply her makeup more quickly while still being half asleep. The best thing about her new hours was that her dad wasn't up to harass her before she walked out the door.

When she stepped out of the house to make the walk to work, she was relieved that it wasn't raining. The darkness still made it feel cold and damp, though, and Cece was slightly creeped out by the eerily empty streets. She walked through the puddles of light cast by the streetlamps, hurrying along the residential streets.

The back lane behind the bakery had a few streetlamps, but not enough to dispel the darkness completely. That stretch felt like the final hurdle to reach safety. Her heart was pounding when she finally let herself in the back door.

After that walk through the darkness, Cece wanted to buy a car before she did anything else. However, even though she didn't know much about finances, she was pretty sure that an apartment would be a better investment and cheaper.

In the meantime, she had to tackle the baking so that Brooke didn't regret giving her the promotion and raise.

A few hours later, Cece let Mia in the front door.

"Good morning, Cece," Mia said with a wide smile. "How's the baking been going?"

"It's fine. Should have plenty for the customers."

Mia followed her into the kitchen, disappearing briefly into the small staff room. When she came back out, she said, "Do you attend the same church as Andy?"

Cece glanced up from the cooled cinnamon buns she was icing. "No. Why?"

"I was just curious if I'd see more than one familiar face there."

That got her attention more fully. "You're planning to attend Andy's church?"

"Yep. I looked up the church using the information he gave me and watched some of the services, and I think it looks like a good church."

"I'm sure if Andy attends it, then it is." Cece thought of the invitation that Andy had extended to her. Apparently, he'd invited Mia as well. Jealousy burned through her, and she wasn't sure why.

Cece had learned that Mia had a husband, so it was unlikely that Andy was looking at her as a potential girlfriend. However, maybe he was looking for more friends. Ones that weren't as messed up as she was.

"Ben and I will probably visit the church on Sunday to see how we like it. I also plan to ask Andy if he knows of any apartments that might be for rent."

The jealousy already burning inside Cece grew even more. It seemed like they were in a position to afford a place of their own, even though they were a bit younger than her. And Andy would probably happily help them out.

"Do *you* know of any places that might be available?" Mia asked. "We'd just need a one-bedroom, I think."

"Sorry. No," she said with a shake of her head as she picked up the icing to finish the cinnamon rolls. "But Andy probably will, or maybe some people at his church might."

"That would be great," Mia said. "We're living with Ben's parents at the moment, and while they've been great, we need our own space."

Cece listened as Mia prattled on about her wonderful life with her wonderful husband and wonderful in-laws, even though she was missing her wonderful parents and wonderful siblings. Just... wonderful.

Finally, Mia left to start her preparations to open, and Cece was happy to see her go. She knew her attitude was why she only had one long-suffering friend. But given what was currently going on in her life, it felt far too difficult for her to be happy for someone else's wonderful life.

Blinking back tears of frustration, she focused on the one thing that *was* going well in her life. She couldn't mess this up because if she had a hope of attaining a wonderful life for herself, she needed to be able to save up some money.

"Hey, Cece," Mia said a couple of hours later from where she stood in the doorway of the kitchen. "Someone here to see you."

Cece frowned for a moment, then remembered that Andy had said he'd say hello when he came for his coffee. Setting aside the cookie dough she was preparing, Cece made her way out of the kitchen to the front. Andy turned to her with a smile on his face and a cup of coffee in his hand.

"Good morning," he said as he walked toward her. "How's your day been so far?"

Cece felt exhausted from having been on her feet for hours after such a brief night of sleep. However, in light of Mia's perky happiness, she didn't really want to be seen as a complaining whiner. "So far, so good. Haven't burnt anything, which is a plus."

"I worried you might be tired. I probably shouldn't have kept you out as late as I did."

"It was fine. I had fun," she told him. "I can always take a nap when I finish here."

"Everything..." He glanced over his shoulder to where Mia was serving another customer. "Everything okay at home?"

"For now," she said, appreciating his discretion. He'd never embarrassed her by revealing the things he knew about her that no one else did, so it was no surprise that he wasn't doing that now.

"Well, let me know if it isn't later."

She nodded, though she didn't know what good it would do. "Hope you have a good day at work."

"Well, I'm off to a good start," he said, lifting his cup of coffee. "And I've also got a cinnamon bun to take with me."

He rarely picked up something to eat along with his coffee, so his support in picking up one of the cinnamon rolls she'd made touched her. Like so much of what he did.

"I hope you enjoy it."

"I'm sure I will." He gave her another smile. "I'd better get to work. Those books aren't going to sell themselves."

"And that one isn't going to write itself."

Andy chuckled. "Nope. But I got a chapter written last night, thanks to you."

"Nice! I can't wait to read it."

As she watched him leave the bakery, Cece wished that she could go with him and spend her day in the bookstore. It amazed her sometimes that he thought she was good enough to be his friend. At one time, she'd thought she was better than people like him, but over the years, she'd come to realize that Andy was truly special.

"I don't believe you," Mia said.

Cece turned to her, frowning as she crossed her arms. "About what?"

"That you and Andy are just friends."

"We *are*," Cece told her. "We've never dated."

"That must be your fault," Mia said. "Because I'm pretty sure that if Andy thought you'd say yes, he'd ask you out pronto."

"I doubt it. Andy's smarter than that."

"What's that supposed to mean?"

Cece knew that Mia would never understand, and there was no way she was going to explain her situation to someone she barely knew. She'd never even explained it to people she'd known for years, like Sarah or Jillian.

"Andy and I have known each other for a long time. Believe me, friendship is as far as our relationship is going to go."

Thankfully, someone walked in, drawing Mia's attention away from her. Cece escaped back into the kitchen and returned to the cookies she'd been working on. She really hoped that Mia wouldn't keep harping on the subject of Andy. There was no way she would ever explain the details of her life to the upbeat woman.

She knew that dealing with customers required a certain level of cheerfulness, but Mia's level seemed excessive. Cece had worked the same job without being over-the-top cheerful. No one had ever complained about her customer service.

She wondered what Andy would say if she asked him if she should be more cheerful. He'd never told her to be happier. Sometimes he'd hinted that she needed to be a bit nicer, but he'd never said it when other people were around.

None of it mattered. Her lot in life didn't seem to require things like cheerfulness or being nice. Geof and her dad hadn't cared. All they wanted from her was obedience and for her to take care of herself, so she looked good. Apparently, her appearance reflected on them.

Geof hadn't cared if she was nice. Most of the time, he filled the time they were together talking about himself or his interests. He never asked anything about her life. And his last words before they entered any social event he'd been invited to had always been *keep your mouth shut and look pretty.*

It was how her mom had always operated with her dad. Whenever Cece had gone with them to social functions, her mom had always been beautifully made up, but she'd rarely said anything. Instead, she'd stood silently at Cece's dad's side, slightly behind his elbow, and smiled continuously while her dad had talked and talked and talked...

Before she'd started dating Geof, her dad had insisted that Cece go with them. Apparently, in his mind, it gave him more status to have a beautiful woman on each arm. Or maybe he'd hoped that Cece would catch the eye of a rich man at one of those events. Which was exactly what had happened.

Cece was wiping down all the counters in the kitchen in preparation for the next day when Mia appeared again.

"Hey, Cece, there's someone out front asking for you. Yet another handsome man."

Her movements stilled, and her stomach clenched. "I'll be there in a minute."

She was almost as angry as she was scared. Geof would know that she wouldn't want a confrontation at her place of work. He was going to take advantage of that, she was quite certain. The idea of this meeting playing out in front of not just Mia, but also Brooke, who was meeting someone for a wedding cake consultation, made Cece feel a little sick.

"He can't hurt me. He can't hurt me. He can't hurt me." Cece repeatedly murmured the words as she rinsed out the cloth she'd been using, then washed and dried her hands.

Just before she walked through the door that led to the front, she paused and took several deep breaths, pulling up the front she'd seen her mom use with her dad and that she herself had used plenty of times with Geof.

"Darling!" he exclaimed when she appeared. "I thought I'd surprise you with a visit and some flowers."

Cece swallowed against the nausea that tried to climb up her throat as she spotted the large bouquet of blood-red roses in his hand. Some might see it as a sweet gesture. She knew better.

She'd had thorns slice into her arms. She'd had petals rain down around her. She'd had flowerless stems flung at her.

Flowers from Geof, especially right then, were a reminder. A reminder that there were consequences to standing up to him. To not doing exactly what he wanted.

"Thank you," she said, though she made no move to accept the flowers.

The corners of Geof's eyes tightened as he took a couple of steps toward her. The rest of the shop faded away as she watched him, looking for the tells in his expression or actions to know what he was going to do.

He held the flowers out to her, and Cece reached to take them. She wrapped her fingers around the stems, but he didn't let go. Instead, he glared at her, anger distorting his features.

Since his back was to the others, no one else could see his expression. Geof knew he was safe. It made her mad that he was still manipulating her.

She let go of the flowers and stepped back. "I guess they're not for me after all, huh?"

Yeah, it was a bit like poking the bear, but she was *so* tired of him creating havoc inside her. She hated how she'd let him control this part of her.

"Maybe I just wanted a kiss," he said, keeping his tone light. Even flirtatious.

"Sorry, but this is my place of work, and I'm still on the clock."

"Then I guess I'll just give you the flowers and collect the kiss later." Again, with the flirty words and tone.

When he held out the bouquet again, she hesitated a moment before she took it. He let go of them this time, though his gaze was still narrowed on her.

"I'll see you later, beautiful Cecelia."

She hated it when he called her that, but she still smiled at him. "Thanks again for the flowers."

It wasn't until he left the bakery that she took a deep breath and blew it out. Clutching the roses, she felt the thorns dig into her palm.

"That is one beautiful bouquet," Mia said. "I guess he's why you're not dating Andy."

"Something like that," Cece said, struggling to keep the smile on her face. The last thing she wanted was for Mia to dissect her interaction with Geof.

Before Brooke could add to the conversation, her appointment walked in, distracting her.

"I'd better finish up in the kitchen." With a stiff smile, she turned and went back into the kitchen. She wanted to put the flowers in the garbage, but that would bring questions from Mia or Brooke. Instead, she put them in a large glass filled with water, planning to drop them in a dumpster on her way home.

The big problem she had now was that Geof was probably sitting out in front of the bakery in his expensive sports car. He knew that she would be walking home, so it was unlikely that he was just going to leave her alone.

As she finished cleaning up, she thought about her options. The most obvious one was to see if she could somehow make it to the bookstore. She knew Andy would let her hang out in the break room there. Probably without asking any questions.

The unfortunate thing was that she'd told Geof in the past that if she was working in the kitchen, it was because she'd started her shift early, so she would then be off work earlier than usual. So since he'd seen her come from the back while someone else was working the front meant that he would know she was off soon.

Why did her life have to be so complicated?

She slowly finished her cleaning, trying to work out a plan. Once everything was done, she sent Andy a text.

Can you look out the back door and see if there's a car sitting down by the bakery?

CHAPTER NINE

Andy frowned as he read the text from Cece. He didn't like the sound of that.

He cracked open the back door and peered around it, glad that the bookstore wasn't very far from the bakery. The sight of a familiar expensive car idling just outside the bakery's back door drew a growl of anger from him.

As he stepped back inside, he tapped out a message to Cece.

Yes. He's there. Come in the front.

Andy made sure the rear door was locked, then went back to the main part of the store. He stood near the front door, watching for Cece. When he spotted her leaving the bakery, he pushed open the door and held it so that she could scoot right inside.

Clutching a bouquet of flowers, she didn't even hesitate to walk straight to where the shelves were so that she wasn't as easily seen from outside. He followed her more slowly.

"What happened?" he asked, positioning himself between her and the front window.

"Geof paid me a visit at the bakery and brought me these." She lifted the flowers. "I figured he might be waiting for me."

"You should talk to the police," he said.

She lowered the flowers down by her leg. "He hasn't done anything reportable."

"That's a lie, and you know it." Andy was angry at Geof, but he was also getting angry at Cece. "He's hurt you. I know he has. And you must feel threatened by him, or you wouldn't have texted me like you did."

Cece turned away from him, facing the shelf they were standing next to. "I have no proof."

"You didn't take pictures of the bruises he put on you?" For some reason, Andy felt sure that she had.

"Even if I did, what good would they do? I have no proof that it was him that did it. I can't even prove that it's me in the pictures." She frowned, her chin dipping down. "Plus, if my dad finds out I reported Geof, he'll probably kick me out."

"If Geof finds out you left the bakery, is he going to be waiting for you at home?"

"I don't know." She shrugged. "I just... don't know."

Andy hesitated, then did something he rarely did with her. He slid an arm around her shoulders, and when she turned toward him, he fully hugged her. He kept his embrace loose, so if she wanted to step away, she could, but he just needed to offer her some sort of comfort.

The shuddering breath she took as she leaned against him stabbed at his heart. He'd known for a long time that the prickly exterior she showed to the world protected a vulnerable heart and spirit.

He'd seen it for the first time when he'd found her sobbing under the bleachers. When he'd realized who he'd heard crying, Andy had immediately apologized, planning to leave her alone. Even as a teenager, she'd had a reputation for chewing up and spitting people out, especially those who ticked her off for some reason.

Instead, in a moment of apparent desperation, she had grabbed onto his arm, stopping him from leaving. He hadn't known what to expect. They moved in completely different circles, and as far as he knew, she had no clue who he was.

Although maybe she'd just been so desperate for help that she hadn't been thinking clearly. In that moment, she'd confessed her fear that she was pregnant, and how her dad was going to kill her if it was true.

At the time, Andy had assumed that her comment about her dad was just an expression. However, more recently, he'd realized that perhaps she'd been serious.

Just like he had that day under the bleachers, Andy softly asked, "How can I help you?"

Before she had a chance to respond, there was a pounding on the back door. Cece stiffened in his arms.

"Let me get that," Andy said. "Go hide in the office."

It was tempting to ignore the back door, but he knew that doing so would just raise Geof's suspicions. Instead, he walked toward the door, glancing back to make sure Cece had disappeared from sight.

When there was more pounding on the door, Andy yelled, "Hold your horses! I'm coming."

He jerked open the door, then pretended to be surprised when he spotted an irate Geof. "Geof? Sorry, man, I thought you were the delivery guy."

"Where is she?" Geof demanded.

Though he didn't like to lie, he made an exception in this particular case. Geof absolutely didn't deserve the truth. "Cece? She's probably at the bakery."

"Do I look stupid?" Geof demanded. "I already checked there."

Andy really, really wanted to answer his question, but antagonizing the man would likely delay his departure. "Sorry, I can't help you, and I need to get back to the store."

Before Geof could respond, Andy closed and locked the door. As he passed the office, he poked his head inside. "Just hang out in here for a bit."

Something told Andy that Geof was going to come around the front, just to mess with him some more. He went to his spot at the counter and pulled up a stack of books from the worktable behind the counter.

It didn't take long for Geof to reappear. When the bell jangled over the door, Andy looked up.

He sighed loud enough for Geof to hear him. "What do you want now? Back with more threats?"

"I'm not sure why you've appointed yourself as Cece's protector. She's not worth it, you know."

"She must be worth something," Andy said. "After all, you seem to be quite determined to hang on to her."

"She won't give you the time of day, dude," Geof scoffed.

"We're going to go over this again?" Andy shook his head. "I got bored with this conversation the first time. This is a place of business. You need to leave."

Geof glared at him, but apparently, he had no argument to come back with to dispute his statement. He pointed a finger at Andy. "Don't get involved."

Andy arched a brow at him but didn't respond verbally. As he watched Geof walk to where he'd parked his car, Andy wondered to what extremes the man was going to go in order to get Cece back. Each time Andy encountered him, Geof seemed to be losing his mind a bit more. Which was a very scary thought.

It wasn't until Geof had driven away that Andy left the counter and went to the office. Cece was sitting with her head resting on her arms, which were folded on the desk. She lifted her head and sat back, letting out a long sigh.

Andy crossed his arms and leaned against the doorjamb. "I'm not sure you should go home just yet. I have a feeling that's where Geof is headed next."

"My dad's at work, so I doubt he'd go there."

"Are you going to go home, then?"

"I don't think I should. He might not be at the house, but he's probably watching to see if I'm walking home. He knows I don't have a car anymore."

Andy felt a wave of helplessness. He didn't know how to help Cece. Geof knew too much about her life, so it seemed like the only thing that would protect her would be her quitting her job and leaving town.

For all the bravado that Cece showed most of the time, Andy wasn't sure that she'd be able to leave town. Her parents had done a terrible job preparing her for adulthood. And honestly, she hadn't done a great job educating herself, either. She probably hadn't realized how little she knew about the more practical side of life.

It wasn't like she'd had a lot of friends who had struck out on their own to show her the way it was done. Even he still lived at home. Sarah and Leah had also lived with their mom until they got married.

For a moment, he considered asking Sarah if Cece could move out to the lodge. He was pretty sure that there were two empty rooms there since she and Leah had moved out. Unfortunately, it wouldn't work well with Cece's job since she had no car. He couldn't offer her a bed at his place since they didn't have any spare rooms.

"Do you want to stay here until I close up?" Andy asked. "Then I can give you a ride home."

"You don't mind?"

"Not at all. You should probably hang out in here, so if Geof comes back, he doesn't see you."

"I might take a nap," she said, gesturing to the small couch in the office. "I was up so early this morning."

"What time?"

She wrinkled her nose. "Three."

"Yikes. Are you going to have to get up that early all the time?"

"Yeah. I'm going to have to go to bed around seven in order to get enough sleep."

He found it weird to think of living that type of schedule, but maybe it would work in her favor. "Will that give you enough time if I drive you home?"

"It'll be fine. I'll just go straight to bed."

He gestured over his shoulder. "I'll get back to work and let you rest for a bit."

At her nod, he left the office, pulling the door closed behind him. As he prepared some online orders to be mailed out, he couldn't seem to keep from thinking of how to help Cece. Thankfully, there was no further sign of Geof. Andy hoped that meant he'd given up and gone home.

Cece ventured out of the office around five, still looking tense and tired.

"Were you able to sleep?"

She shrugged. "Not much, but that's okay. If I slept too much, I probably would have ended up not being able to sleep later."

"Will you have time to eat before you need to go to sleep?" Andy asked.

Cece stared at him for a moment, her blue gaze intense, her expression unreadable. "Why do you care about stuff like that?"

"What do you mean?"

"Why do you care if I'll have time to eat or if I'll get enough sleep?"

Andy wished he could tell her the reason was that his heart ached for her, but he settled for the other reason. It was just as real as the love he felt for her but probably more acceptable to her. Maybe.

"God commands us to share His love with the world. You are a big part of my world, and showing concern for your welfare is the only way I know how to show you that God loves you."

"It just seems so strange."

Given what she'd shared with him recently about her life, he could imagine that was true. "God's love for us isn't something that makes sense until we experience it for ourselves."

"Why does it matter if I know about God's love?"

Andy felt a moment of fear, worrying that he wouldn't have the right words to share with Cece. It was the first time they'd ever ventured into a serious discussion of his faith. In the past, all he'd been able to do was pray for her and hope that she'd see God in his life through how he treated her.

Please, God, give me the right words to say.

"Because God cares about you, and He wants you to experience that love and His peace in your life."

She rolled her eyes at that. "I really doubt He cares about me. If He did, why did He let me end up in this situation?"

"Life isn't perfect for any of us," Andy said. "But having God in our lives and depending on His strength and wisdom can help us get through the difficult times."

"Like when your dad died?"

He nodded. "It was a horrible time for us, but we knew that God was with us, and we knew my dad was in Heaven."

"I've never really understood about God," she said. "But you're... different from other people. Even Sarah was different before things went bad at that stupid dinner."

"What happened that night?" Andy asked.

He knew that things had fallen apart between the two, but Cece had never given him the details, and he'd never asked her for them either. Sarah had warned him about how mean Cece could be, but honestly, it hadn't been anything he hadn't already known about her.

It wasn't until the last couple of years that Cece had started to interact with him where people could see them. Prior to that, their interactions had been more sporadic, and if they communicated, it was via text.

Cece crossed her arms and looked away from him. "Jillian ordered fries or something, and I told her that maybe she shouldn't be eating junk food. I don't remember exactly what I said, but it was basically directed at her because of her weight."

Andy winced. "Have you ever apologized to her?"

"No."

Just the one word. No defense of the words that she'd uttered to Jillian. No defense of herself at all.

"Maybe you should."

"Yeah. Maybe."

"We're all carrying a burden, and the world becomes a better place when we choose to offer support rather than condemnation."

"Like you did when you offered to get me a pregnancy test because I didn't dare buy one myself in case my dad found out?" She glanced at him. "You could have judged me for being in that position, but you didn't."

"I might not have agreed with what you'd done to end up in that position," Andy said. "But judging you wouldn't have helped you in that moment."

"Sometimes I think you're too good to be true," she said.

"If there's any goodness in me, it's because of God."

"Do you have any faults?"

Andy gave a laugh. "Sure. I get frustrated and impatient with people, especially with Phoebe."

"And me?" she asked. "Do you get frustrated and impatient with me?"

"Not impatient, really," he replied, debating on how honest he should be. But she'd asked. "I do get frustrated with you on occasion."

She nodded. "I'm not surprised. I get frustrated with myself sometimes."

"I usually get frustrated with you for not seeing your own worth. For thinking that you deserve the bad that's happening to you."

She didn't say anything in response to that. "Well, I still think you're too good to be true."

Andy wasn't sure what to say to that. Clearly to Cece, *too good to be true* meant relegating that guy to the friendzone, because that's where he'd definitely ended up. But he wasn't sure how to change that. His parents had impressed on him the importance of being a nice person, and to some degree, his natural personality leaned in that direction. It was who he was, and he wasn't going to become a mean guy like Geof in order to get a girlfriend.

If he came in last because he was a nice guy, so be it.

"I'm not perfect. I struggled with anger and questioning God after my dad died. I just couldn't understand how He could let that happen to us. And then my mom started to get sick..." He swallowed hard. "Sometimes I get scared that she's going to die and leave me and Phoebe on our own. I don't want to think God would allow that to happen."

"It kind of sucks," Cece said. "I'm sure the world would be a whole lot better with your dad still in it, and it would also be a lot better without people like my dad and Geof."

Andy winced as Cece essentially wished her dad was dead, but he couldn't entirely fault her for feeling that way. "I wish I understood better why God has allowed certain things to happen, but I just have to believe that He is still in control. If I'm willing to trust Him in the good times, I have to trust Him to carry me through the hard times."

Cece fell silent after that, wandering away from the counter to her favorite section of the bookstore, and Andy let her go. He felt the weight of trying to convey God's love to someone who, it seemed, had never felt love in her life. His heart cried out to God, pleading with Him to give him the words to say to Cece to offer her hope in the midst of the storm in her life.

Soon, he spotted her curled up in one of the comfy armchairs he'd added to the store awhile back. She had a book in her hands, and he didn't bother to interrupt her reading until it was nearly six.

"I'll be ready to go in about ten minutes."

She looked up from the book and nodded. "Okay."

He returned to the front counter and finished his cash out, then went to the office to put the cash drawer in the safe. Thankfully, he never had much cash in the store since most people paid with their credit or debit card. Cece was in there gathering up her jacket and purse. Once he was done locking everything up, they climbed into his car.

"Are you sure you don't need dinner?"

"I'm sure."

Andy had to accept her word for it, so he backed out of his spot behind the store and headed for her house.

"Can you let me off down the block?" she asked.

"You don't want me to drive you to your house?"

"I think it's probably better that you don't. If Geof talked to my dad, he might be watching for me, and it would be better if he didn't see me getting out of a guy's car."

It surprised Andy that she'd actually admitted that. And if she suspected that was possible, he wasn't going to do anything that would aggravate her dad and put her in a difficult position.

After he turned onto her street, he pulled over to the curb. They were almost a block away, but she seemed fine with where he'd stopped.

"Thanks for letting me hang out," Cece said.

"Anytime. Seriously. Anytime. You're welcome to come by the store whenever you want."

"Thanks." She opened the door, then glanced back at him over her shoulder. "Have a good night."

"You, too."

Worry knotted Andy's stomach as he watched her walk away, her steps slow as she headed toward her house. He didn't know if she truly felt safe in her home, or if she just felt like she had no other option. It didn't seem like a place where a man like her father lived and where a man like Geof had access to her would be safe. However, he couldn't force her to leave.

There had been points in their friendship when he'd been concerned for her, but it had been more that she'd seemed unhappy. Over the past year or so—ever since Geof had entered her life—his concern had turned more to her safety, not just her happiness.

Even after she'd disappeared into the house, Andy stayed parked for a few minutes, praying that God would protect her. The helplessness he felt in this situation felt similar to how he felt regarding his mom's health.

He hated to not be able to help the people he loved. That often caused him to struggle with resentment. God gave him such a caring spirit, but then he was faced with situations where he just couldn't do *anything*. It about killed him to admit his helplessness.

As he drove home, he hoped that his mom had had a better day than Cece, but he knew it was very likely she hadn't. They were both fighting battles... different and yet still both were heart wrenching for him to witness.

CHAPTER TEN

Cece knew that she wasn't going to be able to sneak downstairs, so she was already bracing herself for her dad's yell when she walked in the door.

"Cecelia May Albrecht, where have you been?" he demanded from where he stood in the doorway that led from the landing by the backdoor into the kitchen. It confirmed her suspicion that he'd be watching for her.

"I was at work, then I hung out with a friend for a bit."

"You need to come home as soon as you're done with work."

She frowned at him. "Why?"

"Until you've accepted that you need to get back with Geof, you go to work, and you come home." His hands clenched at his sides. "Nothing more."

"You're grounding me?" Things were reaching a whole new level of crazy if he thought he could do that. "You can't ground me. I'm an adult."

"Try me," he growled with a fierce glare. "Just try me."

Cece felt a bolt of fear shoot through her, and she knew that at least for the time being, she needed to back down. With a jerky nod, she headed downstairs to her room.

People who knew her would probably be surprised at how she backed down when dealing with her dad. For the most part, she never backed down from anyone. She would go toe to toe with them, and *they* would be the ones to back down. Never her.

Yet there she was, slinking her way down the stairs to her room, her tail between her legs. Weak. So weak.

Anger burned inside her, making her want to lash out at the world. This wasn't who she was. This wasn't the person she wanted to be. But because she'd been born to a jerk and a weakling, she would never be able to reach her full potential.

She'd never be able to find happiness.

Once in her room, Cece locked her door and went straight to her bathroom, peeling off her clothes as she walked. She started the shower, ran the water as hot as she could handle, then stood under the spray. She let the water flow over her hair and face. And if her eyes burned and tears fell, no one would know. And she could just pretend it was water from the showerhead that slid down her cheeks.

Except that her heart ached. Oh, how it ached. And she didn't know how to get rid of it, since the water didn't wash the ache away.

Though she wanted to stand under the spray until the water ran cold, she knew it would give her dad just one more reason to rail at her. So, when she felt like she'd regained control of herself, she quickly washed her hair and body, then got out.

Though she'd told Andy she would eat at home, she had no appetite. Once she was done with her nighttime routine, she crawled into bed. Maybe the next day would be better. It certainly didn't feel like things could get much worse.

"Good morning," Mia chirped cheerfully as she came into the bakery's kitchen the next morning. "How's the baking going?"

Lousy. That was what Cece wanted to say, but instead, she said, "Fine. I'm just finishing up with the Danishes."

"Those seem quite popular. Same with the cinnamon rolls. And the cookies..." Mia laughed. "Actually, everything here is popular. And having tasted most of it, I can see why."

Cece gave her a wan smile. "Brooke has definitely set a high standard. People come from the surrounding towns to pick up their favorites."

She turned her attention back to the Danishes, not needing yet another burnt item on her hands. Burning a batch of muffins had been a poor start to the day. She'd had to make a strong cup of coffee and give herself a stern talking to about keeping her focus, and she'd managed to not burn anything else since.

"Are you doing okay?" Mia asked.

"Hmm?" Cece looked up at her.

"You seem like you're tired or stressed or something."

"Tired," she agreed readily enough. "Definitely tired. This new schedule is taking some getting used to."

"What time do you get up?"

"Around three or three-thirty."

"Wow. Why so early?"

"I have to be here by four-thirty."

"No wonder you're tired."

"Yep. But I'll get the hang of it, eventually."

"If you need a cup of coffee, let me know."

"Already had two, so not sure I should have any more."

"Well, if I can help, just tell me what to do."

Cece might have taken her up on that if her brain was working well enough to figure out something for her to do. "I'll let you finish stocking the case once the last of the baking is ready to go."

"Sounds good. In the meantime, I'm going to make sure everything is clean."

It said something about how tired she was that she didn't even have the energy to be irritated by Mia's upbeat attitude. She really hoped that Geof didn't show up that day because she wasn't sure she'd be able to deal with him without bursting into tears.

Clenching her jaw against yet another yawn, Cece focused on the task at hand. Once the early morning baking was done, she could take a short break before tackling the rest.

She kind of hoped that Andy didn't come into the kitchen to talk to her because she wasn't sure she could stay strong when faced with his gentle concern. But at the same time, she really wanted to see him. She had to keep from begging for another hug, just so she could lean into his strength.

He showed up a short time later, coffee already in his hand. Mia had apparently told him to just head into the kitchen, because he appeared in the doorway and startled the life out of her.

"Hey there." His smile came easily, but she could read the concern in his gaze.

"Hi." She let out a sigh and leaned a hip against the worktable, crossing her arms. "This schedule is kicking my butt."

"Yeah? Didn't get enough sleep?"

"My brain seems wired to not fall asleep so early. Sooner or later, I'll get the hang of it."

She wanted him to buy what she was selling. That her tiredness was strictly because of the new schedule, and not from tossing and turning. Unfortunately, she knew he wouldn't be as easily convinced as Mia was.

Unlike Geof, however, Andy seemed to respect that she was at work because he didn't comment on her state of mind. He just said, "Feel free to come to the bookstore after you're done here."

She might, just for a couple of hours. She wouldn't stay as late as she had the previous day. Until her dad realized that she was going to work early and thus, was off earlier than she used to be, she'd spend that time in a place where she felt safe. After Geof's appearance the previous day, the bakery didn't feel as safe as it once had.

"I'll probably stop by. Did you want me to pick you up something from *Norma's* for lunch?"

He considered it for a moment, then nodded. "I'll phone in an order if you want to swing by and grab it."

"Yep. I can do that."

He smiled again. "Perfect. I'll see you in a couple of hours, then."

She watched as he disappeared, then heard the low rumble of his voice as he spoke to Mia. The urge to run after him was strong.

Her neediness where Andy was concerned was starting to aggravate her. She didn't want to need anyone. For most of her life, she hadn't had someone who was there for her. But then Andy had come along. It was hard to not lean on him when he'd been the one good constant in her life for so long.

At one time, she'd tried to convince herself that he was like a brother. However, that hadn't sat right with her. Given that he was the one person who'd stuck by her, she'd decided to claim him as her best friend. It was unlikely that he thought *she* was *his* best friend, but she could live with that. Even if she wasn't his best friend, he clearly considered her some kind of friend, or he wouldn't have stuck around for so long.

With the idea of spending time at the bookstore spurring her on, Cece found the energy to push on. Since she enjoyed her job, she didn't usually look forward to leaving the bakery, but she was that day.

"See you tomorrow," she called out as she walked out the front door when her shift was done.

After a quick glance around, she jogged across the street and headed toward *Norma's*. Hopefully Andy had remembered to phone in his order. She hadn't called ahead for hers, but usually they could throw an order of fries and a milkshake together for her pretty quickly.

The restaurant was fairly busy when she walked in, but the woman at the front greeted her with a smile. "You here to pick up Andy's order?"

"Yep."

"It should almost be ready."

Cece headed to the counter to place her order and pick up Andy's. "Hi Missy."

"Hey there, Cece," the other woman said with a smile. "Here for Andy's order?"

"Yeah. And I wanted to pick up a couple of things for myself."

"I'm pretty sure that Andy took care of that already." Missy turned and picked up a drink tray and a paper bag from the counter behind her. "Unless he's drinking two milkshakes and eating chicken strips and a hamburger by himself."

Why did that make her want to cry? "Ah. I guess he did."

"He's such a sweetie," Missy said with a smile.

That was something that Cece would never argue about. "Yeah. He is."

Too bad no one would ever say that about her. Picking up the drink tray and the bag of food, Cece thanked the woman, then headed out of the restaurant. She glanced around again, then crossed the street to get to the bookstore.

"You didn't have to get me lunch," she said when she set the food down on the counter in front of Andy.

"I know." Andy grinned. "But I wanted to. I didn't want to eat in front of you, and I wasn't sure if you planned to get anything."

"I did plan to get something, but then I didn't need to." She paused. "Thank you."

He glanced up from where he was looking through the contents of the bag. "You're welcome. Let's eat in the break room."

Cece picked up the drink tray while Andy grabbed his phone and the food bag. Her stomach rumbled as she inhaled the aroma of the food. It had been too long since she'd last eaten, and suddenly, she was starving.

Sitting down across from Andy, Cece eyed the chicken strips and French fries with reluctant appreciation. This wasn't the type of food she should eat, but right then, she didn't care. It smelled good, and she wanted to eat every last bite. Still, she waited for Andy to pray for his food, then she grabbed a fry and shoved it into her mouth.

Cece began to relax, only then realizing how stressed she'd been about running into Geof as she'd walked along the street. She felt safe enough with Andy that she could let everything else go. Too bad she couldn't just spend all her non-working hours camped out in the bookstore.

Partway through their meal, the bell on the door at the front jangled, so Andy got to his feet and left the room. Cece heard the murmur of voices but couldn't tell who Andy was speaking with. He ended up being gone for about five minutes, and by the time he got back, she had finished most her fries.

"That was Jillian," Andy said, making Cece wince a bit. "She was looking for a specific book for her class."

"I keep forgetting she's a teacher," Cece said.

"From conversations I've had with her, she seems to really love her job."

"I don't think I could ever have been a teacher. My patience level isn't high enough."

"Well, it's always good to know our limitations," Andy said with a laugh. "I think I have lots of patience, but I've never wanted to be a teacher either. Although I do teach Sunday school at church when they need someone."

It didn't take much for Cece to imagine Andy teaching children. Geof, on the other hand... "Do you *want* kids?"

Andy's brows rose as he swallowed the bite of hamburger he'd taken. "Sure. I mean, I've always hoped to have kids someday. I know my mom would love to have grandchildren."

"Guess you need to get a girlfriend." As soon as she said it, Cece wanted to take the words back.

He shrugged. "I've been trying, but so far, it hasn't really worked out."

Cece lowered her milkshake to the table. "You have?"

He hadn't said anything about dating, and she really didn't like the idea. *Really* didn't like the idea. He was her one friend. If he got a girlfriend, what was she going to do? No woman would want their boyfriend hanging around with another woman.

"I've been out on a few dates," he said, oblivious to the fact that she was melting down a little inside. "Even went out with the same woman a couple of times over the past month, but I just didn't feel much of a connection."

Cece didn't even know how to respond to that. While she was dealing with her mess of a life, he was trying to find a woman to spend the rest of his life with. A woman who he'd actually want to spend time with. And probably someone whose life wasn't the dumpster fire hers was.

Her dad had always said that the only men of value to her should be ones who were rich and influential. The ones who could support her because she was never going to amount to anything.

There had been times she'd wanted to ask him what his value in life was then. Because they were far from rich, and he definitely wasn't influential.

As she stared at Andy, she came to a realization. Andy might not be rich or influential, but he was dependable. He was stable and caring. His wife might always have to work outside the home, but Cece was sure that the two of them would be a team. They'd work together to build a life for themselves and any children they had.

There was a time coming—and it appeared to be sooner than she'd imagined—that she wouldn't have a place in Andy's life anymore. He'd been in her life for so long that she couldn't even imagine how she'd live without him.

"So... uh... how are you meeting these women?" Cece asked. "Church?"

Andy gave a laugh. "No. There aren't a lot of single women in the church at the moment. I'm using dating apps."

Cece wondered if they'd get matched if they were on the same app. Somehow, she doubted it. But strangely enough, the idea of being matched with Andy stirred something inside her. A spark of longing to be the woman he wanted to spend the rest of his life with.

But Cece knew that wasn't her destiny. If Andy had any interest in her like that, he would have said something already. Not that it mattered. If she got free of her father and Geof, she wasn't going to have anything to do with men again. Except Andy.

"I'm not sure that dating apps are for me, but it seems the easiest way to meet women these days."

"So if you don't use a dating app or church, what are you going to do?"

He shrugged again. "Not sure. I guess I'll just have to leave it for the time being. Maybe God has another plan for me."

Though she wasn't sure about trusting some distant God with one's future, Cece was very relieved that Andy wasn't going to be exiting her life anytime soon. Hopefully.

"You can hang out here, if you want," Andy said as they cleaned up the remnants of their lunch a short time later.

"Are you sure?"

"Very."

"Then I think maybe I'll take a bit of a nap."

Andy nodded. "No one will disturb you in the office."

After he'd returned to the store, Cece settled onto the couch in the office. It wasn't the most comfortable place to sleep, but with a full stomach, she was feeling even more tired.

She'd barely closed her eyes when her phone pinged with a message. Since she doubted Andy was texting her—and he was the only person she would want to hear from—Cece was tempted to ignore it. But there was some sort of morbid curiosity within her that made her reach for the phone and flip it over to see the screen.

Geof: *Where are you? I'm at the bakery, and they said you're done for the day.*

Distance made Cece brave, along with an intense desire to be strong enough to stand up to Geof. She'd been able to do it a couple of times, but he just wasn't taking her seriously.

She had to keep trying, though. If she ever hoped to be free, she had to keep trying.

Leave me alone. Where I am is no longer your concern.

After hesitating a moment, she turned her phone completely off so she wouldn't be tempted to check any more messages he sent. Maybe it was time to get a new number so that he couldn't keep messaging her. Only she'd have to give it to her parents, and then her dad would give it to Geof. Which would totally defeat the purpose.

Sleep was a little longer coming after that exchange, but eventually Cece managed to drift off, hoping that she'd dream of happy things and what her life might be like one day if she could just get free of Geof and her dad.

CHAPTER ELEVEN

Andy got to his feet when the church service ended. He'd come on his own once again since his mom hadn't felt up to joining him, and Phoebe had gone to spend the weekend with her friend.

"How's life been treating you?" Tanner Mikkelson asked him as they walked with Emma, Tanner's fiancée, up the aisle to the foyer.

"It's been alright. How about with you two?"

"I just got back from a speaking engagement in Florida," Tanner said. "I never imagined that public speaking would be something I'd enjoy doing, but it's not too bad."

"Did you go with him, Emma?"

"Not this time. I'm more of a homebody."

Tanner slipped his arm around Emma. "I figure she'll remember how much she appreciates me if I go away occasionally."

Emma laughed, giving him a light slap on his chest. "I appreciate you just fine."

It had been interesting to see how Emma and Tanner had managed to get beyond what had happened in their past to build a relationship. Andy hadn't known what had happened, but Tanner had shared about it with him after he and Emma had started dating.

Part of him wondered if Tanner would have any ideas on how to help Cece. They had dated for awhile, which might make it kind of awkward to ask, but Andy was getting desperate. His fear for Cece was increasing because he'd continued to have run-ins with Geof as he searched for Cece if she wasn't at the bakery or her house.

Cece had said she was okay, but for how long? He didn't want to hear that she'd decided to get back with Geof in order to stop him from stalking her. No doubt that was Geof's end game. He probably assumed that if he kept after her enough, she'd cave.

And Andy could see that Geof's obnoxious persistence was wearing on her. It didn't help that she was still adjusting to the new hours and responsibility at the bakery.

Finally, he decided that he had to see if Tanner or Emma could give him some advice or insight. "Hey, guys, I wonder if I could talk to you for a minute about something."

Tanner's brow furrowed, but he nodded. They moved off to the side, out of the way of the other people in the foyer.

"What's going on?" Emma asked.

He'd gotten closer to Tanner and Emma since they'd all spent time together during the planning and the events of the reunion the previous summer. They might not have been friends during high school, but Tanner seemed to have no problem being his friend now.

"It's about Cece," he said.

Tanner's brows rose, and he glanced at Emma. "What's going on with her?"

Andy hated talking about her behind her back, but he thought he could trust Tanner and Emma. Taking a deep breath, he told them about the recent events in Cece's life.

"I knew I didn't like that guy," Tanner said. "I ran into him in the gym once, and he was flirting with anything that moved. Well, females, anyway. I called him out on it, and he really didn't appreciate that."

"Well, he hasn't appreciated Cece breaking up with him, either." Andy sighed. "Did you ever meet her parents when you dated her?"

"Yeah. They showed up at one of my games that Cece was cheering at. Afterward, her dad was really drilling me about my future plans, like if I thought I'd make it big in football." Tanner grimaced. "Of course, back then, I was cocky enough to say that was the plan."

"The cockiness was obviously well placed," Andy said with a laugh. "Guess he was sizing you up."

"Guess so, but I had no intention of maintaining a long-distance relationship when I left for college. There was never going to be a future with me and Cece."

"I sure wish she'd ended up with someone like you," Andy said. "Even with the way you were back then. At least then she'd be with a guy who wouldn't hurt her."

"But don't you have feelings for her?" Emma asked with a frown. "Why would you want her to be with another guy?"

Andy's shoulders slumped. "I'm never going to be the type of man she wants."

Tanner reached out and laid a hand on his shoulder. "Except that I think that the type of man she keeps ending up with is who her dad thinks she should be with, not who *she* wants."

Andy wasn't so sure, but he didn't say that. "I'm just not sure what I can do to help her. I feel like she's not safe living at home, but she's not able to move out because her dad is holding her hostage financially."

"I am so grateful that I had a wonderful dad," Emma said softly. "And even though my mom can be a bit of a pain sometimes, I know she loves me."

Andy nodded. "I struggle to understand how a man could treat his only child—a daughter, no less—the way Cece's dad treats her. It's like he sees her as a commodity to use to secure his own future."

"I guess that kind of explains why she is the way she is."

Andy agreed, though he hadn't even told them everything Cece had revealed about her family.

"I'm not sure how we can help her," Tanner said.

Andy nodded. "Yeah. I guess I just wanted to see if I was missing something."

"Cece's a very proud woman, so I'm not sure she'd accept help from me, or anyone else, for that matter," Tanner said. "You're probably the only person she trusts. I'm glad that she's had someone like you as a friend all these years."

"She needs more friends," Andy murmured. "And a bigger support group. I don't mind being there for her, but I think she needs more than just me. Even if she doesn't think so."

"What happened with her and Sarah?" Emma asked. "They used to be close."

Andy wasn't going to reveal those details. "They had a falling out of some sort."

"I think she's had a falling out with a lot of people," Tanner said. "I just hope that doesn't end up happening with you."

"I don't think it will." Andy wasn't sure what might make him walk away, but they hadn't even come close to reaching that point.

Though he hadn't really expected Tanner or Emma to have a solution, Andy was disappointed that he still had no idea what to do. However, it had felt good to get some of it off his chest.

"We'll be praying for both of you." Emma reached out and gave his arm a light squeeze. "And if something specific comes up that we can help with, don't hesitate to call."

"I appreciate your willingness to help," Andy said. "Especially given your experiences with Cece."

"Honestly, what you've shared has given me a different view of her and a better understanding of why she might act the way she does," Emma said.

Tanner nodded. "It even explains some stuff that happened back when we were dating."

The couple again assured him of their prayers, then they left the church hand-in-hand. Andy couldn't help but feel a little jealous of the relationship they shared. He was happy for them, but he longed for something like that for himself, too.

Andy said hi to a few more people, then headed home to see how his mom was doing.

She was sitting in the living room when he got there. "Hello, darling. Did you enjoy the service?"

He sat down on the ottoman in front of her. "Yep. It was good. You enjoy the stream?"

"Yes. The music was lovely."

"It was," Andy said, not surprised that was what his mom had commented on. Back in the day, she'd been part of the worship team at church. Music was something she enjoyed a lot, whether she was creating it or listening to it.

"Mary is coming over with some food in a few minutes," she said.

"Really?" Andy had thought he'd hang out with his mom, but if she had company coming, he could do something else. "If you're okay with Mary, I think I'm going to head out for a bit."

"That's fine, darling."

As he headed downstairs to his room, he considered what to do. He was concerned about Cece not having work to escape to or a car to go anywhere on her days off, so maybe he should see if she wanted to do something. She liked to go to movies, so he went to his laptop and checked to see what was playing that she might like.

A few minutes later, he sent her a text. *Want to go to the movies? There's a Back to the Future marathon going on at a theater in Everett.*

Cece: *Sure.*

It starts at three. We could grab some lunch first.

Her response to that was a little slower. He'd almost accepted that she was going to say no when her reply popped up.

Cece: *Okay.*

Cece: *Someplace cheap tho.*

That she added that told him how dire her situation was. But at least she wasn't trying to keep up appearances with him.

I'll be by in about thirty minutes. Should give us enough time to get something to eat before the movies start.

Cece: *Pick me up at the corner.*

He sent her back a thumbs up, then did a quick check of his bank account. He was quite sure that she was going to protest him paying for everything, but he wanted to at least be able to offer it. She probably assumed he'd think it was a date if she let him pay.

Little did she know that he had no expectation of them ever dating. And under normal circumstances, he wouldn't fight to pay. However, knowing that she was trying to be better with her money, he wanted to help her as best he could.

When he went back upstairs, he found Mary and his mom sitting in the living room with food on TV trays in front of them. There had been a time when his mom would never have let them eat like that in the living room, but there were days now when sitting on a chair at the dining room table was too painful for her.

"Hello, Andy," Mary said with a smile. "How is life treating you these days?"

"Very well. How about you?"

"I'm doing great."

"I'm glad to hear that. Thanks for hanging out here." Andy turned to his mom. "I'm going to catch a movie marathon, so I might not be home until late. I'll have my phone on vibrate though, so if you need me, just call."

"Have fun, darling."

He said goodbye to the ladies, then headed out to his car. It wasn't too long before he pulled to a stop at the curb where Cece had asked him to meet her. She wasn't there yet, but he was a little early.

After turning off the car, he kept watch in the direction of her house, praying that she wouldn't have any issues with leaving. It felt weird to be thinking that about someone who was his age. His mom never gave him grief about leaving the house, and she rarely asked him where he was going. She respected that he was an adult and that he didn't have to account for every move he made.

He felt bad that Cece didn't have that same respect from her parents. Or at least her dad. The man treated her like she was a child, and until she got married, she was his possession.

Anger burned inside him again. Not that he would ever be that type of father to begin with, but he would remember this in years to come and make sure that he prepared any daughters he had to function well in the world.

As the minutes clicked by, he began to worry, even though she wasn't late. But at this point, he wouldn't put anything past her dad. What would he do if she didn't show up? Did he have the courage to knock on the door and confront her dad? Would she want him to do that?

Thankfully, it ended up being a moot point because he spotted her headed his way. He got out of the car and walked around to the passenger side, watching as she approached him. She wore a pair of jeans with a light green sweater under a jean jacket and a pair of black boots. Her blonde hair hung loose in long curls.

As she neared him, she gave him a quick smile. "Hey."

As usual, his heart skipped a beat when she smiled at him, like it did every time after not seeing her for awhile. It was like it hoped that *this* time, she'd see him as more than just a friend. It didn't take long for his heart and mind to snap back into sync, allowing him to put aside his feelings for the time being.

He opened the door for her. "Thanks for coming with me."

Gripping the edge of the car door, she lifted an eyebrow. "Sure. Anytime."

Chuckling, Andy waited while she settled herself in the front seat, then he shut the door. He jogged around to the driver's side and slid behind the wheel.

"So... fast food for lunch?" he asked as he started the car.

"Yeah. It's not the healthiest, but it's cheap."

As Andy steered the car toward the street that led out of town, they debated the merits of each of the fast-food options they had. He let her make the final call since he didn't really have a huge preference for one place over the others. She was the one who was more concerned for health and budget reasons.

By the time they reached the restaurant she'd settled on, they had just over an hour before the first movie started. Though he tried to pay for her meal, as expected, she declined.

As they sat down at a table with their trays of food, Andy said, "The movie marathon is on me."

"Why?" she asked as she plunged a straw through the lid of her drink.

"Because I invited you. If you had invited me, I would have made you pay."

Cece rolled her eyes. "Yeah, right."

"I would have had to go on my own if you hadn't agreed to come."

"You could have whipped out one of your apps. Might have found a woman up for watching a *Back to the Future* marathon."

"I'm starting to think I shouldn't have told you about that. Besides, I knew that you liked those movies, so I thought I'd see if you'd want to go with me. I'd rather watch them with someone I know."

"Well, thanks for thinking of me." She took a sip of her soda. "I was bored at home. I hate being without a car."

"Was there something else you'd rather do?" Andy asked. He wasn't against forgoing the movie marathon, though he didn't exactly enjoy shopping, which was probably what she'd want to do instead.

"Nope. Movies sound good to me."

"Then that's what we'll do," Andy said as he opened the box holding his burger.

"Did you go to church today?" she asked after he'd said a prayer for his food.

"Yep."

"Were Mia and her husband there?"

Andy frowned. "Uh... I'm not sure. To be honest. I didn't look for them."

He probably should have since he'd invited Mia, but he'd had other things on his mind. Thankfully, he knew that members of the congregation would have noticed the unfamiliar faces and greeted them. He would have to remember to talk to Mia about it on Tuesday when he went by the bakery for his coffee.

"Do people make a big deal out of it when you visit?" Cece asked.

"Not really. Used to be they would welcome visitors and have them stand, but that was a long time ago. Like when I was a kid. I think they realized that not everyone liked the attention."

"But some did?"

"Sure. I think there are always some who like that kind of attention."

"Geof would like to be asked to stand and be welcomed like that."

Andy grimaced. "Yeah. I can see that. He probably wouldn't even have a problem walking into a church and getting everyone to like him."

"In the short-term, anyway," Cece said. "Problem is—or maybe it's a good thing—he can't hold the act up for long. Sooner, rather than later, people would see his true colors."

"Is that what happened with you?" Andy asked.

She glanced at him before focusing on her chicken wrap. "Yeah. He seemed nice enough when my dad introduced me to him, but it didn't last. If nothing else, he's taught me not to take people at face value."

"Guess I was lucky to sneak in before you learned that."

"Shut up," she said with a laugh. "Pretty sure what you see is what you get with you."

Andy knew he should take it as a compliment, but frankly, it kind of felt like she was saying he was boring. Which, okay, was true. It wasn't like he led a very exciting life.

"How about you?" he asked. "What you see is what you get?"

She rewarded his question with a hard stare. "I don't matter enough to anyone for them to care whether what they see is what they get with me."

"That's not entirely true," Andy told her. "I care about you, and I think I know you pretty well."

She nodded. "Probably the only person who does. My folks and Geof don't care who I am, they just want me to play the role they've cast me in."

"Well, I have no expectations of you when we're together, so just be who you are."

She smiled at him then. "You might regret that."

"I haven't yet."

Andy was glad that she seemed relaxed. Hopefully that meant her weekend hadn't been bad so far. He wanted to ask her about it, but he also didn't want to bring up anything negative when their time together was going well.

CHAPTER TWELVE

Cece didn't want to move when the credits rolled for the last movie in the marathon. When Andy had texted to ask her if she wanted to go out, her answer would have been yes, regardless of what he'd suggested.

Thankfully, she enjoyed the *Back to the Future* movies. She wished that there had been another one because she wasn't ready to go home yet.

Neither she nor Andy had to work the next day, but she doubted he'd want to stay out super late. The next day was going to be a trial since she didn't have work to get her out of the house, and Andy probably wasn't going to suggest they hang out together again. When she'd had a car, she used to go to Seattle or one of the other towns that weren't too far from New Hope, to run errands or shop.

"Ready to go?" Andy asked.

"Sure." She got up and followed him down the row to the aisle.

He stepped out and then waited for her to exit. She walked in front of him up the aisle, then out of the theater to the foyer area. It wasn't one of the fancy newer theaters, and the décor showed its age. She wouldn't be surprised if this theater had been a new one back when the first *Back to the Future* movie had come out in the eighties. Still, the nostalgic look suited the movies.

Outside, they walked to where Andy had parked earlier. The sun had set while they were watching the movies, and the air held a chill. The night was clear, though, so there was no rain.

Once they were on their way back to New Hope, Cece said, "If you could travel back in time, would you change anything?"

"Hmmm." Andy didn't answer right away. "I don't know. Maybe I'd try to do something to prevent my dad from dying. And I wish we had realized there was something more significant to the stuff my mom was going through when she first got ill."

"Do you think it would have made a big difference for your mom?" Cece didn't know a lot of details, but from things Andy had said, they still didn't know exactly what her medical issues were.

"Probably not. But maybe we'd be further along on the journey to finding out what's going on with her." Andy sighed. "I really miss my dad when dealing with my mom's health issues. I feel like I'm failing her because she doesn't want to share everything with me the way she would have shared with my dad. She tries to shoulder it herself and not be a burden to me and Phoebe."

Cece could hear the sadness in his voice, and it made her want to give him a hug. She wished that she could help him, but there was nothing she could do. She had nothing to offer him.

"What about you?" he asked.

"What about me what?"

"What would you change if you could go back in time?"

Cece sank back into her seat, staring out the passenger window at the lights flashing by as Andy drove. "I don't know if there's anything I *could* have changed. Maybe I could have tried to stop my parents from getting together. No them, means no me."

"I wouldn't like that," Andy said. "Maybe you could have avoided getting together with Geof."

"I suppose. But if it wasn't Geof, it would just be someone else."

"How about the events that led up to what happened at the bleachers that day? Would you change that?"

"No." The answer came immediately.

Andy glanced at her. "Really?"

"Really. Changing that would mean that we wouldn't have met." It was a bit surprising how much that idea distressed her. She wasn't sure she would have survived the years since then without his friendship.

"I wouldn't change that either."

Warmth suffused her at his words. He was the only person in the world who made her feel like she wasn't just a waste of space. If she could change anything, maybe it would be to have met Andy sooner.

"I can't let myself dwell too much on how things could be different," Andy said. "It would just make me feel more negative about my current circumstances."

"Yeah. Since I feel like there's really nothing I can change, I don't think much about it either." Cece turned to look at Andy. "I do wonder what my life might have been like if I'd been born into another family."

Andy nodded. "I can see why."

Cece couldn't begin to imagine how much more different her life would have been if she'd had loving parents who had only wanted what was best for her. Who had wanted her to thrive in life.

"Thanks for today," she said. "I enjoyed getting out of the house."

"Do you have plans for tomorrow?"

"I'm not sure. Can't really go anywhere."

"I have to go to some appointments with my mom in Seattle, but you could hang out at the bookstore if you wanted," he said. "I could pick you up before we go to her appointments and let you in. If you need to leave, I can turn on the alarm from my phone."

Cece considered the idea. It was very appealing. "I think I'd like that. If you're sure it's okay for me to be in there without you."

"I know you're not going to mess with stuff. I trust you."

"I would love to just be able to hunker down and read all day."

"So if I pick you up around nine, would that be okay? I have to have Mom in Seattle for her appointment by eleven. We'll need to leave by nine thirty to give us enough time."

"That would be perfect."

With a plan in place for the next day, Cece felt lighter. She knew that her issues with Geof and her dad hadn't disappeared, but she would be able to avoid the pair for another day. She doubted they'd even think that she'd go to the bookstore since it was closed on Mondays.

"Do you want me to drop you off at your house or the corner?" Andy asked as they drove down Main Street to her street.

"At the corner." She had no idea if her dad was watching for her. When she'd left, he'd been on the phone, so he hadn't been able to hassle her about where she was going.

"Just for the record, I hate letting you off at the corner like this. It goes against everything I've been taught regarding how to treat a woman."

"It's for the best," Cece said as he pulled to the corner and stopped. "Respecting what I want is a good thing to do too, though."

"That's true." Andy put the car in park and turned to her. "I'll be praying that your dad doesn't hassle you when you get home."

"Thanks." She wondered if he prayed for her without mentioning it. In a way, it was weird to think about that. That would mean he thought about her when they weren't together, and she hadn't ever really considered that.

"So I'll be here at nine. Okay?"

"I'll be ready," she said.

"Sounds good."

Cece found it difficult to open the door because she didn't want their time together to end. Finally, she curled her fingers around the door handle, then glanced back at Andy. "Have a good night."

"You too. Maybe text me that everything's okay?"

"I will."

She pulled the handle, and a rush of cold air greeted her. Though she really didn't want to get out, Cece forced herself to stand up outside the car. She closed the door, then headed down the sidewalk to the house.

Since it wasn't really late, there were still lights on inside the house. She took a deep breath, bracing herself for the possible confrontation. As she approached the house, she glanced back and saw that Andy still hadn't left. It made her feel a little more courageous. Like she really wasn't alone.

As she unlocked the door, her shoulders tensed. Pushing it open, she quickly spun to lock it again, then headed down the stairs. When she made it to her room without her dad making an appearance, she wondered if Andy's prayers really worked.

Before she got ready for bed, she put some stuff together in her bag so that she was ready to go in the morning before remembering she was supposed to text Andy.

I'm home and everything is fine.

Andy: *Great! Hope you have a good night. See you in the morning.*

Yep. Thanks again for today. Goodnight!

She wasn't going to sleep yet, but she wanted to be comfortable, so she went through her nighttime routine and changed into her pajamas. As she did that, Andy lingered in her thoughts.

For the first few years of their friendship, she'd taken him for granted. She'd had other friends, so she hadn't always depended on Andy. But when she'd needed someone to vent to or talk with, he had always been a safe place for her. No matter how much time passed between their texts or conversations, he'd always responded.

Since she'd torpedoed her friendship with Sarah and the others, Cece had leaned more and more on Andy. And he had stepped up to fill the void in her life without complaint. She knew that he had other friends because he talked about the Bible study he attended with people from his church, including the McNamaras. Still, he made time for her.

Cece was sure there would come a day when Andy tired of her issues and just stopped responding. Her heart hurt at the idea. He was the most important person in her life.

She froze at the thought, staring at herself in the mirror. How was it that no matter who she dated, Andy was still the person she relied on the most? She'd never cared about any of the men she dated as much as she cared about Andy.

Cece wasn't sure what to do with that revelation.

Sadly, she knew that despite being the most important person in *her* life, he had others in *his* life who were more important than her. Particularly his mom. And she knew without a doubt that if he found a woman to date seriously, that woman would be more important to him than Cece.

Her heartache was reflected in her eyes. She could see it in the mirror as she stared at herself, her face stripped bare of the makeup she always wore to elevate her appearance. No one ever saw her like this. No one knew the longings that she'd tried to bury deep inside her, knowing that they'd never be met.

Stripped bare of everything that she used to protect herself from the world as best she could, Cece had never felt more vulnerable and worthless. She squeezed her eyes shut and turned away from the mirror. Moving slowly, she finished getting ready for bed.

As she settled under her covers a few minutes later, Cece realized that if it weren't for Andy, she would have just given up already. She would have just gone along with her dad's plan. Accepted that she and Geof would have a relationship until *he* decided he didn't want her anymore.

Andy had shown her what it was like to be treated well, even as just a friend, and she wanted that. Cece didn't want to end up like her mom. She wanted someone to respect her. She wanted to know what it was like to be loved.

And she wanted to love someone, too. Unfortunately, she wasn't sure she knew how. She read plenty of romance novels, but she wasn't sure how to apply what she read to her everyday life.

If only she had someone she could talk to about these things. Someone other than Andy. She could only imagine how weird it would be to ask Andy about how to fall in love with a guy.

Her phone chimed with a text. Hoping it was Andy, she grabbed it off her nightstand.

Geof: *I am out of town for a couple of days, but I expect you to be ready for me when I get back.*

Cece stared at the message, but she didn't reply. At least she was going to have a reprieve from him. She wasn't surprised that he was going out of town. At almost forty years old, he ran a successful business with offices in New York and Dallas. It wasn't unusual for him to be gone for up to five days at a time. Unfortunately, he always came back. If only he would just move to one of those other cities.

Setting her phone back on the nightstand, Cece picked up her tablet and opened her eBook app. Geof was probably going to get upset that she didn't reply, but she didn't care. She had to stand up to him when she could, and in the safety of her bedroom, she felt strong enough to do that.

The next morning, Cece pulled herself together, determined not to carry her emotions from the night before into the new day. After getting ready, she headed up to the kitchen to grab some food to take with her to the bookstore. Her dad should have already left for the day to wherever he called an office these days, so she didn't have to worry about running into him.

"What are you doing?" Of course, her mom was still there.

Cece glanced at her, taking in the perfect hair and makeup. Her dad pretty much required it of her, even if she didn't leave the house. "I'm going out for a bit, and I want to take some food."

"Where are you going?"

Cece knew her mom was going to share whatever Cece told her with her dad. "Just out. I don't have money to buy food, so I want to take some with me."

She put the items to make a sandwich on the counter. The urge to give more details to her mom was there, but she kept her mouth shut. It was hard, though, because she wanted to confide in her mom. But she'd proved over and over that she told her husband everything.

"I'm not sure your father would want you to go out."

She glanced over at her mom, where she stood near the counter, her arms crossed. "I'm an adult, Mom. There's absolutely no reason for me to have to spend my time off in my room, never leaving the house. If you choose to stay cooped up in here, that's your decision. I'm choosing *not* to be cooped up here."

Her mom narrowed her eyes. "You should be more grateful for what your father is doing for you."

Cece swung to face her more fully. "Grateful? Grateful!? Are you kidding me? He takes nearly all of my paycheck to cover living here. He's not letting me stay here out of the goodness of his heart. He yells at me all the time, and he's forcing me to date an abusive man. Why on earth should I be grateful for that?"

"He's trying to make sure you have a financially stable future."

Cece scoffed at her words, then turned back to her sandwich prep. "I'd rather be with a poor man who treated me well than with a rich one who doesn't."

"You'd change your mind on that when you can't buy what you want."

"That's already what my life is. And Dad doesn't make much money, otherwise he wouldn't need to take my money, and we'd live in a nicer house."

"Your father has worked hard at his businesses. It's not his fault that they've failed, and now that he's working with Geof, things will be much better."

Cece hadn't realized how bad of a businessman her dad was until recently. He had lofty dreams, but somehow, he never managed to carry out the steps necessary to succeed.

At the moment, he was tied up in cryptocurrencies and NFTs. None of which Cece understood. And it was entirely likely that her dad didn't understand it all either, but he'd jumped on it as the latest fad. He and Geof had discussed it ad nauseum, and Cece and her mom had had to sit there and listen.

Only Cece had long ago learned how to tune them out. If only she could tune Geof right out of her life.

Once she was done with the sandwich, she grabbed some granola bars and an apple. She was pretty sure that Andy had water at the bookstore, so she didn't bother with any drinks.

"I'll see you later," Cece said after she'd put the food in her bag.

"When will you be home?"

"Not sure." She picked up her bag and headed for the door.

Before her mom could say anything more, she slipped out the door and headed down the block to where she was going to meet Andy. It was a gray day, but there was no rain yet.

Andy's car was already parked at the curb, so she jogged toward it. Andy got out and came around to the passenger side. He was wearing black slacks and a black blazer over a light blue shirt. He looked very professional, and she wondered if he dressed like that to get the doctors to take him more seriously.

"Good morning," he said with a smile.

She couldn't help but smile back at him. "You look nice."

Andy's brows lifted and a flush stained his cheeks. "Oh..." He looked down at himself. "Uh... thanks."

Seeing him so flustered made Cece realize that she had never complimented him before. He'd told her she'd looked nice on occasion, but for some reason, she'd never returned the compliment. She was truly a horrible friend.

"You always look nice," Cece said as she got into the car.

Andy laughed. "No need to lay it on that thick."

He closed the door, then went around to get in the driver's side. Starting the car, he pulled away from the curb. "No problems leaving the house?"

"Nope. Dad was off somewhere, and I got a text from Geof last night telling me that he was going away for a few days."

Andy glanced at her as he braked at a stop sign. "You haven't blocked him?"

"No. I figured it's a good way to monitor his moods."

They didn't have time to discuss it further because it was a super short drive to the bookstore from her house. She suspected Andy had a definite opinion about her not blocking Geof, but he didn't say anything more.

Once they got to the bookstore, he parked at the back, then got out. She followed him to the back door and waited as he unlocked it and disarmed the alarm with his phone.

"I'm not going to turn on the lights in the front," he said. "Just so no one gets confused and thinks the store is open."

"I'll just stick to the back. I have some stuff to do, so I won't need to go to the front."

"Sounds good. Text me if you have any issues or if you're going to leave," Andy said. "I'll set the alarm on my phone."

"I don't want to distract you from your appointment."

"I'll have my phone on vibrate, so it'll be okay."

"Thanks again for letting me hang out here. So much better than being at home."

Andy smiled. "Anytime."

The quiet that descended over the store when he left was weird since normally there was music playing. Thankfully, that was easily remedied by putting music on her phone. She settled onto the couch with her tablet and set her phone down beside her as it played her favorite playlist.

It was odd being there without Andy, but Cece decided to embrace the serenity, grateful that once again Andy was providing that for her.

CHAPTER THIRTEEN

Andy waited for his mom to get settled in the front seat of his car, then he helped her with the seatbelt before he closed the door. As he walked around to the driver's side, he flexed his hands, trying to work out the tension that had built up during the appointment.

"It's going to be okay," his mom said as he slid behind the wheel.

It was a lie. He knew it. She knew it. But it was a lie they had to tell themselves in order to keep going. They tried to subscribe to the theory of *no news is good news*, but it really wasn't. Especially when she seemed to be getting worse between appointments. Not significantly, but steadily enough that it meant that over time, it became significant.

On the hour's drive back to New Hope, they talked about everything but the appointment. Andy let her guide the conversation, not sure that he could come up with a topic if she left it up to him. She mainly talked about the visit she'd had with Mary the previous day. He was so thankful that she still had friends who came to spend time with her.

When they got home, she declined to eat anything. That wasn't unusual after an appointment, but hopefully she'd eat more for dinner.

"I'm just going to sleep for a bit," she said once they were home.

That also didn't surprise Andy. She never slept well the night before an appointment. And neither did he.

He helped her to her room, then went to his own room to change into jeans and a T-shirt. Before leaving the house, he checked on her to make sure she didn't need anything else from him.

"Text me if you need anything. I'll be home around five with supper."

"Sounds good," she said, then lifted a hand to cover her yawn. "Get me soup and French fries, please."

"Will do." Andy bent and kissed her cheek. "Love you, Momma."

"Love you more, darling," she murmured, sleep already working to claim her.

He locked the house, then headed to the bookstore to check on Cece. As he entered the back door, he heard music and smiled. He poked his head into the break room, but she wasn't there, so he went on to the office. She was sitting on the couch with a tablet in her lap.

"Hey," he said as he walked into the room.

She looked up and smiled, then set her tablet aside. "How did it go?"

Andy sank into his office chair at the desk with a sigh. "It didn't."

Her brow furrowed. "What do you mean?"

"They still couldn't tell us what's wrong. So next up is more blood work. More scans."

"How can they not know what's wrong?"

Andy had the same question, but he didn't voice it anymore because there was no answer to it. Just like there wasn't one to what was wrong with his mom. It was a struggle, however, to accept that they still didn't have any specific answers. He had almost resigned himself to never having an answer to what was plaguing her.

"They've had some ideas, but then the treatments for those diagnoses don't work like they should, so they have to move onto something else."

"Is it... is it possible that her illness will never be diagnosed?"

Andy shrugged as he leaned back in his chair. "They do think it's a neurological issue. Her organs are all fine so far. Her blood-work to date hasn't helped with a diagnosis. She just has weakness and pain throughout her body."

"I'm sorry," Cece said. "I'm sure that must be so difficult for all of you."

"Yes, but especially for Mom. She hates feeling like she's a bur-den on us."

Andy tipped his head back against the chair and closed his eyes. Sometimes he felt the burden keenly, but it was only because he felt like he wasn't doing enough to help her.

"When do you go back?"

"Next month. She has to get some more scans and tests done."

"I wish I could do something to help you," Cece said, her voice soft.

Andy lifted his head and stared at her. He wasn't sure what to make of Cece recently. The earlier compliment about how he looked had taken him completely off-guard. And now she wanted to help and seemed so caring. He didn't know what had prompted the changes in her attitude, but he wouldn't mind if they were per-manent.

"It's fine," he said. "There's nothing any of us can do but just keep moving forward."

"I can't even imagine how things would be if my mom had health issues like your mom has. I doubt my dad would have had any patience with her, and I wouldn't be surprised if he divorced her over it."

"No better or worse for them, huh?"

"Oh, there is better or worse. My dad expects my mom to stick with him through the worse, and he'll stick with her through the better."

Andy didn't even know how to respond to that. His parents had shown him a very different type of marriage, and it was the kind he hoped to have one day. Cece's example of marriage had been the opposite.

"I figured out that Geof has the same views as my dad," Cece said. "After seeing what my mom has gone through with my dad, I decided that I didn't want that kind of relationship."

"I can't believe that there is anyone who would."

Cece nodded. "But you know most relationships that end up like that don't start out that way. Men like my dad and Geof would never get a woman if they acted badly right from the start. Geof was a gentleman to me at first, and I assume that was probably true for my mom and dad, too."

"Sometimes it seems like the jerks get the girls," Andy muttered.

"Well, the jerks have just enough charisma to outshine the nice guys, at least at the beginning."

"But if you know that, why do you keep going for the jerks?" Andy wasn't sure she'd answer him. It was the first time he'd really called her out on the men she'd chosen to date.

She wrinkled her nose as she frowned. "I don't know. I guess I just keep hoping that the charisma is genuine. I mean, if Geof had been as nice as he'd portrayed himself at first, we would have had a great relationship. It should have been more of a red flag that my dad really liked him."

Cece certainly had a type, and that type *wasn't* Andy. He wondered how long it would be before he had to watch her start dating *men with charisma* once again. Though she seemed a bit different after having dealt with Geof, he wasn't sure that any of this would lead to a lasting change in how she approached men and relationships.

"I have to say that you are the only reason I don't hate every man on the planet."

Andy gave a huff of laughter. "There are plenty of good men out there. You know that. Just because they haven't been interested in a relationship with you doesn't mean they're bad."

"You're talking about Tanner and Eli," Cece said with a scowl.

"Yes. They're both good men. As are other men that I know."

"So, is it just me?"

"What do you mean?" Andy asked.

"Is there something about me that attracts the jerks instead of the nice guys?"

Andy went back and forth on how to reply. "It's not that you just attract jerks, it's that you don't look past the surface to see what they're truly like. The things you're looking for in a man are things that jerks can fake until they get you hooked."

"But I haven't attracted any non-jerks," Cece said.

Andy gave a shake of his head. "That's not entirely true. What's more likely is that they were either too scared to approach you or figured they didn't have a chance, so didn't bother to try to talk to you."

Cece frowned. "Too scared?"

Andy held up his hand. "Don't even try to tell me you don't know that you can be a bit... uh... intense."

"Intense?"

Andy didn't want to hurt her feelings, especially when she was dealing with so much in her life already. But they'd never had a conversation like this before, and he wanted to use it to get her to see why she didn't have friends and seemed to keep ending up in relationships with men who treated her badly.

"People worry about ticking you off or getting on your bad side."

"You make me sound terrible."

"Not terrible," Andy said. "Like I said, you're intense. You say what you think, and there are times that isn't well-received."

"That's not my fault."

Andy shrugged. "Sometimes you have to weigh whether what you want to say is really necessary. Not everything needs to be said. Telling someone that the outfit they're wearing doesn't flatter them isn't necessary unless they've actually asked for your opinion."

"But if it's the truth..."

"Still doesn't need to be said," he told her, feeling slightly emboldened by her lack of anger in response to what he was saying. "Has anyone ever told you that you were wearing an outfit that looked bad on you?"

"Yeah. My Mom. My dad. Geof."

Andy rolled his eyes. "How about a friend? When you used to hang out with Sarah, did she ever tell you anything like that without you asking for her opinion?"

"Not really. She rarely said anything like that to anyone." Cece's gaze dropped to her hands. "I didn't ask for her opinion on my clothes or stuff like that because I didn't care what she thought."

"Here's the thing," Andy said. "It's not that you should lie to people. I'm not saying that at all. All I'm saying is that you don't need to blurt out opinions, especially if they're negative. People will begin to feel negatively about you, and most of us avoid people who make us feel that way."

"Two questions," Cece said as she held up two fingers.

"Okay?"

"First, why have you never said anything about this before? And second, if I'm such a horrible person, why are you still around?"

Andy leaned forward, resting his arms on his knees. "You are *not* a horrible person. You've just managed to push people away because you aren't aware of how your words make them feel. As to why I'm still around... I think I've told you that already."

"And why haven't you said this to me before?"

"I don't think you would have been as receptive to hearing it before."

She frowned again. "What do you mean?"

"You seem different recently. Like you're realizing some things about yourself and your life, and you're wanting to do things differently."

She seemed to consider that before nodding, her gaze flicking up to meet his for a moment. "Well, I suppose that's true."

"Because of that, I felt like maybe you are ready to hear this."

The big question was whether she'd be interested in making any changes. He wasn't holding his breath. She'd been dealing with a lot over the past little while. He wouldn't blame her if she struggled a bit to make changes. And sadly, he wouldn't be shocked if she decided to not make any changes at all.

He prayed that wouldn't be the case, but he had to be realistic. She had been a certain way for a long time and apparently hadn't seen anything wrong with it. He wouldn't harp on her about the change. It was something that she needed to decide for herself without pressure from anyone else.

All he could do was point things out as she asked and continue to pray for her. Sadly, their conversation had only reinforced Andy's place in the friend zone. It was disappointing, but not something he would dwell on. He had other things that needed his focus.

He rested back against the chair, lacing his fingers over his stomach. He hadn't updated Phoebe on the appointments that day yet. She had a harder time with the unproductive appointments, getting frustrated and angry at the lack of answers.

"Do you need me to go?" Cece asked, seemingly having picked up on his shift in thoughts."

"No." He gave her a quick smile. "You can hang around if you want. I'm going to do a little work before I leave."

She picked up her tablet. "I'm just going to do some more reading, so I won't disturb you."

Andy swung his chair around to face the desk. He had some invoices that he needed to input, along with some other bookwork that was easier to deal with when the store was closed. Cece's music continued to play, and while it didn't include songs he usually listened to, it wasn't too bad.

It was kind of nice not being alone in the store when it was closed. And as promised, Cece didn't bother him as he worked.

"I'm going to have to get going soon," Andy said after about an hour. "I promised Mom I'd bring supper home tonight. She was pretty wiped after the appointment."

Cece looked up from her tablet. "Yeah. I should probably head home, too."

She didn't seem entirely happy about the idea. Not that he blamed her.

Before they left, Andy called in an order to *Norma's*, then he took Cece home.

As he parked down the block from her house, Cece let out a sigh. "Thanks for giving me somewhere to hang out today. It was nice to be in a calm place with no chance of someone bothering me."

"You're welcome to hang out there whenever you want."

"Thanks." Cece picked up her bag from between her feet and opened the door. "Maybe I'll see you tomorrow."

Once again saying a prayer for her safety, Andy watched until Cece disappeared into her house before heading back to pick up his order from *Norma's*. When he walked into the house a few minutes later, he saw that Phoebe had arrived home.

"Hey, Pheebs," he said as he walked into the kitchen. "I brought you food."

"Good." She came over to stand next to him as he put the bag of food on the counter. "I'm starving."

"Is Mom still in bed?"

Phoebe nodded. "Yes, but she's awake. She's just on her phone with Cilla."

Andy left Phoebe to unpack the food and went to check on her. She was propped up against a mountain of pillows and looked up from her phone when he walked in.

"Hello, darling."

He bent to brush a kiss across her cheek. "Did you manage to get some sleep?"

"I did. I got enough to feel better, and not too much that I won't sleep tonight."

"That's good. Did you want to eat in here or in the living room?"

She considered it for a moment, then said, "Maybe just in here, darling."

"Sounds good. I'll be back in a couple of minutes."

Back in the kitchen, he got the tray he used for his mom's meals when necessary and began to put the food on it. "Mom wants to eat in her room. Are you going to eat with us?"

Phoebe nodded. "Sure."

Andy was glad, since she didn't always want to join them when their mom stayed in bed to eat. It seemed that was too much of a reminder of their mom's frail health.

He also knew that Phoebe wouldn't want to talk about the appointment. For some reason, she preferred the head-in-the-sand approach when it came to what was going on with their mom. He tried to talk to her about it, but she just brushed him off, telling him that when there was actually something figured out, then she'd listen.

There were times when he envied her. He and his mom didn't have the option of ignoring the situation. They had to face it head-on whether they wanted to or not.

He carried the tray of food down the hall to his mom's bedroom, and Phoebe followed with their drinks.

"Oh lovely," his mom exclaimed when she spotted them. "I'm hungry."

They got the food all sorted out, then Andy and Phoebe settled into the chairs beside her bed that had been put there for that exact reason. Though he'd had a burger from *Norma's* not that long ago, Andy still appreciated his first bite.

"How was school today?" his mom asked Phoebe.

"It was alright. It was pretty much a Monday, though, you know?"

Since the bookstore was closed on Sunday and Monday, Andy actually enjoyed Mondays. Not that he minded any day of the week, really, since working at the bookstore was his ideal job. He was eternally grateful that Drake had hired him back in high school and had believed in him and trusted him enough to leave him in charge of the store.

Also, he had time to work on his writing, since the bookstore wasn't super busy. As long as he was caught up on everything, he knew Drake wouldn't mind him using that time to write.

Phoebe hadn't decided exactly what she wanted to major in yet, but Andy knew she was leaning toward something in fashion design. Though he was clueless about fashion, he knew that Phoebe had some talent for drawing and design. She'd been doing it since her early teens. Since he'd been fortunate enough to get his dream job, he hoped that hers worked out for her, too.

His mom ate all the soup and fries he'd brought her, which was encouraging for Andy. He assisted her to the bathroom, making sure she had her walker nearby, then waited for her to finish.

"I'm going to read for a bit, then sleep," she said when she came back out, using her walker to get to the bed. "Still feeling a bit tired."

Andy helped her get settled in bed. "Hope you sleep soundly. Do you want me to bring you some water?"

"That would be nice," she said.

He grabbed the insulated cup on her nightstand and went to the kitchen to fill it with fresh water. Once he'd taken it back to her bedroom, he said goodnight, then went down to his room.

Part of him wanted to text Cece, to check on her and chat a bit, but it was close to her bedtime. Plus, he wasn't sure that she'd want that after their conversation earlier. Their friendship seemed to be evolving, but he was going to let her lead the change.

So instead of reaching out to her, he settled into his recliner with his laptop with a plan to write. His story binder was on the end table at his elbow in case he needed to refer to it. After loading up some music, he read through what he'd written most recently, then dove into the story, eager to get into a world where there were problems he *could* solve.

CHAPTER FOURTEEN

With Geof out of town, Cece relaxed slightly. Her dad was even leaving her alone, for the most part. Still, she went by the bookstore every day after work and hung out there until around five. After that, she went home, had some dinner, then got ready for bed.

On Friday, she got her first paycheck since her promotion. When she went to the bookstore after her shift, she handed it over to Andy.

"What's this?" he asked as he looked down at it. "Oh. Your paycheck."

"Yep."

He pulled a notebook out of the drawer, then motioned toward the back. "We'll go into the office and do this."

She nodded and followed him to the back of the store. "My dad asked why I was getting up so early and going to bed so early."

"What did you tell him?" Andy asked as they walked into the office.

"That I had been moved to a new position in the kitchen, but I didn't tell him I got a raise."

Andy set the notebook on the desk as he rounded it to reach his chair. "He didn't suspect anything?"

"Yeah, I think he did, but he didn't ask me specifically. You forget that he thinks I'm too dumb to understand finances." She shrugged. "He's going to figure it out, eventually."

Andy stared at her for a minute. "If you hope to get out from under his thumb financially, you're going to have to figure out a way to keep him from finding out stuff like how much you're paid. How do you pay him for your rent?"

"He just transfers it from my account to his."

Andy's eyes widened. "He has access to your bank account?"

"Yeah. It's the account he set up with me when I was younger."

"I want to tell you to go into the bank and have his name removed from that account, but I also don't want to put you in a position where he'd get angry with you."

Cece slumped down in the chair opposite his. "Then what do I do?"

"My suggestion would be for you to set up another account under just your name, so you have somewhere to keep your money away from your dad. You won't be able to save anything as long as your dad has access to your money."

Cece felt *so* stupid to have not figured that out on her own. "So, what should I do?"

Andy sat in silence for a moment, his brow furrowed. "Is your bank the one here in town?" She nodded. "Okay. Go over there now and tell them you want to set up another account. Transfer out all the money in your other account except for what you usually pay your dad. Then, have them give you updated information for your direct deposit. Give that to Brooke, so that on your next paycheck, the whole amount goes into your new account."

"My dad is going to be pissed," she said.

"Yes, and I'll understand if you don't want to deal with that. However, he's been controlling you by making it impossible for you to survive on the money he leaves you with each paycheck. This is the only way to make sure he can't take more than what he already is."

"He told me once that he was putting part of the money he took from me into another savings account." She hunched her shoulders. "He said I wasn't smart enough to save on my own, so he was going to help me."

"Have you ever asked him how much you have in that savings account?"

"I'm pretty sure that the balance is zero," she said. "I'm smart enough to know that the likelihood that he was saving my money for me is zero."

Andy nodded. "I'm inclined to agree with you."

"And even if he has saved up some money, I doubt he'd just hand it over to me."

"You're the only person who can decide how to work this out," Andy said. "You're the one who has to deal with the consequences, so no one else can tell you what to do."

"But you think I should set up the account," Cece stated.

Andy sighed, his blue-gray eyes showing compassion that was edging toward pity, which Cece didn't want. The idea of Andy pitying her made Cece feel a little sick to her stomach.

"I will not tell you what to do," he said. "You've had too many people do that to you already. You're smart enough to figure this out."

She sincerely doubted that. "You're the only person who I trust to have my best interests at heart when telling me what to do."

"Honestly, I think you should go do the new bank account set up now." He flipped open the notebook and jotted something down on the page. When he was done, he ripped it from the notebook and held the paper out to her. "Let me know if that makes sense."

She read over what he'd written, momentarily distracted by how neat his penmanship was. Forcing herself to focus, she finished reading the to-do-list.

"He'll still be able to see how much money went into your account today, but once you've moved everything but the rent money—which is all he's entitled to—into the new account, he can't touch it."

They talked the plan over for a couple more minutes, Andy doing the math to figure out how much she needed to leave in the account for her dad, and how much she needed to transfer out.

When she left the bookstore a short time later, she felt more confident than she ever had before when it came to her personal finances.

Cece knew that what she did at the bank that day was going to have consequences. The thought made her stomach knot, but this was necessary. The future she wanted for herself was worth upsetting him. She was just fortunate that for once in her life, she had someone who was helping her gain that future instead of trying to sabotage it.

The woman at the bank was super helpful, and thanks to Andy's list, everything went smoothly. By the time she left there almost an hour later, Cece was nearly euphoric. It was a great feeling to know that her money was now secure. If she was careful with her spending, that balance would continue to grow, and hopefully, it would eventually be enough to help her take the first steps toward personal independence.

When she walked back into the bookstore, Andy looked up from his laptop. She smiled at him and skipped to the counter.

"All done?" he asked.

"All done!"

He closed the lid to his laptop. "That's great."

"All I have to do is give Brooke the direct deposit information, and my next check will go into my new account." Cece wasn't sure when she'd last felt so good. "I should have done this ages ago."

"At least you've done it now."

She nodded. "And I'm going to try and be better about what I spend."

"Not having a car might help with that."

"Maybe. However, there's this thing called online shopping. Ever tried it?"

Andy chuckled. "I have, in fact. And it is definitely an easy way to spend more money than we should."

"It's fun, too." She leaned against the counter. "But maybe I should pay for that pen I had you set aside."

Andy opened the drawer and pulled the bag out. "Make sure you still want it."

She took it from him, but as she looked at the pen inside, Cece realized that even though it wasn't *that* expensive, being able to resist buying it would be a good step. "I'm going to put it back."

As she spun on her heel, Andy said, "Good plan."

When Cece returned to the counter, she fought the urge to go to Andy and throw her arms around him. This man... He was so amazing, and she'd been fortunate to have him in her life for so long. He had ended up being one of two good things in her life. The other being her job.

The bell over the door jangled, and Cece looked over to see a woman about her age walk in. She didn't recognize her, but then, it wasn't as if she knew everyone in New Hope Falls.

The woman looked at her for a moment, then turned her attention to Andy. She smiled at him with a familiarity that Cece wasn't sure she liked.

"Hi, Andy," she said as she stepped closer to the counter.

Andy didn't look as thrilled to see her as the woman did to see him. "Hey, Lynne. What brings you by?"

"Thought I'd stop by and see your store. It sounded so lovely when you told me about it over dinner."

"Oh. Well, I certainly like it," Andy said.

Lynne looked at Cece, then back to Andy. "I'll just look around while you finish with your customer."

"I'm not a customer," Cece stated. "I'm a friend of Andy's."

"Oh." The woman held out her hand. "I'm Lynne."

Cece didn't want to shake her hand, but knew she'd probably disappoint Andy if she was rude to the woman. "Cecelia."

"Nice to meet you."

"You, too."

"Can I talk to you for a couple of minutes?" the woman asked Andy.

Cece didn't want to leave them to talk, but when Andy looked at her, she knew that he wanted her to excuse herself. "I'm just going to hang out in the office."

She was tempted to hide herself by one of the bookcases and listen, but she needed to be a better person. So, she did go to the office like she said she would, but she didn't close the door. Unfortunately, all she could hear was the distant murmur of conversation.

That woman had to be from the dating app. Andy hadn't seemed thrilled to see her, which made Cece glad. If he'd been happy to see her, Cece wasn't sure how she would have felt.

While she waited for the pair to have their conversation, Cece paced around the office. She'd been having *such* a good day, and then that woman had to come along and ruin it. If Andy had told her he wasn't interested, why would she show up?

What was it with people who couldn't take rejection? She understood that being rejected wasn't great. Tanner's rejection of her back in high school had stung a lot. But if someone told her that they didn't want to be with her, her pride would make it difficult to beg them to stay with her.

It wasn't that she thought she deserved better. It was just that she wanted to be wanted by someone. Geof wanted her, but he also wanted other women as well. She didn't want to be one of many.

Pausing mid-pace, Cece looked toward the door. What if the woman was able to talk Andy into reconsidering his decision to step away from dating? She doubted that Lynne would want her hanging around Andy as much as she did. Cece knew that she wouldn't like Andy hanging around with another woman all the time if he were her boyfriend.

The way her heart skipped a beat at the idea made her frown. Andy as her boyfriend? That was laughable. He knew her far too well to ever love her or want her to be his girlfriend. How she felt about it really didn't matter.

When she heard the doorbell jingle, she held her breath, wondering if Andy would come back to the office, or if that was just another customer entering the store. Not wanting Andy to find her hovering near the door, she hurried over to the couch and sat down.

Pulling out her phone, she stared down at it. As she waited, she scrolled through her social media, not really seeing anything. When Andy didn't appear right away, she wondered if someone had come into the store.

She didn't want to walk back out there if the woman was still there. Maybe she should just slip out the back and head for home. If Lynne was going to be hanging around, Cece didn't want to be the third wheel. She never wanted to be the third wheel when it involved Andy and another woman.

When Andy still hadn't appeared after a couple of minutes, Cece gathered up her stuff and left the office. Instead of going to the front, she slipped out the back door and walked down the back lane, heading for the street that she needed to take to get home.

As she approached the house about ten minutes later, her phone's text alert went off. She ignored it as she let herself in the side door. Before she could head down the stairs to her room, her mom appeared.

"Your dad called and said that if I saw you, I needed to tell you that we're going out for dinner."

"Have fun," Cece said.

"Uh... no. You're coming with us."

"Uh... no, I'm not."

"Your dad will be very upset if you don't."

"I have to be up at three-thirty tomorrow morning since I do the morning baking. There's no way I can go out for dinner when I have to work in the morning."

Her mom crossed her arms and looked down at her from the kitchen entrance, which was up two stairs from the landing where Cece stood. "I'm just conveying your father's message. You know there will be consequences if you don't do as he asks."

"He's not *asking* anything," Cece retorted. "He's telling, but that doesn't make any difference. It's important that I keep my job, so I'm not willing to risk losing it by not getting enough sleep and then making mistakes."

"Why would you agree to a position with such ridiculous hours, especially if they're not paying you more?"

"I happen to like the work," Cece told her. "I enjoy doing the baking. Plus, Brooke is pregnant, so she didn't want to have to come in so early. I don't have a choice but to be up early, which is why I *won't* be going to dinner with you two and Geof."

Her mom frowned. "I didn't say that Geof was going to be there."

"You didn't have to," Cece said with a scoff. "You think I don't know both men by now? I know you think otherwise, but I'm not actually stupid."

"What am I supposed to tell your dad?" her mom called after her as Cece turned away and started down the stairs.

"Give him my regrets," Cece said.

When she got to her room, she blew out a long breath. The bravado she'd shown her mom bled away. Her dad was going to be livid, and Geof was going to be, too.

She dropped her bag onto the bed, then remembered the text that had come in. Sinking down on the edge of the bed, she looked at her phone.

Andy: *Where'd you go?*

Cece debated what to say. *Figured you were going to be busy so might as well head home. Need to do a few things anyway. Laundry is the big one.*

Andy: *Okay. Just wanted to make sure you're okay.*

She sent him back a thumbs up. *I'll probably come by tomorrow after work.*

Andy: *See you then. Have a good night.*

You, too.

She had kind of hoped that he would tell her about his conversation with the woman, but she wasn't going to ask.

Setting her phone aside, she went to her dresser to get something to change into. Once she was in her comfy clothes, she gathered up her laundry. She hadn't lied to Andy about needing to do it, and since she was home earlier than usual, she might as well tackle it.

She also dusted and vacuumed and changed the sheets on her bed. Once she'd transferred the laundry from the washer to the dryer, she went to take a shower.

As she sat at her makeup desk drying her hair, there was a pounding on her door. She knew who it was and was tempted to ignore it. But if her dad was angry enough, he'd probably kick the door in, which would leave her unable to lock it afterwards.

"Just a minute," she called out, then crossed to the door to open it.

"Get ready, right now," her dad said, his face flushed with anger.

"I'm not going out. I have work early tomorrow, and I need to be in bed by seven."

"Too bad. You can go to work a little tired. Get ready."

"No. I'm sorry, but my job is important to me, and it's even more important that I be alert now that I'm doing the baking. You'll just have to have dinner without me."

"If you'd just get back together with Geof, you wouldn't have to work. He said he'd be fine with paying all your bills if you quit."

"I enjoy my job, and I have no intention of quitting."

"Geof might have something to say about that."

Cece didn't argue with him. She just wanted him to leave her alone. If she reiterated that she wasn't going to get back together with Geof right then, it would only pour gasoline on the fire of his already blazing temper. She didn't think he knew yet about her bank accounts because if he did, he'd probably be throwing that in her face, too.

"You don't work on Sunday, so you will go to dinner tomorrow night."

She didn't agree, but she also didn't tell him no. Maybe Andy would let her sleep in the bookstore overnight. All she knew for certain was that she couldn't go to that dinner either. She couldn't allow herself to be trapped somewhere with no way of escape.

It wouldn't surprise her at all if the dinner wasn't actually at a restaurant. It was likely that Geof had arranged the meal at his house, then her parents would leave her there after the meal.

There was no way she could allow that to happen. She'd leave and walk all the way back to New Hope if she had to.

But hopefully it wouldn't come to that.

CHAPTER FIFTEEN

Andy smiled at Sarah McNamara as she chatted excitedly about the plans she and her family were making for her mom's upcoming birthday. She'd come in that day to pick up an assortment of items for her mom's present.

"Mom doesn't usually like us to do much for her birthday," she said. "But this year, I think we all are just looking for a reason to party."

"Even Leah?" Andy asked skeptically.

Sarah laughed as she nodded. "Surprisingly enough. I think Gavin is rubbing off on her."

The door to the store opened, and Andy looked over to see Cece walk in. Her gaze locked onto Sarah, and she frowned.

"Hi, Cece," Sarah said cheerfully. "How are you doing?"

Cece's frown deepened. "Why do you care?"

Sarah's smile didn't fade at all. "I do care about you, Cece."

"Couldn't prove it by me."

Andy suppressed a sigh at Cece's words. He knew that the women had had a falling out, but he had hoped that they'd one day be able to get past it. Cece could definitely use a friend besides him, but he had a feeling that she'd tell him that she wasn't interested in that friend being Sarah.

"Come on, Cece," Sarah said. "You know you deserved to be called out for what you said. It was your choice not to apologize for it and to distance yourself from us."

Cece crossed her arms and lifted her chin. "I only told Jillian the truth."

"It was a truth that didn't need to be said. It was a truth that she hadn't asked for. I'm pretty sure that it's a truth that *no one* would ask for."

"I was only trying to help."

Sarah gave a shake of her head. "No. You weren't."

Andy waited for Cece to get defensive again, but instead, she just scowled at Sarah.

"I'd love for us to all be able to hang out together again," Sarah said. "But you really need to think about how you interact with people."

"What's that supposed to mean?"

"When I'm interacting with friends, I always want them to leave our time together feeling better about themselves or to have experienced some encouragement."

"I'm not going to leave our time together here feeling better about myself," Cece said. "Just so you know."

Sarah sighed. "I'm sorry about that, Cece. I do care about you. Enough that I want to help you understand how you can be a more positive influence in people's lives. Have you made some new friends?"

"I don't need new friends," she said. "I have Andy."

Sarah smiled as she shot him a look. "Andy is a sweetheart. You're very fortunate to have him as a friend. I know that I appreciate his friendship."

"You just have to be friends with everyone, don't you?" Cece said.

"My philosophy is that I'd rather have someone be my friend than my enemy. Life is a lot easier when you're at peace with those around you. If at all possible. I understand that there are circumstances when friendship is not a good thing, but I'd like to at least try to be a friend before writing someone off completely."

Andy hoped that what Sarah was saying would sink in with Cece. She'd been more open to things that she wouldn't have been in the past, so he had a small glimmer of hope that she'd at least think about what Sarah was saying. Whether she did something with it or not was a whole other question.

"Well, I'd better go," Sarah said. "I need to pick up the cake at the bakery."

Andy rang up the items she'd chosen and laid on the counter before Cece arrived. "If your mom doesn't want any of this, she's welcome to return or exchange it."

"I think she's going to love it all. Especially the books. She's always talking about that author. She just discovered her recently."

Once Andy had it all rung up, Sarah paid for it. He put all the items into a bag, then handed it to her. "Tell your mom happy birthday from me."

"I will. See you on Sunday." Sarah turned to Cece. "It was good to see you again. Call me if you ever want to hang out."

Cece just nodded and moved away from the entrance. She turned to watch as Sarah left the bookstore and headed down the sidewalk in the direction of the bakery.

Andy waited to see if she'd say anything, not wanting to push her to talk about what Sarah had said.

"She can be so annoying," Cece muttered. "How can someone be happy *all* the time?"

"It's a choice."

Cece's brow furrowed. "A choice? You're telling me she *chooses* to be happy all the time?"

"Well, I do think she is, by nature, a happy person, but I also think there are times where she chooses to have a positive outlook even when facing problems in life."

"I'm not sure she has any problems. I mean, she's got siblings to support her. She's got a great mom. She's married to a rich man, who treats her well. Yeah, she's got all kinds of problems."

Andy knew it appeared that way from Cece's perspective, since her situation wasn't very good. He could compare his life with

Sarah's and resent the fact that his mom was struggling so much when hers was happily celebrating her birthday. He would guess that his mom and Nadine were probably close to the same age, so it was hard to see his mom struggling to even leave her bed some days.

It wasn't fair, but that was just how life was. The McNamaras hadn't lived a totally problem-free life. Their parents' divorce and everything that had happened with Eli after his girlfriend had disappeared had been challenging for them. So they had problems and struggles, just like everyone else.

He understood, though, that Cece was right in the middle of a huge storm in her life, so it was hard for her to see beyond that.

"It sounds like she'd like to see you again," Andy said.

"She's probably just being nice."

"I don't think she'd say that if she didn't mean it. You know her better than that."

"Yeah. She usually means what she says." She shrugged. "Sarah used to be my best friend, though I realize now that I wasn't hers. To her, I was just one friend among the many she had. I think she's closer to Jillian now than she ever was to me."

"She's asked me about you," he told her. "So I know she still cares about you."

"What did she ask?"

"Just how you were doing."

"And what did you say?"

"I told her that you were doing okay."

"You didn't tell her about my issues with my dad and Geof?"

"Of course not. I would never disclose those details about your life."

"You're my best friend now," Cece said.

"I'm your *only* friend," Andy said with a laugh.

"Well, I suppose that's true," she agreed with a small smile. "But even if I had more friends, you'd still be my best one."

Andy appreciated that she saw him that way, but he really hated that she had relegated him to the friend zone. Sarah had actually warned him about Cece at times, but she didn't know about the connection they'd forged back in high school.

"You have lots of other friends, so I'm probably not your best friend, either."

"Next to my family, you're the person I spend the most time with. You're special to me, Cece, more than just a best friend."

She stared at him for a moment. "I'm glad for that. I don't know what I'd be doing right now if it weren't for you."

"Sarah would be a good support for you, too," Andy said. If she had another friend, would she be willing to look at him as something more than just a friend?

"Did you get your laundry done yesterday?" he asked, deciding that maybe a subject change might be good.

"Yep. Laundry done. Cleaned my room. It was very productive." She paused, then said, "Did you have a good conversation with Lynne?"

Okay. So maybe he should have stayed on the topic of best friends. "Not really."

"Why?"

"Well, I had told her that I didn't think things would work out for us, after I'd gone on a couple of dates with her. She didn't feel the same way."

"So she was here to convince you to keep dating?" Cece asked.

"Yeah. I guess she thought if she came here and showed an interest in what I did that I might reconsider."

"What was wrong with her? Why didn't you think things would work out with her?"

Well, he couldn't be completely honest with Cece. "I just didn't feel a real connection between us. She was nice and everything, and I did invite her on more than one date, hoping that maybe the relationship would grow."

"You really wanted something to grow with her?" Cece asked, a frown on her face.

"It's not that I wanted something with *her*, but I felt like I should give it a chance in case it took more than one or two dates for something to develop between us."

"As opposed to love at first sight?"

"Yeah."

"Have you ever loved someone?" she asked. "I mean, I've never heard you talk about dating in the time we've known each other, but then we haven't always spent as much time together as we do now."

"Yes. I have loved someone, but we've never dated."

"If it was Sarah, I don't want to hear about it," Cece said with a wave of her hand.

"It wasn't Sarah, but I'd rather not talk about it."

"Just tell me if it was someone I know?"

"I don't want to talk about it. Maybe later I will, but not right now."

"I hope so because now I'm curious."

"Curiosity killed the cat," Andy said.

Cece laughed. "Oh, but cats have nine lives, so I think I'm okay."

He just shook his head, glad that she didn't seem to be determined to pry that secret from him. If there was one thing that he was pretty certain of, it was that things would change between them if she knew how he felt about her, and it wouldn't be a positive change.

"So, how was your day at the bakery?" Andy asked, going for yet another subject change.

Cece settled down on the stool he'd moved to the front for her and proceeded to tell him about her day. He wasn't sure how long she'd continue to come by the bookstore each day, but he really enjoyed her visits.

"Do you have any big plans for tonight?" he asked, more to keep the conversation going than because he thought she would have something going on. Except she grimaced in response. "What's wrong?"

"My dad told me that we're going out for dinner tonight."

"You're having dinner with your parents?" Andy asked. "Just your parents?"

"I don't think so. I think Geof is going to be there." She paused. "Actually, I think that we're going to end up at Geof's house, and that my parents are probably going to leave without me, stranding me at his house."

"Oh no," Andy said. "That's not going to happen."

"I'm not sure how to avoid it."

"Can you just not go with your dad?"

"I tried that last night, and he was furious. I'm scared to think what he'd do if I refused again tonight."

Andy considered how to help her. "Okay. Can you tell me with one hundred percent certainty that you *don't* want to stay with Geof? That there would be no reason that you'd want to stay with him."

"I don't want to stay with him at all, but the threats are hard for me to deal with."

"Here's what I'm thinking," Andy said, abandoning the order he'd been putting together as they talked. "I'll come to Geof's house and park outside. Then, if I see your parents come out and leave without you, I'll wait for you to come out. If you're not able to leave within fifteen minutes of when your parents do, I'll call the cops and tell them you're being held against your will. But that will only work if you really are being held against your will. I don't want to call the cops and have them show up, only for you to say that you want to be there with him."

Cece didn't look entirely convinced. "Why would you do that?"

"Do what?" Andy asked. "Try to help you?"

"Yeah. You're going to a lot of trouble for me."

"I care about you, Cece, and I don't want you to be in a dangerous position. You shouldn't be forced into a situation that you don't want to be in."

"I suppose you'd help anyone in my position," she said. "That's why everyone likes you."

Andy wished he could tell her that he'd only do it for her, but that wasn't true. He would try to help anyone who was in need. If it had been Leah or Sarah, or any of their friends, he would have been just as willing to help.

"I just want to make sure you're safe," Andy said. "Will you be willing to go along with my plan?"

"I wish I could just not go, but I'm afraid of what my dad might do to me."

"Has he hit you before?" Andy asked.

Cece frowned. Then, after a long moment, she shook her head. Andy didn't buy it, but he understood why she would deny it. Admitting that her dad had hurt her would be something she wouldn't want people to know.

"I don't know what to do," Cece said. "I don't want Dad to get into trouble with Geof, but I also don't want to be with Geof just so things will work out for Dad."

"I don't think that you should have to sacrifice yourself for your dad's poor business dealings. We're not living in medieval times here."

"I know." She sighed. "I just wish I could live my life the way I want."

Andy already knew that if Cece agreed to the plan he had in mind, he was going to be contacting Kieran to make sure that the cops would take it seriously if he called them to rescue Cece.

"So you'll really be there to help me if I need it?"

"I will. You just need to tell me when you're leaving home and what Geof's address is."

"His place is about halfway to Seattle."

"Wherever it is, I'll be there."

"What about your mom?"

"I'll make sure that I've taken care of her before I leave."

"I just want a normal life," Cece said with a sigh, her shoulders slumping.

"You're taking important steps to get to the life you want," Andy reminded her. "You're strong and determined. I believe you'll be able to get the life you want."

Another customer came into the store just then, so Cece disappeared into the back while Andy dealt with them. After the person left, Andy stayed at the front of the store, working on a new order for some books that someone had asked him to order.

He continued to be amazed that people came to him to order books when they could so easily just use one of the online sites. But he was also very grateful, because he knew Drake wouldn't keep the store open if it began to lose a lot of money.

If that ever happened, he didn't know what he'd do. Leaving New Hope wasn't an option, so he'd have to hope to get another job in town or in the nearest city.

If his own books took off, he wouldn't have to worry so much about what might happen to the bookstore. So far, he had a small following of readers who bought everything he published. Their purchases helped him with some bills, but he still needed his work at the bookstore to make ends meet.

Throughout the rest of the afternoon, Andy continued to work, periodically checking in on Cece. She was curled up on the couch with her tablet.

Since it was Saturday, the store closed at five instead of six. After locking the front door and turning off the *Open* sign, Andy went back to the office. "What time are you going with your parents?"

"Mom texted me to say that we're supposed to be at Geof's at seven for dinner."

"So she said for sure that you're going there?"

Cece nodded, and he could see the tension on her face. "I'm scared."

Andy sat down beside her and, after hesitating for a moment, he slipped his arm around her shoulders. She slumped against his side, her head pressed into his neck.

As he held her, Andy prayed for her and the whole situation she was facing. He prayed that God would help him rescue her if that became necessary. He was scared, too. Scared that even his best efforts wouldn't be enough.

"Would you be willing to do something for me?" Andy asked.

"Sure," she said without hesitation.

"If I have to call the cops, it might make things easier if I have something from you that says that you don't want to be in Geof's home."

She looked up at him, her eyes suspiciously damp. "What do you mean? You want me to write something?"

"How about I take a video of you? Just something that would explain the situation and then say exactly what you do and don't want."

Cece looked skeptical, but finally, she nodded, and Andy pulled out his phone. They talked for a minute about what all she should say, then Andy opened up his camera to the video setting.

"Don't worry about getting it perfect. I think it's best if it appears to be natural, so just say how you feel about everything, okay?"

She nodded, then took a deep breath. When he motioned for her to start, she began her recitation of what was going on with Geof and her wishes in the situation. She started to cry near the end, shredding Andy's heart.

Once she stopped talking, Andy set the phone down and reached for her again. He held her while she cried, tears stinging his own eyes. *Please, God, protect her tonight.*

He hoped they were overreacting. There were probably plenty of people who would think they were, but his own experiences with Geof led him to believe that they couldn't be too safe. The need to control Cece was making Geof lose his mind.

"I'd better go," she said a few minutes later. "I still have to get ready."

"Try to get out of it again," Andy said. "But don't push the issue if it makes your dad too upset."

She nodded. "I just want this to all be done."

Andy wished that it was all over, too. That she was free from the oppressive relationships she had with her parents and Geof.

Maybe this night would be a turning point for her.

CHAPTER SIXTEEN

Andy drove Cece home, stopping down the block as usual. Each time he watched her walk away, he had a sick feeling in his stomach. She was so brave to keep going home when she knew that at any moment, she might have to face her dad or Geof's anger.

He just wanted to protect her from everything, but he knew he couldn't. She was the only one who could extricate her from this situation. But he was going to be there for her in any way he could, even it meant sitting outside Geof's house for however long it took to make sure that she was safe.

They'd added another step to their plan for that night, one that would give her the chance to send him a clearer message. He just hoped that she'd be able to communicate with him, or he would lose his mind.

Before he pulled away from the curb after Cece had disappeared into her house, he sent a message to Kieran.

Would it be possible for me to talk with you for a few minutes?

Without waiting for a reply, Andy drove home. He needed to make sure that he had enough time to get some supper for his mom. He prayed that she'd had a good day, because he really needed to be able to go to Geof's to support, and possibly rescue, Cece.

When he got home, he went right in to where his mom was seated in the living room. She looked up at him with a smile. Phoebe also sat on the couch near her.

"How was your day?" he asked as he bent to kiss her cheek. "Anything exciting happen?"

"Phoebe got asked out on a date," she said with a glance at her daughter.

Andy looked at his sister. "Really? By someone you actually want to go out with?"

She nodded with a smile. "It's Aubrey's brother's best friend."

"So you know him already?"

"Yep. He's been there when I've hung out with Aubrey."

"That's good," Andy said. "I guess I'll need to have a little chat with him."

"Nope." Phoebe held up her hand in a stop motion. "There's absolutely no need for that."

"I think Dad would be extremely disappointed if I just let you date some dude without me having a talk with him."

"I have to agree with Andy, darling," his mom said.

Phoebe rolled her eyes. "He's a nice guy."

"Then there's nothing for you or him to worry about if I talk with him."

"Whatever," Phoebe said with a huff.

Andy and his mom both laughed at her response.

"So what's for dinner?" Andy asked. "Or do I need to make it?"

"I thought maybe we could order pizza tonight," his mom said. "We haven't had that in awhile."

"I'm going to be out for a couple of hours tonight," Andy said. "I have to leave around six-fifteen. Maybe even a little earlier if I have to make a stop on my way."

"Going on a date?" Phoebe asked. "Is it someone I need to lecture?"

"Nope. Not a date. Just a friend who needs some help."

"Well, I'll take care of ordering the pizza if you need to get ready to go," his mom offered.

"Thanks, Mom. That would be great."

The text alert sounded on his phone, and he pulled it out to see that Kieran had replied to his message.

Kieran: *Sure thing. Did you want me to come to your place or do you want to come here?*

I'd rather come to your place if that's okay.

Kieran: *That would be fine. I'm home now, so anytime.*

Andy looked at the time and realized he probably should go right over in order to make sure he had time to arrive at Geof's before Cece and her parents did.

"I'm going to head out now," he said. "Are you sure you're both okay?"

His mom reached out and took his hand. "We're both fine. I just hope that you are. Is everything alright?"

Andy sighed. "I just need to help a friend out of a difficult situation. I can't go into more details than that, but if you want to pray for safety for them, I'd really appreciate it."

"Are you in danger too?" his mom asked with a frown.

"No. I'll be fine." He hoped that was true. But even if it wasn't, he'd put himself between Cece and Geof in a heartbeat if he had to.

His mom squeezed his hand, then let it go. "I'll definitely be praying for them."

"Thank you."

As he drove to Kieran's a few minutes later, Andy felt anxiety creep up his spine into his shoulders. He didn't deal with anxiety on a regular basis, but the situation with Cece was really testing his ability to trust God for a positive outcome. Instead, he was more worried than he'd ever been before.

When he reached Kieran and Cara's house, Andy didn't hesitate to get out of the car and approach their front door. Kieran opened it right away and invited him inside.

"Hi, Andy," Cara said as she walked past them toward the stairs, their son, Jayden, in her arms.

After greeting her, Andy followed Kieran into the living room.

"What's going on?" Kieran asked, his expression serious. "Something happening with Cece?"

Andy nodded, then instead of telling the man himself, he loaded up the video and handed Kieran his phone. Hearing Cece's voice tremble as she spoke ramped up his anxiety even more.

"So she's being forced to go to the home of the man who's been threatening her and you?" Kieran asked at the end of the video. "Why doesn't she just say she won't go?"

Andy tried to explain as best he could the situation she was in with her dad and Geof. "She wants to get away, but her dad has made it so it's financially impossible for her to gain her independence."

They talked a bit more about the plan that Andy had come up with, then he asked if it was possible that the cops wouldn't come if he called them to say that Cece was being held against her will.

"It's out of my jurisdiction, but I know some people from that district. I'll make a couple of calls, then I'll let you know if you should just call 911 or if one of the staff will take your call directly."

"Thanks," Andy said. "I just don't want anything to happen to her. We both think it's likely her parents will leave her there, and then she won't have a way to leave."

"Some parents are a real piece of work, I have to say," Kieran said with a shake of his head.

"Tell me about it. I know people don't like Cece and don't understand why she is the way she is, but she's had a hard life with her parents. She's kept it all hidden because of her pride, but everything is reaching a crisis point now, and I'm the only one she has to help her." Andy swallowed hard. "I worry that I won't be able to do it."

"You're not the only one now," Kieran said. "I will do what I can to help as well, and maybe it's time to talk with a few other people to see if we can come up with an option for her."

"She's been trying to take some steps to at least gain control of her money, but it will all be for nothing if her dad and Geof manage to beat her into submission... emotionally, if not physically."

"You go do what you need to," Kieran said. "Send me a copy of that video, and I'll call you as soon as I've talked to my contacts. One way or another, Cece will not be left in a place where she doesn't want to be."

As he sent the video to Kieran's number, Andy sighed in relief, and his anxiety eased slightly. He just hoped that Cece would follow through on leaving if it did become necessary for him to call the cops. Worst case would be that she'd let her dad and Geof talk her into staying with Geof.

He didn't think his concerns were unfounded since Cece had already stayed in that toxic environment for years. He hoped that she would remember the steps she was taking to move on with her life.

"Okay. I'm going to head to Geof's. I want to be there when they arrive so that if she wants to leave right away, I'm available."

"Don't engage the guy or her parents by yourself. That will probably just escalate the tension which will benefit no one." Kieran rested his hand on Andy's shoulder. "I know you want to rush in and save her, but it will be better for her if you're not tangled up in this. Call the cops and let them take care of things. Cece will need you to be available for her afterward, which, if you get into it with either man, might prevent that."

He nodded, even though he wanted to be able to physically deal with Geof if he had to. As he walked to his car, Andy prayed that he was doing the right thing. He prayed that Cece would stay strong and follow through on the plan they'd come up with.

Finding Geof's house wasn't difficult. Unfortunately, it wasn't in a super busy neighborhood. The expensive homes in the area weren't pressed right up against each other, and there were hardly any vehicles parked on the street, though large driveways held quite a few.

His old car was going to stand out, there was no denying that. Hopefully, no one noticed that he was sitting inside his car. They might call the cops on *him*, which would definitely throw a wrinkle into the plan.

He decided it wouldn't be smart to park right in front of Geof's house, but he also didn't want to be too far away if Cece came out looking for him. Finally, he pulled to the curb on the far side of the house just before Geof's. Thankfully, it looked like the people in that house were having some sort of gathering, as their driveway was full of vehicles. He hoped that would make it easier for his car to blend in.

There were no cars in Geof's driveway, however, so he hoped plans hadn't changed. He'd been sitting there for around five minutes when he got a text from Cece.

Cece: *Almost there.*

He sent her back a thumb's up, then slid down in his seat, keeping an eye on his side mirror so he'd see the car as it approached. He didn't know what her dad's car looked like, but there hadn't been any cars going past him in the time he'd been sitting there.

If so much hadn't been at risk, Andy might have enjoyed his first stake out. But he found absolutely no joy in what he was currently having to do. He just wanted all of this to be over and for Cece to be safe.

Sadly, he knew that even if things were settled with Geof tonight, Cece would still have to deal with her parents. Which could be just as bad, since she'd have no escape from them, yet.

When he saw the car appear in the side mirror, he tensed. He stayed slouched down, not wanting her parents to see him, though Cece would probably recognize his car. That would be good since then she'd know where to find him if necessary.

Once they'd parked, he pushed himself up enough to see out the front windshield, lifting his phone to video what was happening. He watched as Cece climbed out of the back seat while her parents got out of the front. She trailed after them up the wide stone steps to the large front door. It swung open almost immediately, and Andy felt a wave of anger wash over him as he spotted Geof.

When the door closed behind them, Andy fought the urge to run up to it and storm inside.

And so, the real wait began.

Except, fifteen minutes later, the door opened again, and Cece's parents walked out. Andy gripped the steering wheel. His thoughts scattered as he watched them get into their car. That wasn't how it was supposed to happen. He'd thought they'd have a couple of hours before things would start moving.

What did he do now?

Pull yourself together, Andrew! You can do this! You have *to do this.*

Okay... Fifteen minutes. He glanced at the clock, making note of the time.

He was supposed to give Cece fifteen minutes before sending the text. He'd told Cece to delete all the text messages between them, and then change the name attached to his phone number to read *Mia* instead of his name. It would never have held up to a police search of her phone, but it would hopefully pass Geof's inspection if he went through her phone, provided she'd remembered to delete their messages from just a few minutes ago.

The only issue might be if he'd looked for Andy's number because he wasn't anywhere in her phone. When he brought that up as a problem, Cece said that she'd tell Geof that Andy had gotten annoying, so she'd deleted his number. Andy had figured that Geof was probably dumb enough to buy the explanation.

But now he was worried that he wouldn't be. Maybe they'd been the dumb ones, believing that they actually knew and understood a crazy man.

He opened up his text app and found Cece's name. But after a moment, he backed out and searched for Kieran's number instead.

Cece's parents have come and gone already, leaving her with Geof.

Kieran: *Send the text to check on her, then let me know what she says.*

Andy knew that they'd agreed to wait fifteen minutes, but he just couldn't. Anything could be happening to her.

Back on Cece's number, he tapped out the agreed upon message.

Hey, Cece. Any chance you could cover the first hour of my shift for me tomorrow morning? I'll owe you forever!

He sent the message, then sat staring at his phone as he waited and prayed for a good response. He wanted to see the door open and her come out and head his way.

I've sent the message, Kieran. No response from her.

Kieran: *Okay. Sit tight. My buddy said he'd come and see if he can defuse the situation. If not, he'll call for a squad.*

He's a cop?

Kieran: *Yep. He has a special interest in DV situations.*

Andy's heart thumped hard against his ribs, feeling like it was going to explode.

He should have tried harder to talk her out of going. Except he hadn't wanted to be telling her what to do, since she'd already had so much of that in her life. But right then, he really wished he had convinced her to go into hiding from her dad and Geof.

As the minutes ticked by without a response from Cece, Andy felt sicker and sicker. How was this going to have a good ending if she couldn't even reply to his message? It meant that Geof or her dad had taken her phone, essentially making her a prisoner.

By the time a car pulled to a stop behind his, Andy was sure he was going to throw up. The man who got out and approached on the driver's side of his car was big. Similar in build to Geof, in fact.

Andy rolled down his window as the man rested an arm across the top of his car and bent forward.

"You Andy?"

"Yes."

"Kieran called me about the situation," he said. "Has anything else happened?"

"No. She didn't reply to the text I sent her, and she hasn't come out."

"You're sure she's in there?"

Andy quickly found the video he'd taken earlier, then handed his phone to the man. "This was when she arrived with her parents. They stayed about fifteen minutes and left without her."

"I'm going to go have a conversation with the man and see what he has to say. Can I send this to my phone to show him we have proof that she went into the house?" After Andy nodded, the man focused on his phone for a moment, then he pinned him with a stern look. "You stay in your car. Don't approach the house or show your face. We need to keep this focused on her, okay?"

"Okay." It would be hard, but he needed this to have the best resolution possible, and if that meant standing back while the professionals dealt with it, so be it. He'd had a role in getting things this far, so it wasn't like he hadn't done anything to help her.

He watched the man walk back to his car, then he drove around him and up into Geof's driveway. Andy gripped the steering wheel and prayed like he'd never prayed before.

The door didn't open right away when the cop pressed the doorbell. The man didn't leave, just continued to ring the doorbell and knock on the door.

Finally, the door jerked open, and Geof stood in the doorway. After a moment, he tried to close it again, but the cop prevented him.

Andy wished he could hear what they were saying, but he'd promised not to get out of his car. All he could do was watch and pray.

Suddenly, the cop pulled his gun and pointed it at Geof, then entered the house. The pair disappeared inside, leaving Andy at a loss as to what was going on. Minutes ticked by, though it felt like hours. It took everything within him to keep from running to the house, and the desire to do that only ramped up when cop cars rapidly approached with lights and sirens, followed by an ambulance.

An ambulance?

Along with the fear he'd been dealing with, he was now filled with a deep sense of failure. If Geof had hurt Cece, then all the things he'd come up with to help in this situation had been for nothing.

Andy had told the cop that he'd stay in his car, but he just couldn't.

He pushed open the door and got out. Glancing around, he could see that some of the neighbors were also curious about what was going on. They probably didn't get many visits from the cops in a neighborhood like this.

Jogging closer, he stayed clear of the cops and EMTs who were heading for the house. He texted Kieran to see if he knew what was going on, but then all he could do was watch and wait, pleading with God to spare Cece any serious injury. It was clear that someone had been injured if the ambulance was necessary.

Though he hoped the ambulance was for Geof, courtesy of the cop, Andy knew Geof wasn't afraid to use his strength against Cece. His gut told him that despite all the planning, he'd failed to keep Cece safe from harm.

When the door opened again, the EMTs came out with the wheeled gurney. Andy darted forward, reaching out as he neared them.

"Cece? Is that Cece?"

"Andy?"

When he heard her voice, he wanted to elbow the EMTs out of his way to reach her.

"Sir, you need to move out of the way."

"She's my friend."

"Andy?"

As they got to the back of the ambulance, he was able to get close enough to see her. His heart fell when he saw her beautiful face, swollen and bruised. Anger made him want to turn around and find Geof so he could take a bunch of swings at the guy.

But his love for Cece overrode his anger at Geof.

"I'm right here, sweetheart," he said, taking her hand and bending close. "Everything's going to be okay now. Everything's going to be okay."

He wasn't sure that was really the truth, but he'd do everything in his power to make it so that it was.

CHAPTER SEVENTEEN

Andy slumped in the chair beside Cece's hospital bed, still feeling overwhelmed by what had happened the night before.

Thankfully, she didn't have any broken bones. Her wounds consisted of mainly bruises and some broken skin. *However,* she should never have suffered those injuries in the first place.

There was a knock on the open door, and Andy looked up to see Kieran approaching them.

"Hey, you two."

Andy was so grateful that Kieran had taken his concerns seriously, and that the cop who had come to Geof's house had been willing to take Andy's word for what was going on. If neither of them had, things could have been so much worse.

Unfortunately, the wounds Cece bore weren't just physical. She'd barely said anything since she'd been admitted to the hospital the evening before.

"How are you doing, Cece?" Kieran asked as he set a duffel bag on the floor beside the bed.

"I'm fine."

Kieran frowned as he glanced at Andy. "I hear that the doctors are letting you go home today."

"Yeah," she murmured. "Not sure *where* I'm going, though. I doubt my dad will let me go back home after this."

"That's kind of why I'm here," Kieran said. "Cara wants to offer you the apartment over her dance studio. It's just sitting there empty at the moment, plus, it has an excellent security system, so you should feel safe there."

"Geof's not out of jail, is he?" Andy asked.

"Not yet, but it's likely that will happen later today or tomorrow. We're working on a restraining order against him."

"How about her parents?"

"Well, they're denying everything, saying they didn't know what Geof had planned."

"And you believe them?" Andy asked.

"No, I don't. Not at all."

"How will Cece get her stuff?" Andy frowned. "I'm worried they won't let her in the house."

"You don't have to worry about that. After church, I went to your parents' house with a couple of officers, along with Sarah and Cara. While they packed up everything in your room, I told your parents what had happened and warned them to keep their distance from you."

Cece's eyes widened. "You did?"

"I hope you don't mind that we took the initiative to do that, but none of us thought you'd want to see your parents after what happened yesterday. We removed all the furniture as well. We weren't sure if it was yours or theirs, but your parents didn't say anything when we took it."

"Where is it all now?"

"Everything is in a trailer that's parked at Beau and Sarah's. If you want to move into Cara's apartment, we can bring it all over there. You don't need furniture, as it's fully furnished."

"Why hasn't she rented it out?" Andy asked.

"To be honest, I'm not sure. We've talked off and on about it, but because it's above her studio, she didn't really want to rent it to a stranger. Now it seems that maybe God knew that you'd need a place, which is why she didn't feel right about renting it out prior to this."

"But why would she want to rent to me?" Cece asked.

"I know that you've had some difficulties with Sarah and Jillian, but we, as a Christian community, know that we should set aside hard feelings and help when we know there is a need."

"How much will the rent be? I'm not sure if I can afford it."

Andy reached out and laid his hand on hers where it rested on the mattress. "You can. There's no reason for you to give *any* of your money to your dad now. You're out of their home, and you owe them nothing. Your new account is all set up, so you don't have to worry about your dad getting his hands on your money."

She stared at him for a moment before looking back at Kieran. "I guess if it really is okay."

"It is more than okay," Kieran assured her. "I'll have the trailer moved over behind the building, and we can start unloading your things."

"Thank you," Cece whispered. "I appreciate it."

"You're very welcome."

Kieran left the room then, and Cece fell silent once again, closing her eyes as she sank back against the pillows on the bed. Andy didn't know what to say to her. He'd already apologized for not being able to do more to protect her from Geof, though she'd brushed his apology aside.

And now that she had a safe place to go, Andy hoped that things had turned a corner for Cece.

After another hour, Cece was released to leave the hospital. Thankfully, Sarah had thought to send along some clothes with Kieran for Cece to wear home. Andy left the room so the nurse could help her dress, then they were on their way back to New Hope.

There were so many things on the tip of his tongue that he wanted to say, but all of them felt so insignificant. He wanted to assure her that everything was going to be okay, but honestly, he didn't know what to think anymore. Though he'd been aware that

Geof had hurt her in the past, for some stupid reason, he hadn't thought the man would actually get *that* physical with her.

"Do you want to get something to eat?" Andy asked. "I can go through the drive-thru."

She shook her head, which didn't surprise him. Still, he decided to pick up something for himself. He hadn't had anything to eat yet that day and was feeling the effects of it. Knowing her as he did, he decided to get her a milkshake. Even if she wouldn't eat something, maybe she'd drink her favorite milkshake. It was such a measly thing, but he just didn't know what else to do for her.

When they gave him the order, she took it from him and held it in her lap while he pulled away from the drive-thru to a parking spot to sort it out.

"The mint milkshake is for you, if you'd like," Andy said. "The rest is mine, but if you'd like any of it, help yourself."

She tucked one of the orders of fries into a cup holder, along with his vanilla milkshake. He said a prayer for the food, then unwrapped the burger he'd ordered for himself and took a bite. After the previous night, he hadn't been sure he'd ever feel hungry again. But now, he was just so glad to have Cece out of the hospital and on her way to somewhere safe, that his appetite had returned.

Not that he thought the whole situation was over by a long shot, but hopefully Cece wouldn't face another physical altercation like this one had been.

"So, you plan to eat the wrap, too?" Cece asked.

"Sure, unless you want it," Andy said. "I'm more than happy to share."

"I'm sure you are," she murmured.

He knew that she'd get why he'd ordered her favorites along with his. But if she couldn't be tempted to eat it, he wouldn't force it on her.

"I guess I'll help you out," she said and picked up the chicken wrap.

"I really do appreciate that."

He finished his burger, then backed the car out of the parking spot. "Anywhere you want to stop before we head to New Hope?"

She shook her head, then took a sip of her milkshake. He supposed that as long as her face bore the signs of what she'd endured, she wouldn't want to see anyone. He was just glad that she wasn't trying to hide it from him.

By the time they pulled up behind the studio building, the trailer was there and the garage door into Cara's building stood open. He recognized everyone there, and quickly put the car into park and turned off the engine.

He'd pushed his door open, then glanced over to see Cece sitting with her head bent. Shifting to face her, he said, "Would you rather go to the bookstore and wait there until everyone has gone?"

Her shoulders slumped as she let out a little sigh. "I don't know."

"Why don't you just sit here while I give them a hand?" Andy suggested. "If you feel like getting out, you can. But if not, I know the others will understand."

Her bent head gave a small nod.

He reached out and gave her clenched hands a light squeeze. "Just think. In a matter of hours, you're going to have you very own space. A safe home where no one can hurt you."

A smile briefly crossed her lips as she glanced at him. "I can't wait."

"I'll see if they need some help. Lock the doors when I get out, okay?"

She nodded, and he waited by the car after he got out, waiting until he heard the locks engage. Then, with a quick wave at Cece, he jogged over to the trailer where Beau and Kieran were unloading some boxes.

"Hey there, Andy," Kieran said with a smile. "Cece with you?"

"She's staying in the car for the time being. I think she's reluctant to face people looking the way she does." Andy gestured to the boxes. "Let me grab one."

"The ladies are upstairs putting away the dishes and groceries they picked up for her."

"Did you already take the bed up?"

"No, we just moved it into the garage for the time being. If she wants it upstairs, we can move it later, but there's room in here to store it for now."

Andy took one of the boxes, then, after a quick look in the direction of his car, he followed the guys up the stairs to the apartment. He'd never been there before, but when he got his first look at it, he knew Cece was going to love the place.

"Hi, Andy," Sarah said as she came to give him a hug. "How're you doing?"

"I'm fine."

"And Cece?"

"Still struggling. She's waiting in the car because I don't think she wants to see anyone while she's bruised and swollen."

"I can understand that," Cara said. "We'll get some of this set up for her, then she can unpack the rest of her stuff and put it where she wants it."

"I got her some groceries, based on what I remember her liking," Sarah said. "I figured she wouldn't want to worry about groceries just yet."

Cara waved at the cupboards. "The kitchen is fully furnished with plates and pots and pans, so she shouldn't need anything."

"Thanks so much for doing this," Andy said. "I know she hasn't always been the easiest to get along with, so no one would have blamed you if you hadn't done all of this stuff for her."

"I think she needs more people to show her God's love, not fewer," Sarah said. "And perhaps I should have tried harder to do that after what happened with Jillian. I guess I just hoped she'd come to see the error of her ways, but she can be stubborn when she wants to be."

"Do you have instructions for the alarm system so I can explain it to her?" Andy asked, not wanting to discuss Cece's personality right then. "I don't think she'll come in until everyone has left."

"Yep. Come over here, and I'll show you what to do," Cara said. "It can also be monitored from an app that I'll give you the info for."

While Cara showed him how the alarm worked, Sarah helped the guys bring in the last of the boxes. When everything was done, Andy thanked them all again, then went back down to the car. The others waved at them as they climbed into their vehicles and pulled away.

Andy guided his car into the garage, then got out and closed the overhead door behind them. Cara used the garage during the times she was teaching a class, but that wouldn't be an issue since Cece didn't have a vehicle yet.

He got out and went around to open the door for Cece. She moved slowly as she exited the vehicle. Andy followed her up the stairs, then stood beside her as she stopped in the kitchen and looked around the open layout of the apartment.

"This is really nice." He headed into the living room area. "Cara said that people can't see in these windows, so you'll have lots of privacy."

"I still can't figure out why they've done this for me," Cece said as she went to the large windows that looked out over Main Street.

"I'm pretty sure it's because they've seen a need, and God wants us to help when we see that."

"So it's just a God thing?"

"That's definitely part of it," Andy said with a nod. "But for me, and probably for Sarah, it's also more than that. We care about you."

She glanced at him, and he tried not to wince at the swelling on her face. But more than that, the deep sadness in her gaze tugged on his heart.

He hated what Geof had done to her. He hated what her parents had done to her. The people who should have loved and protected her had handed her over to a monster, and he'd broken her. Not just physically. He could see that her spirit had also been broken.

He never would have imagined Geof would go so far, and he doubted that Cece had either. Or at least he hoped she hadn't. If she had, and had still chosen to put herself in harm's way like that...

In that moment, he wanted to wrap his arms around her and tell her that he loved her. That he cared for her. That she mattered to him. And that even if she had no one else in the world, she had him.

Would she believe him, though?

"Do you want some help unpacking your things?"

She looked around, then said, "I guess it's all in the bedroom?"

"Let's check it out and see."

He led the way to the bedroom door. It was a large room, and the boxes and bags that Sarah and Cara had packed up for her were stacked against the far wall.

"Sarah said that she put the bag with stuff she thought you might want for tonight on your bed."

Cece slowly moved to the bed and sat down beside the small suitcase. She unzipped it and flipped the lid open. As she looked through its contents, Andy went to the stack of boxes and read what was written on each in black marker.

Normally, he wouldn't feel comfortable being in Cece's bedroom with her. But since she hadn't made the space her own just yet, it didn't feel like he was intruding.

It looked like Sarah and Cara had labelled the boxes with great detail, so hopefully Cece would be able to find everything. They'd told him that they'd taken everything they'd found, including the cleaning supplies and the rolls of toilet paper from under the sink in the bathroom.

He imagined that once Cece got over the shock of what had happened, she might be a bit upset at what she'd see as an invasion of her privacy by Sarah and the others. But right then, he figured she was just glad to not have to be around her parents.

"You don't need to stay now," she said. "I think I'm just going to take a shower and maybe try to sleep a little."

Andy frowned. "Are you sure you don't need help?"

"No. I'll just do a little at a time over the next few days."

"Cara and Sarah said they stocked the kitchen with food, so when you get hungry, you have stuff here."

She nodded. "Okay."

"If you need anything, just call me."

"I need to talk to Brooke about work. Since I'm in the kitchen now, I could probably go to work even looking like this." She waved a hand at her face.

"I'm sure she'd understand if you need to take a couple of days off."

"Maybe, but I think I need to work."

Andy could understand why that might be. "Come back out to the door so I can show you how to manage the alarm."

She got up and followed him to the panel by the door. He explained everything about the alarm system and the corresponding app for her phone, even as he marveled at how extensive Cara's security was. It seemed overkill for the small town of New Hope Falls. Whatever Cara's reason, Andy was glad that it was there for Cece. She would definitely feel safer with it in place.

Once he'd shown her everything on the panels, both in the apartment and down in the garage, he knew it was time to leave her.

"Are you sure you're okay here?" Andy asked.

"I'll be fine," she said, giving him a small smile. "I'm just really... tired."

Andy nodded. "Text or call if you want to chat. Maybe I'll see you tomorrow."

"Maybe."

Andy hoped so. She followed him down the stairs, then waited to close the garage door after he pulled out. He gave a wave but didn't pull away until the garage door had fully closed.

He had such a mix of emotions as he left Cece. Though he was glad that she was in a safe place, he hoped that her being completely by herself wasn't a bad thing.

Anger still burned inside him when he thought of what had happened. And it wasn't just anger at Geof and Cece's parents. He was angry at himself for not having tried harder to convince her to avoid that "dinner" at Geof's. Part of the responsibility for what had happened felt like it should land on his shoulders.

When he got home, he spent a couple of minutes just sitting in his car, trying to gather up his scattered emotions. He didn't want his mom to worry about him, which was what she'd do if she saw him visibly upset.

All he could do was hope that Cece's life had turned a corner. That from this point on, she would be in charge of her own future instead of what her parents wanted for her. He hoped her stubbornness would reassert itself and keep her from even considering letting her parents or Geof have any sway in her life.

She deserved to have a chance at the life she wanted, and if Andy could help her with that, he'd do whatever he could.

CHAPTER EIGHTEEN

"What happened to your face?" Mia exclaimed when she came into the kitchen.

"I was mugged," Cece said, having already decided that she had no desire to share what had actually happened with anyone who didn't have to know.

"Really? Here in New Hope?"

"No, it wasn't here."

Mia came closer to the table and rested a gentle hand on Cece's arm, concern clear on her face. "Are you okay?"

"I'm fine."

Her quick response brought a frown to Mia's face. "Are you sure?"

Cece nodded. During her nights, there had been moments when she'd been jerked her out of sleep, panic robbing her of breath and infusing her with fear. Falling back asleep had been difficult, leaving her tired and with her emotions far too near the surface.

At the same time, during her waking moments in the apartment, she'd never felt safer. Knowing Geof couldn't reach her there had allowed her to heal a bit over the past few days, both emotionally and physically.

She'd taken Tuesday off work, which had given her plenty of time to unpack her things in the apartment. If she could have, she would have liked to take more time off. It pained her to be seen with the bruises and swelling that even makeup hadn't been able to hide completely, but she needed the money.

Though she still had pain in her ribs and shoulder, it was getting better. She knew she was lucky that Geof hadn't been able to inflict more damage on her before the cop had shown up. Things had deteriorated rapidly when she'd realized that her parents were leaving without even staying for dinner.

Despite having had physical altercations with Geof before, it had gone up a level on Saturday night. But Andy had come through. He'd said he'd be there for her, and he was. She knew he blamed himself for not getting her help sooner, but all that mattered was that he'd gotten someone there to help her.

"I'm glad that you're okay," Mia said. "There are some really terrible people in this world."

Cece couldn't argue with that. If only Mia knew that Cece had had the misfortune of being born to two of them. She wasn't going to share that with her, however.

"Brooke said you weren't feeling well," Mia added. "She didn't say that you'd been hurt."

Brooke had proven to be the soul of discretion. When Cece had phoned to let her boss know that she wouldn't be able to work on Tuesday, she'd been concerned, since Cece had hardly ever missed work. Cece had given her a watered-down version of what had happened. Thankfully, Brooke had decided to not share even that much with Mia.

"I guess she decided to let me make the choice of what to share with people."

"Andy must know too, since when I mentioned you were out sick when he came in for his coffee, he didn't seem surprised."

"Yes. He knows what happened."

"He'll be happy you're back to work, I'm sure."

Cece didn't bother to tell her that Andy had been checking up on her, and that he didn't need her to be at work to be able to see her.

"Well, I'd better get back to work," Mia said. "I'm glad you're doing okay."

As the other woman disappeared through the doorway, Cece stared after her. It really seemed like Mia cared about how she was doing. For so long, she'd been focused on keeping her home life a secret, that now that her home was a lovely apartment all to herself, it felt like she didn't need to be as focused on herself.

She hoped that now that she'd moved out of her parents' home, and Geof had a restraining order against him, that Andy could relax. He had been worried about her long before that night at Geof's.

He deserved better than that, and Cece hoped that he'd focus on something else now. Not that she didn't like his attention on her, but it felt wrong to keep wanting that attention when he'd given so much of it to her already. Plus, he had someone in his life who actually needed his attention for more serious reasons than Cece's.

If she was a better person, she'd tell Andy that she was fine and that she didn't need him coming around so often. She should encourage him to get back to his dating apps to find a woman who was worthy of his time and attention, not to mention his love.

But she was still selfish enough to want to keep him in her life. After all, he was the only real friend she had. Although it seemed like Sarah was interested in maybe becoming friends again, and for the first time since that disastrous evening when Cece had been so rude to Jillian, it felt like friendship might actually be possible.

However, even if it was, and she ended up with more friends, she would always count Andy as her best friend. She might have thought that Sarah was, once upon a time, but Andy was the one who had seen the worst of her and still stuck by her side.

"Hey."

Cece looked up from the cookies she was scooping out on trays to see Andy standing in the doorway, a takeout cup in his hand. "Hi."

"How's it going being back at work?"

"It's been good," she told him.

"How are you liking the apartment?"

"It's very nice, and so quiet, even when Cara has a class downstairs. And just... having my own space that no one has access to without my permission, means everything."

Andy smiled, his expression holding warmth and affection. "That's great. You deserve that."

"And I think it will work with my budget, right?" she asked.

He nodded. "Yep. You should still try to save some money each month, though, just for unexpected expenses and if you want to buy a car at some point."

"I do want a car," she agreed. "Maybe you could help me figure out how much to save so I can get one soon."

"Sure. Come by the bookstore one afternoon, and we'll work on it."

"I'd like that," Cece said.

"I would too." He smiled again. "Well, I gotta get the store open. I guess I'll see you later."

"You will." Cece knew she shouldn't take up more of Andy's time, but she just didn't want to imagine her life without him in it.

"Good. I hope the rest of your day goes well."

With another smile, Andy left the kitchen, and Cece turned her attention back to the cookies she needed to get done for the afternoon.

It was weird to know that when she was done for the day at the bakery, all she had to do was walk out the back and down a few doors, and she was home. And it was such a beautiful home. Over the past couple of days, she's spent time at the window, watching as people went about their lives.

She'd never thought she'd enjoy people-watching, but with nothing else to do, she'd started doing it because she'd needed something to fill her time when she wasn't unpacking. The pain in her ribs and shoulder necessitated her taking frequent breaks.

It had been interesting to watch people go about their business on Main Street without them being able to see her. Maybe it was a little creepy, but it had helped her get through the past couple of days.

"How're you doing, Cece?"

She closed the door of the oven where she'd just slid the pan of cookies into, then turned to face Brooke. "I'm doing okay. Better."

"That's great," Brooke said as she came over to the worktable. "I don't want you to overdo it. If you need help, just let me know."

"Thanks for covering for me on such short notice."

"You're welcome. It really wasn't a problem, and if you need more time off, I can cover for you again."

"I think I'm good to go now."

"I'm glad to hear it."

They chatted for a few minutes, then Mia came into the kitchen to tell Brooke that someone was there to see her.

Over the next couple of hours, Cece managed to get all the baking done, even though she'd needed to sit down periodically. It felt great to be back to normal. Well, mostly, normal.

When she was done cleaning up the kitchen, she gathered her things together and said goodbye to Mia and the other girl who had come in to cover the afternoon shift.

As she walked out the back of the bakery, she glanced in the direction of the bookstore, but decided to go back to the apartment. She felt a bit worn out after working a full shift when she still wasn't feeling one hundred percent.

She let herself in the back door, then made her way up to the apartment, disabling the alarm as she passed by the panel. It was such a good feeling to know that Geof wouldn't be able to reach her once she got behind the door of her apartment. The only place she felt remotely vulnerable was making the short walk from the bakery to the apartment.

Unfortunately, there was no way to avoid that, since she didn't want to have to walk through the dance studio to get to the door in the garage. Andy had loaded the app on her phone that allowed her to access the exterior security cameras so she could check them before leaving the bakery if she wanted.

Even though she wanted to be confident that Geof wouldn't break the restraining order, she wasn't. He was a jerk who believed that his money allowed him to make people do what he wanted.

But Cece didn't want to dwell on the man. She just wanted to get past everything and move on to her new life. Andy had suggested that maybe she should get some professional counseling, but she didn't want to. She'd survived lots of bad times with her parents and previous boyfriends without ever seeing a counselor.

Honestly, she just wanted to forget her parents. Forget Geof. Forget her past life and focus on the new one she was trying to build.

She texted off and on with Andy throughout the afternoon while she sat curled up in front of the window. When her text alert dinged just before six, she assumed it was Andy again, but when she glanced at the screen, it wasn't his name she saw.

Sarah: *Hey Cece! Feel up to company tonight?*

Cece stared at the message for a minute, not sure how she felt about the idea. She had the perfect excuse not to... which wasn't really an excuse, since it was the truth.

Unfortunately, I'm in bed by seven most nights now that I'm doing the morning baking at the bakery.

Sarah: *You have to get up early for that?*

Yep. I get up at 3:30 now.

Sarah: *That is crazy! I only see 3:30 in the morning if I'm working through the night. I never see it because I get up early.*

I never would have thought I'd like getting up that early, but I enjoy doing the baking. Plus, it's nice and quiet.

Sarah: *So you don't work out front anymore?*

No. Brooke hired a new employee to cover my old shift. She's just focusing on the cake decorating side of the business now.

Sarah: *That's great! I'm glad you're enjoying the baking. Not something I would ever be able to do.*

I didn't know that I'd like it, but when Brooke started to teach me, I discovered it was something I really enjoyed.

Sarah: *That's great that you've been able to find that out.*

Sarah: *So if evenings don't work for you, would around 4:30 or 5?*

Just you?

Sarah: *If that's what you prefer. I think Jillian would like to talk to you sometime, too.*

Cece frowned as she stared out the window, tapping her phone against her chin. She felt like they were preparing for a confrontation or something. Thanks to Andy helping her become more self-aware, she realized that she owed Jillian an apology. However, she wasn't sure that she was ready for that yet.

Sarah: *No pressure, Cece. Whenever you feel up to hanging around with us, just let me know.*

It probably won't work until Saturday or Sunday when I don't have to get up early the next day. I'm still feeling a little tired, too, after what happened on the weekend.

Sarah: *That's understandable. Just know that if you want to talk, I'm here. Also, if you need to go anywhere and Andy can't take you, give me a call.*

I'll keep that in mind.

Sarah: *Great! And now I guess you'll be getting ready for bed since you're going to bed earlier than my baby nephew.*

Haha... I think I'm going to bed earlier than most kids.

Sarah: *But it's for a good reason, so that should make it easier.*

Yep. It does. Plus, having no social life means going to bed earlier is not an issue.

Sarah: *Well, maybe it's time to change the no social life thing. But we can talk about that later. Hope you have a good sleep. We'll chat again later.*

Yep. Talk to you later. Have a good night.

Cece sat for a moment, staring out the window as she thought back over the conversation with Sarah. She really didn't have any expectation that she would have a close friendship with Sarah, let alone Jillian. Cece had seen the two of them together plenty over the past couple of years. Enough to know that they had become close, and there was likely no room for her in that friendship.

But maybe she needed to apologize for what she'd said before she'd be able to move forward and find new friendships. She was only now beginning to truly understand how the things her parents had said to her had impacted her interactions with other people.

It had made perfect sense to her to focus on Jillian's looks because that's what she heard about the most from her dad, and to a lesser extent, her mom. Now, however, she understood that just like she was more than her looks, so was Jillian.

Having accepted that she needed to have a conversation with both Sarah and Jillian, Cece began to mentally prepare for it. She needed to find the strength to be vulnerable with them because vulnerability had always been something she'd avoided if possible.

She wondered if she should tell Andy about her conversation with Sarah, then gave a huff of laughter. Of course, she'd tell him. For some reason, she wanted him to know that she was trying to be a better person.

Since she'd already said she'd meet with him to discuss her budget, she figured she'd just talk to him about it then.

Temporarily abandoning the window, she went to the kitchen and opened her fridge. She was going to need to get some more groceries soon. Especially fresh stuff. Not seeing anything there that appealed to her, she grabbed a can of soup from the cupboard, opened it and dumped it into a soup mug.

Once it was heated, she went back to the window and set the mug on the small round table beside the chair. As she ate, she couldn't help but wonder about her parents. She'd blocked her dad's number, but for some reason she couldn't bring herself to block her mom's. She had definitely blocked Geof's number this time around. It wasn't that she really cared what had happened to her parents, but she *was* curious.

It was kind of hard to accept that she was now completely on her own. Maybe that was why she couldn't keep from wondering what was going on with them.

But she refused to let herself think too much about it, especially this close to bedtime. Her dreams were already not that great, so she didn't need to add to them by thinking about the scary things she'd dealt with lately.

Once she'd finished eating, she cleaned up her dishes, then made sure the alarm was correctly set. The only reason she could fall asleep without being plagued with worry was knowing that the alarm was set. There was no way that Geof could get in without her approval. Not even an apartment building would have been as secure as the apartment Cara had rented her.

She was incredibly grateful, which, honestly, wasn't a mindset she'd had much of in the past. However, considering what had happened, she'd become aware of the many things in her life she should be thankful for.

Her dad would probably laugh at her for even thinking something like that. Cece hoped that she'd learn from her parents' mistakes so that she would have a happier life than they did. Now that they were out of her life, she felt like she actually had a chance at that.

She might have still been in some pain, but Cece didn't think she'd ever felt more hopeful in her life. Whether or not that feeling would last was debatable, but she'd try to enjoy it for the moment.

CHAPTER NINETEEN

Andy stared at Geof, unable to believe the guy had the nerve to show his face in New Hope. It wasn't a surprise he'd managed to get himself out of jail. It had been a week since that horrible night, but as far as Andy was concerned, they should have thrown away the key to whatever cell they'd shoved him into on that Saturday night.

"What do you want?"

"Where is she?"

"Are you *stupid?*" Andy asked, but then waved his hand. "Don't answer that. I can already see that you are. Why else would you actually think that I'd give you any information about someone who has a restraining order against you? Someone you beat up? Get out of here."

"Who's going to make me? You?" Geof asked with a laugh. "I could break you with one hand tied behind my back."

"We already know that you don't pick fights with people who have a shot against you. There's probably no chance that you'd actually win in a fair fight."

"A win is a win," Geof said with a shrug.

Andy pulled his phone out. "I think you need to leave. Or maybe you'd like to have a chat with the police chief."

"You tell Cece that this isn't over yet."

"Oh, but it is. She's made the decision that she doesn't want you in her life, so you need to just accept that and move on."

"If you think this means you get a chance at Cece, you're the stupid one." With that zinger, Geof turned and left the store.

As he watched the man leave, Andy wondered if there was a way to get a restraining order for himself, so that he could keep Geof out of the bookstore.

It wasn't good that Geof was in New Hope Falls. Andy worried that Cece would assume he wasn't around and wander out, only to come face to face with him. He didn't want to worry her, but at the same time, he didn't want her caught off-guard.

Since Cece was still at work, he texted her instead of calling, and hoped that she'd see it before she ventured out of the bakery. He wasn't sure why Geof had come to the bookstore rather than the bakery since he knew that's where Cece worked. Not that he wanted Geof to go to the bakery. He much preferred to be the one to deal with the man.

Just a head's up, Geof stopped by. I'm not sure if he's left town yet or not.

He watched the screen for an answer, but when a minute passed without her replying, he set his phone to the side. Geof's visit had unsettled him, and he didn't like not knowing where the guy was.

Walking to the front window, he peered out at the sidewalk in front of the store, trying to see if he could spot Geof's car. He even pushed the door open and stepped out onto the sidewalk, smiling and nodding as Mary passed him on the way to her store.

"Enjoying your day, Andy?" she asked as she touched his arm.

"For the most part," he said. "Just had someone stop by that I'd rather not have seen."

"We all get those encounters, I think."

Andy hadn't given his mom many details about what had happened with Cece, and he wouldn't share them with Mary, either. The last thing he wanted was his mom telling him that he needed to steer clear of Cece if she had dangerous people in her life.

"I talked your mom into having a ladies' night at your place tonight."

Andy smiled. "She mentioned that. I think she's looking forward to it."

"You're going to have to entertain yourself somewhere else," she said.

"I think that can be arranged." Andy figured he could hang out with Cece, or maybe Tanner.

"I'll make sure that we leave you some of the food, though."

"Oh, that would be nice. The food you lovely ladies bring is always   delicious."

Mary beamed at his words. "Well, I should get back to the store."

"Take care," Andy told her, thankful that she was a good friend to his mom.

He watched her walk down to her antique store, then swept his gaze over the area again. There was no sign of the car Geof usually drove, but that didn't mean anything. Andy was pretty sure he had more than one car.

Back in the store, he checked his phone and saw that Cece had replied.

Cece: *Thanks for letting me know. I'll be on the lookout for him when I go home.*

I'm not sure what he's hoping to accomplish coming around here when he knows he's not supposed to.

Cece: *Just trying to make sure that I know that he's still in control.*

Cece: *Maybe I'll come by the bookstore after work. Would that be okay?*

Definitely okay. Want to hang around and have pizza later? I'm banished from my house since Mom is having guests.

Cece: *That sounds good. Maybe I'll go home first, for a bit, then come to the bookstore.*

That works. See you then.

Andy felt better now that Cece was aware that Geof was wandering the streets of New Hope Falls. It would probably be better if she just always assumed that he was in the area and be mindful of the possibility of running into him.

Wanting to know if there was something more he could be doing, Andy decided to call Kieran.

When the man answered, he said, "Hey, Kieran. It's Andy."

"Hey. How's life treating you?"

"Well, it was fine until Geof waltzed into the bookstore a few minutes ago, wanting to know where Cece was."

"Was she in the store with you?"

"No. She was still at work. I warned her that he was around, but is there anything else I can do so he doesn't keep showing up?"

Kieran sighed. "I'm not sure that there is at this point. Did he threaten you?"

"Yeah. Said he could break me with one hand tied behind his back." Andy gave a huff of laughter. "I mean, he's not wrong, but still, he's such a jerk."

"No argument there."

"I don't understand why he is so focused on Cece. Why is he so determined to have her when she is equally determined not to be with him?"

"It has nothing to do with Cece as a person, or that he's in love with her," Kieran told him. "It has everything to do with control. In Geof's mind, their relationship will only be over when *he* says it's over. His pride won't allow him to accept that a woman might not want him."

"But how does that even work? Is he just going to keep harassing her indefinitely?"

"I'm not sure. That's why it's important for Cece to stick to her guns and support the charges against him. If you sense that she's backing away from that, try to encourage her to push through. I know it's not easy, but it really is necessary. Geof needs to experience consequences for his actions."

"He won't be able to just get off, given how rich he is?"

"He'll definitely have a good legal team, but that doesn't necessarily mean he'll get away with what he's done."

Andy wanted to scream his frustration, but instead, he just sighed.

"Andy, I know this is frustrating, especially since I know you care for Cece. The best thing you can do is just be there to support her and encourage her to stay strong regarding the charges against Geof. In too many instances like hers, the charges don't stick because the victims refuse to testify against the accused."

"I can't force her to do anything, but I'll try my best to encourage her to carry through. So far, I get the feeling that she's determined to get Geof out of her life."

"Then I hope she'll be willing to testify, if necessary," Kieran said. "And if Geof keeps coming to the store, let me know and maybe we can look at setting up some cameras, so we can catch him threatening you."

"So far, he's been all threats and no action. With me, anyway."

"Let's hope it stays that way."

Andy assured Kieran that he'd let him know about any future interactions with Geof, then he ended the call. Though he didn't like discussing Geof every single time he was with Cece, he really wanted to make sure that her mind was set on following through on testifying against Geof, if it got to that point.

Since he had a couple of hours before Cece showed up, Andy tried to keep focused on his job. Thankfully, he had several customers who kept him busy. Well, technically, a couple of them hadn't been customers. One had been Tanner, who happened to be picking up some stuff in town for his mom, so he had stopped in to say hi. Sarah had stopped by as well, checking in with him on how Cece was doing.

"I wish we could hang out with her," Sarah said. "But I think she feels like she has enough to deal with right now without having to deal with us, too."

Andy nodded. "She knows that she needs to talk with you and Jillian. But yeah, I think she's not sure exactly how to do that when she's struggling with a lot already."

"I never imagined that this would be where she'd end up." Sarah frowned. "I hate that it came to this for her."

Andy didn't explain the issues Cece had had with her parents. That would be something only Cece could share with others.

"She's strong, and she'll get through all of this," Andy said with confidence. "It will just take some time."

Sarah nodded. "She really is strong and focused." Her eyes narrowed briefly. "Are you still in love with her?"

Andy just stared at her, not about to confirm or deny anything like that to her. He'd never actually told her in blunt words how he felt about Cece, and he wasn't about to do that now.

She just laughed, then said, "Maybe you should invite her to come to the Bible study on Sunday. She'd know a bunch of us there, so it's not like she'd be surrounded by strangers. I mean, she used to come sometimes."

"I'll think about it, but I'm not going to pressure her into anything."

"Yeah. I wouldn't expect you to."

The door to the store opened, and Beau walked in, bringing a smile to Sarah's face.

"Hey there, Andy," he said. "How's it going?"

"Going good. How about with you?"

They chatted for a few minutes, then the couple left, hand-in-hand. Andy was happy that Sarah had found love with Beau, but he wished that he could have that, too. Given all that had happened with Cece and Geof, Andy figured that the likelihood of Cece wanting a relationship any time soon was slim to none. And even less likely she'd want a relationship with him.

It was hard to accept that, but he understood that even the strongest person would have trouble moving past what had happened that quickly.

So... friendship was it.

Cece showed up around four, still bearing traces of her encounter with Geof on her face. She probably still had bruises on her ribs from him as well, but she hadn't said anything about them. She actually hadn't given Andy any details about the attack. What he knew came from Kieran. It was almost as if she figured that if she didn't mention it, they'd all forget what happened.

Or maybe she hoped she'd forget what happened.

Andy was pretty sure that wasn't how it worked, but he hesitated to push her to talk. He'd mentioned that maybe she should get some counselling to help deal with the trauma of the attack, but she'd just brushed his suggestion aside.

"I brought dessert," Cece announced as she came into the store, lifting the large bakery bag she carried.

"What is it?"

She smiled, and Andy felt a sense of relief at the genuineness of it. "You'll have to wait and see."

"Lucky you, I'm a very patient person. Maybe I should make the pizza a surprise for you."

Setting the bag on the workbench behind the counter, she climbed onto the stool he had there for her. "I doubt you'd ever order me something you knew I didn't like."

"That's true." She smiled at him as she crossed her legs. "So, how's it been here today?"

It looked like she'd changed clothes after work since she was wearing a pair of leggings and an oversized sweater. Her hair was braided back off her face, and though she wore makeup, it didn't completely cover the bruises. However, she looked infinitely better than she had on the previous Saturday.

"It's been good. Sarah came by for a bit while she was waiting for Beau to finish up some stuff."

"I'm supposed to line up a time to talk to her and Jillian," Cece said with a frown. "I'm not sure I'm up to that conversation just yet."

"You know, it doesn't have to be a conversation. You can just hang out with them."

Cece shrugged. "It kind of feels like I need to apologize before we can do that."

"Is something holding you back from apologizing?" Andy asked.

She sighed as her shoulders slumped. "I feel like I need to give a reason for why I acted the way I did, but I really don't want to. I don't want to talk about my life with my parents. It's bad enough that you know."

Andy frowned as he sank down to sit on the other stool he kept behind the counter. "Why is it bad that I know?"

Shrugging, she said, "I don't know. I'd just rather that people didn't know that kind of stuff about me."

"It doesn't make me think any less of you," Andy assured her.

She glanced at him and gave a humorless laugh. "You probably didn't think too highly of me to begin with."

"That's absolutely not true," he told her. "I don't know why you'd think that. I have great respect for you, and knowing about your life has only made me understand and appreciate you more."

"Not everyone will feel that way, I'm sure."

"The thing is, you don't need to give an explanation. All you need to do is apologize. It's a guarantee that Sarah and Jillian will accept your apology and forgive you."

She crossed her arms and frowned at him. "How do you know that?"

"As Christians, we're told to forgive when someone apologizes."

"Just like that? What if they do the same thing again?"

"Then we forgive them again," Andy said. "The reality is that it's good to forgive someone, even if they never apologize."

"Why would you do that?" Cece demanded. "That would mean I should forgive Geof and my parents for everything they did."

Andy understood how that would seem nearly impossible to her so soon after what had happened. "Forgiveness helps free you from the pain and anger you might hold toward someone. It doesn't mean you ever have to interact with them again. It doesn't mean you have to let them back into your life. Forgiveness can be the first step to breaking the chains that hold you to those people."

"You mean that I need to forgive them before I can move on?"

"I'm not sure if that has to be the actual order of things, but I'm sure that forgiveness will help you move past what's happened."

"I'm not sure that I can forgive them," she said. "At least not yet."

"And that's understandable. I told you about forgiveness so that you'd understand why Jillian and Sarah have likely forgiven you already for what happened."

"I guess I should arrange a time to meet with them."

"Would you like to come with me to a Bible study group tomorrow night?" he asked. "You'd know quite a few of the people there."

"Is this the hiking and dinner like they used to do? Or the actual Bible study?"

"We don't hike much anymore. We usually have a meal and visit, then yes, we do have a time where we talk about the Bible, though you don't have to participate if you don't want to. Afterwards, we have dessert and visit some more."

"I don't know," she said, her reluctance obvious.

"No pressure," Andy assured her. "Just, if you'd ever like to hang out with some people that you know, you're welcome to come. And also, if you want to go to church ever, let me know."

"I might be more interested in that," Cece said. "What time is the church service?"

"It starts at eleven."

"Do your mom and sister go with you?"

"Not always. It's getting to be too hard for my mom to attend the services, and Phoebe usually goes with her best friend to her church. So if you want to go, I can pick you up."

She seemed to consider it, but Andy figured she'd still turn him down.

"Maybe I should go with you." Cece hesitated, her brow furrowed. "Last Saturday, I prayed to God, asking Him to stop Geof from... hurting me, and that was when the cop showed up."

Her revelation surprised Andy. "That's amazing."

"It was a... surprise," Cece said. "I just felt so desperate and alone."

"I'm sorry I didn't realize right away what was going on. I should have known that he'd resort to violence."

"You did your part, Andy. If it hadn't been for you coming up with that plan, things would have been much, much worse. But there was that short period of time when I thought... Well, I thought that I'd never be free again."

"I spent a lot of that time praying too, and when you came out hurt, I thought God hadn't answered my prayers," he said. "But like you said, it could have been a lot worse."

"So I think I should go to church and see what it's all about."

"I can pick you up around ten-thirty tomorrow," Andy said. "Will that work for you?"

She hesitated, then nodded. "I'll be ready. You'll stick with me, right?"

"Definitely," Andy assured her. "There's nowhere I'd rather be."

When she smiled at him, Andy readily embraced the warmth that filled him. He prayed that her coming to church would help her see God in a way that she could understand and appreciate.

CHAPTER TWENTY

Cece stared at herself in the full-length mirror, trying to see herself through others' eyes. She'd texted Andy that morning to ask what she should wear, and he hadn't been much help.

After much debate, she'd settled on a pair of fitted black jeans, a white cotton blouse with a collar, and a black cropped jacket. She didn't have much to wear for jewelry, as most of what she'd once owned had come from Geof, which she'd returned, along with the car. So all she had were a simple gold chain, gold hoops, and three rings, all of which she'd bought herself.

As the clock ticked closer to ten-thirty, Cece began to second guess her decision to go to church, even though Andy had assured her that he would stick with her. However, she was going to follow through, at least once, because she kind of felt like she owed God that much. She hadn't really believed in Him until that moment when she'd pleaded with Him for Geof to stop hurting her, and then the doorbell had rung.

Her phone dinged, and when she picked it up, she saw a text from Andy that he was leaving his house. She sent back a thumb's up, then pulled on her ankle boots and grabbed her purse.

After locking the apartment, she went downstairs and watched the camera angles at the back of the building on her phone, waiting until she saw Andy's car before stepping out. She was still hyper-aware of her surroundings, and probably would be until she knew that Geof was out of her life for good. Unfortunately, she had a feeling he wasn't going to get punished like he should be for what he'd done to her.

"Good morning," Andy said with a smile as he got out of his car. He came around the car and opened the door for her.

She slid into the seat, then looked up at him. "Thank you."

When he'd settled back behind the wheel, he said, "How are you doing?"

"I'm good." She turned her attention to the security app and made sure that everything at the building was armed. "How are you?"

"Great!" The smile he gave her lit up his face, and she felt a little flutter in her heart in response to it.

As they drove to the church, he talked a bit about what to expect, probably assuming the information would make her feel more at ease. It did, sort of, but she was also still anxious. She felt like everyone would know that she didn't really belong in church.

All too soon, they were pulling into the parking lot of the large brick building. After they parked, Cece stayed in her seat, watching groups of people moving toward the church.

Andy opened her door, then dropped down onto his haunches, gripping the door with his hand. "Did you change your mind?"

She glanced at him, then shook her head. "I said I'd go, so I will."

"You're not doing this alone. I'll be right beside you, and we'll sit at the back."

Cece liked that idea, so she took a deep breath, then swung her legs out of the car. Andy stood up and offered his hand to help her out. She gripped it, reluctant to let it go even after she got out and shut the door.

He didn't pull his hand away, but she knew they couldn't walk into the church hand-in-hand. As they neared the steps that led to the front door, she let go of him. He glanced at her but didn't say anything.

When they reached the door, he opened it and waited for her to step inside before he followed her. She felt his hand land lightly on her back, guiding her through the people who were gathered in small groups in the foyer area, chatting.

Geof had often used a hand on her to make her go where he wanted her to, but Andy's touch was different. It felt like what he was doing was more protective, even though he was guiding her to where they needed to go. She spotted a few familiar faces in the crowd, but no one approached them.

Inside the sanctuary, as promised, Andy led her to the back pew and let her go in first before he followed her in. As he sat down beside her, Cece edged closer to him, drawing comfort from the press of his arm against hers.

She spotted Leah playing the piano at the front of the sanctuary. It was odd to see the people she knew in a completely foreign environment. She'd been aware that Leah was a talented pianist but hearing her actually play in church was a new experience.

Cece noticed information was being shown on the large white screens at the front of the sanctuary. She read through each slide, quickly realizing they were announcing programs and events at the church.

As more and more people filled the pews in front of them, Cece lowered her head, not wanting to meet anyone's eyes. She was still convinced that this wasn't a place anyone but Andy wanted her to be.

"Cece!"

Cece looked over and saw Mia scooting into the pew towards her with her husband, Ben, trailing behind her. She sat down beside Cece with a big smile.

"How great to see you here." She leaned forward a bit and waved at Andy. "Hi, Andy!" Then she motioned to her husband. "This is Ben, my husband."

The man gave them a warm smile as he slipped his arm around Mia's shoulders and angled himself toward them. "Nice to meet you."

"You too," Andy said.

"Thank you for recommending this church, Andy," Mia said. "We've really enjoyed the services so far. We're hoping we can get involved with a small group soon, too."

"I can probably help you with that. After the service, I'll introduce you to a couple of people who help facilitate the groups."

"That would be wonderful," Mia said. "And I'm so glad to see some familiar faces. I know we'll get to know more people as we keep attending, but I like seeing people I know."

Before Cece could respond, a couple more familiar faces appeared in the pew in front of them.

"Cece! I can't tell you how happy it makes me to see you here," Sarah said with a big smile. Beau smiled at her as well as he sat down next to his wife. "And you too, Andy."

Andy chuckled. "Nice to see you again. It's been far too long."

"Yeah. Not even twenty-four hours," Beau said with a laugh.

"Sarah, this is Mia and her husband, Ben," Andy said, motioning to the couple next to Cece. "They're new to New Hope. Mia works at the bakery with Cece."

Cece watched as the pair greeted each other with smiles and handshakes. It all seemed to come so easily to them to interact with strangers... quickly turning them into friends. Andy could do the same. Cece, however, really struggled with that.

"Why don't you come to our small group this evening?" Sarah asked Mia. "It's at our place, and we'd love to have you. And Cece, you're more than welcome to come too."

It wasn't like it would be her first time to hang out with that group. Before everything had fallen apart with Sarah and Jillian, she'd gone on hikes with them. Back when she'd had a useless crush on Eli. Even if Eli had returned her feelings, her dad would never have approved of the relationship. Eli was probably the first guy that she'd actually had real feelings for. She'd seen firsthand how he treated his sisters and his mom, and she'd wanted that for herself.

Now, of course, she knew that Eli would never have wanted someone like her. He'd ended up with a woman who was super nice and friendly. Just like the other women in his family.

Her crush on Eli had drawn her to church a few times, so this really wasn't her first time there. It just felt like it was because her intent this time around was different.

She wasn't there because her friends were.

She wasn't there because the guy she had a crush on attended there.

She was there because she felt she owed it to God.

Whether she would come back again, Cece wasn't sure yet.

When a man walked up on the platform along with several other people who took their places at the instruments, the two couples seated around her settled into their spots on the pews. Cece felt awkward, surrounded by people who knew what to expect when she was floundering.

But she was determined to pay attention and not daydream like she had in the past when she'd attended services there. Out of the corner of her eye, she saw Andy looking her way, as if to check on her. She was glad that he was beside her because she wasn't sure she would have been able to come by herself, even if there were other people she knew there.

After a time of singing, the man at the front drew their attention to the announcements that had been on the display. A teenage boy read a bit from the Bible, then one of the women who'd been part of the worship team stepped forward with a mic in her hands. She looked familiar, though Cece couldn't remember her name, and she appeared to be quite pregnant.

As she stood with her head bowed, Leah began to play the piano.

Andy leaned over and murmured, "That's Alessia Morgan. She's married to Cara's brother, Gio. He's an assistant pastor here at the church. I think he's preaching today."

When the woman lifted the mic and began to sing, chills swept over Cece.

Pass me not, O gentle Savior,
Hear my humble cry,
While on others Thou art calling,
Do not pass me by.

When another voice joined Alessia's, it took Cece a moment to realize the person harmonizing with her was Leah. Alessia lifted a hand as she tipped her head back, her eyes closed.

Savior, Savior,
Hear my humble cry;
While on others Thou art calling,
Do not pass me by.

Gripping the mic with both hands, Alessia once again sang alone.

Let me at Thy throne of mercy
Find a sweet relief;
Kneeling there in deep contrition,
Help my unbelief.

"If you know the chorus, please sing with us," Alessia said as words popped up on the screen.

Though people joined in, Alessia and Leah's voices were still the strongest as they sang together again.

Savior, Savior,
Hear my humble cry;
While on others Thou art calling,
Do not pass me by.

Though Cece had never heard the song before, she found that the words and melody were becoming familiar enough to hum along.

Trusting only in Thy merit,
Would I seek Thy face;
Heal my wounded, broken spirit,
Save me by Thy grace.

Alessia encouraged them to once again join her and Leah as they sang the chorus, and that time, Cece sang along with them. The words spoke deeply to her, reminding her of those moments when she'd pleaded for God to hear her.

Leah stopped playing, and she and Alessia sang the last verse together without any accompaniment.

Thou the Spring of all my comfort,
More than life to me,
Whom have I on earth beside Thee?
Whom in heav'n but Thee?

The words seemed old-fashioned to Cece, but they still resonated with her. *Whom have I on earth beside Thee?* Was that possible? To have God when she felt like she had no one else?

But she did have someone. Glancing over at Andy, she recalled his words about being a reflection of God, so that people could see God in their lives. Maybe God had put Andy in her life all those years ago so that she could see Him in a real way.

The chorus was also sung without the piano, and tears pricked at Cece's eyes as she was moved in a way she'd never experienced before.

Once the women stopped singing, a tall man walked up to join Alessia on the platform as she put the mic she'd used back in its stand. She turned and gave him a smile as he pulled her in for a brief hug. He held her hand and helped her down the stairs, then walked back up to stand behind the podium.

"For those who might not know, that was my lovely wife, Alessia," the man said with a smile. "I just didn't want you to think I go around hugging random women. Just one very specific woman and the baby girl she's carrying."

There was clapping from the congregation, and people called out congratulations.

"Yes. That was our very high-tech gender reveal," Gio said with a laugh. "We hadn't planned to find out, but at the scan this week, the temptation was just too much. So now you know too. Jayden is going to have a little girl cousin."

After more applause, Gio asked everyone to bow their heads for prayer. Cece had assumed that the older man, who was pastor of the church, would preach, so now she was curious about the younger man.

"When I prepared for preaching this week, I wasn't entirely sure what God wanted me to share with you. But it just so happened that I heard Alessia practicing the song she just sang, and it really resonated with me. So, thank you to Alessia and Leah for performing that so beautifully before I spoke today."

There was some applause before he continued to talk.

"I'm sure I'm not the only one who has, at times, felt very alone. Convinced that everyone, including God, has forgotten about them. When I counsel with people as part of my responsibilities here, often they mention being lonely and feeling like they have no one who really cares for them.

"I understand that because I've been there myself," Gio said. "There was a time in my life when I was estranged from my family, trying to piece together a life for myself that didn't include them. It was an extremely challenging time for me, and I questioned a lot of things, including my newfound faith in God."

Cece stared at the man who seemed to have so much together in his life. A beautiful, talented wife. A baby on the way. A career he seemed to like. A sister who was generous and loving.

"Even people who normally have very full lives can have moments of feeling alone or times of questioning if God is there for them. The writer of that song gave words to the cries of many hearts."

Cece had always assumed that when people believed in God the way Andy did, they'd never struggle to believe God was there for them. Because she didn't have God in her life like that, it would have made sense if He hadn't answered her cries for help. But it was odd to think that people like the pastor might doubt that God was there for them.

"I want to share with you some passages of scripture that show us that even people mentioned in the Bible at times felt they had been deserted by everyone, even God," Gio said. "And then I have some verses that encouraged me personally when I felt very alone in the world."

Cece didn't have a Bible or even a Bible app on her phone, but thankfully, the verses he read were flashed onto the screen. She didn't know any of the people he talked about in the verses, but the words he attributed to them were things she could definitely relate to.

As he spoke, she realized that the faith Andy embraced was a very real thing. It wasn't just perfect people getting together to talk about how great God was. There were people who loved God and believed in Him who struggled with hurt and loneliness.

Andy had tried to talk to her about how Christians weren't perfect, that they relied on God to help them deal with things in their lives. And sometimes, they didn't do so well trusting God and tried to take care of things themselves.

She'd thought that maybe he'd said that as a way to reassure her that she could be a Christian, too. But now, listening to this man, Cece was left to wonder if maybe it really was possible that God would welcome her, even with all her issues and her messed up life.

"I know that I'm not preaching about anything new, really," Gio said after speaking for another twenty minutes. "But after the conversations I've had recently, along with hearing Alessia sing that song, I felt like maybe God was telling me that there were others who needed to be reminded that they are not alone. We are not alone during the trials of our journey through life. God never leaves us. Our heavenly Father never forsakes us."

Cece frowned at the idea that God played the role of father, even a heavenly Father. Her own experience with a father figure hadn't been good, so it was hard to embrace God as Father. Maybe Andy could help her understand that.

Gio closed out his preaching with a prayer. Then he had the musicians come back up on the stage. "This hymn came to mind as I was praying about this sermon, and at my request, the worship team graciously agreed to sing it for the closing song."

After a smile at his wife, Gio picked up his Bible and left the stage to stand by the front pew as the worship leader asked the congregation to stand.

As they stood to sing the final song, Cece stood close to Andy. The song wasn't one she knew, but she followed the words on the screen, searching for meaning in them.

What a friend we have in Jesus
All our sins and griefs to bear!
And what a privilege to carry
Everything to God in prayer!

Oh, what peace we often forfeit,
Oh, what needless pain we bear,
All because we do not carry
Everything to God in prayer!

Have we trials and temptations?
Is there trouble anywhere?
We should never be discouraged,
Take it to the Lord in prayer.

Can we find a friend so faithful
Who will all our sorrows share?
Jesus knows our every weakness,
Take it to the Lord in prayer.

As she listened to the song, Cece knew she wanted that friend. She had such a good friend in Andy, but there were moments when he wasn't around. She wanted to know that she had someone with her always. What Gio had shared, along with the words of the song, made it seem that God would be there for her, even when others might not be.

But was she willing to take on everything that becoming a Christian seemed to entail? Or would she just fail at one more thing in her life?

CHAPTER TWENTY-ONE

Andy had had no expectations of how Cece would handle the service when she'd agreed to go. Instead of trying to figure that out, he'd focused on praying that God would prepare her heart to hear whatever He wanted to say to her through the service.

He'd been pretty sure that even though she'd agreed to attend, her decision was likely made with the intention of only going once. However, if that was the only time she was going to go, he wanted it to be a positive experience for her.

Once the service was over, Andy thought Cece would be eager to leave. And maybe she was, but between Mia and Sarah, she didn't really have much of a chance to escape.

"So, do you think you'll come this evening?" Sarah asked as she turned to face them once the service was dismissed. "We'd love to have you."

Mia glanced at her husband, who gave her a smile, then looked back at Sarah. "I think we'd like to come."

"That's great." Sarah focused on Cece. "How about you?"

"I'm not sure."

"That's fine. If you decide to come, Andy can bring you." Sarah smiled at him. "Right, Andy?"

"Definitely."

"Perfect." Sarah reached out and patted Cece's arm. "Seriously. We'd love to have you there."

Cece just nodded but didn't say anything more. Leah and Gavin, who had been walking up the aisle from the front, paused at the end of the row next to Sarah.

Leah's eyes narrowed briefly when she spotted Cece, but then her attention shifted when Sarah introduced her to Mia and her husband. "This is my sister, Leah, and her husband, Gavin. Mia works at the bakery with Cece."

"Nice to meet you both," Gavin said as he leaned forward to shake their hands. "Are you new to town?"

Mia nodded. "We just moved here a couple of months ago."

As the people around them chatted, Andy leaned close to Cece. "Want to leave?"

She glanced up at him, but then just shrugged. Andy didn't know what to do with that response. He didn't want her to feel trapped if she was anxious to leave.

Soon enough, Leah and Gavin moved on, then Sarah and Beau got up and followed them.

"Do you think you'll go tonight?" Mia asked once it was just the four of them in the pew.

"I really don't know," Cece said, which Andy was pretty sure was a no.

"It would be nice to have someone I know there."

"If Cece isn't up to going, I'll still be there," Andy said, trying to take the pressure off her. "And the group has lots of other friendly people. They won't be strangers for long."

Mia and Ben both smiled at that, then Ben said, "We'd better go. We told my mom we'd be home for dinner."

"It was great to meet you," Andy said as they headed toward the foyer. "Hope to see you tonight."

The pair nodded, then crossed the foyer hand-in-hand toward the doors leading out of the church.

Andy turned to Cece. "Ready to go?" When she nodded, he said, "Do you want to grab a bite to eat?"

"I think I'd like to go home."

"Sure thing," Andy said. He felt a bit disappointed, but he reminded himself that he needed to be grateful that she'd come to church at all and not be greedy for more time with her.

As they walked out of the church, he waved to a couple of people, but he didn't stop to chat. He didn't think that Cece was up for more introductions, especially considering people might make assumptions about what was going on between them.

He wanted to ask her if she had questions about the service, but he was reluctant to press. In the past, she'd shown that if she wanted to know something, she'd ask him about it.

"It seems that all areas of my life are colliding," she mused as he drove to the lane that ran behind her building.

"Is that a problem?"

She sighed. "I'm not sure. I guess I figure that Sarah will tell Mia how unfortunate it is that Mia has to work with me."

"I don't think she'll do that." In fact, Andy was certain that she wouldn't.

However, he knew that Cece wasn't quite willing to trust people yet, especially people who she felt had a reason to treat her badly because of how she'd treated them. As long as she didn't understand that God wanted them to pursue forgiveness and not revenge, she wouldn't understand why Sarah wouldn't badmouth her to others.

Sarah *had* warned him about Cece, but he knew that it was because they'd both had experience with her. She had worried that his feelings would cloud his judgment. That concern was valid. However, Andy had come to see Cece's faults as well as her strengths. He knew she wasn't perfect, but then, no one was.

It wasn't that there weren't Christians out there who might think they were entitled to talk bad about someone who had mistreated them. But he knew Sarah and Jillian, and he was confident that they would rather make amends with Cece than speak badly about her to others.

He pulled his car to a stop at the back of the building, then put it into park.

"You don't have to get out," Cece said, laying a hand on his arm.

Andy paused with his hand on the door handle. "My dad taught me to open doors for the ladies."

"I think you can save yourself the effort on my behalf."

Actually, Andy felt like of all the women in his life, Cece was the one he needed to make the effort for. She needed to know that she was worth someone's time and effort. His mom knew that. Phoebe knew that. Cece, he was pretty sure, didn't.

Because of that, he opened his door, then jogged around to the other side of the car. Cece had already opened the door a crack, so Andy grabbed the door handle and opened it fully.

"You are a stubborn man," Cece commented as she got out of the car.

"I am," he agreed. "Just like you're a stubborn woman, when you choose to be."

Cece grinned at him. "I'll own that."

"Keeps life interesting, that's for sure."

His heart lightened at the sight of her smile. While he'd always liked to see her smile, since that night at Geof's, her smiles had been few, so he treasured each one.

"I'll be heading to Sarah and Beau's around five-thirty since they have a meal prior to the meeting. So, if you want to come with me, just let me know by five-fifteen. That way, I'll have time to swing by and pick you up."

"Okay." She pulled her keys out. "Thanks for taking me to church today."

"I was happy to, and if you ever want to go again, just let me know."

As Andy watched her open the door, then disappear inside with a quick wave, he said a prayer that she'd be willing to go to the group later. However, if she decided not to, he'd still be thankful she'd gone to church that morning.

Back home a few minutes later, Andy found his mom sitting in the living room with a bowl of stew on a small tray in front of her chair. "Did you manage that yourself?"

"I did." She smiled up at him. "That new walker Mary suggested I get works better for transporting things."

"That's great. I'm gonna go grab myself a bowl. I'll be right back."

After he'd heated a bowl of stew for himself, he grabbed two biscuits that his mom had obviously made fresh and slathered some butter on them. He filled a glass with water, then returned to the living room.

"This is so good," his mom said as he set his food and glass on the coffee table, then sat down on the carpet, stretching his legs out.

"Anything you make with the ladies is tasty," Andy said, then bowed his head to say a quick prayer of thanks for the food and the day overall.

"I really enjoyed the service today," his mom said as he took his first bite. "Alessia and Leah did such a lovely job with that song."

"And it tied in really well with Gio's sermon."

"I didn't see you," his mom said.

"I sat at the back with Cece and Mia, the woman she works with, and Mia's husband, Ben."

"How did Cece find the service?"

He shrugged as he broke off a piece of the biscuit and dipped it in the stew. "She didn't volunteer any thoughts, and I didn't want to pressure her to share."

As he ate the biscuit, he waited for his mom to comment on that. But instead, she just took another bite of food. He wanted her to like Cece, but he knew that because of how she felt that Cece had taken advantage of his friendship over the years, it wasn't easy for her.

"Do you have your Bible study group tonight?" she asked.

"Yep. It's at Beau and Sarah's. Mia and Ben were interested in joining a small group, so they'll be there tonight."

"Mia is the woman that works with Cece?" Andy nodded. "And they're new in town?"

"Apparently. Ben's parents live in the area, I think. Brooke hired Mia at the bakery to take over Cece's position at the front, then she promoted Cece to do the baking."

"That's nice to have some new people to add to your group."

"Yeah, it is. I think Eli and Michael will decide to split the group soon though. We've already outgrown a few of the homes that we used to rotate to."

"That's definitely a good problem to have."

It was, but Andy enjoyed the closeness of their weekly group, and he'd hate to lose anyone from that.

"Is Cece going tonight as well?"

"Sarah invited her, but when I dropped her off, she still wasn't sure."

They chatted a bit longer about the week ahead. Thankfully, his mom didn't have any appointments. Not that he didn't want to go with her in hopes that they'd hear some helpful news, but the appointments were always stressful and exhausting for her.

"Cilla is coming to visit on Wednesday," his mom said.

"Really?" His mom's sister didn't visit often and hadn't been there since his mom had started to struggle physically.

"Yep. She called me a bit ago to ask if she could come visit."

"Where's she going to stay?" It wasn't as if they had extra space in the house unless she wanted to sleep on the couch.

"Mary said she could stay with her."

"How long will she be here?" Andy asked.

"She didn't say." His mom frowned. "I think she and Roy are having some issues."

Andy wasn't sure how to respond to that. While his mom had married a great guy, her sister had definitely... not. Roy was a lazy man who spent most of his non-working hours at the closest bar, spending his paycheck getting drunk. His aunt had to work hard to pay for food and bills.

"Plus, she got fired."

"Fired? Why would they have fired her?"

"Roy kept showing up and making a scene at her workplace. It happened a few times before they finally fired her."

"Well, that's just terrible."

"I'm hoping that if she can find a job in the area, she might be willing to move here."

"What are you thinking?" Andy narrowed his eyes at his mom. "And don't tell me you haven't been thinking, because I'm sure you have."

"Cilla said she'd be willing to help me while she's here," his mom said. "Maybe having her here would allow you or Phoebe to move out."

"I don't want to move out," Andy assured her. "But I'm sure Phoebe would love to."

"That's what I figured. I'd love to have Cilla close by, even if she wasn't able to help me. Just having her nearby again would be wonderful."

Like him and Phoebe, his mom and her younger sister were several years apart. He knew that it had bothered his mom to see Cilla married to such an awful man. Not that he'd been awful at the start. Somehow, he'd managed to hide his true character at first.

After what had happened with Cece, the thought of Cilla going back to Roy made Andy feel a little sick. "Hopefully, she packs her car with everything that's important to her."

"That's what I told her to do. Plus, I told her to not let Roy know she was coming here."

"He'll figure it out." Which meant Andy was going to be dealing with two crazy, angry men trying to threaten the people he loved and cared for.

"Yes. I'm sure. I just hope that all his drinking has made him forget our address. He hasn't been here since your dad died."

Just one more thing to pray about. And one more thing that Andy worried he wouldn't be able to deal with the way he should.

After they had finished eating, he gathered up their dishes and took them to the kitchen. He put them in the dishwasher, then made sure everything was cleaned up. If he didn't take care of it, his mom would try to do it herself, exhausting what little energy she had.

"Do you need anything, Mom?" he asked once he was done.

She looked up from the needles and yarn she held. "Nope. I'm good. I found a new cooking competition show, so I'm going to binge watch that while I work on this blanket."

"Okay. I'll be down in my room if you need anything."

Satisfied that his mom was fine, Andy went down to his room. Grabbing his laptop and binder, he settled into his recliner, deciding that he'd fill the hours until the Bible study doing some writing. He hadn't been able to do much that week, what with everything else that had happened.

Escaping into the dystopian world he'd created with Cece's help felt good. Writing was always something he enjoyed, so being able to spend a few hours doing it was a nice break from his normal responsibilities.

He kept an eye on the time as he worked, and as five-fifteen approached with no word from Cece, Andy realized she wasn't going to attend. He'd really hoped that she would want to go, but realistically, he had known she wouldn't.

Setting aside his laptop, Andy got out of his recliner and went to freshen up for the evening. After checking that his mom didn't need anything, he set out for Beau and Sarah's.

There were lots of cars there already when he arrived. Andy found a spot and parked, glad that there was plenty of available space in front of the large house.

Beau opened the door when Andy rang the doorbell, greeting him with a smile. "Hey there, Andy. C'mon in."

There was a good turn-out that night, but Andy couldn't help but wish that Cece had wanted to be there, too. He really hoped that her attending church with him that morning hadn't been a one-time thing. While he was grateful that she'd come at all after not attending with him before, he was greedy and wanted her there more.

But more than that, he wanted her to want to be there to learn more about God and how her future—both in life and after death—would be so much better with Him in it.

CHAPTER TWENTY-TWO

Cece carried a tray of cookies out to the front to add to the bakery case. Mia was serving a couple of customers but still gave her a smile before handing over the cups of coffee to the man and woman standing on the other side of the counter.

"Thank you," the woman said while the man paid, then the pair left the bakery with their coffees in hand.

"Is there more stuff to bring out?" Mia asked as Cece transferred the cookies into the display baskets.

"I have some muffins cooling," Cece said. "If you want to finish with these, I'll go get them."

Mia nodded and took over the cookies while Cece went back into the kitchen. She was surprised that she hadn't burnt anything that morning. She'd had a couple of restless nights, which had left her tired and a bit scatterbrained.

After she'd decided not to attend the Bible study, she'd spent the evening wishing she'd gone. She wasn't even sure why she hadn't, except for not wanting to be around Sarah and Jillian just yet.

"Did you go to the Bible study on Sunday night?" she asked Mia when she set the tray of muffins down.

"We did," Mia said with a big smile. "What a wonderful group of people. Ben really enjoyed getting to know some of the guys. He likes to socialize, but he often finds it difficult to get past the first meeting, so this was great. Andy introduced him to several men at the study."

"That's good. I'm glad you enjoyed it."

"Why didn't you go?" Mia asked. "Aren't they your friends too?"

Friends was definitely a stretch when referring to the women at the study. "I've known several of them for years, and Cara is my landlady."

"Sarah mentioned that you used to be cheerleaders together."

Cece nodded. "Feels like eons ago, though. I'm not sure I could turn a cartwheel now."

Mia laughed. "You mean it isn't like riding a bike?"

"I don't know. To be honest, I haven't tried to do a cartwheel in a long time. I haven't had a reason to."

"I never had the nerve to try out for the cheerleading team when I was in high school."

"How long have you been a Christian?" Cece asked, realizing after she'd asked the question that she'd abruptly taken the topic of their conversation in a totally different direction. But it was something she'd wondered about the other woman, and the question had just spilled out.

Mia gave her a curious look, but then said, "For as long as I can remember, to be honest. I was raised in a Christian home, so I became a Christian as a child. How about you?"

Cece realized then that she shouldn't have asked Mia that. Of course, she'd turn the question back around to her.

"I'm not a Christian." Cece figured she wasn't going to be able to bluff her way through being one, so being honest with her answer was probably the best route.

Mia's eyes widened briefly. "Oh. Sorry. I shouldn't have assumed."

"Church just wasn't a part of my life. My parents aren't Christians, so I wasn't raised with it."

"Well, I hope that you'll consider becoming a Christian," Mia said. "I'm sure Andy and Sarah have shared what it means."

Andy had tried off and on to talk to her about his faith. Sarah had, to some degree, as well, though all of that had changed when Cece had cut off contact with her. Cece had always known that church was important to those around her, but she hadn't been interested in it herself.

She'd been fairly certain that she'd never find the type of man her dad would want her to marry at church, so it had felt like a waste of time to go there.

"They have talked about it over the years," Cece said, skirting around a direct answer.

"Well, if you have any questions, you can talk to me about it, too." Mia smiled at her. "I'd love to be your friend. I had a bunch of friends where we used to live, but I don't have any here yet."

Cece had a hard time believing that anyone would actually want to be her friend. She'd never thought she had the qualities that anyone would want in a friend. After all, the one person—aside from Andy—who had been her friend the longest, had been quick to drop her in favor of someone else.

She wasn't sure that she was interested in befriending someone again, only to be dropped when she didn't act like they wanted her to. It wasn't that she didn't understand that she hadn't been a good friend to Sarah and Jillian. It just felt like no matter how good she was, she was just one mistake away from being cast aside.

On top of everything else, she just couldn't take that pressure, and she was sure that Sarah and Jillian would be better friends for Mia than she'd be.

"I think the consensus is that I'm not a great friend," Cece told her as she stacked the trays together.

Mia crossed her arms and frowned at her. "Who told you that?"

"Let's just say that of all the friends I had in high school who still live here, Andy is the only one who still wants to spend any time with me. And before you ask, I have no idea why he sticks around."

Mia gave a laugh. "Oh, I think I know why he sticks around."

Cece knew what Mia thought, but the woman didn't know what Andy had put up with because of her. "He's apparently a sucker for punishment."

"So you're not friends with Sarah and Leah?"

"I wasn't friends with Leah. She's never liked me. And Sarah and I had a falling out awhile ago."

"But she was talking to you at church on Sunday," Mia pointed out. "She seemed to want you to go to the Bible study."

Cece shrugged. "I think she's trying to figure out if she wants to give me another chance."

"Why do you think people don't want to be your friend?" Mia asked.

For a moment, Cece debated whether she should just tell her the truth and get it over with. However, when the door to the shop opened and a customer came in, she took it as a sign that she shouldn't. Or at least not right then.

The look Mia gave her said that the conversation wasn't over, and strangely enough, Cece was okay with that. Maybe if she was upfront about all the horrible stuff she'd done, Mia would just back off and keep their relationship professional.

While Mia focused on the customer, Cece took the trays back into the kitchen. That was the last of the baking for the day, so she tackled the cleanup, making sure that everything was spotless and ready for the next day or in case Brooke came in later to do some baking or decorating.

Mia was still busy with customers when Cece was ready to go. She popped into the front of the store to say goodbye before she went to the back door.

She stayed there for a moment, checking the security cameras to make sure that Geof wasn't lingering in the lane. Seeing that all was clear, she remotely unlocked the back door of her apartment the way Andy had shown her, then she pushed out the door of the bakery and made a mad dash along the lane to the dance studio building.

When she reached the door, she jerked it open and hurried inside. Frustration bubbled inside her as she locked the door behind her and went up to the apartment. She hated that Geof had reduced her to darting fearfully between safe spaces. But as long as he was wandering around freely, she didn't know what else to do. It had already been proven that he could do some serious damage to her if he got too close.

Upstairs, she went into her bedroom and changed into a pair of leggings and an oversized T-shirt, then she made herself a sandwich. As she'd been doing recently, she took her sandwich and a glass of water to the table by the window. Sitting there watching the citizens of New Hope go about their lives made Cece feel as if she was part of that world, even though she was still scared to be out in it.

From behind the window, she even saw familiar faces occasionally. Usually, they were coming out of *Norma's* since that was across the street from the apartment so she could see them more clearly.

As she ate her sandwich, Cece debated going to the bookstore. She hadn't seen Andy since he'd dropped her off after church on Sunday. He'd texted her the previous day, and they'd had a brief conversation. She wanted to see him, though. Which was a pretty good indication that she should just stay in the apartment.

She didn't think she should rely on him so much, but she just felt so alone. Plus, Andy knew everything there was to know about her, and he was still there for her. And out of all the people in the world, she felt safest with him. He was the best man she'd ever known.

Cece rubbed her hand against her chest, trying to ease the ache that lingered there.

Ever since Geof and her parents had been removed from her life, she felt as if, for the first time ever, she was seeing how healthy relationships should work. She saw it in Mia and Ben's marriage. And even Sarah and Beau's, and Jillian and Carter's. None of them had a relationship like the one she'd had with Geof or that her parents had had with each other.

Andy deserved to find a woman who could give him that type of relationship, and Cece was sure that would never happen if he was tied up constantly with her. She leaned on him far more than she should, but he'd always been there for her. And he was nice enough that things would probably continue on that way, even if they shouldn't.

Cece knew that she needed to learn to stand on her own two feet. She wasn't sure that she could do it yet, but hopefully, with the help that Andy had already given her—working with her to create a budget and understand her finances better—she'd be able to.

Her heart ached at the idea of not being around Andy much, but she'd proved to be a lousy friend to him, and he was just too nice to tell her to take a hike. Now she just had to convince Andy that he didn't need to keep such a close eye on her anymore.

When her eyes stung and her throat tightened, Cece tried to brush it all off as a pending cold or allergies. There was no way she was going to get emotional and shed tears over the idea of losing a friend. Friends had never been the most dependable people in her life.

Rather than go to the bookstore or spend time texting Andy, Cece took her dishes to the kitchen and put them in the dishwasher. Then, after a moment of consideration, she opened a cabinet and began to pull everything out.

It didn't take long to empty all the shelves, then she filled the sink with hot soapy water. Climbing up on a stepstool she'd found in the pantry, she wiped down all the shelves, even though they didn't really need cleaning.

When her text alert interrupted her thoughts, she glanced at where she'd left her phone on the corner of the counter, but she hesitated to get down and check it. Unfortunately, the need to see who was messaging her was overwhelming.

With a sigh, she dropped the cloth she was using into the sink and got off the stepladder. After drying her hands, she picked up her phone and tapped the screen to bring it to life so she could see who the text was from.

Mom: *You need to talk to your father.*

Cece's regret was instant. Why hadn't she blocked her mom's number when she'd blocked Geof's and her dad's? Probably because she'd assumed her mom would never contact her. But of course, she'd make the effort at the behest of her husband.

I don't think so. I have no interest in anything he'd have to say. Anything either of you have to say, actually. Goodbye.

As soon as she sent the message, Cece went to her contact page and blocked her mom's number. She was counting on her dad being too lazy to go through the process of getting a new number just to message or call her. So far, he'd been too lazy to walk into the bakery to talk to her. She didn't have a restraining order against him, so there was nothing keeping him from approaching her.

Of course, she had a restraining order against Geof, and he was still trying to track her down.

With a sigh, she sat down on the top of the small stepladder. Her first instinct was to contact Andy to talk to him about her mom's message, but she had to be strong and resist. She still had plenty left to do with the cupboards. Unfortunately, now her thoughts were all tangled up in that mess again.

Getting up, she went to the television and after a bit of searching, she found a true crime show on a streaming service that she could binge-watch—or binge-listen to—as she worked.

It was nearly five o'clock when her phone chirped again. By that time, she'd wiped down all cupboards, both upper and lower, plus the pantry, and returned all the contents to them. She had moved onto the fridge and currently had its meager contents spread across the counter.

Andy: *Hey! Want to join me at the bookstore for dinner? Planning to get something from Norma's.*

The temptation to go to him was tremendous. She had a fierce argument with herself, but in the end, she knew she had to stay strong for Andy's sake.

She didn't *want* to, but she would.

Would love to, but I'm in the middle of a cleaning spree. She took a picture of her empty fridge, thinking that would support her excuse better than the jug of milk, carton of eggs, and some butter and cheese that currently sat on her counter. After attaching the picture, she sent the message.

Refusing Andy's invitation honestly made her want to cry, but she needed to learn from him and be less selfish.

Andy: *Was the place that dirty?*

Not really, but I started to clean one area and it just kind of spread and became a thing.

Andy: *Can't say I've ever had that issue. Cleaning one area is usually more than enough. Lol*

Cece smiled, but her smile quickly faded. *Usually, yeah. It's kind of weird having a space that's all my own. I mean, I always cleaned my bedroom and bathroom, but Mom cleaned everything else.*

Andy: *Phoebe and I have a schedule, so we take turns on most things. Mom does what she can, but it's exhausting for her.*

And Cece had added even more to Andy's plate by being so needy. If she didn't think that Andy's mom probably hated her, she might have offered to go help clean. Even though she and Andy had known each other for years, she'd never met his mom, just like he'd never met her parents.

Maybe he hadn't told his mom much about her. She hadn't told her parents about Andy because she'd known what her dad would say about him. And even though she hadn't really cared much about other people's opinions, she'd known that Andy hadn't deserved that.

Andy: *Guess I'll leave you to your cleaning then. Hopefully I'll see you tomorrow when I pick up my coffee. Not wanting to run late two days in a row!*

Andy: *Maybe we can do supper tomorrow night?*

Cece gave an exasperated laugh. How was she supposed to give Andy more freedom from her when he was so persistent about spending time with her? There was no denying that after all she'd been through, Andy's determination to spend time with her was like a balm to her hurting heart.

Sounds like a plan.

Andy: *Perfect! I'm sure you're still going to bed at a toddler's bedtime, huh?*

Yeah. Only way I can function enough to do the baking. So once the cleaning is done, it'll be time for bed.

Andy: *Sleep well! And I'll see you tomorrow.*

Cece told him goodnight, then set her phone down. She was so weak. Not even strong enough to tell Andy she couldn't hang out with him.

She'd have to try harder the next time.

CHAPTER TWENTY-THREE

Something was off, but Andy struggled to put his finger on it. Ever since he'd dropped her off after church on Sunday, things had been different with Cece.

She'd had a legitimate reason for not coming by the bookstore the previous afternoon since she'd been in the middle of cleaning. And he knew that with her earlier bedtime, waiting until later to get together hadn't been a viable option.

Unfortunately, he was going to have to take a raincheck on the dinner he'd arranged with Cece for that evening. He'd forgotten that his aunt was arriving, and he wanted to be there with the family.

For that reason, he was determined not to miss stopping by the bakery that morning.

"See you later, Mom," he said from the doorway of her room. "Text me when Cilla arrives."

"I will, sweetheart. Have a good day."

As he climbed into his car, he said a quick prayer that Cilla would be able to get away from Roy without any issues. It was hard to be unable to do anything himself, and he knew that his mom was feeling the same way. Once Cilla was with them, they'd be able to do more to protect and help her.

After he parked his car in the back of the building, he went through the store to go out the front door. It was a dreary day, so he was really looking forward to his coffee.

"Morning, Andy!" Mia called out when he walked in. "How is your morning going?"

"So far, so good. How about you?"

"Can't complain. We're going to look at a couple of apartments after I get off work. I can't wait."

"You've been living with Ben's family?"

She nodded as she began to prepare his coffee. "They're great, but I miss just being the two of us, you know. We've only been married just over a year."

Though he knew that his place was with his mom for the time being, there was a part of Andy that wondered what it would be like if he had a place of his own. His mom had tried to tell him that she was okay with moving into a long-term personal care home, but he hadn't wanted her to do that. Plus, his dad wouldn't have wanted that for her either.

"Well, I'll pray that you find a place that works for you," Andy said.

"Thanks." Mia flashed him a smile as she set his cup on the top of the bakery case. "Want a cinnamon bun to go with that?"

"Sure. Why not?" Andy said with a laugh. "Is Cece in the back?"

"Yep. Hard at work, as usual."

Andy picked up the cup and took a sip. "I'll get the cinnamon bun on my way out."

He walked around the end of the case to the door that led into the kitchen. Not wanting to get in Cece's way, he stopped by the door. "Morning."

Cece looked up from the worktable where she was dumping out loaves of freshly baked bread. "Hi."

"How's your day been?" he asked. "Burnt anything?"

She scowled at him. "I really don't burn things that often."

He grinned. "I know, which is why I have to ask. I'll mark it on my calendar when you do."

"You're mean," she said. "I should tell Mia you're not allowed any coffee for a week."

"As long as I can still get a cinnamon roll or muffin, I can make coffee on my own."

"That's because you're not a coffee connoisseur."

Andy shrugged. "You're right about that. I'm much more of a cinnamon bun connoisseur."

"Are you getting one today?" she asked as she deftly positioned the loaves to sit upright on the cooling racks.

"Yep. Mia sold me on it."

"She does a much better job of upselling to customers than I ever did," Cece said. "She just flashes that smile and people suddenly feel like they need a cookie or a Danish."

Andy might have thought she'd say that with a bit of resentment, but she didn't. Instead, she smiled as she said it. It made him wonder what might have brought about the change. They hadn't had much of a chance to talk in depth since the attack, and it pained him that they might not be able to do it that day, either.

"Listen," he began. "I know we decided to have supper together tonight, but it slipped my mind that my aunt is arriving today. I should be home for dinner with my family."

She gave him a smile. "That's fine."

"How about if I order some lunch from *Norma's* and you bring it by after you're done here? Then we can hang out at the store for a bit."

It took her longer to respond to that than he'd thought it would, but finally, she nodded. "Okay. Lunch will be my treat, though."

Andy frowned. "I don't expect you to pay since I suggested it."

"I'll take care of phoning the order in and paying for it," she said. "It's that, or no deal."

"You drive a hard bargain," Andy groused.

"Do we have a deal?"

"Yeah. I guess."

"Good." She gave a nod of her head. "I'll see you in about three hours."

"I'm looking forward to it." And he really was. Going for more than a couple of days without seeing or talking to her wasn't something he liked. "Guess I'd better go. Don't want to keep the customers waiting."

Cece laughed, the sound light and happy, and it made Andy smile in return. He hoped that she'd find some happiness in her life now that she was away from her parents and Geof. But he didn't doubt that she was still having some struggles. Andy just hoped she'd lean on him and the others when she had those moments.

He spent the hours between opening the store and Cece's arrival with their lunch, compiling reports for Drake. Once a month, they had a conversation about what was going on with the store. Sometimes, Andy approached the meetings with trepidation if sales were low, but so far, Drake hadn't even hinted that he wanted to close the store.

By the time he was done with the reports, a delivery guy had dropped off an order of two boxes. Andy quickly unpacked them, flipping through a few of the books that looked interesting. Some were earmarked for customers, but a couple of titles were coffee table books that he thought might sell well.

As the time neared for Cece to join him, Andy wandered over to the front window, watching for her. There was no sign of Geof, but he wouldn't put it past the man to lie in wait for Cece.

He saw her cross the street and disappear inside the restaurant, but then a customer came in looking for coloring books for her granddaughter and that distracted Andy. He was happy to show the lady the selection of good quality kids' coloring books he had in the store, especially since she decided to buy several of them.

Cece arrived just as the woman was leaving and greeted her with a smile. Andy took the drink tray from her, then they went into the break room.

"What all did you get?" he asked as he watched her set the bags she carried on the table. "This seems like a lot for just the two of us."

"I brought you some stuff from the bakery." She motioned to the white bag with the bakery logo on it. "Some bread and muffins."

"You didn't have to do that." Though she'd given him muffins or a cinnamon bun with his coffee sometimes, this was the first time she'd brought stuff that was obviously for him to take home and share with his family.

She shrugged. "Hopefully you'll like it."

"I'm sure we will," he said. "As long as you didn't burn it."

"Like I'd bring you burnt stuff," she scoffed as she pulled food out of the bag from *Norma's*. "The only people who would get the burnt rejects would be Geof and my parents."

Andy frowned. "Have you run into them?"

"No, but my mom texted me that I needed to talk to my dad."

"What did you say?" He worked the drinks free from the tray and set one in front of her before sitting down.

"I told her that wasn't going to happen, then I blocked her." She set the empty bag on the counter by the sink, then sat down across from him.

"Are you curious about what he wanted?"

She shook her head. "I'm sure it has something to do with the fact that I've closed the account that he had access to, and Brooke has made sure that my paycheck is now going into my new one. They don't have my money anymore, and I'm sure it's hurting them financially."

"Well, you don't owe them anything, especially since you aren't living there anymore."

She jabbed her straw into the lid of the cup and nodded. "I'm kind of surprised neither of them has come by the bakery. But it's possible that now that I've blocked them both, my mom will show up."

"Not your dad?"

"He probably thinks I'd be more receptive to my mom."

"But you're not?"

"She never stepped in to help me when my dad was being...aggressive. I realize that she was as trapped in that situation as I was, but I was her child. She should have done more to protect me. Instead, she left me vulnerable and scared. I don't even think she loved me. She certainly never told me she did."

Andy's heart ached for her. He couldn't imagine not being secure in a parent's love. He'd never questioned if his parents loved him. Every single day, they'd told him and Phoebe that they loved them.

It saddened him to think that Cece had never experienced that.

As they ate, she talked a bit about her day, and Andy shared what he'd done.

"Mia's decided she wants to be my friend," Cece said.

Andy took a sip of his drink. "She told you that?"

"Yep."

"And... what did you say to that?" He figured she brushed her off, but maybe she was more open to new friendships now.

"That she shouldn't want to be friends with me. That I made a lousy friend."

"What?" Andy frowned at her. "Why would you say that?"

"Because it's true?"

"No, it's not."

"Andy, you are the friendship unicorn. The one person who has seemed to tolerate me when others haven't been able to."

"I don't just *tolerate* you, Cece," he insisted. "And I think you should give Mia a chance."

Cece shrugged as she dipped a chicken strip into the sauce she'd ordered with them. "I'm going to tell her why Sarah and Jillian aren't my friends anymore."

"You don't need to do that," Andy said.

"Why not? She deserves to know the sort of person I can be."

He set his burger down on the paper it had been wrapped in, then he leaned forward, his arms folded on the table. "The person you *used* to be."

"What?"

"Can you tell me with one hundred percent certainty that you would react the same way now as you did back then?"

Her brow furrowed, and she didn't reply right away.

"I think you've grown and softened. You've come to see things differently."

"I still don't think I know how to be a good friend."

"As someone who has been your friend for years, I believe I'm uniquely qualified to comment on the type of friend you are."

"And?" She lifted a brow, as if daring him to be honest.

Andy considered his response. If he didn't acknowledge the rough parts of their interactions as friends, she was going to dismiss everything he said.

"I'm not gonna lie," he began. "You have been difficult at times. But that hasn't been the case recently. And even with that, I've never regretted being your friend."

"You've never wished you could go back in time and avoid the bleachers that day?"

"Never." He couldn't tell her that his love for her played a large role in his lack of regret.

"You deserved to be treated better than I've treated you sometimes."

"I think you'll find that that is true for most long-term friendships. There are always ups and downs."

"I wouldn't know," she said.

"Give Mia a chance," Andy encouraged.

"Maybe. I still think I need to be honest with her about what happened before."

"If you feel like you have to. I think Mia might surprise you."

"I just want her to make an informed decision," Cece said. "I want her to know what she's getting into."

The bell on the front door jangled, and Andy got up to go see who it was. He wondered how long it would be until Cece saw worth in herself. He wished his words were enough to build that up for her, but he knew that she needed to come to that understanding herself.

"Hi, Andy," Carter said when he spotted him.

"Hey. How're you doing?"

"Just great. And you?"

They talked for a couple of minutes, exchanging pleasantries. Andy had gotten to know Carter over the past couple of years, but it hadn't been easy. The man had been reserved, rarely volunteering information about himself. However, it seemed like Jillian's presence in his life had helped him open up more.

"Jilly asked if I could come by and pick up some books she had you order for her."

"They're just over here," Andy said, walking to the counter.

"Those look lovely," Carter said, running his hand over the shiny cover of the top book.

"Yes. The illustrator for these books did an amazing job. I'm sure the kids are going to love them."

"How's your writing going?" Carter asked.

"Not too badly. Cece helped me brainstorm a sticking point, and that really helped."

"I read the first two you wrote," he said.

Andy laughed. "Really?"

"Yep. After you told Sarah about them, she told Jillian, and Jillian told me. I thought I'd check them out. You've done great with the stories. I like how even though the world in your books seems hopeless, you've created characters that are still hopeful. I can't wait for the next one. Is it close to releasing?"

"Uh... not very close. I still need to finish writing it, then I have to polish it up and run it by my editor."

"So what? A couple of weeks?" Carter's grin told him he knew his suggestion was ridiculous.

"Luckily, ideas are flowing more smoothly now, thanks to Cece, so it won't be as long a wait as it might have been without her help."

"Well, just know that you have people eagerly waiting for the next book."

"I do appreciate that," Andy said. "I'd been reluctant to share about my writing, but then I kind of spilled the beans inadvertently with Sarah and now everyone knows."

"I'm glad we found out. We're your friends, man. Let us support you."

"Next thing, Sarah will want to throw a book launch party for me."

"You should let her. That would be fun."

"Nah. I like a more low-key release. Social media announcements are good enough."

"Well, don't be surprised if Sarah overrules you on that."

Andy just shook his head, since he knew Carter was right. He rang up the books as they continued to chat.

"Thank Jillian for ordering here," Andy said as he handed Carter the bag. "I really appreciate the business."

"We're both happy to support you and the store."

Once Carter said goodbye and left the store, Andy returned to the break room. Cece looked up from her phone as he walked in and sat back down.

"Do you want to heat your food up?" she asked.

"Maybe my fries, but my burger is fine."

She reached over and picked up the container of fries. Getting up, she went to the microwave and put it in, pushing buttons to start the machine.

"Was that Carter?" she asked.

"Yep. He came to pick up some books that Jillian had ordered for her classroom."

Andy waited for her to make a comment on the couple, but she didn't say anything. When the microwave beeped, she took the fries out and brought them over to him.

"Thank you," he said, smiling at her.

She sat down again and picked up her milkshake to take a sip. "You're welcome."

"How are you doing overall?" Andy asked, needing to know if she was struggling with anything.

"I'm good. It's... weird living on my own. Which is dumb because it's not like I interacted much with my parents when I lived at home."

"But you're sleeping okay?"

She nodded. "For the most part. You know how it goes."

He might not have dealt with a situation like hers, but he'd dealt with plenty of worry and had struggled with adjustments after his dad had died and then again when his mom's health began to decline.

"Would you tell me if you were having problems?" Andy asked.

Her hesitation hurt him, but he was careful to not let it show. He wouldn't be yet another person making demands of her, forcing her to share things with him.

"You've done so much for me already, Andy," she said, her voice soft. Her gaze dropped to her cup, and his heart began to pound. "I appreciate everything you've done, but I think it's time I learn to stand on my own two feet. And you need a chance to find someone who makes you happy. You've carried my burdens along with your own for too long. I know your mom is needing you more and more. You don't need to be so tied up in my problems."

Andy didn't know what to say to that. How did he tell her that he *wanted* to be there for her without revealing his feelings for her? He wasn't sure that she was ready to hear about them yet.

"I think you need to focus on your own life," Cece continued. "Your own happiness. Maybe give that dating app another whirl."

He felt sick at her words, but he knew he shouldn't. After all, he'd accepted long ago that he wasn't the sort of man she'd want a relationship with. Perhaps she was getting tired of him constantly being underfoot. She was making it seem like this was for his benefit, but maybe she was just tired of him.

Regardless of her reasoning, he had to respect her wishes.

When she left a few minutes later—far sooner than he'd wanted—he stood with the back door propped open, watching to make sure she made it safely to the door to her apartment. With each step she took away from him, Andy felt the ache in his heart expand. And when she disappeared inside without looking back, he struggled to take a breath past the pain in his chest.

She'd been such a huge part of his life over the past couple of years, more than at any other time in their friendship. He'd accepted that there would be no romance between them, but he'd assumed they'd always have a friendship.

But now he wasn't sure they even had that anymore, and the realization broke his heart.

CHAPTER TWENTY-FOUR

"Did something happen with Andy?"

Cece glanced over at Mia, then turned her attention back to the macarons she was piping onto a baking sheet. "What?"

"He hasn't been by for the past couple of days," Mia said. "I just thought maybe something was wrong."

"His aunt is in town visiting," she said, as if that was the reason.

Mia's hum in response held a skeptical note to it. "You'd think he could spare a minute to come by and get a coffee and say hi."

"I'm sure he'll be back soon." The lie almost choked her.

"Are you sure nothing happened?" Mia asked again. "You've seemed quieter than usual."

Cece laid the piping bag down and tapped the tray on the work-table. "I've got some stuff going on in my life that's kind of distracting me."

"Anything I can help with?"

Cece gave her a quick smile, then moved to set the tray onto the end of the worktable. She picked up another bag with a different flavored batter and began piping on another tray. "No. But thank you for offering."

"That's what friends do," Mia stated.

Were they friends? She'd never gotten around to telling Mia why her friendship with Sarah and Jillian had failed. Right then, she just didn't want to have anyone in her life. It was easier that way.

Easier, but harder, too.

Her thoughts had taken dark turns several times over the past few days. The struggle to find a reason to exist had been real. About the only thing that had any meaning anymore was her work at the bakery.

Brooke seemed appreciative of her work, and Cece was glad that she could help her. Even though she was happy for her boss, it was also hard to see her glowing and happy. For the first time in her life, she wondered what it might be like to have kids.

As long as her dad had been controlling her life and her future had seemed to include men who would hurt her more than love her, Cece hadn't allowed herself to think about having a family of her own. She hadn't wanted to bring children into a relationship like the one she'd had with Geof.

Now, though, she wondered what it might be like to have a relationship that was secure and loving enough to bring a child into it. She wasn't sure she would know how to be a good parent.

Andy would, though. He would make a great husband and dad. The thought hurt, but she refused to show Mia that emotion.

"You know, you can tell me anything," Mia said. "I'm good at keeping confidences."

Cece finished with the second tray, tapping it a few times before setting it aside and focusing on the next one. "I'm not used to sharing things."

"Even with Andy?"

He had definitely been the one person who had known the most about her. "Andy is aware of what's going on."

"That's good." Mia wandered closer to where she was working. "Do I annoy you?"

Cece paused, resting her hands on the worktable as she looked at Mia. "What?"

"Do I annoy you?" she asked again. "Sometimes people tell me that I'm annoying."

"No, you don't annoy me," Cece answered truthfully. "Although your perpetually upbeat attitude can be a bit... distracting."

Mia laughed. "Sorry. You're not the only person who has mentioned that."

"It's probably not the worst personality trait to have," Cece said as she focused again on her work. "I'm sure people would rather hang around someone who is always happy than someone who is more... dour."

"You're not dour, if that's what you're trying to say."

Cece wasn't sure what she was trying to say, but maybe it *was* that she saw herself as dour. "Maybe dour was the wrong word."

"If I had to pick one," Mia began, her expression turning thoughtful. "I'd probably say you're reserved."

She could be. The thing was, she could be a lot of things, depending on who she was with and how much effort she wanted to put into impressing someone. Being a cheerleader had taught her how to put on a smiling face, even when she definitely wasn't happy inside.

The bell over the front door jangled, drawing Mia out of the kitchen. Cece sighed once she was alone again. She had a feeling that Mia was going to persist in trying to be her friend. Cece wasn't as opposed to that idea as she might have been in the past, but at the same time, she was feeling a bit raw, emotionally.

Everything that had happened with Geof still lingered in the back of her mind, periodically pulled to the forefront, which overwhelmed her. She was always able to pull herself together again, but it took time and often left her feeling exhausted. But she was surviving... not thriving at the moment... but surviving, for sure.

Mia stayed busy with customers at the front, so she didn't come back into the kitchen for the remainder of Cece's shift. Once she'd finished cleaning everything up, she made sure that everything was stocked up at the front, then she said goodbye to Mia and left for the day.

Just like the previous days, Cece didn't know what to do with her time. The apartment was spotless, so she didn't need to clean anything. She couldn't go anywhere because she had no car, and it wasn't safe for her to walk around town. There'd been no sign of Geof, but that didn't mean he wasn't out there somewhere.

Maybe she needed to find a hobby. She'd never really had one before, but she needed something to fill her time. If she didn't come up with an idea, she was going to lose her mind.

She got her laptop and took it to the table by the window. Before she could open it, her attention was grabbed by the people she saw approach the dance studio, then disappear inside. Cara must have had a class starting soon.

For a moment, Cece toyed with the idea of joining the class. It would certainly help to pass the time. However, she just couldn't see herself being part of a group like that.

She spotted Sarah getting out of a parked car and walking toward the dance studio. If she'd been serious about joining the class, Sarah's presence would definitely have changed her mind.

Though she couldn't see the bookstore since it was on the same side of the street as the apartment, she leaned her head against the window and stared in that direction. She missed Andy more than she could ever have imagined. More than anything, she wanted to walk down the sidewalk and into the bookstore, where she'd talk with Andy about her day. And maybe he'd need help with something in his book.

When her vision blurred, she blinked and felt the warmth of tears as they slid down her cheeks. She knew she'd done the right thing for his sake. But man, his absence in her life hurt.

As tears continued to flow, Cece thought of the sermon she'd heard, and how the pastor had said that God was there for people who felt alone. Would He be there for her? Even though she wasn't a Christian?

She wiped a hand across her cheeks, trying to understand how that was possible. How exactly would she not feel alone when God wasn't a visible person? None of it made sense, and she wished she could talk to Andy... or someone, about it.

As she sat with her head tipped against the window, Cece zoned out. Her thoughts were a jumble. She felt emptied of everything. The anger and pain she'd felt for so many years were gone, but there was nothing to take its place. Nothing to replace those emotions.

She was a shell.

Fragile and brittle.

And she didn't know what to do about it.

She'd thought that if she somehow managed to get free of her parents and Geof, everything would be perfect. That her life would be this wonderful thing that would bring her so much happiness.

Instead, she was lost. Unable to find purpose and direction in her life.

She didn't know how long she'd been sitting there when she heard a knock on the apartment door. For a moment, she wanted to ignore it. But on the off chance it was Cara, she figured she'd better answer it. Cara wasn't someone she could ignore since she was her landlady.

She walked to the door and opened it, frowning when she saw who stood there.

"Hey!" Sarah said with a smile. "Mind if we come in?"

Cece hesitated, then stepped back. "Sure."

Jillian followed Sarah into the apartment, smiling at Cece as she passed her. Cece closed the door, leaning against it for a moment before she turned to face them.

"How are you doing?" Sarah asked as she sat down on the couch with Jillian next to her.

It looked like they were planning to stay awhile. Cece went back to her seat by the window, angling herself to face them. "I'm fine."

Sarah gave her a skeptical look. "You know it's alright if you're not."

"You can't go through something like you did without it leaving you with issues to deal with." Jillian's tone was gentle, but her words were spoken with conviction. "I know what it's like to be attacked physically. I know the scars it leaves on the inside, even after the visible ones have faded."

Cece stared at Jillian for a moment. "What do you mean?"

Sarah laid a hand on Jillian's arm, and the woman looked over at her. "You don't have to talk about it."

"I think I do." Jillian gave her a small smile. "It feels right."

Cece remained silent as she watched the interaction. She still wasn't sure how she felt about the pair showing up unannounced.

"Have you heard about the Portland Predator?" Jillian said.

Frowning, Cece tried to remember if she'd ever heard anything about them, but nothing came to mind. "I don't think so."

"He was a man who kidnapped, tortured, and killed several women," Jillian explained. "I was one of his victims. I was fortunate to survive my time with him. However, the ordeal left me with scars that have taken a while to heal. There are days when I don't think about what happened at all. But then there are times when the hurt and memories overwhelm me, and the scars simply pulse with the memory of what I endured."

"I didn't know," Cece murmured.

Jillian smiled. "Most people don't. I didn't want that to be what people thought of when they saw me. But it means that I understand how it feels to be hurt physically."

"But I chose to be with Geof."

"You choosing to be with him didn't give him the right to treat you the way he did," Jillian said. "He is the only one responsible for his actions. It's not wrong of you to expect to be treated well."

Cece stared down at her hands. "I made mistakes with him."

"That still doesn't mean you deserved what happened," Jillian said. "Don't let your mind convince you that you did."

"I haven't always been a good person." Saying those words made Cece feel a little sick. It was the first time she'd admitted that out loud to anyone but Andy. And these two hadn't needed her to put into words what they already knew.

When neither of them argued the point, Cece clenched her hands. Of course, they wouldn't argue. They, more than anyone else, had been witness to her horrible behavior. What she'd said to Jillian at that dinner had been the final straw, but there had been plenty of other times when she'd made snide or critical comments to them and others.

"I hope that you don't believe that we think you deserved what happened to you because of things you've done," Sarah said. "That is not how we feel at all."

"It wouldn't be surprising if you did."

"But we don't," Jillian said. "I might not understand why you act the way you do sometimes, but I don't carry hate in my heart toward you."

Cece glanced up and saw the sincerity on Jillian's face. "I am sorry for what I've said to you. I had no right."

"I won't lie and say it's fine because it did hurt," Jillian murmured. "But I've chosen to let that go. It took me a little while, I won't deny that, but I have already forgiven you for what happened."

Andy's words came back to her then. He'd known that Jillian and Sarah would forgive her. She hadn't been so certain because she didn't understand. If someone had said something like that to her, she would have had a much more difficult time letting it go. She was pretty sure she would have held a grudge against them.

That was just more proof that she wasn't a good person.

"I'd like it if we could put all of that behind us," Jillian said. "And maybe we could become friends again. Better friends."

Cece frowned. They wanted to be friends with *her?* Now they were starting to sound like Mia. Why was everyone wanting to be her friend? She had nothing to offer anyone. She didn't want to be the person she'd been before, but she still didn't know who she was apart from all of that.

But what could she say? *No, I don't want to be your friend?*

The reality was, she *did* want friends. Desperately. But she was scared that they'd have expectations of her that she wouldn't be able to meet. That she wouldn't know how to be a good friend. And in the end, she'd just be alone again.

"Why don't we just start out simple?" Sarah suggested. "Jillian and I are running into Everett to grab some groceries. Do you want to come with us?"

From a strictly practical point, she needed to go with them. Her cupboard and fridge were nearly bare, and she didn't have a car to go to the store. She could shop at the grocery store in New Hope, but she knew that prices were higher there. As much as she'd like to support a local business, right then, she needed to save some money.

"Are you sure?" she asked. "I can't be gone too long. I have to be in bed by seven since I have to get up early to do the baking."

"Oh, we'll be back before six," Sarah assured her. "Jillian wants to get back in time to visit Carter at the station for supper."

"So you're going right now?"

"We'll go as soon as you're ready."

"I can go now."

"Perfect," Sarah said. "Let's go."

The two women got to their feet, and Cece followed suit. "I just need to go to the bathroom really quick."

"We'll go get the car and meet you at the back door."

After the women had left, Cece went into her bathroom to freshen up. She winced at how pale and drained she looked. Though she didn't have much time, she quickly grabbed her makeup and tried to lighten up under her eyes and hide some of the redness around her nose.

She was just going down the stairs when Sarah sent her a text letting her know they were there. Cece locked up behind her and stepped out into the back alley. She opened the door behind the driver's seat and slid into the car.

Sarah was driving the luxurious vehicle, which Beau had no doubt bought for her. Cece tried not to feel jealous, but it was hard.

As they drove, Jillian and Sarah talked about a variety of things, most of which Cece was clueless about. Instead, she took the time to make a list of things to buy, so she didn't forget anything. It was the first time she'd shopped like this for herself, and it made her wish that Andy was with her.

She checked the notes that she'd made when she'd been working on her budget with Andy. Biting her lip, she went back to her list and re-worked it, prioritizing the items to make sure that she got what she needed before her budgeted grocery money ran out.

After they'd parked in the large lot, they walked into the store together and each of them got a cart.

"Do you think an hour will be enough time for you?" Sarah asked.

Cece had no clue, but she nodded.

"Okay. We'll meet on the other side of the cash registers when we're done."

With that, the other two moved in different directions, leaving Cece to look around to decide where to start. The bright signs hanging from the ceiling helped, and soon she found herself in the grocery section of the store.

Not being familiar with the store meant it took her a bit longer than it should have to find the things on her list. Keeping a running total of the cost of what she was buying also added to the time it took for her to mark things off her list.

Still, she felt a sense of accomplishment when she finally made it to the cash registers. She'd managed to find everything on her list, and she'd even resisted the urge to buy things she hadn't really needed.

Well, except for the chocolate bar she'd picked up, but she figured she deserved a treat.

Cece glanced around for the two women and spotted them on the other side of the registers already. Sarah waved at her with a smile. Cece nodded to let her know she'd seen her, then focused on putting her items on the conveyor belt. The total was just under what she and Andy had budgeted for food, which made her feel good.

After they loaded the bags of groceries into the car and left the store, Cece opened her text messages with Andy. The urge to tell him what she'd done was *so* strong. She knew without a doubt that he'd be proud of her. That he'd understand why she felt like she'd accomplished something major.

Jillian tried to draw her into a conversation on the trip back to New Hope, and Cece did her best to respond. She wanted to show the two women that she was trying to change. The hard part was that she still felt so empty and unsure of who this new version of herself was supposed to be.

"Thank you so much for this," she said to Sarah after they climbed out of the car a short time later. "I really appreciate it."

Sarah smiled at her, then approached her with her arms open. Hugs hadn't been a regular part of Cece's life, so she wasn't sure what to do.

"Take care of yourself," Sarah said as she squeezed her tight. "And call me if you need anything or if you need to go anywhere. My schedule is fairly flexible."

"Okay." She glanced at Jillian. "Sorry again for what I said."

Jillian waved her hand in the air. "No more apologies. It's in the past now, and I'm looking forward to spending more time with you."

She seemed sincere, so Cece decided to take her words at face value. After they helped her carry her bags into the garage, the women said goodbye and left.

Cece mulled over the past couple of hours as she carried her groceries upstairs and put them away. It was hard to believe life was as simple as they made it out to be. They forgave her, and everything was fine?

She really wanted to talk to Andy about it. He would know how to help her understand how this was supposed to work.

But she needed to learn how to do this stuff on her own, no matter how much she struggled and how much it hurt to not have Andy to constantly lean on for support.

CHAPTER TWENTY-FIVE

Andy listened to his mom and his aunt discuss the upcoming changes for their family. Changes that he was more than okay with.

It had taken surprisingly little to convince his aunt to move to New Hope. They'd had a family meeting to decide exactly how to proceed, with Phoebe volunteering almost immediately to move out with her friend so that Cilla could have her room.

Like he'd done with Cece, Andy had sat down with Phoebe to go over her finances to make sure she knew what she had to work with. He didn't want her to end up in a bad financial situation in her desperation to get out of the house.

It was good he had something to focus on or else he'd be constantly thinking about Cece and wondering how she was doing. He was still struggling to accept that she didn't want him in her life anymore. There had been times over the years when contact between them had lapsed, but it had never held the finality that this did.

The way she had cut him off had come out of the blue and had been like a knife to the chest. Straight into his heart.

He might struggle with it, but she'd made it clear that this was what she wanted. Maybe this change would help the love he held in his heart for her to finally fade away. Because if she didn't want his friendship, she certainly wasn't going to want anything more.

Unfortunately, Cece removing herself from his life didn't alleviate the worry Andy had for her.

Had Geof tried to contact her again? Or her parents? He'd kept an eye out for Geof but hadn't seen any sign of the man. He really wanted to believe that situation was over, but it seemed unresolved.

Maybe it would feel like it was over once Geof had his day in court... which hopefully led to time in jail.

"Are you doing okay, darling?" his mom asked.

He looked up at her from where he'd been staring at his phone. "I'm fine."

"You seem... distracted."

"Well, there is a lot going on," he reminded her. "Just thinking about it all."

"Anything you're specifically concerned about?" she asked.

"I didn't mean to add stress to your life by coming here," his aunt said.

"You're not." Andy smiled to reassure her. "I just want to make sure that we cover all the bases."

"You're very much like your dad," Cilla said. "He always thought everything through, considering it from every angle."

It pleased Andy to be compared favorably to his dad. He always hoped that his dad would be proud of how he'd stepped up to take care of their family.

"He is very much like him," his mom agreed, a soft smile on her lips. "I am blessed in the men God gave me for a husband and a son."

Andy appreciated the kind words from his mom and aunt, but they were definitely biased in their opinions of him. He had always tried to live up to the high standard his dad had set, but apparently not everyone could see the value in that, or in him.

"Do you have a girlfriend?" Cilla asked.

Andy tried not to wince at the question. "No."

"Why not? Any woman would be lucky to have you."

That was the thing, he hadn't wanted just any woman. His heart had been set on one woman for years. "I've got quite a lot going on in my life at the moment."

"Aren't there any single women in your church?" Cilla asked.

"Not as many as there once was," his mother said. "It seems as if there've been quite a few getting married lately."

"That's true," Andy said. "Many of them are my friends, and they've each found a great guy."

"*You're* a great guy," Cilla said. "My favorite nephew."

"Ha. I'm your *only* nephew."

Cilla shrugged. "That doesn't negate you being my favorite."

Andy was glad that his aunt had come, and it was a relief to see that she was relaxed and safe. She hadn't spoken much about what had brought her to them, but he suspected she'd talk more about it with his mom. He just hoped that Roy had forgotten where they lived so that he didn't show up to try to convince Cilla to return to him.

And it wasn't just that. He didn't want the unstable man to be anywhere around his mom. Given her weakened state, she wouldn't be able to protect herself like she might have in the past.

"He has a... special friend," his mom said with a sidelong glance at him.

"You do?" Cilla asked, curiosity edging her voice. "Tell me about her."

"Mom is referring to someone I've been friends with since school."

"Oooh. A high school romance?"

"Not a romance," Andy said. "We're just friends."

"Hmmm. Friendship is always a good foundation for something more," Cilla said. "I wish I'd followed that path to a relationship. I know there are people who meet and fall in love in a matter of days and go on to have a wonderful relationship. That just wasn't my experience."

"If this friendship was going to turn into something more, it would have done so long ago," Andy said. "She's just getting out of a relationship that's not unlike yours with Roy."

Cilla frowned. "That's not good."

"No, it's not," Andy agreed. "But she's safe now."

Or at least he hoped she was.

"You haven't talked about her over the past few days," his mom said, her brow furrowed.

Andy debated what to say in response, but finally decided on the truth. "She's asked for a little space as she adjusts to her new life. Her parents were also part of the problem, so she's cut herself off from them as well as the ex-boyfriend."

"But why would she need space from you?" his mom asked. "You've done so much for her."

If only he had the answer to that question. "Well, she actually said that was part of the reason she wanted space."

"What do you mean?"

"She said I've spent too much time helping her. That I deserve to have time for myself. To date and find a girlfriend."

"And you didn't tell her that you'd like *her* to be your girl-friend?" Cilla asked.

"Of course not. She's never viewed me like that. I think she assumed she was doing me a favor."

"It doesn't sound like you feel that way."

"I have long ago accepted that there would be nothing romantic between us. I don't need time apart from her in order to find a girlfriend. I've gone on dates even while she was still in my life."

"Nothing came of them?" Cilla asked.

"No. The women were nice enough, and I even went on more than one date with one of them, but there was just no connection between us."

"Well, I definitely think it's this girl's loss," Cilla said. "You would be a wonderful boyfriend. And you're even attractive, which is just a bonus when you're a nice guy."

Unfortunately, Andy felt it was his loss, too. He knew that people didn't understand what he saw in Cece, and that was fine. They didn't need to. The problem was that Cece didn't understand it either. Or maybe she finally understood that he had feelings for her, and she just didn't want to deal with that.

That was the only thing that made sense to him. And it hurt his heart. Andy had known he wasn't her type of guy, and he'd accepted that. He'd just thought he'd have her friendship, if nothing else. He had tried to keep his feelings out of their friendship, but he must have done something that tipped her off.

"It's fine," Andy said. "I think she needs friends, though, so I hope she's reached out to the other people we know."

His aunt patted his hand. "If it's meant to be, things will work out."

Andy wasn't so sure, but he didn't argue with her.

"Are you going to go with Phoebe tonight to look at that apartment she and Aubrey are interested in?" his mom asked.

"Yeah. I'm meeting her there after she's done work."

"I'm glad she is willing to look at places here in town."

Andy nodded. "I was surprised, but I think they both realized it's cheaper here."

"Are you sure I shouldn't be the one looking?" Cilla asked with a frown.

"No," his mom said. "Phoebe's been wanting to move out for ages."

"As long as you're sure. I'd like to be here to help you."

Andy was glad that Cilla was willing to help his mom. There were things that he knew his mom struggled with but that she would never ask for his help with. If Cilla was there, she could help his mom with those things.

When his phone text alert chirped, he couldn't stop his momentary prayer that it was Cece. Unfortunately, that was a prayer that was destined to be unanswered.

"Phoebe's off in five minutes." Andy got to his feet. "I'm going to head out to meet her and Aubrey."

"Okay, sweetie," his mom said.

He drove the short distance to the building where Phoebe and her friend were looking at an apartment. The three-story building was in an older part of town, but it looked like it was well maintained. He knew his mom would be a lot happier about Phoebe moving out if she lived in an apartment in town rather than in a bigger city.

Phoebe approached him as he got out of his car, a skip to her step revealing how excited she was about this new chapter in her life.

"Is Aubrey coming?" he asked.

"Yep. She's gonna be here in a couple of minutes."

They chatted as they stood on the sidewalk, waiting for Aubrey. It was pretty clear that Phoebe was totally hoping that this was going to be the place for them.

When Aubrey finally arrived, the two girls hugged and squealed, making Andy smile. He wasn't sure he'd ever been that excited about anything.

He followed behind them as they walked up the sidewalk to the door. Since this was their deal, Andy let them take the lead on everything.

As he climbed the stairs with them and the apartment manager, his thoughts went to Cece, and he was glad that she was in an apartment that was safer than these ones since Geof was still on the loose.

This place would be safe enough for Phoebe and her friend, though, with a security system in place on the entrance doors and, interestingly enough, on each floor. No one could access a floor unless they had the code for it. That was a definite point in the building's favor.

The manager addressed his comments to the girls, which Andy appreciated, since it showed he was taking it seriously that they were the ones interested in living there, not Andy.

"This has two bedrooms and a nice sized bathroom," the man said as he opened the door to the apartment. "It's been freshly painted, and we had to replace the carpet throughout because the previous tenants..." He clicked his tongue as he shook his head.

There was a lingering aroma of paint in the air as they stepped into the apartment, but it wasn't overwhelming. Andy trailed behind the girls as they investigated the bedrooms and the bathroom.

It seemed like the perfect place, and he hoped that they'd get it. They could clearly see themselves living there as they discussed who'd get which bedroom.

"You're related to one of them?" the man asked as they stood in the kitchen while the girls took a second tour of the place.

"Yes. Phoebe is my sister."

"Do you live here in town?"

"Yep. My mom also lives here. I work at the bookstore on Main Street."

The man nodded. "I've seen the store, but don't think I've ever been inside."

"Have you had any other interest in the apartment?" Andy asked.

"A couple of people, but they weren't sure it was the right location for them."

"Can we fill out the application?" Phoebe asked as they returned from the bedrooms. "We really like this apartment."

"Sure thing," the man said. "Though I have to mention that if you don't have a rental history, it might be necessary for you to have a co-signer. Will that be an issue?"

Aubrey shook her head. "My dad already said he'd do it."

Phoebe glanced at Andy, so he said, "My mom or I will co-sign for Phoebe."

"That's good," the man said.

He gestured to the counter where a couple of pieces of paper lay. "You can fill these out now, if you'd like."

"While you do that," Andy began, "I'm going to take a few pictures for Mom. You know she's going to want to see this."

Phoebe nodded, then said to the man, "My mom is disabled, so she couldn't come see this herself."

"Sorry to hear that," he said.

Andy left them to talk as he pulled up the camera app on his phone. He took some photos as well as a video, knowing that his mom and Cilla would love to see the apartment. He sent them off to his mom, then went back to where the girls were.

"When do you think we'll know if we're approved?" Phoebe asked.

"Provided everything checks out, probably in a day or two."

"Okay. Thank you very much for showing us around."

The man walked them back to the entrance of the building, where they said goodbye.

"Thanks for coming, Andy," Phoebe said.

"Anytime." He looped his arm around her shoulders and gave her a hug. "I'll see you at home."

He left the girls talking on the sidewalk and went to his car. Rather than head straight home, he found himself driving toward Main Street. He pulled to a stop along the street between the bookstore and the dance studio.

The windows above the studio were dark, and he knew that was probably because of the window glazing that prevented people from being able to look inside when it was night, and the lights were on inside. He glanced at the clock and saw that it was almost seven, which meant the darkened apartment could also be because Cece had gone to bed early.

He knew that it bordered on stalkerish to sit and stare at Cece's windows, but he just missed her so much. Andy had no idea if this was just a temporary break in their friendship or if Cece was viewing it as a permanent thing.

The loss of their friendship hurt a lot. It was a loss he felt deeply, and he didn't know how to deal with it. His dad's death had stunned him, leaving him in shock. But afterwards, he'd had a direction in which to move. He'd known that his dad wasn't coming back, and he had no choice but to move forward. To do what he could to help his mom and sister as they dealt with their shared loss.

This situation with Cece, though... it felt unfinished.

His dad's death had been a defining break in their lives. Cleanly marked as being the end of his presence in their lives.

Cece's absence from his life felt more frayed. As if their lives were still connected, albeit only by the thinnest of threads. But maybe that was only how he viewed it because he didn't want things to be over. It was possible that to her, it was completely done between them.

No friendship.

No nothing.

CHAPTER TWENTY-SIX

"What's happened between you and Cece?"

Andy froze, then lowered his cup back to the counter he was standing next to in Eli's house. "What?"

"You haven't been by the bakery all week," Mia said, her brows drawn tight together. There was no smile on her usually cheerful face. "Cece said it was because you had family visiting, but I'm not buying that."

"Something happened with you and Cece?" Sarah asked, turning away from the conversation she'd been having with Leah and Gavin.

"I do have family visiting," Andy said. "My aunt is here."

Mia's expression was full of skepticism. "And you don't have two extra minutes to spare in the morning to swing by the bakery and get your usual cup of coffee?"

"What's going on, Andy?" Sarah asked as she crossed her arms and pinned him with a firm look.

Andy lifted his cup of coffee and took the sip that Mia's question had interrupted. He might have been able to get out of explaining anything to Mia, but now that Sarah was part of the conversation, he didn't have a hope.

"Cece feels that she's taken up enough of my time, and that helping her has prevented me from dating and finding a girlfriend."

Sarah's brows rose. "She thinks you want a girlfriend?"

"I told her that I'd gone on some dates using a dating app."

Sarah grabbed his arm. "Say what?"

"I went on some dates," he repeated. "What's so surprising about that?"

"All kinds of things." Sarah's serious expression made her look more like Leah than usual. "I thought you had feelings for Cece."

"The problem with that is that Cece doesn't have feelings for me," Andy said, trying not to choke on the words. "And I'm pretty sure that she just used me dating as an excuse to get me out of her life."

"I don't know..." Sarah shook her head. "Cece has seemed to lean on you more than any other person. In fact, there's been times when I thought she was just using you, but I'm not sure that really was the case. Given what I know about other things, I think it was more that you were a harbor for her. A safe place to go when the storms of her life became too much."

Andy rubbed a hand against the back of his neck, then dropped his gaze to the cup he still held. "I don't know what to think. The only thing I know for certain is that I'm not going to force my presence on her."

Sarah leaned her head against his shoulder for a moment before smiling up at him. "You've always been such a wonderful man, Andy."

"Which doesn't explain why no woman has ever expressed much interest in me," he scoffed. "Even you."

"We've already established that a relationship between us would never have worked," Sarah said. "But I'd certainly talk you up to any woman if I thought they had a chance."

"Cece's different," Mia said. "I mean, she's different from when I met her for the first time, and that's not even been that long ago."

"What do you mean?" Sarah asked. "I've seen it myself, but I'm curious to hear it from someone who's just met her."

"She seems a lot... softer." Mia frowned. "And at times, it's like she's just a shadow moving through her life."

Those words were like a hammer blow to Andy's already aching heart. "Please explain."

"She's very focused on her work and rarely speaks to anyone unless they say something to her first. If she happens to be in the front loading the cases when someone who knows her walks in, she'll respond to their greeting, but then she doesn't pursue any further conversation." Mia tilted her head to the side. "Has she always been that way?"

"For the most part," Andy said. "She can be outgoing, if she needs to be, but that isn't her usual personality."

"Jillian and I spent some time with her earlier this week," Sarah said. "We took her grocery shopping with us."

Andy was relieved to hear that, since he'd wondered how she was going to manage without a vehicle if she wasn't going to rely on him for help. "Thank you for doing that for her."

"She has changed," Sarah agreed. "But I'm not sure how much is because she's adjusting to a lot of changes in her life and how much is going to be lasting."

"Maybe you should come by for coffee this week," Mia said. "I really don't think she'll be upset if you do."

Andy wasn't so sure about that, but he also really wanted to see her again. To see for himself that she was doing okay. "I'll think about it."

"I hope you will, because I really do think a visit from you will be good for her."

But would it be good for him? He wasn't sure how many rejections from her he could take.

With a smile and a squeeze of his arm, Mia wandered off to join her husband. Sarah, however, stuck close by, moving him off to the side of the room.

"I didn't want to go into details that Cece might not want Mia to know, but I do think Cece is still struggling with what happened to her."

"That's to be expected," Andy said. "I don't think someone can go through something like that and immediately be fine."

"Yeah, but now she's without the one person she's always relied on."

"I didn't step away by choice," Andy reminded her. "You don't know everything that's gone on in her life, but believe me when I say that it's very important for her to have control of her own life. I'm not going to force myself on her."

"But what if she really does feel that pushing you away is for your own good? What if she feels like she's been a burden to you for long enough? What if all she wants is for you to have a chance at happiness?"

"But I'm happier *with* her than I am without her," Andy said. "Even if it's just friendship."

"She may finally see you for the great guy that you are, but in her mind, she might think she's not good enough for you, even as a friend." Sarah paused. "I got the feeling from talking to her with Jillian that she might think she deserves what's happened to her."

Andy frowned. "I've never wanted her to feel that way because it's not true at all."

"I know that, and you know that, but from the sound of things, she's heard a very different message throughout her life."

He could hardly deny that. "I don't know how to be there for her without her feeling like I'm overriding what she wants."

Sarah let out a sigh as she shook her head. "*Talk* to her. I'm not saying you have to tell her how you feel. But honestly, I feel like the two of you are both so afraid of scaring the other one off, that neither of you are being honest about things."

Andy considered her words, and he realized that he didn't have a whole lot to lose. He was already being left out of her life. If he approached her and she still wanted him out of her life, then he'd just be in the same position he was currently in.

"I've never really known what you've seen in her," Sarah admitted. "Or how you've managed to stand beside her while she's dated other guys, feeling about her the way you do. But if she's honestly doing this because she thinks it's the best thing for *you* and not for herself, maybe she *'s* come to realize how special you are."

"It hasn't been easy," Andy admitted. "And I've always known that there was going to be a time when she would fully commit to a guy. I just hoped that he would be a decent person. I think I stuck close because she kept getting involved with guys who were jerks, and I wanted to make sure she was okay."

"She has had horrendous taste in men," Sarah said. "And yes, I'm including Tanner in that because, even though he's great now, he wasn't so great back when they dated."

"Trust me, he was actually one of the better ones. Tanner might not have been interested in anything long term with her, but he'd never have hurt her physically."

When Tanner had returned, Andy had wondered if Cece might try to get back together with him. However, Geof's grip on her life had been too tight by that point.

"I'll stop in on Tuesday for a coffee and to say hi. That way she'll know I'm not pressuring her for something right then as I have to go to work too."

"Just try to have an actual conversation with her. For both your sakes."

"I will. Thank you for talking me through this."

"Anytime," she said with a smile, then gestured to his cup. "Now put that down so I can give you a hug."

Laughing, Andy set his cup down on the nearby counter and accepted Sarah's tight hug before she stepped back from him.

When he left the Bible study later that evening, Andy's heart felt lighter than it had in awhile. Though he hadn't planned to talk to anyone about Cece, it had helped tremendously to speak with Mia and Sarah. He would take Sarah's advice because she was right. If Cece thought that this was what he wanted, then she needed to know that it wasn't.

~ * ~

Cece finished filling the cases, then turned on the rest of the lights in the front part of the store and flipped the sign to open. She was going to have to handle the front of the shop until the end of her shift, since Mia had called in sick. Brooke had said she'd come in to do the baking for the afternoon, so it would be just like in the old days, except that the afternoon shift person would be on their own for a couple of hours when Mia would usually have been there with them.

Many of the regulars asked after Mia, but they also said it was good to see Cece behind the counter again. She truly hadn't thought that anyone would miss her, but it seemed that maybe a few had.

Just after nine, the woman who had sung at church with Leah showed up with Cara.

"Hi, Cece," Cara said with a warm smile. "Haven't seen you on coffee duty in awhile."

"Mia's sick today, so I'm doing part of my shift up front."

Cara gestured to the pregnant woman at her side. "This is my sister-in-law, Alessia. This is Cece. She's renting the apartment."

"It's nice to meet you," Alessia said. Her smile was as warm and friendly as Cara's.

"You, too. I really enjoyed your singing at church with Leah. You have a beautiful voice."

Alessia's smile widened. "Thank you. I was surprised that I didn't have to bug Leah too much to sing with me."

"You sounded great together," Cara said. "And that song was a wonderful choice."

Cece wanted to share how it had touched her, but she didn't know how to put it into words. It was easier to focus on the obvious, which was the talent that Alessia had for singing. Anything more than that, and Cece felt a bit lost at conveying her feelings.

"What can I get for you?"

The ladies discussed their order, then Cece got busy preparing it for them.

"I thought you'd bring Jayden," Alessia said as they waited.

"I was going to, but then Rose said she'd watch him, and I decided to take advantage of her offer. It will be easier to do our errands without worrying about him fussing."

"We'll probably be done a lot sooner since it's just the two of us."

"That's what I thought," Cara said with a nod. "I hope you've got your list."

"Gio made sure that I did. He said that I better come home with everything on it, or we'll be going right back out."

Cara laughed. "I'm sure he just wants to know for certain that you guys are ready for the baby to arrive. Kieran was the same. I think he was nesting as much as I was in the last month."

Once Cece had finished with their drinks and packaged up the pastries they ordered, Cara paid for everything. "Thanks so much, Cece."

"You're welcome," she replied. "I hope you have a great day."

"You, too."

"It was nice to meet you, Cece," Alessia said. "I hope to see you in church again."

Cece gave her a smile without committing one way or another. Rather than watch the women leave the store, happy to be moving on to the next part of their day together, she turned away and cleaned up the counter around the coffee machines.

When the door opened again a short time later, Cece looked up to greet the customer. Her heart slammed against her ribs when she saw Andy walk into the shop. She gripped the edge of the counter to keep herself from running to him and throwing her arms around him. She had missed him *so* much more than she'd even realized was possible.

"Hey there," he said with a soft smile.

"Hi."

He shoved his hands into his pockets, shifting from one foot to the other. "How've you been?"

"Fine. How about you? How's your aunt's visit going?"

Some of the awkwardness eased from his posture, and his shoulders lowered. "It's actually turned into a move."

"A move?" Cece asked.

"Yeah. Her husband is a real piece of work, and Mom and I encouraged her to consider moving away from him. Once she got here, she agreed, and so she's going to move in with us. Phoebe is getting an apartment with her friend, so Cilla can have her room."

"That's good it's worked out for her," Cece said.

Andy nodded. "And it's good for us too, because she wants to help Mom, which is a relief for me. There are things Cilla can help her with that I just can't."

"So it works out well for all of you."

Andy smiled. "Yeah. It has, and Mom is really happy to have her sister with her again."

As an awkward silence bloomed between them again, Cece's gaze dropped, then she said, "Uh, did you want some coffee?"

"Sure. That would be great." As she got to work preparing his coffee just the way he liked it, Andy said, "Has everything been okay for you? No trouble?"

She glanced over at him. "Everything has been fine. I haven't seen my parents and there's been no sign of Geof. I got a call yesterday from a lawyer. A prosecutor, I think. She said that Geof's lawyer had been talking to them about a deal or something. She said it would mean he wouldn't serve any jail time, but he'd have to pay a fine, do some community service, and take a course."

"What did you say to her?"

"I didn't really know what to say. The woman did mention that the order for him to stay away from me would still be in place, and she said that she would make it clear that should he violate the order, he'd face consequences."

"So, jail time?"

"I don't know."

"At least they're taking the situation seriously, and I would think that Geof's lawyers realize that if you testify against him, it might not go very well for him."

Cece set his cup on the counter, but she kept her hand wrapped around it. "I don't know how I feel about any of it. I'd like him to spend some time in jail, but he would probably be so angry with me when he got out, I'd be at even greater risk. And while I'm glad that there's a protective order in place, it won't mean much if he gets to me and hurts me before I have a chance to call for help."

Andy nodded, and she appreciated that he didn't dismiss her concerns. "I hate that you have to keep checking over your shoulder. But being vigilant is the best thing you can do. And try not to go anywhere that you'll be alone."

"The only places I go are work and home. I did go to Everett with Jillian and Sarah, but I had people around me all the time."

"Did you get everything you needed?"

Cece nodded. "It was my first time buying groceries like that for myself, but I think I did okay."

"That's great." Andy smiled broadly at her. "I'm glad you could go with them."

She wanted to be happy with how proud he seemed to be of her doing something as easy as grocery shopping, but all she felt was chagrin. It was ridiculous that she was learning to do all of this when she was in her late twenties.

But it was her own selfishness that had created that situation. She could have helped her mom more. She probably would have taken Cece with her when she did things like grocery shopping. But Cece hadn't wanted any of that.

Her dad had impressed upon her the importance of snaring a rich man, using the idea of her never having to do housework as the incentive. Of course, now she realized that he wanted her to marry a rich man for *his* sake, not hers. Likely, he'd figured that he had to make his suggestion appealing to her in order to make it happen.

Learning how to grocery shop and cook at this point in her life was not something she was really proud of. Even Phoebe was doing things at the right age. Going to school and working. Getting her own apartment when she was barely out of high school. Phoebe could definitely be proud of the strides she was making in her life.

"Here you go," she said, pushing the cup of coffee closer to him. "My treat."

Andy frowned. "You don't need to do that."

"Coffee's my treat, but if you want anything else, you have to pay."

His laughter at her comment was such a wonderful thing to hear, and Cece wanted him to keep laughing and smiling. It made her heart feel lighter, and for the first time in days, she truly wanted to smile.

He had always been able to make her smile, so it felt good to be able to do the same thing for him.

CHAPTER TWENTY-SEVEN

Andy picked up his coffee and took a sip. "I think this also calls for one of your cinnamon buns."

Cece nodded, then went to where the cinnamon buns were in the bakery case. He watched as she picked out the biggest one and put it on a piece of parchment paper. It was a small thing, but he took hope from it. If she didn't care at all about him, she wouldn't be giving him free coffee and picking out the best cinnamon bun.

"Where's Mia?" he asked as she rang it up.

"Ben called me last night to let me know that she'd been throwing up all day and running a fever, so it wasn't likely she'd be feeling well enough to work today."

"That's too bad. I saw her Sunday night at the Bible study, and she seemed okay then."

"From what Ben said, she woke up yesterday morning feeling badly."

"Here's hoping she gets over it quickly, and that no one else comes down with it."

"Yeah. I'd really rather not be sick," Cece agreed. "And I'm sure you wouldn't want to be either."

"I don't care so much about myself, but I would hate if I took something home to Mom." He tapped his debit card on the machine, then took the small bakery bag she'd put his pastry into. "Thanks."

A fleeting smile crossed her face. "You're welcome."

"It was good to see you again," he said softly. "I know you want some space, but I hope you know that if you need *anything*, you just have to call."

She nodded. "I will."

Andy hesitated, then said, "Promise?"

Another smile curved her lips. "I promise."

"Okay. Well, I'd better go. Thanks for these." He lifted his cup and the bakery bag. "Hope the rest of your day goes well."

"Yours too."

Andy wasn't keen to leave, but he needed to get the store open. As he walked down the sidewalk to the bookstore, he breathed a sigh of relief. That could have gone so much worse, and it gave him hope that they could continue their friendship, even if it wasn't in the way he'd hoped.

When Andy went into the bakery the next morning, Mia was back behind the counter. She greeted him with a wide smile.

"Hey, Mia. How're you feeling today?"

"So much better," she said. "That was a rough couple of days. I'm just glad that Ben didn't catch whatever I had, even though he was taking care of me, and neither did his parents."

"Have you guys found an apartment yet?"

"Yep. We're going to be moving at the beginning of the month."

"If you need any help, let me know. I'm sure I can wrangle up a truck or two along with some guys to help move the heavy stuff."

"We'd really appreciate that," Mia said. "Ben's dad has a bad back, so he isn't able to help much."

"Do you have a lot of furniture?"

"Yeah. We had a moving truck bring our stuff, and we just put it in a storage unit. So we'll need to empty that."

"Give me the details of when and where you need us, and I'll arrange things with Eli and some of the other guys."

"I can hardly wait to get into a place of our own." When she handed him the cup of coffee she'd poured for him, she asked, "Did you want a pastry?"

Andy leaned to look at the contents of the case. "A blueberry muffin, please."

"Did you want to see Cece?" Mia asked.

He was torn on that. "I won't bother her today. Just tell her I said hi."

Mia frowned. "Are you sure?"

"Yep. I spoke with her yesterday when I came by."

The woman didn't seem to be convinced, but she didn't argue with him. "Here you go."

Andy paid for his purchases, then left the shop. All the way to the bookstore, he questioned if he'd done the right thing by not going into the kitchen to chat with Cece. They may have talked the previous day, but he still didn't know what exactly she would accept from him in interactions.

As it got closer to noon and the end of Cece's shift, Andy debated what to do. Finally, he picked up his phone and found his last text conversation with her.

Want to come hang out for a bit at the bookstore this afternoon?

He knew he should put the phone down and not focus on it while he waited for her to reply, but instead, he stared at it. Drumming his fingers on top of the counter, Andy willed a message to appear on the screen.

When it finally came, his heart gave a hard thump as he read it.

Cece: *Okay. Should I bring lunch?*

Andy grinned. *If you'd like, but it's not necessary. I can call the order in, if you don't mind picking it up.*

Cece: *Sure. That works. I'll be there around one.*

Sounds good!

Now that that was settled, his heart felt lighter. He just hoped she wasn't coming to reiterate that she didn't want him around. Like Sarah had said, they needed to have an actual conversation about their friendship, and he hoped that wouldn't push her to cut him off again.

When she appeared around one, Andy felt a sense of relief. He took the drink tray from her, then followed her into the break room.

As they settled down at the table, he said, "So, have you been keeping busy?"

She sighed, then took a sip of her drink before responding. "It's kind of been a struggle, especially since I can't go out much. I've been watching a lot of cake decorating videos."

"Are you hoping to do some of that eventually?"

"I've been thinking about it. Maybe if I can learn how to do it, Brooke would let me take on some smaller decorating jobs."

"I'm sure you'd be great at it," Andy said.

Cece frowned. "How would you know that?"

"Because you've already proven your ability to learn new things and do well at them," Andy said. "Like the baking. Brooke wouldn't have given you the position if she wasn't confident in your abilities."

"Decorating is a bit different than baking. It requires some artistic talent, which I'm not sure I have."

"You'll never know unless you try."

"True." Cece focused on her chicken wrap. "I just need to find some things to fill up my time."

"Are you bored?"

She shrugged. "I mean, I basically have nothing to do once I'm finished at work for the day. I don't have a family, and I don't have a car to go anywhere." Her expression saddened. "I'm struggling a bit with that."

"Do you wish you were back with your parents and Geof?"

The brief hesitation before she answered made Andy frown.

"It's not that I want to be back with them. After all, I'd already broken up with Geof before everything else happened. I just..."

She sighed. "I just keep seeing people around me with these great lives, and I've got... nothing."

Andy wanted to tell her that she didn't have *nothing,* but he didn't. It wasn't his place to tell her that. "Do you *want* what those people have?"

Cece rolled her eyes at him. "Well, I wouldn't mind a car."

"And that's it?" Andy asked. "A car?"

"It would be the most helpful thing right now. I feel trapped without one."

"I realize it wouldn't be your own car, but if you need to go somewhere, you can always borrow mine."

"You'd let me take your car?" she asked. "Or do you mean you'd drive me somewhere?"

"I don't mind driving you, but I'm also willing to let you just take the car."

"You're too nice," Cece told him. "People will take advantage of you."

"If I'm agreeing to something, then they're not taking advantage of me. Or if they are, I have no one to blame but myself."

"Have you lined up any more dates?"

The change of subject took Andy off-guard for a moment. "Uh... no. I've had other stuff going on. Plus, I'm just not sure that apps are the way for me to find a woman."

"How else are you going to?" Cece asked.

Andy shrugged. "I don't know. In the past, people met without the use of a dating app, so it's not like that is the only way to go."

"Tell me what you like in a woman."

This was really not something that he wanted to discuss with Cece, but he supposed she was fine with it because it was something friends would talk about. Thankfully, the bell at the front jangled, saving him from having to answer just yet.

"I'll be back," he said, then barely managed to keep from running away from their conversation.

"Hey, Cilla," he said when he spotted her standing near the door.

His aunt smiled at him. "Hey. I thought I'd come by and see how business is."

Andy gave her a hug. "Business is slow at the moment."

"This is a great place." She wandered toward the display he had of coffee table books. "I can see why you love to work here. You've always liked books. Just like me."

"Yep. Which is why I've written a couple as well."

They chatted for a few minutes about the sections of the store before Cilla said, "Are you really okay with me hanging around? Taking a room in your house?"

"I'm more than okay," Andy assured her. "I think Mom will be a lot happier having you here where she knows you're safe."

"I just don't want to make you feel like I'm intruding into your family. I can get myself an apartment."

"Nope," he said with a shake of his head. "And I think Phoebe would lose her mind if we told her that you were going to take the apartment instead of letting her have it."

Cilla laughed. "Well, maybe this will give you more time to woo that lady you're interested in."

"Woo? I'm not doing any wooing," he said, hoping that Cece didn't hear what Cilla said.

"Maybe that's the problem. You should be. How are you going to win her heart if you don't try to woo her?"

"It's complicated."

"No, my dear," Cilla said. "*My* relationship is complicated. You're just starting out. It shouldn't be complicated yet."

"Trust me, it can be complicated just starting out." Especially when he was pretty sure it wasn't going to actually go anywhere.

"If you ever want to talk to me about her, I'd be happy to listen."

"I'll keep that in mind." And then absolutely not do it.

"I promised your mom a treat from the bakery, so I'd better go. I'm making supper tonight, so I hope you'll be hungry."

"I'm sure I will be. Just remember that I won't be home until a little after six."

She nodded, then headed for the door, waving a hand in the air as she left the store. Andy watched her walk toward the bakery, then returned to the break room.

"My aunt stopped by on her way to the bakery to pick up a treat for my mom."

"Hope there's some good stuff left."

"You mean it's not all good?" Andy said as he sat back down.

"It's a matter of preference, I suppose. Although you seem willing to eat anything from there."

Andy shrugged. "All of it tastes good to me. I haven't tasted anything yet that you've made that I don't like."

She gave him a peculiar look, then crumped up the wrapper from her meal. "How's your writing going?"

Andy didn't know if she'd heard what Cilla had said and was just ignoring it, or if she really was interested in his work in progress. Either way, he didn't care. He just wanted to steer clear of the subject of what he liked in a woman.

As he finished his food, he caught her up on what little writing he'd been able to do. Once again, she gave him stuff to think about when it came to a couple of issues he'd been considering.

When they spent time together, talking about things that they both enjoyed, Andy struggled not to feel so frustrated that she couldn't see how good they could be together. But then he reminded himself that she didn't look for stuff like that when choosing a boyfriend.

"You need to get this book written," Cece said. "I know I'm not the only one getting impatient for you to finish it."

Andy laughed. "No pressure."

"Of course, I'm going to pressure you. You'd probably never get it done if I didn't."

"You are cruel," Andy said. "*So* cruel."

"Nope. I pressure you because I care. I know you actually do want to get this book done, so I'm just lighting a fire under you."

Andy sighed. "I really appreciate it. I just haven't been able to focus on it in the past week or so. Every time I've sat down to work on it, my brain takes a side trip. Maybe now that a few things have been settled, I can focus a bit more."

"You mean because of what's been going on with me?" Cece asked with a frown.

"A little bit, but also my aunt coming. Finding an apartment for Phoebe. Just... stuff."

"Sorry that you've had to deal with all my issues on top of that."

"Don't apologize, Cece," he said, then hesitated for a moment. "The thing is that I could have walked away at any point over the past ten plus years."

"Were there moments when you considered it? Or did you actually walk away, and I just didn't realize it, and then you were too nice to tell me to take a hike when I texted you?"

"Nope. Never walked away." It had never seriously crossed his mind.

There had been times when he figured she'd forgotten all about him, and while he hadn't enjoyed the thought that he was so forgettable, he'd accepted it. Then, out of the blue, she'd text him. She'd ask about an assignment in one of their classes, or sometimes she'd needed a ride somewhere.

Yes, she'd probably used him. And yes, he'd allowed it, which might have made him a wuss. But as he looked back over the years, he was glad he hadn't brushed her off.

It was only in more recent years that they'd been in contact more regularly, and she'd taken their friendship into the public eye.

For some reason, she'd been willing to spend time with him with others around them.

"So, are you going to answer my question?" she asked.

"Which question was that?"

"What do you look for in a woman?"

Oh... How was he supposed to answer that? His feelings for her—however futile—hadn't been based on her checking the boxes on some list he had. Beyond her looks, a lot of what would normally be on a guy's list didn't necessarily apply to Cece.

Andy rubbed a hand across his chin. "Uh... I need someone I'm comfortable with. That shares some of the same interests I have. I like someone who can make me laugh."

"That's it?" Cece asked, a skeptical look on her face. "No physical preferences?"

Andy had no problem with that question. "No. For me, it's more important that our personalities mesh. I don't want to be with someone who's beautiful but constantly wants to argue with me."

"Most guys want a pretty girlfriend."

"Just like most girls want a handsome boyfriend."

That made Cece frown. "I suppose, though I've come to realize that being handsome and rich doesn't necessarily mean that a guy is good."

Andy wished that meant he had a chance, but he wasn't going to get his hopes up. "That applies to women as well."

"You don't want to have to deal with a high maintenance girlfriend."

Andy was ready to move on from the conversation. It was rather pointless, as far as he was concerned. As long as they could stay friends, he'd be happy. And maybe, just maybe, someday his feelings for Cece would fade, and he'd find a woman he could love who would love him in return.

Or maybe not.

His mom had always told him and Phoebe that being married shouldn't be the ultimate goal in his life. That seeking God's will and using the talents He'd given them to touch other people's lives could bring fulfillment.

Andy was well aware that people might look at his life and think that he shouldn't be happy. After all, he still lived at home and had to take care of his mom and his sister. He'd also never aspired to leave the small town he'd grown up in.

He wondered if Cece's newfound freedom would lead her away from New Hope. It was entirely possible, and if it came to that, Andy knew that it would break his heart. Leaving might give her a better chance at happiness, away from Geof and her parents, and he could never begrudge her that.

CHAPTER TWENTY-EIGHT

Cece frowned as she stared out the window in the direction of the bookstore. For all her good intentions to give Andy space, she'd caved easily enough when he'd suggested they hang out together.

Selfish. That's what she was. *Selfish.*

How was she supposed to become *less* selfish?

Maybe Sarah could help her understand. Cece was quite certain that Sarah would be happy to tell her all the ways she could improve herself. And maybe she was just desperate enough to make herself that vulnerable to the other woman.

She picked up her phone and tapped out a text to Sarah.

Got any free time?

As she waited for a response, Cece sat with her chin in her hand and watched the world below her. In some ways, it felt as if she lived in an ivory tower, watching people live their lives below her, while she was stuck hiding behind mirrored windows.

Sarah: *Sure. I can come by now, if that works.*

Cece hadn't expected her to be available so soon, but it didn't make sense to push it off since she had nothing better to do that afternoon.

Yeah. That works.

She didn't really have anything to offer her to eat or drink, and figuring she had a few minutes before Sarah arrived, Cece hurried down the back lane to the bakery. From past experience, she knew what drink Sarah liked, so as she chatted to the woman who worked the afternoon shift at the bakery, she made drinks for her and Sarah, then also bought an assortment of cookies.

Once she'd paid for everything, she headed back to the apartment using the lane behind the building. She didn't do her usual check before leaving the bakery, and she was almost to the door of her building when she spotted a familiar car moving slowly toward her.

Her heart started to pound, fear making her hurry to the door that led into the garage. Had he been moving around town, just watching for her? She hadn't seen him, but then she'd been keeping a low profile herself.

Please, God. Please, God. Don't let him hurt me.

Fearful that Geof was going to accelerate and run her over, Cece fumbled to pull her phone out so she could use it to unlock the door. She kept a grip on the drink tray with the pastry bag looped over her wrist as she looked down at her phone.

But then she realized that if she went in the door, he'd know where she lived now. Cece didn't want that, so instead, she called the number Kieran had given her to use in case of an emergency.

"Kieran speaking," he said when he answered.

"It's Cece. Geof's in the lane behind the apartment."

"Where are you?" he asked.

"I'm in the back lane, too. I was going from the bakery to the apartment, but I don't want to go in now, though, because he'll see where I live."

"Hang on," Kieran said.

By this point, Geof had nearly reached her. He wasn't going any faster, but she was. She didn't look into the car as it rolled past her. It was hard to walk past the door to the apartment and the safety that it offered.

Keeping her head bent, she waited until the car had moved past. Once the car was behind her, she lifted her phone and took a picture over her shoulder, keeping her face in the frame but focusing on the license plate of the car.

The good thing about this happening in the back lane was that there was no room for him to turn his car around. He would have to get out of the car if he wanted to follow her. She wouldn't put it past him to do that, though, so she hurried toward the end of the lane where it opened onto a road. If she could reach there, then she could make it to Main Street.

Since he hadn't stopped or tried to talk to her, Cece guessed he was there to just remind her that he could get to her if he wanted to. It was probably to scare her. Which he'd definitely succeeded doing.

"Cece?"

"Yeah?"

"Where are you in relation to him?"

Cece glanced over her shoulder. "I'm almost to Robbins, then I'm going to go to Main Street. He's heading in the opposite direction."

"What's he driving?" Kieran asked. "His usual car?"

"It's actually the car he gave me, that I returned to him." She gave him the info about the car, then said, "I took a picture of the license plate."

"Now? Send it to this number."

She managed to send it one-handed, still clutching the drink tray in her other one. "It's mirrored, so you'll have to flip it."

"Not a problem. Hang on a minute."

The road neared, and she turned toward Main Street, glancing back down the lane. The car was reaching the far end of the block, and he also turned toward Main Street. She wasn't sure if Cara had a class that day, but she hurried to the door of the dance studio and pulled on it. When the door swung open, relief flooded her. She stepped inside to see Sarah standing there with Cara.

"Hey," Sarah said with a smile that faded into a frown. "What's going on?"

Cece's hands trembled, and she thought she was going to drop the drink tray. "I saw Geof in the back lane."

"What? Did you call the cops?" Sarah came toward her. "Here, let me take those."

"I'm on the phone with Kieran right now." Cece lifted her phone as Sarah took the food and drinks from her. "I went to get us something to eat and drink."

"You didn't need to do that," Sarah said as she set the drinks and pastry bag on the small desk in the corner.

Cece turned to look out the front window, then took a step back when she spotted the car slowly driving in their direction. Instead of continuing toward the studio, however, the car pulled into a spot down by the bookstore. Fear spiraled through her at the thought that he might hurt Andy.

"Kieran?" she said into the phone. "Kieran?"

"Yep. Sorry, I'm just getting one of my guys to run the plate."

"He's parked down the street. I think he's in front of the bookstore."

"Okay. Are you somewhere safe?"

"I'm in the dance studio with Cara and Sarah."

"Perfect. Stay there. We'll take care of this."

"I can hang up now?"

"Yes. But don't leave the studio."

"I won't."

Sarah came and slipped her arm around Cece. "Are you okay?"

Until she asked, Cece hadn't realized how badly she was shaking. Was this how it was going to be for the rest of her life? Feeling threatened by Geof just rolling past her in a car? Worrying that he was going to hurt someone who was super important to her?

She clenched her hands, tightening the muscles all over her body, hoping to stop the trembling.

"I need to warn Andy." She focused on her phone's screen and managed to bring up her messages with Andy.

Geof is around town again. I think he might be parked in front of your store.

"Andy will be okay," Sarah said, giving her a squeeze.

"He wouldn't be in danger if it wasn't for me."

"No. If anyone is to blame, it's Geof. You're Andy's friend. You were Andy's friend long before Geof was in your life."

"I'm just so stupid," Cece muttered. "I should have known better."

"It's going to be okay."

"The cops are there," Cara said from her spot by the front window. "Andy's on his way."

"What?" Cece stepped away from Sarah and went to the window, just in time to see Andy approach the studio.

He pushed the door open and walked inside. "Cece?"

She went to him, and when he opened his arms, she didn't hesitate to step into them. "I'm sorry."

"No. Don't apologize." His arms closed around her, and she sank against him, clinging to the safety he offered her. "Are you okay?"

"I'm fine. He didn't hurt me," she said. "Seeing him just scared me."

"Kieran is taking care of him right now."

"I hate him."

"I know." He loosened his embrace and stepped back, keeping his hands on her upper arms. "But we're here for you. All of us."

Cece's shoulders slumped. "I don't know why. All I do is make things a hassle for everyone."

"We care about you. That's why."

She tilted her head up to look at him. "I don't understand why you care."

"Friends care," Andy said. "And we're friends, right?"

She nodded, though she'd never cared as much about any of her other friends as she did about Andy. And none of her other friends—not that she'd had many—had ever seemed to care about her the way Andy did.

"Why don't we go upstairs and wait for Kieran?" Cara suggested.

Cece frowned at the drink tray where it sat on the desk. "I don't have drinks for everyone."

"Don't worry about that," Andy said.

Sarah picked up the drinks and the pastry bag. "Let's go."

They went upstairs to the apartment, and Cece immediately went to the window where she could look down at what was happening without worrying that Geof could see her. "Will they arrest him?"

"I hope so," Andy said as he stood next to her. "He violated the protection order."

"He's got rich lawyers helping him. He'll probably get off."

Andy didn't argue with her, which didn't make Cece feel any better, but she appreciated that he didn't try to make it sound unlikely. "Even if he does, we'll make sure that you're safe."

She didn't want to keep appearing vulnerable and needy to him. More and more, she wanted him to view her as competent and his equal. Unfortunately, Geof just kept throwing her into these scenarios that made her look weak.

Perhaps he did it so easily because she really *was* weak. The idea made her want to throw up. She swallowed hard against the urge.

"Here. Drink this." Sarah handed her the iced coffee Cece had gotten for herself at the bakery.

"Thanks." Cece stood there, trying to figure out what to do next. "Can you ask Kieran what's happening?"

She hadn't addressed the question to anyone in particular, but Cara said, "I'll give him a call."

Glancing at the woman, Cece said, "Thank you."

Cara moved to the kitchen as she put her phone to her ear.

Cece felt weary. Physically, emotionally, and mentally worn down. While she was glad she wasn't alone, part of her just wanted to crawl into her bed and pull the covers over her head. She didn't want to deal with the world right then.

"Was there a reason you wanted to hang out?" Sarah asked as she stood next to her with a coffee in one hand and a cookie in the other.

Cece frowned, trying to remember why she'd asked Sarah to come by. The near run-in with Geof had completely refocused her.

"Oh." She looked down at her cup. "I wanted to talk to you about how to become less selfish."

"You think you're selfish?" The surprise in Sarah's voice was unexpected.

"You don't?"

"I think we all tend to be selfish at times," Sarah said. "Being aware of our own selfishness is important."

"Why do you think you're selfish?" Andy asked, his voice gentle.

She looked up at him. "It seems that all I'm doing right now is taking from people."

"That's not selfishness," he said, and Sarah nodded. "Allowing others to help when you're in need isn't being selfish at all."

Cece wasn't convinced, but he was right that she was in need. If she'd had a choice, she wouldn't have had to rely on him and the others. It made her feel like she owed them, and she was off kilter because of it.

"I don't want people to think I'm not appreciative of what they've done for me," she said. "I am."

"I think you're in a very challenging time of your life," Andy said. "This will pass. You won't always need to have help."

"You'll be able to stand on your own soon enough," Sarah said with a confidence that Cece didn't feel. "But for now, let us help you. None of us resent you for needing that from us."

Andy's hand rested on her back. The gentle warmth of his touch soothed and comforted her. "You are strong, Cece. What you're going through now will only make you stronger. Take each moment as it comes, good or bad, and just keep moving forward. You'll get past all of this. I know you will."

Cece allowed his words to sink into her heart, calming the fear that lingered there. She didn't know how she would have survived any of the turmoil of the past couple of years without him.

"Thank you." When he frowned down at her, she said, "For everything you've done for me. I don't deserve it."

"You don't have to keep thanking me for doing what a friend should do. I'm not happy you've had to go through what you have, but I've been happy to help however you've needed me."

"And thank you, too," Cece said, directing her words to Sarah.

Sarah grinned, then gestured to Andy. "What he said."

"Well," Cara said as she joined them again. "It didn't take long for the lawyers to get involved. Kieran doubts Geof will spend time in jail right now, but this breach of the protective order will definitely be presented to the judge."

That didn't surprise Cece. "I don't care if he goes to jail, but I sure wish he'd just leave me alone. I'm tired of him popping up in my life, and I don't want to have to constantly be looking over my shoulder."

Cara nodded. "That's a difficult way to live."

"Do I have to move to a new city in order to get away from him?" she asked. It wasn't something she wanted to do, but she was beginning to think it might be the only way she'd ever get free from him.

"I hope you don't have to do that," Cara said. "I had to move in order to get away from a bad situation, and while it ended up being okay in the end, it was a difficult thing to have to do."

She didn't know much about Cara, having only interacted with her briefly when she came into the bakery. It sounded like she had a story of her own.

Cece hadn't thought much about other people's lives, except for when she'd compare them to hers. And usually all she saw was how their lives were great, while hers was awful.

"Have you talked to the prosecutor about Geof?" Sarah asked a few minutes later.

Cece glanced out the window one last time, then went to sit on the loveseat. Andy settled down beside her. Sarah and Cara sat down on the couch, expectant looks on their faces.

Before she had a chance to say anything, there was a knock on the apartment door. Cara got up, then looked at Cece. "I'm pretty sure that's Kieran. I'll just go let him in."

When they returned a couple of minutes later, Kieran's expression was one of annoyance. His lips pressed flat. He grabbed a chair from the dining room table, then sat down, while Cara sat back down on the couch.

"What's going on?" Andy asked.

"We're just waiting for someone from the main station to come get him."

"You're not keeping him in jail here?"

"We're not really equipped for that," Kieran said. "Especially in a situation like this."

"So what's going to happen to him? Is he going to come back again?"

"I gave him a pretty stern lecture, reminding him what a protective order is," Kieran said. "Then he said something about it being a free country, and he could drive wherever he wanted. Showing him the picture we had of his car behind you was pretty damning. He has no reason to be driving the back lanes of New Hope, especially when he knows where you work."

"And he knows that she hangs out with me sometimes," Andy added. "He's come into the store a time or two asking where she is."

"I'm hoping his lawyer will talk some sense into him because, at this rate, he's definitely going to end up doing jail time. If he'd just been willing to walk away, he might not have ended up with a threat of jail time."

"Men like him should always have to do jail time," Cara muttered. "They just don't learn otherwise."

"I'm not going to argue with you over that," Kieran said, reaching over to take his wife's hand. "Unfortunately, rich guys like Geof clean up really well, and they have slick lawyers who know what to say and do to get their clients off."

"Are judges really swayed by stuff like that?" Sarah asked.

Kieran sighed. "Some are. They look at someone like Geof, who has a good financial standing and is well spoken, and they think that whatever they're being accused of was an aberration. They want to give him a second chance."

"It wasn't an aberration," Andy said.

Kieran looked at Andy, then at Cece. "He'd been physical with you before?"

Cece's shoulders slumped as she stared down at her hands. It felt like admitting she was weak for not leaving him the minute he hurt her the first time. "Yes, but never as bad as last week."

Kieran nodded, as if that made sense. And maybe it did. She probably wasn't the first woman he'd met who had stayed in a relationship when she should have left.

"Hopefully, he'll get a judge who truly wants to teach him a lesson."

"Not sure that Geof will ever learn that lesson," Andy muttered. "He's a real piece of work."

"You did the right thing earlier, Cece," Kieran said. "Don't ever hesitate to call if you see him around town, even if you recognize his car but don't see him. Pretty sure it's better to be safe than sorry."

"I will," Cece said. She was done giving Geof the benefit of the doubt, and she wanted him *out* of her life. If that meant she had to call the cops if she even got a whiff of his cologne, she would do that.

It may have taken her awhile to get free from him, but now that she was, there was no way she was going back. But even as she wanted to be free of everything negative in her life, she couldn't help but wonder what was going on with her parents. It felt like she was waiting for the other shoe to drop where they were concerned.

She wasn't sure when she was ever going to be free of her troubled past, and that thought was wearying.

CHAPTER TWENTY-NINE

Even though she had Sarah and Cara with her, Andy didn't want to leave Cece. Unfortunately, he needed to reopen the store. Closing it during the middle of the day wasn't something he'd ever done before, but it had felt necessary once he'd realized what was going on.

"I'll talk to you later," he said when Cece walked him to the door of the apartment. "Are you going to be okay?"

She looked a bit like the fight had gone out of her, at least for the moment. And he didn't blame her for that at all. "I'll be fine. It just shook me up a bit to run into him like that."

"I'm glad that it wasn't any worse."

"I'm going to need to go to church again on Sunday."

Andy's brows rose at the change in subject. "I'm happy to hear that, but why?"

"I asked God to help me again when I saw Geof," she said. "And I think He did."

"I'm glad He answered your prayer again."

"Me, too. I think I'm going to start asking Him to do something about Geof."

"I'm already praying about that." Andy smiled. "I'd better go."

When Cece stepped forward and hugged him, Andy froze for a moment before wrapping his arms around her. He wasn't sure she'd ever initiated a hug with him before, and emotion choked him as he held her.

"Thank you for coming."

He let her go as she stepped back. "I will always come if you need me."

When she smiled at him, Andy didn't want to leave, but he did, taking the memory of that smile and hug with him.

Sunday found him outside the back door of the studio building, waiting for Cece. Andy wasn't sure that she'd carry through on her observation that she needed to go to church again because God had answered another prayer, but then she'd texted him on Saturday to ask if he could pick her up.

His answer, of course, had been yes. He'd prayed that one day she'd develop an interest in his faith and want to go to church, and he'd invited her off and on over the years. Pretty much any time he'd asked, she'd said no. Things had changed for her, though, so maybe this change of heart would affect all areas of her life.

He was glad that Sarah was part of her life again. Even though it was a good thing that Cece had more friends, Andy selfishly still wanted to be the most important one to her. He wanted her to call him when she needed help.

So far, she was still texting and calling him as much as she ever had—except for those few days when she was trying to give him the space he hadn't wanted. She'd also come by the store a couple of times. However, they still hadn't had the discussion that Sarah had told him they needed to have. They'd just kind of slid back into things.

It was like it had always been, though this time they didn't talk about her boyfriends. Part of him figured it was only a matter of time before some guy asked her out, and she'd say yes because Cece had never liked being without a boyfriend, even if he treated her badly.

He got out of his car and went around to the passenger side, leaning back against the car while he waited for Cece. He pulled out his phone and began to browse social media, checking on the bookstore's accounts, which he was more active on than his own personal ones.

There usually weren't a lot of messages waiting for him, but he noticed he had a couple. Expecting them to be related to the bookstore, he frowned when he realized that they were both from Geof.

You better stay away from Cece or you'll regret it.

You may think she's going to stay with you, but she's mine.

Andy frowned at the messages. He had no idea how to deal with someone as delusional as Geof was proving to be. It really concerned him. He took a screenshot of the message, just in case he needed it.

The door opened, and he slipped his phone into his pocket and smiled at Cece as she walked out. "Good morning."

"Hey." Cece greeted him with a smile. She was dressed in a denim skirt that ended just above her knee and a light pink blouse under a white sweater. "Everything okay?"

There was no way that he was going to tell her about the message from Geof, but he was going to talk to Kieran about it. "Everything is fine."

He opened the passenger door for her, then waited for her to settle into the seat before rounding the front of the car to slide behind the wheel. As Andy drove to the church, Cece told him about a conversation she'd had with Brooke about trying her hand at cake decorating. He loved hearing the excitement in her voice, and he hoped that maybe this was something she could do to occupy more of her time.

Once at the church, they went right into the sanctuary and found seats in the same pew where they had sat the last time she'd attended. It wasn't where he usually sat, but if being near the back of the sanctuary was what made her comfortable, that's where he'd sit.

She didn't seem as tense as the last time she'd been there, and Andy was glad for that. He didn't know if she'd ever attend regularly, but having her at his side was encouraging.

"Doesn't Leah play the piano every Sunday?" she asked when someone else began to play.

"No, not every Sunday. Sometimes she travels with Gavin, so she shares piano duties with a couple of other people."

"Is it the same with the worship team? Will Alessia be part of it again?"

"That is also a shared responsibility. They've had enough people interested in serving on the worship teams that they've been able to have more than one team."

Cece nodded as if she understood, then she said, "So what do you do here?"

The question kind of took Andy by surprise, and he didn't really have a good answer for her. "Uh... Nothing, really, at the moment. I've taught Sunday school, and I've helped Pastor Evans with stuff around the building sometimes. Also, people know that if they need me to do anything, I'll say yes if I have the time. Which I usually do."

"Does everyone have to do something around the church?" Cece asked.

"It's not a *have to* type of thing. People are encouraged to find a way to plug in, whether it's helping with the music or in childcare. There are lots of opportunities for anyone who wants to help. It's very much community centered."

Cece had a contemplative look on her face as the worship team walked onto the stage. Andy liked that she was curious about things. That she wanted to know how being a part of this Christian community worked.

While she had been in situations that should have offered her a supportive community, Andy was quite sure that she hadn't leaned on them. When she'd been a cheerleader, the girls in that group had seemed to move as a single entity, and Cece had always been in their midst.

He'd known then, like he knew now, that even when she was part of a group, she rarely connected deeply with people. She hadn't ever believed that anyone would truly be there for her. But maybe, with Sarah and others back in her life, she'd begin to see that she didn't have to be alone. If she could bring herself to trust them again.

Sarah had called him after the incident with Geof, and she'd expressed that she had made a mistake in not working harder to keep up her friendship with Cece. That even though Cece had distanced herself, she should have tried to maintain contact with her.

As the service progressed, Andy kept praying that God would work in Cece's heart. He wanted so much for her to experience the peace and joy of having God in her life.

Pastor Evans spoke that day, and it was a sermon focusing on living an authentic Christian life so that others who saw were drawn to God. It was something Andy's dad had always focused on when he'd talked to him about spiritual things. And it was something that Andy had always tried to embrace.

There will be times, son, when how you act will speak louder than any words you might say.

So much of the sermon brought his dad to mind, and Andy had to take a few deep breaths to loosen the band of emotion that thinking about the man brought to his heart. His dad had been friends with Pastor Evans, and he'd had the highest respect for the older man.

You would've liked this sermon, Dad.

He knew his dad couldn't hear him, but it felt right to acknowledge the message he'd so often spoken with Andy about. The memory of the man was stronger than usual, and Andy was grateful for it. So many years had passed since his dad had died that memories of him were faded most the time.

But not that day.

Sitting in the place that his dad had loved, listening to a man he had admired preaching a sermon on a topic his dad had fully embraced, Andy felt closer to his dad than he had in ages. The idea of it made him smile.

Once the service was over, they talked with the usual group before they headed out of the church.

"That sermon was all about you," Cece said as Andy put his key in the ignition.

Without starting the car, he turned to her. "What do you mean?"

"The man talked about showing God's love by what you do." Her words were spoken haltingly, as if she didn't really understand what she was saying. "That explains why you do what you do."

Andy rested his arm on the steering wheel, uncertain how to respond.

"It explains so much about you," she said. "If someone asked me to explain God using you, I'd say that He was patient, caring, and good."

Well, that certainly didn't help him find words to respond. He looked away from her, staring out the front windshield as he cleared his throat.

"Did I say the wrong thing?" She sighed. "I guess I don't understand what it all means."

"You didn't say anything wrong," Andy said, turning to look at her again. "It's just that my dad used to always tell me to live my life in such a way that people saw God in me."

"You've done that, I think."

Andy smiled at her. "It makes me happy to hear that."

Cece lifted a brow. "Did you really not think that you were living that way?"

Andy wished he could say that he was a great representative of God every single hour of every single day, but he knew there were times he wasn't.

He reached forward and turned the key in the ignition. "I've always tried to, but I'm only human. I know I haven't succeeded all the time."

"If this was something your dad wanted, you have made him proud, I think."

"I hope so. I really hope so." He backed the car out of the parking spot. "Do you want to grab lunch somewhere?"

"Sure. That would be nice."

After a bit of discussion, they made their way to Everett, where they decided on a sit-down family-style restaurant. Andy struggled not to view times like that, when it was just the two of them sharing a meal, as a date. Especially since they were happening more frequently.

Cece seemed relaxed as they settled down in a booth with menus from the server. Andy wasn't sure how the latest run-in with Geof would affect her, but it seemed that for the time being, she'd put it aside.

He didn't ask because he didn't want the man to intrude on their time together. Geof had done that enough as it was.

As he drove her back home after they'd shared a leisurely meal, Andy asked her if she wanted to go to the Bible study.

"I... uh... I'm not sure," she said. "I don't think so. I'm not sure I'm ready for that."

Andy didn't pressure her. Having her go to church had been enough, and he wouldn't try to force her to do more than she was ready for. "If you change your mind, you know my number."

"I do," she said with a smile.

He didn't want their time together to end, but all too soon, he was stopping behind her building. After she got out, he waited until she was safely inside before he pulled away and headed home.

The next day would be busy as he was helping Phoebe and her friend move into their new apartment. Once they'd been approved to rent the apartment, things had moved quickly. Phoebe was excited to be in her own place and able to gain a new level of independence. Cilla would move in later that same day, and Andy knew his mom was looking forward to that.

Life was changing for so many of the people around him. His, on the other hand, seemed to be staying pretty much the same. Work... Home... Church... It seemed like not a whole lot had changed for him in years. The only thing that seemed to be changing was the extent to which people relied on him.

With people stepping into Cece's life that she could depend on, she wouldn't need him as much. And now Cilla was going to be there to help with his mom.

Andy had mixed feelings about it all. He knew it was good for Cece and his mom to have people other than him to depend on, and he needed to focus on that. It was just that helping others had always been important to him, so what would it mean when those closest to him didn't need him anymore?

Tuesday afternoon, Andy was shocked to see Cece's mom walk through the door of the bookstore. Maybe he shouldn't have been surprised, but he'd expected that if anyone would have showed up, it would have been her dad.

"Where is my daughter?" she asked. "I need to speak to her."

Andy took in the woman's appearance, noticing all the ways she looked like her daughter. She and Cece shared similar builds and features, and her hair was the same shade as Cece's, but unlike her daughter's long curls, the older woman wore her hair in a sleek bob.

"I'm not sharing Cece's location," he told her, finding it interesting that she hadn't gone to the bakery, since presumably she knew that was where her daughter worked.

"I need to speak to her," she said, her perfectly arched brows pulling together.

"If Cece wanted to speak with you, she would have made sure you could contact her."

She frowned at him. "You are a bad influence on her."

"Uh... Let me get this straight." Andy crossed his arms as he narrowed his eyes at her. "You wanted her to stay with a man who beat her, and *I'm* the bad influence?"

"He only did that because she didn't go back to him."

Andy shook his head. "I can't believe that as a mother, you don't see the problem with that. Do you not love your daughter at all?"

The woman's frown deepened. "Love has nothing to do with it."

"Clearly. Let me tell you this, Mrs. Albrecht. My mom would *never* in a million years let my sister go anywhere near a man who would hurt her. She would protect her from someone like that because that's what a mother does. What a parent does."

Cece's mom straightened her shoulders. "You don't know what you're talking about."

"Actually, I think you're the one who is completely out of touch with reality. I daresay most parents would agree with me. It's only the bad ones who would think it's okay for their daughter to be in an abusive relationship, simply because it benefits them."

"Tell Cece to contact us," Cece's mother said in a sharp tone, then she turned and left the bookstore.

"I won't be doing that," Andy muttered to the empty store, since she hadn't hung around for his response. He just had to put it out into the world that he had no intention of doing as Cece's mother had demanded.

He didn't want to have to tell Cece about this interaction, but at the same time, he wanted her to be aware that her parents wanted to communicate with her. If that meant she would keep an eye out for her parents along with Geof, that would be for the best.

Though he usually enjoyed the size of New Hope, considering everything that had happened with Cece, he was beginning to see the real downside to living in a small town. She didn't have many options for keeping a low profile other than limiting where she went. That would work for a while, but how long would it be before she just wanted to be able to live her life without such constraint?

He didn't like the idea of her moving away in order to escape harassment, but he was bracing himself for that. And he wouldn't try to talk her into staying. Andy just really prayed it wouldn't get to that point.

CHAPTER THIRTY

Cece stared at the message on the screen of her phone, anger swirling inside her.

Andy: *Your mom just stopped by. Wanted to talk to you.*

She couldn't believe how the people she was trying to cut out of her life kept going to Andy to get to her. It didn't make sense, but it did worry her more than a little. If her parents or Geof thought that Andy stood between them and her, they might do something to hurt him. If that happened, she'd never be able to live with herself.

I'll be right there.

Anger consumed her thoughts as she went to her room to change out of the comfy clothes she'd put on when she'd come home from work. If it meant they'd leave Andy alone, maybe she needed to talk to them. It didn't mean she actually had to do anything more.

Andy: *Though I'd love to see you, I'm not sure that you should be walking around right now. Who knows if it was just your mom, or if your dad and Geof are lurking around somewhere waiting for you.*

She stood in the middle of her bedroom, accepting that Andy was probably right. However, she also really wanted to see him. It had seemed like a good excuse to go.

Are you okay?

It was highly unlikely that her mom had done anything physical to him, but Cece needed to be sure.

He sent her back a smiley face, then added, *I'm fine. You look a lot like your mom.*

Cece frowned at that comment. She was aware of the physical similarity, but she really hoped that Andy didn't think she was like her mother in any other way, especially now.

I'm not like her though.

Andy: *I know. You've shown that you're not.*

That made Cece feel better. The day Andy thought she was like her parents was the day he'd probably walk away.

I don't understand why they keep going to you. They know where I work.

Maybe she needed to call her dad and tell him to back off. She didn't want to talk to him at all, but if it meant they'd leave Andy alone, she was willing to do it.

Andy: *I have no clue. I wondered about that myself.*

I'll call and tell them to leave you alone.

Her phone rang almost immediately, with Andy's name flashing on the screen.

"Don't call them," he said when she answered. "It's not a big deal that they come here. In fact, I'd rather they come to me than go to you."

"But it's a hassle for you."

"Not really. All it takes is some time, and that's usually something I have."

"But what if they come with something more than wasting your time on their minds?" she said. "I don't want anything to happen to you."

"I'll be okay," Andy said.

Cece wished he could actually guarantee that. "I hope you're right."

Though Andy had told her not to contact her parents, Cece needed to. He'd protected her often enough, and now she needed to do the same for him.

"How was work today?" he asked. "Burn anything."

"Shut up," Cece said with a laugh.

As they talked a bit more, Cece recalled the sermon from Sunday. She felt like it had given her a glimpse of Andy that she'd never had before. Or maybe that she hadn't been interested in seeing.

She'd always just thought that Andy was a nice guy. That he'd been born with a kind personality. Now she suspected, while that might have been true, it was the result of a choice he had made, too.

As she'd listened to the sermon at church, it had been like a lightbulb had turned on. She might have wondered if Andy had just been that way with her, but from what she'd seen, he was that way with everyone. She'd heard him offer to help Mia and Ben, and they were already Christians.

"Did Phoebe get moved okay?" Cece asked, trying to be better at asking about his life. She didn't want their conversations to be all one-sided anymore.

"She did," he said. "And she was very excited about it. I texted her this morning to see how their first night in the apartment went, and she said it was super. Cilla moved into Phoebe's room yesterday, so I think we're done with the shuffle."

"I'm sure your mom is happy to have her sister close by."

"Yep. They've always gotten along really well, even though they've lived in different places. I think having Cilla with us is going to be great."

"Is she going to be working here?"

"She was a librarian, so I think she's hoping to get a job at the library here, or maybe in one of the towns nearby."

"That would be nice. Does she have any kids?"

"Thankfully, no." Andy grimaced. "That sounds horrible. Cilla would have made a great mom. She loves children. I just meant that because her husband is a real piece of work, them not having kids together is a blessing. It means that she isn't tied to him for years to come."

"Yeah. I can see how that could be an issue."

"This way, once they're divorced, they won't have to interact anymore," he said. "As long as he leaves her alone."

"Guess he's a bit like Geof?"

"Too much," Andy said. "Those two guys are cut from the same cloth, except Roy isn't rich. I'm glad that you've both gotten away from such abusive men."

Had they though? There were moments when Cece felt like she'd never be truly free of Geof, and she suspected that Andy's aunt might feel the same of her ex.

It just felt wrong that such a wonderfully sweet man as Andy had to deal with men like her father, Geof, and his aunt's ex. He deserved so much better.

"Someone just walked in," Andy said. "I'll talk to you later."

After she ended the phone call, Cece hesitated only a moment before going to her dad's contact information. She unblocked his number, then tapped the screen to call him, putting it on speakerphone because she had no interest in hearing him up close in her ear.

"It's about time you called," he said when he answered.

"Why do you need to talk to me?"

"You need to talk to Geof."

"Nope. That's not gonna happen."

"You *have* to," he insisted.

"No, I don't. That man beat me so badly I ended up in the hospital."

"You pushed him to do that."

"I did no such thing. And the fact that you are justifying his actions tells me that you're just like him. Neither of you are men to be desired or admired."

"You are selfish."

"I might very well be," she agreed. "But I'd never ask someone to go back into an abusive situation. You're being selfish telling me to do that."

"Geof is threatening us!"

"Oh. So it's okay for him to threaten and hurt me, but not you?" Cece scoffed at him. "Get used to the idea then, because it's going to continue. I refuse to have anything to do with him or you two. Also, stop bugging Andy. You know where I work, so I'm not sure why you keep harassing him."

"I figured you'd actually listen to him."

"Actually, if I were listening to him, I wouldn't have called you. I'm just not interested in having him know all our business." That was a bit of a lie, but she figured it was something her dad might actually understand.

"Geof has promised to be good to you, and if you go back to him, he won't take everything we own."

Cece sighed. "I can't deal with Geof ever again. So you're just going to have to move on. Pack your bags, move to an apartment, and get on with your lives. You're better off just accepting the situation and moving forward."

If she was lucky, they'd move far, far away from her.

"I didn't raise you to be so ungrateful for everything we've done for you."

"So you've said. Guess you're going to just have to live with the disappointment." She took a breath, then said, "Don't bother trying to get me to call you again. That's not going to happen. This is the last time I'll call you."

Without waiting for his response, Cece ended the call. She blocked him again, then set her phone aside. She hoped the call would get them off Andy's back. If not, she wasn't sure what more she could do. She didn't want to go back to Geof, but if there was even a whiff that they might hurt Andy or his business, she might have to rethink the situation.

Things would have been so different if she'd been born into a better family. One where she had supportive parents who wanted her to fall in love with a good man. A man who would treat her with love and respect. She would have loved having parents whose biggest concern when it came to her and a man was when they'd be getting married and how long after that she'd be making them grandparents.

Cutting her parents off the way she had meant that she had no family. She just had to keep reminding herself that even when they'd been in her life, they hadn't had her best interests at heart. And because of that, she'd already had no family. This was just her physically cutting them off, making that alienation official.

Still... She was left with so many emotions that made her feel weak. Abandonment. Loneliness. Fear.

She'd told her dad to move forward, and she needed to do the same. Focus forward and not look back. It was important to not let the past hold her in chains. She knew Andy would agree.

He was someone that she would always be thankful for. For whatever reason, God had decided that she needed someone like him in her life. And yes, over the past few weeks, she'd come to really believe that God existed in a way she'd never considered before.

Two days later, Cece stopped just inside the door at the back of the studio building. She pulled up the security camera app on her phone to check the back lane and make sure it was clear before leaving to go to the bakery. It usually was, but she didn't want to risk not checking.

It was a dark night... or rather, early morning... but security lights illuminated the back lane enough that she could see if there was anything unusual happening before she stepped out. Normally, there was nothing to see. The back lane between the apartment and the bakery was usually deserted.

That morning, however, there was something on the security camera. Cara had invested in the best system, so the camera showed things clearly, even on Cece's small phone screen.

There was a car moving slowly past the building where she stood. She watched as it approached the bakery, but it kept going. When the brake lights flashed red, Cece tried to figure out where exactly it had stopped. It looked like it was behind the bookstore, but she couldn't be sure.

She didn't recognize the car, but she couldn't think of any reason why someone would be at any of the buildings along the street at three-thirty in the morning. In the time since she'd started working the early shift, she hadn't seen anyone else in the back lane. She always made the short walk from the apartment to the bakery in solitude.

Cece continued to watch the car, frowning as a figure exited the driver's side. They were wearing dark clothes, so it was hard to see them clearly. Her heart pounded as the person moved in and out of the shadow cast by the building. Cece couldn't see clearly what they were doing, but she didn't think it was anything good.

Suddenly there was a flash of light, then the figure ran back around the car and drove away more quickly than they'd arrived. It took Cece a minute to recognizing what the dancing light was, and as soon as she realized, she began to shake.

"Oh, God. Oh, please." She fumbled with her phone as she tried to back out of the security app to where she could use her phone. After dialing 911, she went back into the app for the cameras. When someone answered, she said, "There's a fire in the back lane behind the bookstore on Main Street in New Hope."

The woman got a few more details from her, then told her that help was on the way. Cece wanted to go outside and check what was happening, but she was scared that whoever had started the fire might come back. She had a sick feeling in her stomach as she considered who that someone might be and why they might be targeting where Andy worked.

It was just a matter of minutes before the fire engines arrived on the scene. Once she saw them, she let herself out of the building and walked toward the bookstore, watching as the firefighters got to work. She wondered if Jillian's husband was one of them.

As she neared, she saw that the fire was indeed focused on the bookstore. *God, please let it not be too bad.*

Her throat clogged with emotion, and she swallowed hard, trying to keep from crying. Andy had to know what was happening, and he needed to hear it from her.

"Cece?" Andy's voice was groggy when he answered her call.

"Andy." His name came out on a sob. "I'm so sorry."

"What's wrong?" He sounded instantly more alert. "Are you hurt?"

"The bookstore. Someone lit a fire at the back."

She heard the rustle of movement before he said, "I'll be right there."

The line went dead, and Cece felt like the disconnect went right to her very soul. She was almost positive the fire was her fault, and she wouldn't blame Andy if he decided that this was the final straw in what he was willing to endure because of her.

Was everyone in her life in jeopardy because they were close to her? Was Geof hoping to isolate her by driving away the people around her? If it got that bad, what was she going to do?

Now that she'd escaped it, she didn't want to go back to the life she'd had when she lived with her parents and dated Geof. But would she have any options if she had no one else to turn to? She didn't want anyone to be hurt because of her.

She wrapped her arms around herself, staring through blurry eyes at the flickering flames that crept up the back of the building. It felt like the flames were burning through her life, isolating her and making sure that the one person she'd always been able to count on would realize that staying in her life wasn't a good thing.

She backed away from the fire, then she turned and ran toward the door of the bakery. Her job was the one thing she had left, and for now, she needed to hang onto it. The key to escaping the mess her life had become, was to save up enough money to start over somewhere that Geof couldn't reach her. Then hopefully he'd leave those she cared about alone.

When Cece reached the door, she glanced back at the fire, seeing the sprays of water that were now being aimed at the building. *Please, God, let the damage be minimal. Protect Andy's store, please.*

It was possible that since the fire had been at the back that the contents of the store would escape damage. She prayed that would be the case for Andy's sake. If God would just answer this one prayer, she'd go to church every Sunday and never ask another thing from Him.

Once inside the bakery, she went through the motions of preparing her bakes for the day. She took a minute to bring up the security cameras on the app so she could continue to watch what was happening.

As she worked, she kept an eye on the situation. The cameras on the back of the apartment building were too far away to see much detail, but she saw when the flickering flames began to die down. Somewhere in the group of people milling around was Andy.

She had little doubt that Geof was somehow behind that fire, and Cece couldn't shake the sick feeling at the thought that this was the thing that would make Andy walk away. And she wouldn't... couldn't... blame him for doing that.

Rubbing her cheeks on one sleeve and then the other, she tried to stem the tears that kept slipping free. Right at that moment, more than anything else in the world, she wished she'd been born into a different family. It hurt so much to realize that her parents wanted her to go back to a man who was capable of inflicting so much pain on so many people.

The only person who hadn't inflicted some sort of pain on her was Andy, and now he'd been impacted so greatly that there was no possible way he'd want to remain in her life. She knew she wasn't worth all the hassle, and now he'd realize that, too.

Cece gripped the edge of the worktable as the ramifications of that hit her hard in her heart. How had it taken this moment for her to realize exactly what Andy meant to her? She hadn't been certain what love really was. But if the way her heart felt at the idea of losing Andy was any indication, then love was what she felt for him.

But she didn't want him to be hurt by her presence. So, even if it hurt her, she needed to let him go so that his life wasn't messed up by hers anymore.

It was time for her to be selfless instead of selfish.

CHAPTER THIRTY-ONE

Andy stood with his hands fisted in the pockets of his jacket, watching in horror as the firefighters battled to get the fire at the back of the building under control. He needed to find Cece, but he couldn't drag his attention away from what was happening.

Part of him felt like he must still be dreaming. Or rather, having a nightmare. It just didn't feel real because it made no sense.

Flames licked up the back of the building, affecting the wall of both the office and the break room. Some of the flames looked like they could also be eating away at the second-floor wall where Drake's apartment was. If ever there was a time he wished for an absolute downpour of rain, it was right then. Unfortunately, the cool night air held no moisture.

"Andy."

He shifted his gaze from the firefighters to Kieran as he approached him.

"Hey," Andy said. "How did this happen?"

"It's arson," Kieran told him without hesitation. "I pulled up the security cameras at the back of Cara's building. They showed a car moving along the back lane, then it stopped behind this building. The person appeared to thoroughly douse the wall, then lit the fire."

"Gasoline?" Andy guessed, since the pungent odor of it hung in the air along with the smell of smoke.

"Yep."

"Could you tell whose car it was?"

"I think we got a fairly good shot at finding out. The cameras that Cara has are top of the line, so it's not all the hazy stuff you get from lower-quality cameras."

"What are the chances this is connected to Geof?" Andy asked.

Kieran frowned. "Has he continued to harass you?"

"Off and on. I have some DMs from him on the business's social media. Plus, Cece's mom came by the other day, insisting that I pass on a message to Cece that her dad wanted to talk to her."

"And you did?"

"Yes. I thought Cece should know that they were still searching her out."

Kieran stared in the direction of the building and the firefighters who were spraying water in an arc across the flames. It looked like they were gaining the upper hand over the fire, and Andy prayed that the damage wasn't too extensive. He didn't want to have to close the store for any length of time.

"Why are they coming to you when they know where Cece works? They could just go to the bakery."

"Your guess is as good as mine," Andy said with a shrug. "Geof is trying to get me to back away from Cece. Meanwhile, her parents are trying to reach her through me. None of it makes any sense."

"Well, let's see who the car belongs to. It will be hard for the owner to deny involvement since the license plate is quite clear."

"If it's Geof, will he finally get locked up?" Andy asked. "I hate that Cece has to constantly look over her shoulder because he's insane enough to think that the protective order doesn't apply to him."

"He's not the first guy who has felt that way. I've met a few of them in the course of my job."

Andy glanced around. "Have you seen Cece here? She's the one who called me about the fire."

"I didn't see her in person, but I did see her on the security footage. She watched for a few minutes after the firefighters arrived, then went to the bakery."

For some reason, Andy had thought she'd hang around until he came. But he understood that she needed to work. Brooke was relying on her to prepare the baking for the day. Thankfully, the bakery wasn't right next door to the bookstore, so she should be safe.

"I think she might have been the one who called it in," Andy told him. "Since she called me."

"It would have been a lot worse if she hadn't seen it," Kieran said.

"I guess whoever set it didn't realize that someone would be up and checking their security camera at that hour of the night."

Before Kieran could respond, Carter approached them, decked out in his gear. "Hey, guys."

"Everything under control now?" Kieran asked.

"Yeah." Carter lifted his helmet off and ran a hand through his hair. "If we'd arrived any later, it would have been much worse since these buildings are so close together."

"How much damage is there?"

"I think most of it is confined to the rear of the bookstore. You'll still need to wait for the all-clear before going into the building, just to make sure it's safe."

Andy nodded, realizing he needed to let Drake know, sooner rather than later, about what had happened. He hated the idea of having to tell him, but thankfully, he was pretty sure that Drake had everything well-insured.

Pulling out his phone, he took a picture of the back of the building, which also showed the fire engine and the firefighters. As Kieran and Carter continued to discuss the fire and the likely suspect, Andy took a deep breath, then tapped out a message to Drake.

Had an arsonist set fire to the back of the bookstore.

He sent the text, then added the picture. He didn't know where Drake currently was in the world, so he might not get the message for a couple of hours. If he happened to be in London, like he was sometimes, he would probably get it right away. Andy wasn't sure what he hoped for... an immediate response or a delayed one.

When his phone buzzed, Andy's stomach knotted. He wanted to ignore it, but this business was Drake's, and he'd trusted Andy with it.

Drake: *What on earth? What's the damage?*

Before Andy could type out his response, his phone rang, with Drake's name showing on the screen.

After greeting the man, he relayed what Kieran and Carter had told him, glad that he could say that it didn't appear to be a complete loss. Although, if the contents of the store and apartment smelled of smoke or if there was any water damage, it might all be gone, anyway.

Drake sighed. "This is crazy."

Andy didn't want to have to tell him that it was possible that the bookstore had been targeted because of his friendship with Cece. Though Drake had never spoken about closing the store, it had also never caused him any issues.

Would this be the thing that made Drake think that the bookstore had run its course?

"I'll be there later today," Drake said. "I'll deal with all the insurance stuff when I get there."

"I haven't had a chance to go inside yet to see if there is much damage to the bookstore or your apartment."

"You can hold off until I get there, then we'll go through it together."

Andy rubbed his forehead. "I'm sorry to have to contact you with such bad news."

"Stuff happens," Drake said. "I'm just glad you weren't hurt."

"I'm not sure you'll be able to stay in the apartment. Do you want me to make reservations somewhere for you?"

"No. I'll have my assistant take care of that." Drake paused. "Everything's going to be fine, Andy. Don't worry about anything."

Andy wasn't so sure of that, but he didn't voice his doubts. "Okay. If I'm not at the bookstore when you arrive, just text me. I'm not sure when they'll let us in."

"Sounds good. See you in a few hours."

After Andy hung up, he glanced at Kieran. "Drake will be here later today to deal with this."

"That's good," Kieran said.

"I need to talk to Cece." Andy glanced around again. "I know she's blaming herself for this. Even without the confirmation that Geof is the arsonist, I'm pretty sure she thinks he is."

"Mind if I come with you?" Kieran asked. "I can maybe help assure her that this isn't her fault. I also want to ask her a couple of questions."

Andy nodded, though he wasn't sure there was anything any of them could say that would make Cece not feel guilty about what had happened. The old Cece might have been able to brush it off, but her heart had definitely been softening, and he knew she was feeling vulnerable ever since the attack by Geof.

Together, he and Kieran walked toward the back door of the bakery. When they reached it, Kieran knocked on the door.

"Cece, it's Kieran and Andy," he called out.

Andy worked the muscles of his neck, trying to release the tension that had built up. What sort of state would Cece be in? At one time, she would have been strong enough to handle what was happening. And he had no doubt that she'd get to that point again, but until then, she was far too vulnerable to have to deal with all of this.

When the door opened a crack, Kieran grabbed the handle and pulled it fully open. He motioned for Andy to precede him into the short hallway at the back of the bakery that led to the kitchen.

Cece was already heading back to the kitchen, leaving Andy and Kieran to follow her. There was a quietness to the bakery that he'd never experienced before. Usually there was music playing and sometimes the sound of machines working or the clatter and bang of pans as Cece prepped them.

But right then, there was just an eerie silence.

Once she was by the large stainless-steel worktable, Cece turned to face them. She had pulled the sleeves of her long sleeve T-shirt down over her hands, and she tucked them under her chin, drawing Andy's attention to the devastated look on her face.

"I'm so sorry, Andy," she said, her voice quivering. "I'm going to leave. There's just no way that this wasn't because of me. I can't stay here when I know he'll hurt you as long as I'm around."

The pain Andy heard in her voice struck him hard in the heart, and the idea of losing her hit him even harder. In two strides, he was in front of her, and he reached out to grasp her clasped hands. Wrapping his hands around them, he waited for her to lift her tear-filled gaze to meet his.

"This is *not* your fault," Andy told her with a desperation he'd never felt before. He didn't want her to believe that she was responsible for the actions of an obsessed man. He didn't want her to leave. Even though he had never really had her, he didn't want to lose her. "If the fire was, in fact, set by Geof or someone he hired, then *he* is responsible for that. A normal person who'd gone through a break-up would grieve and move on."

"Andy's correct," Kieran said. "You have the right to end a relationship that's not good for you without having to live in fear afterwards. So anything that Geof has done is not your fault."

"But how do I get him to stop?" She sounded like she was choking out the words. "I don't know how to get him to stop hurting the people I care about."

Andy tugged her forward and wrapped his arms around her. She was stiff at first, then her body kind of went limp against him, like she barely had the strength to hold herself up anymore.

"We have a good shot at figuring out who lit this fire," Kieran said. "And if Geof has any connection to this, we'll find that out, and he'll be charged with arson. The charges are stacking up against him, Cece."

Andy felt her take a deep breath, even though her arms were trapped between them. "The bookstore is going to be fine."

He hoped he wasn't lying. But he really did think that when he explained to Drake what had happened, he wouldn't be upset. At least not at Cece.

"It's getting worse, though," Cece said. "Every time he does something, it's worse than the time before. How long before he hurts someone?"

"He already *did* hurt someone," Andy replied. "He hurt *you*, and that's not acceptable. I'd rather lose the bookstore than have anything more happen to you."

"Why?" she asked. "I just don't understand."

Kieran cleared his throat. "I'll leave you two for the moment. I still need to talk a bit more with Cece, but I can do that later."

Andy watched Kieran leave, then he moved back a bit from Cece. She lifted her head to stare at him, her eyes still damp with tears.

He wasn't sure that he should be honest with her because she didn't seem to be in a good emotional state to deal with that revelation. He'd never been completely upfront about how he felt about her. To do so had never seemed to be a good idea, and he still wasn't sure that it was.

With everything going on, she needed a friend more than another boyfriend—not that she'd ever want him to fill that role.

"We're friends, right?" He waited for her to nod her head before continuing on. "As my friend, I care about you. I care what happens to you. I don't think you realize how much you mean to me. Maybe one day, once things have settled down, I'll tell you about it."

Her brow furrowed. "You shouldn't care about me. I've been a horrible person. Everyone will tell you that."

Andy wondered how many times they'd have this conversation. Until she could see value in herself, she would never understand their friendship. And she definitely wouldn't understand his feelings for her.

"Nope. A horrible person wouldn't have bothered to call me when they saw my workplace on fire. A horrible person wouldn't feel bad about what has happened." Andy gave her a small smile. "You are *not* a horrible person."

"I'm trying to be better," she said, wrapping her arms around herself. "I want to be better. But you'd still be better off without me hanging around."

"I'd miss you a whole lot if you weren't around."

"I really am scared, Andy." Cece slumped down on a stool next to the worktable. "If Geof doesn't get put in jail, I don't know what to do. He just isn't giving up."

Andy pulled another stool closer to hers, then sat down facing her. "I know. It is a bit alarming, but I'm more concerned about what he might do to you."

"It feels like he's losing his mind," Cece said.

"This isn't about you anymore," Andy told her. "Kieran said this is about control. Geof refuses to accept that you have the power to end the relationship. In his mind, he's the only one with that power."

"So what am I supposed to do?" she asked. "Get back together with him?"

"No." He didn't even need to think about that response. "Kieran is aware of what's going on, and I think he'll make sure that you're safe."

Andy hoped that his faith in Kieran and the police wasn't misplaced. Short of having full-time security personnel around her, there really wasn't a way to say for sure that she'd be safe. Unfortunately, the only person who could afford security like that was—ironically—Geof.

Cece sighed, then got to her feet. "I need to check my dough."

Andy watched as she walked over to open a large drawer near the oven and lifted out a big bowl. After peeking under the cover, she walked over to the sink and washed her hands. He was mesmerized watching her work with the dough with a confidence that looked really good on her.

"What are you making?" he asked.

She glanced over at him before focusing on the dough again. "Cinnamon buns."

"Oh. I usually see the end result. This is cool."

That drew a quick smile to her lips. "You're easily entertained."

Andy chuckled, feeling some of the tension in his shoulders release. The whole issue of the fire still loomed in the not-so-distant future, but right then, Cece's smile helped to ease some of his anxiety.

Now if he could just find some way to help Cece deal with all the events that had happened. She'd brushed aside his suggestion that she pursue some counselling, but he had a feeling that was something she could really benefit from. He couldn't even be sure she was talking about all her feelings and struggles with him. And he didn't expect her to, but he wanted her to be talking to *someone*.

"I'm going to go check in with Kieran," he said.

Her gaze shot up to his. "You're leaving?"

"Just for a couple of minutes. I can come back afterward, if you want."

She frowned as she focused on rolling out the dough. "I think I'll be okay. Unless you think there's something I should know."

"If they've discovered anything new, I'll let you know. They probably won't get information on the car that the arsonist was driving until later today. I don't know if they can get that information at night."

Cece shrugged. "I don't know either."

"Drake is flying in later today to deal with the bookstore."

That grabbed Cece's attention, and she paused in her work. "He's going to be so mad."

"I don't think he will be," Andy said.

"Did you tell him *why* there was a fire?"

"No. First of all, we don't know for sure that it's related to Geof."

Cece scoffed. "You're not dumb, Andy. The likelihood of it not being tied to him is pretty slim."

Andy knew she was right, but he didn't want her to worry. "Drake is also not dumb. He'll understand that we can't control the actions of someone like Geof."

"He'll probably wish you hadn't been hanging around someone like me."

"Would you like to meet him?"

Cece gave him an incredulous look. "I don't think so."

It was the reaction Andy had expected, but he'd thought he'd try. "If you change your mind, let me know. He'll probably be here for a few days."

"Not gonna change my mind," she muttered as she focused on the dough again.

Andy stepped up beside her and slipped his arm around her shoulders, giving them a light squeeze. "I'm glad you're okay, and that nothing happened to you. The bookstore is replaceable. You are not."

She glanced up at him, her eyes wide. "You're not replaceable either. And not just to me. There are lots of people who need you to be okay. I don't want anything to happen to you."

"I'll be okay. Geof has had plenty of opportunities to punch my lights out and he hasn't done that yet."

"But he still might."

Andy wasn't going to underestimate the man. Well, not from this point going forward. He'd never thought that Geof would go this far, so clearly, he had underestimated him in the past. And he couldn't help but wonder if the interactions they'd had, where he'd poked at Geof with a few taunts, might have led to this. In that case, it would have been more his fault than Cece's.

Either way, he would not taunt the man anymore, should he have the misfortune of running into him again. Who knew what that might make the man do, and Andy didn't want anything bad to happen to anyone else.

CHAPTER THIRTY-TWO

By the time her shift was done, Cece was exhausted. Fighting through the fear and worry—and the shaking they'd produced—had worn her out. More than once, she'd had to take a break.

When the trembling got too much, she'd had to sit down. She'd struggled to control her breathing so that she didn't get lightheaded. In order to work, she was constantly having to flex her hands, trying to get rid of the shakiness.

Andy had texted her periodically throughout the morning, though she hadn't seen him again. Kieran had reappeared around ten o'clock to ask her some questions about what she'd seen. It was a good thing that she hadn't had to recall much.

Kieran had access to the same security footage that Cece had watched as she'd stood inside the back door of the studio. She hadn't ventured out until she'd seen the fire engine arrive, so she'd had little to add to what Kieran had seen for himself.

After saying goodbye to Mia, Cece stood by the back door, her fingers shaking slightly as she pulled up the security cameras' feed. She could see that the area behind the bookstore was still cordoned off. The large number of people who had been present earlier had dwindled, but there were still a couple of people lingering in the area.

Feeling that it was safe, Cece left the bakery and hurried toward the studio building. She breathed a sigh of relief when she left herself into her apartment. Since she didn't know if Cara had a class in progress, Cece set the alarm for just the apartment and not for the entire building.

Normally, she didn't arm the alarm during the day, since the building's locked doors made her feel secure enough. However, that wasn't how she felt that day.

In her room, she slumped down on her bed, wanting nothing more than to crawl beneath the covers and hide from the world. Before she had a chance to even move in that direction, her text alert sounded.

Andy: *Drake is here now. Would you be willing to meet him? I know you said you didn't want to, but he'd like to meet you. No pressure.*

"Ha. No pressure," Cece muttered. But she would agree because she felt like she owed it to the man. If it weren't for her, the bookstore wouldn't have been set on fire.

Did you want to come to the apartment?

Andy: *If that's what you prefer.*

It was, because the only other place she felt safe was no longer available to her.

Yes. It is.

Thankfully, she kept the apartment clean and tidy, so she didn't have to do anything to prepare for her unexpected visitors. And since she hadn't changed clothes, she wouldn't need to do anything but briefly freshen up.

Andy: *We'll be there in a few minutes.*

Cece wished she'd brought home some treats from the bakery, but there was no way she was going to go out to get some. The last time she'd done that, she'd seen Geof. She didn't even want to take the chance. They'd have to be happy with just coffee.

She dumped some grounds into the coffeemaker and turned it on. She didn't know if either of them would want any, but she could use another cup. Hopefully, the caffeine would chase away the tiredness that plagued her.

Moving to the window, she looked down on the wide sidewalk in front of the buildings on Main Street. People were milling around, but no one seemed to be particularly focused on the bookstore. The damage wasn't likely visible from the front, so people might not even be aware of what had happened.

Not that that would last long. Before the end of the day, she was pretty sure most would know. Small town gossip would make sure of that. She just hoped that her name wouldn't be brought into things.

When she spotted Andy walking toward the entrance to the studio, Cece went downstairs in case she needed to let them in. Cara was apparently in the building because the men were already approaching the stairs leading to her apartment when she stepped out of the doorway.

"Hi, Cece," Andy said with a smile. "This is Drake Swanson. Drake, this is Cece Albrecht."

"Hi," Cece said as she held out her hand to the tall man at Andy's side. "Nice to meet you."

Though Andy had known the man for years, Cece had never met him. He was a serious-looking man with dark hair and piercing blue eyes. He looked like he worked out, but not to the extent that Geof had. Though Drake represented the sort of man she'd dated in the past—rich and handsome—she felt no attraction to him at all.

Andy, however... His caring smile warmed her heart and steadied her.

Waving toward the stairs, Cece said, "Come on up." She led the way up to the apartment, then moved into the kitchen area. "Would you like a cup of coffee?"

"I would," Andy said. "How about you, Drake?"

"I would as well."

Cece pulled three mugs out of the cupboard, lining them up on the counter. After pouring coffee into each of them, she got out the cream and sugar and offered them to Drake.

"I just drink it black, thanks," he said as he picked up the mug she'd slid closer to him.

She doctored her and Andy's coffees, then handed Andy his.

"Thank you." He lifted the mug and took a sip, giving a hum of appreciation. "Lovely as usual."

"Why don't we go sit down?" she suggested, motioning to the living room. She took her favorite seat by the window, while Andy and Drake sat on the couch facing her.

"This is a lovely apartment," Drake said, staring past Cece to the large windows. "Have you lived here long?"

For some reason, she'd thought that Andy would have told Drake everything about her situation. "Uh... Not very long."

Drake shifted his intense gaze to her. "Andy tells me that you think the bookstore fire was set by someone who was striking out at him to get to you."

Cece nodded. "My ex has turned into a bit of a stalker. He hasn't been willing to accept that I wanted to end the relationship. And since Andy is my closest friend, he's targeted him with threats and visits to the bookstore."

"Do you have a protective order against him?"

"Yes. But he seems to feel that it's beneath him."

Drake glanced at Andy. "He's a wealthy man?"

"Yes," Andy said. "He owns several businesses around the country."

"Hmmm." Drake pulled out his phone. "What's his full name?"

While the man focused on his phone, Cece looked at Andy, her brows raised in question. He just shrugged, so Cece gave Drake the information he'd asked for. She knew he was a wealthy man, though she didn't know how rich he was. She'd never really known much about him, aside from the few things that Andy had shared with her.

"I'm going to have someone look into this guy and see what they can find." Drake looked up. "I am no fan of bullies nor of men who don't take no for an answer."

Cece had no idea what that would mean exactly. But so far, Geof had been punching down with his attacks on her and Andy. Maybe Drake would have more success in getting Geof to back off, since it appeared he was on the same level financially as Geof.

"Our biggest fear is that despite what he's done to Cece and now with the bookstore, he'll only get a slap on the wrist." Andy frowned. "Even the cops were saying it was unlikely that he'd spend much, if any, time behind bars for his attack on Cece."

Drake scoffed as he shook his head. "Sometimes I hate the legal system. It feels like all the good work the police do is just tossed aside when people like this guy walk. I can't imagine how frustrated they must get."

"I really hope that they're able to tie him to the fire," Andy said. "If he is responsible."

"Is there any chance that he's not?" Drake asked as he leaned back against the couch, crossing his legs and cupping his mug in both hands.

Andy shrugged. "I suppose it's always possible. It's just that I haven't had any threats from anyone else. As far as I know, Geof is the only person I've ticked off lately."

"It does seem unlikely that it's a random event," Drake agreed.

"I just hope that since Geof is going off the rails, he'll have been sloppy in covering his tracks."

Cece continued to drink her coffee as the two men discussed Geof and the fire. Her anxiety had eased a bit when it became apparent that Drake wasn't there to lay blame on her for the fire. Still, she wasn't one hundred percent convinced that the man didn't have an opinion on Andy's friendship with her, if it put his business at risk.

"Thank you for agreeing to meet me," Drake said as he leaned forward to set his mug on the coffee table. "This has likely been even more traumatic for you, given that Andy is someone you care about. I'm sure you're concerned that Geof may only continue to intensify attacks on him."

Cece swallowed hard against the sudden rush of emotion that tightened her throat. As she blinked back the sting of tears, she nodded.

"Well, first of all," Drake began. "I want you to know that I absolutely do not hold you responsible for what happened at the bookstore, even if it is determined that Geof was behind it. I will hold Geof, and Geof alone, responsible. And if it is determined that he is the culprit, I'll happily look into suing him for the trauma he's caused if he doesn't back off."

Cece was stunned speechless at Drake's words. This wasn't what she'd expected at all.

"And as part of the repairs on the building, I'll be installing cameras throughout the store, as well as along the back and front. If his lawyer gets him out of jail, we'll capture any further attempts on his part to threaten Andy. And if you agree, I'd like to talk to the owner of where you work and offer to pay to put security cameras in there, too. Andy didn't think there were any sort of cameras present in the bakery."

Cece shook her head. "I don't think Brooke ever thought it was necessary."

"And it shouldn't be," Drake agreed. "But I'd rather be safe than sorry."

So would Cece, but she wasn't able to do much to protect those around her. Aside from leaving. That was still an option in her mind, though she knew it wasn't one that Andy wanted to consider.

If she ended up having to leave New Hope, she was sure that Andy would be okay. He had lots of support and plenty of friends who could fill any hole that she might leave in his life.

How she'd survive without him, however, wasn't something she could even begin to fathom.

Drake glanced at the expensive-looking watch on his wrist, then over at Andy. "I need to head back to the bookstore. The security consultant is supposed to meet me there in ten minutes."

When the two men got to their feet, Cece stood up as well. They walked to the door of the apartment, where Drake turned to her.

"It was a pleasure to meet you, Cece," he said with a small smile. "It's clear how important you are to Andy."

Cece felt heat creep into her cheeks because his words seemed to imply that there was more than just friendship between them. "He's important to me, too."

Drake's smile grew at her words, and he clapped Andy on the shoulder. "I can't tell you how glad I am to hear that."

"I'll talk to you later," Andy said, his own cheeks tinged with a light flush.

With that, the two men left her apartment. Cece hurried back to the window and looked down, wanting to catch sight of them as they left the building. As the men stepped out on the sidewalk, Andy glanced up at the window, even though he knew that he wouldn't be able to see her.

Cece pressed her hand against the glass, hoping that when all the mess with Geof was sorted, she would still have Andy in her life.

When her phone rang, Cece flipped it over to see who was calling. Seeing Sarah's name, she debated answering, but finally, she tapped the screen.

"Are you okay?" Sarah asked when Cece answered. "Cara told me there was a fire at the bookstore. Is Geof behind this?"

"Which question do you want me to answer first?"

"Well, even though I really want to know the answer to the Geof question, you'd better tell me how you're feeling, so I don't feel guilty."

Cece gave a huff of laughter, not taking Sarah's comment too seriously. "I'm fine."

"Really?" Sarah didn't sound convinced. "Was Geof involved in starting the fire somehow?"

"I don't think they know for sure yet, but the likelihood is quite high."

"And if he is involved, are you still going to be fine?"

Cece sighed and stared out the window again. "I'm not happy that Andy and the bookstore have been impacted by the stuff happening in my life. I think Andy would be better off without me in his life."

"And then Geof wins."

"What?"

"Don't you think that's exactly what Geof is hoping will happen?" Sarah asked. "He either wants Andy to remove himself from your life or you to remove yourself from his. Geof wants you to have no support so that you'll have no choice but to return to him. Don't let him win."

"But Geof seems to be escalating his attacks. What is going to be damaged next? Or worse, who might be hurt? I don't want anyone else to be negatively affected by a decision I made."

"It was a decision you *had* to make," Sarah said. "And no one begrudges you wanting to be safe. They're also not blaming you for what Geof is doing."

"I'm blaming me," Cece murmured. "It just about killed me when I saw what was happening with the bookstore because I was *positive* that it was tied to Geof."

"Have you spoken to Andy?"

"Yeah. Just after the fire, and then he and Drake stopped by a few minutes ago."

"Wow," Sarah said. "You've met the elusive Drake Swanson?"

"Yep. Seemed like a very nice man."

"Some of us were wondering if he even existed."

"Didn't he go to school around the same time as Eli?"

"I think he was still a year or two older than Eli, and from what Eli has said, he wasn't involved much with anyone at the school. He said he would be there for all his classes, but he'd leave as soon as school was over. Never went out for sports or anything."

"He looks like he could play basketball or something now. Tall and fit looking."

There was a beat of silence, then Sarah said, "Are you... interested in him?"

"No." Cece understood why she asked, and she was glad that she could answer her honestly. "No, I'm not interested in him."

"I'm so glad to hear that."

Cece could hear the relief in Sarah's voice, but she wasn't sure what had prompted the question. "Why?"

"Oh. Well, uh..." Sarah hesitated. "I just think maybe it's too soon since you just broke up with Geof."

"I'm not heartbroken over the breakup with Geof," Cece told her. "I never loved the man."

"Hmmm." Sarah didn't seem to know what to say to that. "So you feel like you're ready for another relationship?"

"I don't know about that." Cece wasn't sure if she'd ever be ready, except that her heart was already full of love for Andy.

No other man had ever made her smile and laugh the way Andy had. She'd always known that he was a safe place in her life. Her rock in the midst of a stormy life. And he'd introduced her to a faith and a view of God she'd never had before.

She just wished that she brought good things to his life. Instead, he'd had to deal with her selfish moments. He'd soothed her when she'd been upset. He'd been there for her when so many others hadn't been. And now he had to deal with a man who was obsessed with her.

But what had she done for him?

Nothing.

"I think you should remain open to having a relationship," Sarah said. "Just be smarter next time about the man you choose."

"I'll keep that in mind. At least now I'm not listening to someone tell me that I need to find a rich man who will take care of me."

"A relationship should involve two people who take care of each other."

"That's how it is for you and Beau?"

"Yes, it is. It took a while for us to figure out what that care looks like. It's not the same for each of us. For example, Beau figured out that I love it when he brings me a cup of coffee in bed. The mornings he does that and cuddles with me for a bit are the best. For him, he has discovered a real love for hiking, so that's a way he recharges. I'll get a backpack ready, then the two of us will go hiking. It isn't something that I really enjoy, but since I know that's what makes him feel good, I go with him when he asks."

Cece had never been with a man who'd ever asked about or cared what things she enjoyed. It was only with Andy that she could talk about the recipes she was learning at the bakery or about the books she'd read and feel like he really cared. He'd even given her books of his own that he thought she'd enjoy. And she was quite sure that some of the stationery products he brought into the store he ordered with her in mind.

Andy was definitely someone she wanted to take care of. She just wasn't sure how. Leaving town so that he would be safe seemed like the best thing she could do for him.

"Anyway, keep an open mind. For all you know, there might be a wonderful man who already loves you."

Cece frowned at Sarah's words. "What do you mean?"

"Just that maybe you've been a bit blind about certain people in your life."

She still wasn't sure what Sarah was trying to say, but before she could probe further, Sarah said, "I'd better go, but if you ever need to talk about anything, you know my number. Don't be afraid to use it. I'm glad that you're safe and that Andy is, as well."

After the call had ended, Cece turned so she could once again watch the world go by, wondering what Sarah had meant. The only wonderful man in her life was Andy. Was Sarah referring to Andy? And if so, did he really love her?

Warmth flooded her heart at the thought, bringing with it a wealth of emotions. It was what she wanted more than anything, but she was so scared to hope for that because she knew she wasn't good enough for him.

CHAPTER THIRTY-THREE

"She seems like a nice woman," Drake observed as they stood together in the bookstore after the security expert had left.

"Who?" Andy asked, confused, since the person they'd just met with had been a guy.

Drake's brows lifted. "Cece."

"Oh. Yes, she is. Not everyone has thought that over the years, but she's really changed over the past little while."

"It's horrible that she was attacked the way she was," Drake said with a shake of his head.

"We didn't realize how badly Geof would take the breakup. It wasn't that he loved her. Kieran said Geof's actions were all about power and control. In Geof's mind, the only person who could end that relationship was him."

Drake nodded. "I've met guys like that."

"How does this end?" Andy asked. "If you've dealt with men like Geof, what's his endgame?"

"I'm not sure."

"If he got Cece back, what does that mean for her? I doubt he would just turn around and breakup with her. He doesn't want her free, and he's regularly reminded me that even if she was available, she wouldn't go for someone like me."

Drake crossed his arms and regarded him intently. "And do you want her to?"

Andy shrugged. "I've always known that regardless of how I feel, we aren't destined to be together."

"Does she have any idea of how you feel?" he asked.

"I doubt it. I'm afraid to let her know because I think it would make her uncomfortable around me, and I really don't want that. She needs me as a friend right now, and I don't want to risk doing or saying anything that would push her away."

"I understand that, but don't write off the possibility of a relationship with her. Something great might slip through your fingers if you don't at least attempt to share your feelings with her."

Andy frowned at him. "Are you talking from personal experience?"

Drake's gaze slipped past Andy. "Perhaps."

Andy waited for the man to expound on his answer, but he didn't. He appeared to be lost in the past, so Andy didn't say anything. Would that be him some day? Living with regret for having not told Cece how he felt?

Unfortunately, his fear of losing her altogether was too great. He'd been hoping that she'd somehow come to understand his feelings by how he treated her.

However, he wasn't sure that she knew what it meant to be loved. From everything he'd seen in her life over the past year, he'd realized that she'd never experienced genuine love. Not just romantic love, but also the love of family.

"Just think about talking to her about how you feel," Drake said as he clapped him on the shoulder. "You might be surprised."

"Or I might be disappointed," he murmured.

"That's life though, isn't it?" Drake asked.

Andy supposed it was. For now, though, he would just continue to take care of her as best he could to get her through this horrible time in her life.

The door to the bookstore opened, ending their conversation. Drake greeted the man he'd called to help with the repairs to the back of the bookstore. Money must talk, because the quickness with which he'd been able to get the insurance and repair people out to the store had been amazing. He must have been offering bonuses if they came and met him that same day.

Listening to the men talking about what needed to be done made Andy wince. Though the damage had been contained to the rear of the building, the back wall needed to be totally replaced. Also, the insurance company was sending in a team to go through the contents of the bookstore and the apartment, checking for smoke and water damage.

Andy suspected it would be a week or more before he'd have the chance to open the bookstore again. And it might reopen with some sparsely stocked shelves at first. He had no idea how much was going to have to be written off.

Thankfully, Drake said he'd stick around for a few days to get everything handled. This was something Andy had no experience with, and he hoped that he never had to deal with it again. But he planned to be part of everything as much as he could be because, even though he hoped to never have to deal with something like that again, he wanted to learn from the experience.

He and Drake were eating supper at *Norma's* when Andy's phone rang. Seeing Kieran's name, he didn't hesitate to answer it, though normally he wouldn't use his phone during a meal.

"Just thought I'd update you on what's transpired today," Kieran said when Andy answered the call.

"What have you found out?"

"We ran the license plate, and unfortunately, it didn't come back to any vehicle Geof owns."

"Really? I was so sure..."

"We were disappointed as well," Kieran said. "But they tracked down the owner of the car and brought him in for questioning. Once he saw the footage of his vehicle being used by the person lighting the fire, he cracked. Considering his car was parked in his driveway, he couldn't even say that it had been stolen. It didn't take long for him to spill that he'd been hired to set the fire."

"Did he name Geof?"

"Not right off the bat. He tried to give some vague description of the guy who'd hired him. But after he realized that he was facing jail time, he decided to give up what he really knew about the person who'd hired him."

"And?"

"He didn't know the full name, but he had the first, which was Geof."

"Where on earth did they meet?" Andy asked. "Is there a website for people looking to hire arsonists?"

Kieran laughed. "No. Surprise, surprise. They met at a bar. Geof was apparently drowning his sorrows, and he told this person all about the guy who was trying to steal his girlfriend. He wanted that guy to suffer. This man sympathized with Geof because he'd had a recent breakup where his girlfriend ended up with another guy really quickly. So when Geof offered him ten thousand dollars to set fire to your business, he was more than happy to help him out."

"Wow. So what does this mean for Geof? Is there any other proof that he's involved?"

"Yep. When the guy let Geof know that he'd set the fire, Geof apparently told the guy he was going to check it out, then send the money. He'd received the payment from Geof in his bank account not long before the cops showed up. They'll be able to track that payment."

"What... what does this mean?" Andy was afraid to hope too much that this might finally take Geof out of Cece's life. "Will he go to prison?"

"I sure hope so. I hope that when the prosecutor presents how attacks have escalated, the judge will see that Geof is a danger to Cece if he remains a free man."

In Andy's mind, it wasn't an escalation, really. To him, the beating Cece had endured from Geof was worse than the fire at the bookstore. However, he knew what Kieran meant.

"What's she supposed to do, Kieran?" Andy asked, desperate to find a way to assure Cece she was safe, so that she didn't have to leave New Hope. "If Geof gets out or even if he just finds another person like this arsonist, how can Cece be safe here? It feels like we're dealing with an insane man."

Kieran sighed. "I understand your frustration. Those of us who have been a part of this continuing saga are also frustrated with how Geof has continued to push the boundaries."

"Yeah. He's finding ways around the protection order. He can afford to hire people to do the dirty work for him."

"He'll probably only do that when you're involved," Kieran said.

"What do you mean?"

"I think that if he decides to go after Cece, he'll want to do it himself."

That idea sent a frisson of alarm through Andy. "Do we need to hire security for her?"

"I'm going to talk to Cara about adding a personal alarm to the account she has for the apartment. Cece could keep it on her, then if Geof ever approached her or if she saw him closer to her than the protection order allows, she can push it to alert the security company that she needs the police."

It sounded like better than nothing, but Andy wished the judge would just toss Geof into jail and throw away the keys. Men like him didn't deserve to walk around free.

"Can we go to his court appearance?" Andy asked.

"Yeah. As long as you behave."

"You mean I'm not allowed to deck him?"

"Nope. At least not unless you want to end up in jail yourself."

"Knowing my luck, the judge would go hard on me and lenient on Geof."

Kieran gave a huff of laughter. "I'd like to tell you that would never happen, but sadly, strange things do happen in the legal system sometimes."

"So have you arrested Geof yet?" Andy asked. "Or do you have to wait for the bank account info?"

"They're bringing him in for questioning while they wait for the forensics on the bank accounts."

"Does that mean he'll be spending any time in jail over this?"

"Probably at least the night," Kieran said. "Then he'll go before the judge again with this additional charge."

Andy knew that the man was entitled to due process, but it was still frustrating.

"I'd better go. I just wanted you to know what was going on."

"Thanks," Andy said. "I appreciate you keeping us up to date."

"You're welcome."

After he ended the call, Andy stared out the restaurant window toward the second floor of the studio building, struggling to know how to tell Cece what had happened and how they were going to make sure she was safe. It was too late now to call her since she'd be going to bed soon, if she wasn't asleep already.

"Everything okay?"

The question startled Andy, having forgotten for a moment that he was out for dinner with his boss. He focused his attention back on Drake. "Sorry about that."

"News about the fire?"

"Yeah. Kieran said that they found the guy who lit the fire, and he's admitted that Geof hired him to set it."

"That's good, right?"

"Yeah. Definitely. However, if they let him out again, Geof isn't just going to leave Cece alone."

Drake nodded. "I know you are concerned."

"I am," Andy agreed. "But I can still do my job."

"Andy. C'mon. You know I'm not worried about that. I wish all the people I employed were as good as you."

"I'm super grateful for the job. It's my dream job."

Drake grinned. "That's great. I'm glad that you feel that way about it. I suppose that's why you're such a reliable and good employee."

Their waitress appeared with an offer of coffee and dessert. Drake seemed interested in the brownie sundae, so Andy ordered one, too.

"I don't want to get your hopes up," Drake began. "But I've got some things in the works that I hope will deter Geof from his focus on Cece."

"Wow. Legal things?"

Drake narrowed his eyes at him. "Of course, legal things. The thing is, men like Geof often like to skirt the line of legal and illegal. The guy I have looking into his business dealings is following some interesting trails of information on Geof."

"Really?"

"Unfortunately, getting to the bottom of it all is going to take a bit of time. But if they uncover illegal business dealings, that could keep him in prison even longer."

"I just want him out of Cece's life. She's in a prison of her own right now, only being able to go to work and back to her apartment. Sometimes she comes by the bookstore. The places she feels safe are few."

"No one should have to live that way unless they want to," Drake said. "So we're going to try our best to give Cece the opportunity to live her life the way she wants."

Andy wished he could give that to Cece, but if Drake's plan was what it took to free her, he'd take it.

After they'd finished their dessert and coffee, they walked back to where they'd parked their vehicles. Drake got into his rental while Andy slid behind the wheel of his car. He was exhausted and ready to go home and crash, though he knew that his mom and Cilla would be interested to know what else had transpired that day.

And since he knew that his mom had been praying that the day would go well, he wanted to give her an update. He'd worried that when he told his mom what had happened, she'd tell him that being around Cece was too dangerous and he needed to keep his distance. Thankfully, that hadn't been the case.

He didn't want to go against his mom, but Cece had so few people she trusted in her life. Plus, his love for her wouldn't allow him to just walk away.

Over the next few days, Andy still spent nearly every day at the bookstore. Drake popped in and out, but he seemed to also be dealing with things unrelated to the bookstore. He left Andy in charge of supervising the people who needed access to the bookstore for repairs and insurance purposes.

Each morning, Andy still went by the bakery to get his coffee. He'd linger to chat with Cece a bit before heading to the bookstore. Usually, most of the people who needed access to the store were done by four or four-thirty.

That afternoon, everyone had left by three, so Andy called Cece. When she answered, he said, "Want to make a run into Everett? Do you need groceries?"

"I do need some groceries," she admitted.

"Let me give you a ride. Get you out of the apartment for a bit."

"Okay."

"How much time do you need to get ready to go?"

"Ten minutes?"

"Sounds good. I'll be there."

Just the idea of spending some time with her lifted Andy's spirits. Even though things were progressing with the bookstore repairs, every day that it wasn't open was unsettling for him. He found it hard to focus on anything other than getting it back open. Even his writing had fallen by the wayside.

It would be nice to do something away from New Hope, just him and Cece. Maybe it would be a nice break for her, too. She hadn't spoken much about the fire. In fact, she hadn't spoken about much, aside to say that she was okay whenever he asked. They both needed a break, away from the reminders of what had happened.

When she came out of the back door a few minutes later, he could see that she was tired. Most likely, worries over what might happen next, since Geof was once again free, kept her awake.

As he drove, he glanced over at her. "Okay. Here's the deal."

"Deal?" she asked.

"Yep. For the duration of the drive to the store, we'll talk about the jerk and what he's done. Once I park and turn off the engine, no more conversation about Geof. We'll spend the rest of our time doing normal stuff and talking about the things we enjoy. Okay?"

"Definitely okay."

As it turned out, she didn't really seem to want to talk much about Geof or the fire at all. Their conversation had turned to other things long before they reached the store. Andy was glad for that because he wanted her to be able to relax and enjoy a few hours of normal.

Once they were at the store, they headed inside. Cece surprised him by taking hold of his arm. He covered her hand with his, giving it a light squeeze.

She didn't let go of him as he pulled out a cart, and together, they walked through the store. The store wasn't too busy, so they could move slowly through the aisles. Cece had pulled out her phone, which had her grocery list on it.

Helping her cross things off her list was a surprisingly satisfying experience. Andy hadn't really thought grocery shopping would feel like anything but a chore. However, doing it with Cece made him think about how much he wished it was something they could always do together.

"I want some ice cream," Cece said as they stood in front of one of the glass-fronted freezers. She looked at him. "What flavor would you like?"

"Am I going to be eating it?" he asked. "Or does ice cream that someone else picks out have no calories?"

Cece laughed and leaned against his arm. "Both?"

"Well, in that case..." Slipping his arm around her shoulders, he stepped closer to the freezer so that he could look at the flavors. He knew she was partial to chocolate, so whatever he picked was going to have chocolate in it. "How about that one? It sounds like rocky road, but instead of marshmallows, it has marshmallow cream in it."

"That does sound good." She pulled the door open and reached inside to grab a container of it.

Since they had left the freezer section until last, once they'd picked up the ice cream and a couple of other things, they were ready to check out.

"Actually, we need to pick up a cooler and some ice," Andy said.

"Are we going camping?" Cece asked, looking like that was the absolute last thing she'd ever want to do.

Andy chuckled. "No. I want to take you out for dinner before we head back to New Hope, so we need something to keep the ice cream and other fridge stuff cold."

They went in search of a Styrofoam cooler and a couple bags of ice, then proceeded to the registers. It didn't take too long to get through the check-out, and soon they were loading the bags and cooler into the trunk of his car.

After a brief discussion, they settled on a place for dinner that wasn't a fast-food joint. Andy knew this wasn't a date, but he wanted her to enjoy the meal, regardless. All he wanted was a couple more hours of Geof-free conversation. And he had a feeling that she needed and wanted that, too.

CHAPTER THIRTY-FOUR

Cece finished with her baking earlier than usual, which wasn't a surprise since she'd come in early after a restless night. After she'd woken up around one-thirty, she'd tried to go back to sleep. However, after twenty minutes of tossing and turning, with her thoughts tangled up in so many things, she'd finally given up.

The walk to work had seemed even darker and lonelier at two-thirty in the morning. In fact, the *walk* had turned into a run fairly quickly. She was glad that the back door of the bakery now had a bright light above it, as well as new security cameras. All courtesy of Drake Swanson.

Brooke had also been more than willing to allow cameras to be installed in the bakery's kitchen and front area. The security man had provided Brooke with stickers and signs to put up, alerting customers to the presence of the cameras. Cece wasn't sure if increased security would dissuade Geof, but she hoped so.

"Are you done already?"

Cece draped the cloth she'd used to wipe down the surfaces over the faucet and turned to face Mia. "Yeah. I was in early today."

Mia frowned. "Is everything okay?"

"Yep. I was just awake well before my alarm went off. Decided that tossing and turning would be a waste of time."

Though she was coming to really appreciate Mia, she still found it hard to confide in her. She hadn't even told Mia about the connection between her and the fire at the back of the bookstore.

"Are you coming to church tomorrow?" Mia asked.

"Probably." She hadn't made up her mind for sure yet, but Cece couldn't deny that there was a desire within her to go.

"Wonderful!" Mia beamed at her as if Cece going to church really made her happy.

She still had to let Andy know so he could pick her up. Part of her wished that she didn't need to inconvenience him for a ride, but she wasn't sure that she had the courage to walk into church by herself. Maybe if she kept attending, she'd get used to it, but for now, walking in with Andy made going easier.

"Do you want me to take these out to restock the case?" Mia asked, gesturing to the tray of cookies Cece had slid into the metal bakery racks a few minutes earlier.

"That would be great. Thanks."

A few minutes after Mia had disappeared through the kitchen door to the front, Brooke walked in.

"Hey, Cece," her boss said with a smile. "How's it going today?"

"Good. All the baking is done. I was in about an hour early this morning, so I got a jump start on everything."

"That's great. So I suppose you're ready to head out."

"I am, but if you need me to do anything, I'm happy to stick around."

Brooke shook her head. "I'm just here for a first birthday cake appointment."

"Oh, fun!"

"Right? I love the challenge of making wedding cakes, but kids' birthday cakes are a lot of fun with their bright colors. We'll see if these people are going to want a theme cake or a character cake."

"Which do you get more requests for?"

"For the younger kids, I get more themed requests, like animals or cars. Pre-school kids tend to want their favorite character from a TV show. Older kids also like character cakes, but now you're adding in games to the TV shows. Fortnite and Minecraft are popular."

Cece had never had fancy cakes for her birthdays. In fact, she'd never had a cake or a party. She hadn't even been able to go to the parties she'd been invited to because her dad had refused to spend the money on a present for some strangers' kid. Even as an adult, her birthday came and went without her or anyone else acknowledging it, let alone celebrating it.

After chatting for a few more minutes, Cece went to get ready to go home. She was tired enough when she reached the apartment that she changed out of her work clothes, then crawled right into bed for a nap.

There was a steady drizzle coming down the next morning as she waited for Andy to pick her up for church. He'd readily agreed to give her a ride when she'd asked him about it the previous evening. Though, honestly, she hadn't expected anything else.

When she saw his car approaching on the camera, she opened the door and popped up her umbrella. Even though it was a short distance from the garage door to the car, she didn't really fancy getting drenched before she even got to church.

When Andy pulled in close to the building, she walked out and opened the car door, maneuvering around so she could slide into the seat, then close the umbrella without getting too wet. After she closed the door, she put the umbrella down by her feet.

"You know, I could have pulled into the garage," Andy said.

Cece turned to stare at Andy before laughing. "Yeah. That would have made sense."

"If it's still raining when I drop you off, we'll use the garage."

"Definitely." She focused on locking the doors and arming the alarm on the building, then said, "Thanks for picking me up."

"I was more than happy to."

They chatted on the short drive to the church. When they reached the parking lot, Andy said he'd drop her off at the front door, but Cece didn't want that. She really didn't want to walk in by herself.

With apparent reluctance, Andy drove on to find a parking spot. No doubt because of the rain, there weren't any spots close to the entrance. After he parked, Andy asked for the umbrella and requested she stay put.

Once on her side, he opened the door, keeping the umbrella over the edge of the car so Cece could climb out without getting soaked.

It was a tight squeeze under the umbrella, so when Andy put his arm over her shoulders, she slid her own around his waist. Laughing, they made their way across the parking lot, dodging around puddles to get to the steps that led to the front door.

They managed to get into the church without getting too wet. They went into a nearby coatroom, where they hung up their damp jackets and left the umbrella.

Andy guided her to the row they usually sat in, and they settled into the pew. Even though there wasn't anyone sitting right next to them, Cece sat close enough to Andy that their arms brushed. She felt comfortable sitting there with him in a way she'd never imagined that she would.

Cecelia Albrecht actually wanting to attend church? Yeah, that wasn't something she'd ever thought she'd want to do. But life had changed significantly in the past little while. And along with those changes, there had been significant changes in her heart, too. And if she was being totally honest with herself, they weren't changes that she hated.

All the things she'd used to think were important and necessary to her happiness had been stripped away. That process had been horrible, but even with there still being uncertainty where Geof was concerned, she felt like maybe she was coming out the other side.

Mia and Ben joined them once again, and as the service got underway, Cece didn't feel so out of place. She still didn't know the songs as well as Andy and the others did, but she was paying attention to the words and the music and was learning.

And when Pastor Evans got up to preach, she didn't try to tune him out. Instead, she focused on what he was saying and even made notes on her phone of the verses he shared, planning to look them up later on the Bible app she'd downloaded onto her phone.

"As I've spoken here today, I've focused on helping you spot the pitfalls you might come across in your life. The weaknesses that could cause us as Christians to stumble. Or perhaps cause those around us to stumble." Pastor Evans closed his Bible and came to the side of the podium, a gentle smile on his face. "But I realize that there may be some in our midst who haven't accepted the gift of salvation that God has offered us through Jesus' death and resurrection."

Cece gripped her phone more tightly, feeling as if the pastor was speaking directly to her.

"John three verse sixteen says, *For God so loved the world that He gave His only begotten Son, that whoever believes in Him should not perish but have everlasting life.* I like to change it up a bit, make it a little more personal. *For God so loved* you *that He gave His only Son.* God so loved me... and you... and you..." With each word, the pastor pointed to someone else in the congregation. "We are part of the world that He loved so much. All of us. He loved... loves... all of us so much that He offers this gift of eternal life. We have but to accept Jesus into our hearts, believing that He paid the penalty for our sins, so that we no longer have to."

As Cece listened to the pastor speak, pressure seemed to build up in her chest. A deep longing rose up inside her to accept that gift and have God in her life the way He was in Andy's, and Mia's and Ben's.

"If you would like to accept the gift of salvation today, please come find me or Pastor Gio after the service. We'd love to speak to you more about it."

With that, the pastor said a final prayer, then the worship team led them in one last song. Through all of it, Cece was a mess of emotions. She wanted this more than anything, but was she good enough? When measuring herself against Andy, she knew she wasn't. But maybe she could be better? Maybe they could tell her what she needed to do to be good enough for the gift.

"Cece?" Concern laced Andy's voice.

She looked up at him through a wash of tears, then reached out to grab hold of his hand. "Will you go with me?"

His eyes widened briefly, hope filling his expression. "You want to speak with Pastor Evans?"

Nerves almost made her shake her head, but she really did want that, so she nodded.

A huge smile broke across Andy's face, and he covered their joined hands with his other one. "I will definitely go with you."

Thankfully, the crowd had thinned out pretty quickly, at least in the aisle next to where they sat, so when they stepped out of the row and made their way to the front of the sanctuary, they weren't bumping into people. Andy kept his arm wrapped around her shoulders, and Cece kept her head bent, not wanting anyone to see the tears she couldn't seem to stop.

"Pastor Evans," Andy said a few moments later. "I wonder if we could speak with you."

"Andy. Of course. Why don't we go into my office?"

Cece allowed Andy to continue to guide her, only looking up when she was sure they'd reached their destination.

"You're Cece, right?" the older man asked with a warm smile wreathing his age-lined face. "We have been praying for you."

Cece swallowed hard, wiping at the tears on her cheeks. "You have?"

"Yes. You're very important to Andy, and he asked us to join him in praying for your salvation."

"I want that," she said. "But I'm sure Andy has also told you that I'm not a very good person."

"Why don't we have a seat?" the pastor suggested, waving to a small couch and armchair in one corner of the room. After they had sat down, her hand still tightly gripping Andy's, Pastor Evans said, "Andy hasn't told me that at all, and he never would. The reality is that we are all born sinners. To God, none of us are very good people, but He loved us so much, He made a way for us to be forgiven of our sin and worthy of eternal life in heaven."

"What do I have to do?" Cece asked.

"You simply have to accept the gift He offers us. In the book of Ephesians chapter two, verses eight and nine, it says, *For by grace you have been saved through faith, and that not of yourselves; it is the gift of God, not of works, lest anyone should boast.* There is nothing we can do through works or behaviors that will gain us salvation. On our own, we will never be worthy of eternal life in God's presence. Nothing we can do can rid us of the stain of sin in our lives other than accepting that Jesus died on the cross for our sins."

"So I just have to accept that Jesus died for my sins?"

"You need to admit that you are a sinner and acknowledge your sins, then believe that Jesus died on the cross for those sins. Invite Him to live in your heart and commit to living your life in a way that honors and glorifies God." Pastor Evans gave her a gentle smile. "Will you allow me to lead you in a prayer for salvation?"

"Yes. Please." Cece glanced at Andy, and she almost started to cry again when she saw that he had tears in his eyes.

After explaining a little about it, the pastor led her in a prayer. Even though Cece was repeating words after the pastor, she felt the sincerity of them and knew that her life by God's grace was changing with every word she uttered. She wanted that more than anything.

The peace she felt as she lifted her head was unlike anything she had ever felt before. "Thank you."

Pastor Evans took the hand she held out, holding it tightly in both of his. "Welcome to God's family. The angels in heaven are rejoicing over the decision you've made here today."

"Really?" Cece glanced at Andy. "Really?"

"Really," Andy said. "God wants us all to accept His gift. Many don't, so there is much rejoicing over those who do."

"Before you go, I'd like to give you something." The pastor got to his feet and went to a bookshelf behind his desk. When he returned, he carried a couple of books. "I know most people use an app to read the Bible, but some like to underline verses and make notes in margins of a physical copy. So I'd like to give this Bible to you. This is also a book that I give to all new Christians to help them understand this new life they have. I am also confident that Andy and others in the church will be happy to walk alongside you as you learn more about God."

Cece took the two books from him. "Thank you."

"You're very welcome."

Andy continued to hold her hand as they left the pastor's office and returned to the sanctuary, entering through a door at the front of the large room. Cece's steps slowed when she saw a group of people standing in a circle, heads bent as they held hands.

She glanced up at Andy to find him smiling. He cleared his throat, which resulted in several heads popping up. Sarah and Jillian abandoned the circle and hurried over to where she and Andy stood.

Sarah gave Andy a questioning look, and when he nodded, she flung her arms around Cece. "What wonderful news! We were praying for you."

Jillian also joined the hug. "I'm so happy for you, Cece."

All Cece could do was return the hugs, her throat too tight with emotion to voice her feelings.

When the two women stepped back, Mia took their place. Cece noticed then that a large group of familiar faces surrounded them.

All of them smiling, happy for her. It felt so surreal, and yet she knew that she had never experienced a realer moment in her life.

Kieran and Cara were also there to tell her how happy they were for her. Even Leah offered her a smile, and it didn't look forced at all. These people, many of whom had reason to dislike her, showed nothing but happiness over the decision she'd just made.

Even so, she was a bit overwhelmed by all the attention. Thankfully, people began to drift away after they'd spoken with her. Soon, it was just her and Andy left to follow Sarah, Beau, Jillian, and Carter up the aisle to the foyer, where they chatted for several more minutes.

It was still raining when they left the church a bit later. But it was just a light shower, and the sun was already peaking through the clouds in spots. Andy held the umbrella as they walked across the nearly empty parking lot.

Letting go of his hand, Cece stepped out from under the umbrella. Closing her eyes, she tipped her head back and lifted her arms. The rain was gentle on her skin, and she felt like God's love was saturating her heart in the same way the rain was sinking into the world around her.

She knew in that moment that even when the tough times came, when the rain in her life was more like a torrential storm, God would be there to make sure that she didn't drown in it. He would be the lighthouse that would always guide her.

Joy filled her and bubbled out of her in laughter. Lowering her head, she opened her eyes to smile at Andy. He stood a short distance from her, still holding the umbrella, a look on his face that seemed like it might match how she felt in her heart for him.

Walking close enough to join him under the umbrella, Cece grabbed his free hand in both of hers and looked up at him. She blinked away the rain that still clung to her lashes because she wanted to have a clear view of the face of the man who meant the world to her.

The man she now felt with certainty that God had sent to her all those years ago to teach her what love truly was. Not just God's love for her, but also what it was like to love another person. To love a man. Not one man in her past had ever filled her heart the way Andy did, and she wanted him to know that, even if he didn't feel the same way about her.

"I love you, Andy."

CHAPTER THIRTY-FIVE

Shock ricocheted through Andy at Cece's words. She stood in the drizzling rain, drenched, but smiling up at him like he'd never seen her smile before.

Andy didn't know how to respond. He'd dreamed of one day hearing those words from her, but he hadn't actually thought it would ever happen. And honestly, he still wasn't sure it really was.

The whole day might have been a dream, playing out his greatest desires where Cece was concerned. But he really, really, really didn't want any of it to be a dream. He wanted Cece to have become a Christian. And he also wanted her to love him.

"Andy?" Cece's hands tightened on his, and her smile dimmed a bit. "I know you don't feel the same way, but I need you to know that you have touched my life in so many ways. You make me smile and laugh like no one else ever has, and during the darkest period of my life, you've brought me light. You've been a safe place for me, and I can't tell you how much I appreciate that. You make me want to be a better person. Someone who might be worthy of your love."

"So... you love me as a... friend?" He needed the clarification. Though, for a moment, he just wanted to imagine that her words meant something more. "And don't be going on about being worthy of my love. You already have my love. Have had it for quite awhile now."

Cece's smile softened with affection, and Andy's heart gave a hard thump in his chest.

"I feel so much right now. So much joy. So much peace. So much love. I never knew that it could be like this, especially when

I'm dealing with so much turmoil. But I have seen it in your life. You've also faced some terribly hard times, and yet you still seem to have joy and peace."

If only Cece knew how he'd struggled at times. He hadn't shared all of that with her because, until recently, he'd doubted that she'd care very much. Knowing now what he did about her life, he understood a bit better why she hadn't been concerned about those around her. She'd just been trying to survive her own life.

But this woman standing in front of him? He was pretty sure that he'd be able to share what was going on in his life with her. Even if it was just as a friend.

He'd been witness to her softening attitude toward others, even before Geof had attacked her. Breaking up with the jerk had shown that she wanted to change her life. She'd definitely walked a rough road to get to this point, and Andy was happy that she'd allowed him to walk alongside her.

What she'd said didn't clear much up for Andy. Sure, it sounded like she admired him, but that didn't mean she loved him in the way he longed for her to.

"Sarah said something to me the other day," Cece began. "It didn't make a lot of sense at the time. And maybe it still doesn't make much sense, to be honest."

Given what Sarah knew about him, Andy wasn't sure if this was going to be embarrassing or enlightening. "What did Sarah say?"

"She asked if I might be ready for another relationship at some point. I told her I wasn't sure, and she suggested that I keep an open mind. That there might be a wonderful man in my life who already loved me."

A chill swept over Andy, and he really wished that Sarah had kept her mouth shut. "Oh, yeah?"

"Yeah." Cece smiled at him again. "And as I thought about it, I realized that there was only one man who Sarah and I would agree was wonderful. I didn't think it could be you, though. I mean, you know the worst about me, and I couldn't imagine that you could have that knowledge and still love me."

"I've always told you how much I care for you," Andy said. "You're special to me."

They were just beating around the bush, and it was setting Andy's nerves on edge.

He thought about what Drake had said, and there was a big part of him that wanted to take the man's advice. But despite Cece's earlier words, there was still a chance of misunderstanding what she'd said. Friends could love each other, after all. And if that was what she meant, he didn't want to take a chance on ruining their friendship by revealing that he felt more.

But maybe it wasn't that much of a risk. Her words and the expressions she'd shown since they'd left the church seemed to indicate that she felt more than just affection for a friend.

"The thing is..." Words failed Andy, making him wish he had someone to write them out for him.

He didn't have any experience with giving voice to feelings of love or affection for a woman he wasn't related to. It would have been easier if he'd had some time to plan what he wanted to say. Write and revise the words to his liking in the same way he wrote his books. Instead, he was standing in an empty parking lot, huddled under an umbrella, floundering for words.

"The thing is...?" Cece prompted him, her expression open and curious.

He was such a confused mess. There needed to be a freeze button for moments like these, at least for him. He wanted to freeze time—and Cece—so he could call one of the guys—maybe Tanner or Carter—to get some advice.

Andy cleared his throat and glanced around. "Do we... uh... really want to have this discussion here? In the rain?"

Cece laughed softly. "I quite like this, to be honest. Just the two of us under this umbrella."

Andy realized then that he just had to be honest. Come what may, he just needed to put it all out there. Hopefully, the recent changes in Cece would help her be a little more sensitive in her response if it wasn't what he hoped for.

"Okay. Here's the deal." He sighed, letting his shoulders slump. "I've cared about you for ages now, as a friend. However, in the past couple of years, my feelings have kind of... changed. I mean, not that I don't care for you anymore. I just care, and also... love you." Andy pulled his shoulders back and lifted his chin, praying he was making the right decision. "I love you. And not just as a friend."

He felt the need to clarify that, because he didn't want there to be any sort of misunderstanding between them. If things were going to change—for the good or the bad—he wanted that change to come from a place of total honesty.

Cece's smile, while always beautiful, was stunning right then. It held so much joy and happiness. The anxiety that had engulfed him loosened at her smile.

"I'm so glad to hear that," she said. "I can't imagine anything more amazing than loving you, except being loved by you."

Andy inhaled sharply, still not convinced that he was awake. Cece loving him felt way more like a dream. But the trickle of rain that dripped down his right shoulder from the umbrella was very real.

"You really do love me?" Andy asked.

Cece reached up and gently touched his cheek with her fingertips. "Loving you is easy and wonderful, Andy, because you are so amazing." Her expression slipped into sadness. "I should be asking you that question, actually, because I know that I'm not an easy person to be friends with, let alone love. No one else in my life has ever loved me."

Though he'd wondered about that, hearing those words from Cece hurt his heart. Everyone should know they were loved by someone. For most people, that would be their parents. But for Cece, it hadn't even been them.

"I can't deny that we have had some challenging moments, but they never made you unlovable in my eyes. That's not how it works for me." He covered her hand, pressing it more fully against his cheek. "I love all the facets of your personality because they're what make you, you."

"But I've changed recently," she said. "How do you know you still love me?"

Andy lowered their hands, lacing his fingers with hers. "Love isn't a stagnant thing that never changes. Two people aren't going to stay exactly the same from the start of their relationship. They'll grow and change as they experience things, so their love also grows and changes. You changing hasn't dimmed my love for you. In fact, as I've watched you deal with everything in your life recently, my love for you has grown even more."

"Were you ever going to tell me?"

"That I love you?" Cece nodded. "Uh... Well, I was afraid it would make things awkward while you were still with Geof. I didn't want to chance losing our friendship, especially when you were going through so much. I felt like you needed a friend more than you needed another boyfriend."

"As usual, you were quite correct," Cece said with a sigh. "I don't even feel like the same person I was a couple of months ago. Even though I was determined to end things with Geof, I never realized that that decision would change my life in the best and worst of ways."

"I can understand that," Andy said. "But I hope that the best is outweighing the worst."

"Just having you by my side through all of this has been the best part, even though I've felt bad about dragging you into my mess."

Andy gave her a hand a gentle squeeze. "You didn't drag me. I was so relieved that you were finally going to be free of Geof that I was more than willing to stick with you through whatever might happen."

Cece's gaze dropped with a frown. "It's still not over."

Andy touched her chin gently, urging her to look at him again. When she lifted her gaze to meet his, he said, "And I'm not going anywhere. Even if we hadn't had this moment, I still wouldn't be going anywhere. I love you and want to be a support for you."

"I want to be that for you too," Cece said, her expression serious. "This has been a one-sided friendship for far too long."

That she had recognized that and wanted to fix it gave him hope that they could make things work between them. Now that he had a shot of a future with her, Andy desperately wanted things to work out for them.

When he told her that, Cece's smile returned. "I want that too."

If someone had told him that morning that later that day he'd be standing in the church parking lot, finally telling Cece that he loved her, he would have told them they were nuts. Knowing that this was the moment that marked such a significant change in Cece's spiritual life was even more amazing than her expressed love for him.

Holding her the way he was, Andy longed to kiss her. But his inexperience left him uncertain about how to convey that. But maybe he needed to approach that just like he'd approached—

All thoughts of that fled from his mind as Cece slipped her hand behind his neck, going up on her toes to brush her lips lightly across his. Andy froze for a moment, then the umbrella dropped to the ground as he let go of it so that he could wrap his arms around her.

Holding Cece close sent a whole new set of emotions cascading through his body. This lingering kiss with her was the first he'd ever shared with a woman, and he was so glad that it was with her. Knowing that she loved him made the moment even more special than he could ever have imagined, and he didn't want it to end.

For certain, he'd never forget that day, and everything that it had held for Cece and for him.

When their kiss ended, Cece blinked away the droplets of rain that had caught on her eyelashes. "I've never kissed a man I loved before. It was like this was my very first kiss."

Andy smiled. "Well, it *was* my first kiss, and I am glad it was with you."

Cece stared at him for a moment, her eyes wide. Even with the rain slipping down her face and leaving her hair in damp strings, she was the most beautiful person to Andy.

Her hands gripped his arms. "I'm your first kiss?"

Andy gave a laugh. "Who do you think I've kissed?"

"I guess I didn't... I didn't think about it. I just assumed you'd been with someone at some point over the years." Cece frowned, tension filling her body. "I know from hearing Sarah and Jillian talk in high school that they weren't going to be intimately involved with a guy before marriage. Is it the same for guys who are Christians?"

Andy didn't want her to feel bad about herself, but he still wanted to be honest. "Yes. As Christian teens, we were taught that God wanted us to only have sex within the bounds of marriage, which meant that we were encouraged to wait. I'm sure not all of us did, but personally, I've found it pretty easy to wait, since I haven't had a serious girlfriend."

"You must know that I've been with several guys," Cece said, her shoulder slumping. "You'd be better off with a woman who waited like you did."

"Cece, you weren't a Christian. I never would have lectured you about adhering to the standards I was taught. I've known you didn't wait for sex. Remember how we met? But since you've become a Christian, your past has been forgiven." Andy hesitated for a moment, praying that what he said next didn't change everything. "One thing I need you to know, however, is that even as an adult, I believe in waiting for marriage before I have sex."

Cece's brows rose at his words. "Oh. Wow. I guess that makes sense since you're still a Christian."

Andy nodded, hoping that she would embrace that as well, since she was a Christian now too. But maybe she'd find it easier to embrace celibacy if she wasn't in a relationship.

"Can you see us married someday?" Cece asked, tipping her head to the side.

That hadn't been what he'd expected her to zero in on. For a moment, he let his thoughts turn towards what that might look like for them, and he found he really wanted that future.

"I can," Andy told her. "I absolutely can."

She stared at him, her eyes wide, seeming to mull over his words. Andy's stomach knotted as he waited to see what her thoughts might be on marriage. He would understand completely if she decided that wasn't what she wanted. After all, she'd only ever dated men who were rich and able to provide her with a life of luxury. Geof had given her a *car*, after all.

Andy knew it was unlikely he'd be able to offer her a life where she'd never have to work. A life with him would mean living on a budget and thinking through any major purchases. He knew Cece was a hard worker, but he also knew that she'd envisioned her future similar to that of her mother, who hadn't worked outside the home.

But he could give her things that none of the other men in her life had, namely love and safety. She'd never have to worry that he'd ever hurt her the way Geof had.

Waiting for Cece to respond made the lump of worry in his stomach grow. Maybe she wasn't interested in marriage. Maybe she couldn't see herself as his wife.

Finding that out would be horrible. To be given his dream, then have it ripped away minutes later would break his heart.

When a smile tipped the corners of her mouth, Andy couldn't help but ask, "What?"

"I'm just imagining what being married to you might be like."

"And?"

"Marriage to a rich man might have been what my dad told me to strive for, but honestly, I wasn't all that interested. Especially when I imagined that kind of life with Geof." Her smile grew. "But marriage to you? Something tells me that would be a wonderful thing. Just thinking about it makes me feel excited. You're the one person I've loved being around. You always make me feel safe and cared for, and I know I can trust you. No one else in my life has ever made me feel that way. You're an amazing man, and any woman would have been lucky to have you love them. I'm just glad that it ended up being me."

It was odd to be discussing marriage when they'd just confessed their love for each other, but it also felt right. They might not have gone on any official dates, but after spending so much time together, they certainly knew each other well enough to figure out if they'd want to be together forever.

"Also, I'm fine with waiting for sex. My past relationships definitely focused on the physical side of things, and I want more than that with you." She tipped her head, and her eyes narrowed slightly. "But does that include things like hugging, kissing, and holding hands? Because I like it when you hug me. It makes me feel safe. Cherished."

Andy smiled as he tugged her into his arms again. Bending his head, he pressed his cheek against her damp hair. "And I like to hug you."

She tipped her head back, her eyes sparkling. "And kisses?"

"Kisses are good as well," Andy murmured, then leaned down to show her that he definitely enjoyed kisses too.

When he'd gotten up that morning to go to church, he'd never envisioned where the day would lead. But he felt nothing but peace when he considered this latest turn in his life.

He might not have thought he'd ever have the opportunity to tell Cece that he loved her—or hear that she loved him in return—but now that they'd expressed their love to one another, Andy felt confident that God had brought them each step of the way. The road they'd traveled had been rough at times, but they'd stuck together, their friendship growing into something solid that Andy was confident would be a good foundation for the future together that he hoped they would have.

EPILOGUE

Andy lowered himself to one knee, leaning forward so his mom could reach his tie. He smiled as she worked to straighten it to her satisfaction. A photographer stood a few feet away, snapping pictures of them as they prepared for one of the most important days of his life.

Once done, she cupped his cheeks in her hands. The sheen of moisture in her eyes did nothing to hide the love in her gaze. "Your dad would be so proud of you, darling. *I'm* so proud of you. I love you so much. Both you and Cece. I'm thankful for how God has brought you to this point."

She pressed a kiss to his forehead, reminding him of all the times she'd done that for him as a child.

His breath caught in his throat as emotion swelled inside him. He was so grateful that this day had finally arrived. It hadn't always been an easy road with Cece, but in the eighteen months since that day in the church parking lot, their love for each other had deepened and grown.

"Are you nervous?" Cilla asked from where she stood at his mom's side.

"Not really," Andy told her with a smile. "I just want this day to go well for Cece's sake. She's put a lot of time and effort into planning everything."

"It's going to be lovely," his mom said.

As his mom leaned back in her wheelchair, Andy got to his feet. "At least it looks like we're not going to get rain, so that's a bonus."

Ben stepped into the living room, having come by earlier to get ready with Andy, since he was his best man. His friendship with

Ben had developed over the past year and a half, much the same as Cece's had with Mia. Of course, they still had plenty of other friends, including Sarah, Beau, Jillian, and Carter. But Ben and Mia had turned out to be great friends for both of them.

The couple were the only two people they'd decided to have stand up with them at the wedding. He had thought Cece might want a big wedding, but when they discussed how long of an engagement to have and what type of wedding she wanted, she'd made it clear that she didn't need months to plan a wedding because it was going to be simple and small.

"Beau texted that he's almost here," Ben told him, holding up his cell.

When Beau pulled up outside the house, Andy and Ben grabbed what they needed for the church, while Cilla and Phoebe helped his mom out of the house and down the ramp they'd had installed when his mom's physical limitations had restricted her to a wheelchair for the most part.

"Congratulations," Beau said with a smile as they reached the SUV. He gave Andy a quick hug. "Cece looks beautiful, and she's very excited."

"I'm glad. I didn't want her to get overwhelmed by all the last-minute stuff."

"She seems to be of the mind that if it isn't done, it just doesn't matter."

Andy was relieved to hear that Cece wasn't getting caught up in the little details.

"Ready to go?" Ben asked once they had his mom settled in the SUV and her wheelchair stowed in the back.

Andy nodded, then turned to his mom. "We'll see you in a few minutes."

His mom nodded, then Andy closed her door. After getting behind the wheel of his own car, he and Ben followed the SUV to the church. The wedding wasn't scheduled to start for another forty-five minutes, so there was only a smattering of cars in the parking lot.

They were greeted in the foyer by Gio and Alessia, who were playing integral roles in the wedding. Pastor Evans had suffered a stroke six months earlier, so he'd be sharing the service responsibilities with Gio. Alessia had eagerly agreed to Cece's request that she sing her down the aisle, while Leah would play the piano at different points in the ceremony.

"Let's head back to the office," Gio suggested. "Pastor Evans is waiting there."

"Will you be okay, Mom?" Andy asked, turning to where she sat in her wheelchair next to Cilla. Phoebe had disappeared as soon as they'd entered the church.

"Yep." She reached out to take his hand. "You go on."

Andy bent to kiss her cheek, then did the same to Cilla. "See you both in a bit."

With Ben and Gio at his side, they headed back to the office, where Andy greeted Pastor Evans. "How are you doing?"

"I'm doing great!" The older man grinned widely, the slight dip on the left side of his mouth the only lingering sign of his stroke. "What a wonderful day this will be."

Pastor Evans and Gio had met with them on a weekly basis for the past three months, offering marriage counseling in advance of the wedding. Those sessions had been super helpful, and Andy was glad they'd had them.

"Why don't we sit?" Pastor Evans said, gesturing to the nearby seating area.

Andy sat down with the three other men, and they chatted for a bit before Pastor Evans suggested they spend some time in prayer.

After taking a deep breath and exhaling it, Andy began to pray, "Heavenly Father, I am so thankful for every step of the journey that has brought us to this day. You know it is both Cece's and my desire to have a God-centered marriage, and I pray that as we stand before You as well as before our friends and family today, that You will bless the vows we make to each other and to You. Help me be the husband that Cece needs, showing her each day that I love her in the same way that Christ loved the church. May our marriage bring You honor and glory, and I pray that those around us will have no doubt that You brought us together in Your perfect will."

Ben and Gio both followed his prayer with ones of their own before Pastor Evans closed.

"I have been involved in a lot of weddings over the years," Pastor Evans said as he reached out to grip Andy's hand. "My emotions for this one are all over the place. How I wish your dad was here. He would have been so happy for you and Cece. As am I. I'm aware that it hasn't all been easy, but God has been so good."

Andy couldn't disagree with that. One of the big things they'd had to deal with was Geof and the abysmally light sentence he'd been given. Cece had been a wreck for a few days, angry and upset that Geof hadn't gotten a harsher sentence for the havoc he'd wreaked in their lives. Thankfully, even though he hadn't been in jail, he'd kept his distance from them. It had helped Cece to feel like she really could put all that behind her.

When other stuff had cropped up regarding the man's questionable business practices, the feds had gotten involved, and soon, Geof was picked up for crimes that, according to Drake, would net him quite a bit of time in federal prison. Clearly, Drake wasn't someone to mess with.

Andy was glad that he could count the man as a friend, especially now that he was no longer his boss. Two months ago, Drake had come to town and over dinner with Andy and Cece, he'd given them the paperwork that turned the bookstore business over to Andy, and along with that, Drake had deeded them the building that housed the bookstore and the apartment, which was where they planned to live once they were married.

Though his writing was still coming along, Andy was thrilled that the bookstore was now his, and he would be forever grateful to Drake for his generosity and friendship.

Drake would be there that day to celebrate with them, and Andy could hardly wait.

~ * ~

"I can't believe you got us a limo," Cece said as she stared out the living room window at the gleaming white stretch limo that was now parked in front of Sarah's house.

Sarah came to stand next to her, slipping her arm around her shoulders and giving her a gentle hug. "I knew that this wasn't something you'd spend money on, but I also knew that it was probably something you would have wanted if you'd have had the money."

Cece glanced over at Sarah and gave her a small smile. "You're right. Thank you. You and Beau have been more than generous with everything."

"What use is it to have stuff like this and not share it?" Sarah said with a wave of her hand at the house. "I'm thrilled that we're able to share it with you and Andy."

Cece blew out a breath, trying to not let emotions overtake her and ruin her makeup. If she was going to cry, it was going to be after Andy saw her, so all the work on her makeup didn't go to waste.

"Are you doing okay without your folks being at the wedding?" Sarah asked quietly.

She had come to terms with the fact that her parents wouldn't be part of this special day from the moment Andy had proposed. Her contact with them had been sporadic and usually only when she happened to run into them in town. They never approached her, and when she'd tried to speak with them, they'd just brushed her off.

"I'm okay. If they can't be happy for me, I don't want them to be a part of this day."

Sarah nodded, and Cece knew that she understood. Her relationship with her dad had been strained to the point that he hadn't been present at her or Leah's weddings.

"Ben just texted and said that they're at the church," Mia said as she joined them at the window.

Mia wore a soft lilac dress that had a fitted bodice and tulle sleeves that flowed around her upper arms. The skirt was full, reaching to mid-calf, and it had a wide band of sage green around her waist. Cece had chosen the colors, but Phoebe had worked with each of them to find a style that they were both happy with for their respective dresses.

Not only had she helped with the style, she'd also sewed both of the dresses. Cece had seen early on in her friendship with Phoebe how much talent the woman had, so when Phoebe had asked if she could design and sew their dresses, Cece hadn't hesitated to say yes.

Cece's own dress was a similar style to Mia's, though it was floor-length, and her tulle sleeves were down to her wrists where there was a satin cuff. The sweetheart neckline framed the white gold necklace with a heart pendant that Andy had given her a few days earlier for her birthday.

He had made sure that both of her birthdays that had occurred since they'd started dating had been celebrated in style. And her friends had been more than willing to help him plan both parties. Although the most recent one hadn't been as large since the wedding had only been a few days later.

"Well, ladies, I think it's almost time to go," Kieran announced from the entrance to the living room. "Andy will be upset with me if I don't get you there on time."

As the man approached them, Cece smiled at him. "Thank you so much for doing this for me."

Kieran's expression softened with a smile. During the months following the fire, Kieran and Cara had stepped up to support her. Kieran especially had done what he could to help them understand what was going on, and the couple had always made sure that Cece felt safe in the apartment over the studio.

After talking it over with Andy, Cece had approached Cara to see if she would mind if Kieran walked her down the aisle. Cara hadn't hesitated to agree, and when Cece had asked Kieran, he had been quick to say he'd be honored to do that.

It didn't take too long to get everything loaded into the limo. Anna, surprisingly, and Sarah had helped Cece organize everything, and Lani, the owner of the flower shop, had helped with all the flowers, offering them to Cece at a significant discount. Brooke had also decorated the wedding cake free of charge, though Cece had insisted on making the cakes to help out since Brook now had her hands full with a little boy who was now a year old.

Cece clutched Mia's hand on the drive to the church, grateful that the woman had become such a good friend. Mia hadn't cared about Cece's past record as a friend. She'd been determined to be the best friend—well, the best *female* friend—that Cece had ever had.

There had been moments over the past week when Cece had been afraid that it had all been a dream. That she'd wake up and still be living in her parents' basement and dating Geof.

The past eighteen months had had their ups and downs, but the one constant had been the love she and Andy shared. For every down they'd weathered, their love had seemed to grow and strengthen. On that day when she'd confessed her love for Andy, Cece had been unaware that she'd be able to love him even more. And yet she had.

When the limo pulled up at the church, Cece stared up at the building, remembering clearly the day when she'd committed her life to God and how that had changed so much in her life. And within the next hour or so, she'd be making yet another commitment in that building.

"Let's do this," Cece said with a glance around at the people in the limo with her.

"Yes!" Sarah punched the air as she grinned broadly. "Let's do this!"

Cece's excitement only seemed to grow as they hustled her into the church and into a side room where she was to wait until it was time to walk down the aisle to join the man she loved. Time seemed to suddenly slow down, each minute dragging as they waited for the signal that they were ready for her.

"Is it okay if I see the bride for a moment?"

Cece turned to see Andy's mom wheel herself into the room in her electric wheelchair. Her smile came readily at the sight of the older woman. Cece knew that Andy's mom had had some reservations about them dating, but she'd never once tried to discourage them from pursuing a relationship.

And it hadn't taken long for his mom to let Cece know that if her son was happy, then she was happy. From that point on, Cece had been welcomed into the Hale family.

"I am so happy for you both today," his mom said, her smile a bit watery with tears threatening to spill over. "I always knew it would take a special woman to make my Andy happy, and I was right. You are a very special woman, Cece. I hope you know how much I love you."

Cece bent to give the woman a hug, blinking rapidly to keep her tears at bay. "Thank you, Mama. I love you so very much too. You've become the mom I always wished I could have."

When Cece straightened, Phoebe approached her to give her a hug. "And now I've got the big sister I've always wanted."

Happiness swelled within Cece, and she didn't know if she could be any happier without exploding. "And I've got the little sister I never knew I needed."

Cilla gave her a hug as well, then the three women left, knowing that they needed to be seated before the wedding could officially start.

Finally, the moment arrived, and Sarah led Cece, Mia, and Kieran to the now closed doors to the sanctuary. Cara was waiting there as well, and Kieran bent down to give her a quick kiss.

Sarah told Cece and Kieran to wait off to the side as she and Cara opened the doors for Mia. Leah's piano playing briefly got louder as Mia walked through the open doorway, then it was muffled once again as Cara and Sarah closed the doors. The two gestured for Cece and Kieran to come over, taking a couple of minutes to fuss over Cece's short train.

The music Mia had walked to faded away, then Leah began to play again. After a moment, Alessia started to sing the song that Cece and Andy had chosen. Because it was a fairly short walk up the aisle, Sarah had timed it so Alessia would sing through most of the first verse before Cece and Kieran would make their entrance.

Finally, with beaming smiles, Cara and Sarah pulled the sanctuary doors open for them. The congregation stood, but Cece only had eyes for Andy. Their gazes met across the large room, and Andy's smile grew, making Cece even more eager to reach him.

Thank you, Father, for this amazing man. Help me be the wife he needs and that You want me to be.

When they reached the front, Alessia's voice trailed away as the song ended. Andy approached Cece and Kieran, and after giving the man a hug, Andy took Cece's hand in his and tucked it into the crook of his arm.

"You look absolutely beautiful," he murmured as they turned to face the pastors on the stage.

"And you're the most handsome man here," she whispered, tightening her grip on his arm.

Together, they climbed the steps and walked toward Pastor Evans and Gio, prepared to pledge their love before their friends and family who had gathered to witness this special occasion.

When it came time to exchange their vows, Cece struggled to contain her emotions.

"Andy, I truly believe that God guided you to find me that day under the bleachers back in high school. You offered me a kindness and compassion that I'd never experienced before. I didn't fully appreciate what it meant back then, but you continued to walk alongside me in the years that followed. Sometimes I'd take for granted that you were there, and time would lapse with no contact between us. But whenever I needed you, even if months had gone by, you were there for me. Thank you for being patient with me. For providing me with a safe place when my world was imploding. For showing me what love is. And for loving me even when I was at my most unlovable. You are an amazing man, and I'm glad that God brought us together. I love you."

Tears shimmered in Andy's eyes as he gazed down at her. He took a deep breath and lifted a hand to wipe his eyes before he spoke. "I had such a crush on you in high school. You were beautiful and always seemed so cheerful. I knew that you'd never notice me, but then one day, our worlds collided. I thought for sure it would be a one-time thing. But then you started to talk to me off and on, and one day, I realized that you actually wanted me around. My feelings for you have grown over the years, from a crush to friendship, and then to love. A love that I was certain you'd never want or return. I have never been so happy to be wrong."

Laughter rippled across the sanctuary.

"These past couple of years, watching you grow in your love for God has been wonderful. Being the recipient of your love has been amazing. You are so beautiful, inside and out, and I love you more than I ever thought possible. I can't wait to love you even more in the years to come."

As they continued through the ceremony, Cece struggled to keep her emotions from spilling over. The happiness she felt was unlike anything she'd ever experienced before.

When Pastor Evans pronounced them husband and wife, Cece happily stepped into Andy's embrace. He wrapped his arms around her, and the world faded to just the two of them as he smiled down at her.

"I love you, darling," she whispered.

"I love you, too, sweetheart."

When his lips touched hers, Cece smiled into the kiss. She couldn't help it. This day was theirs. A celebration of their love and the sometimes-rough journey they'd traveled to get there.

As their kiss ended, they shared a smile, then turned to face all the people who had come to celebrate with them. Many of them were Andy's friends, who had become her friends as well.

A short time later, they were all gathered at Sarah and Beau's home. Tables decorated in lilac and sage were set up across the large stone patio at the back of their house. While the wedding guests were served hors d'oeuvres, the photographer took pictures of Cece and Andy with their close friends and family in the garden which was in full bloom.

When they sat down at their table after the pictures, Cece let her gaze sweep across the people gathered there. That they had come as much to support her as to support Andy still amazed her.

Anna and Eli were there with their two sons, and Anna was part of the current baby boom, as she was due in the next couple of months with their third child. Cece was thankful they had both forgiven her for her attitude toward them when Anna had first come to town and grabbed Eli's attention.

The McNamara family as a whole was growing with Beau and Sarah having recently announced that Sarah was pregnant, though she wasn't showing just yet. Leah wasn't pregnant, but Cece had heard Gavin joking about how he thought it might be time.

Jillian was due any day with her and Carter's first baby, a little girl who Cece knew was going to be loved and cherished by her doting parents.

During one of their conversations about the wedding flowers, Lani had told her that she and Michael were hoping to get pregnant soon with a sibling for their daughter, Vivi, but it hadn't happened yet.

Ryker, Michael's former employee who was now a full-time pediatrician, and his wife, Sophia, were expecting their second child. Sophia was a shy woman, but she'd joined the women's group in the church, where she'd shared that they had suffered a miscarriage. They were all praying that this new pregnancy would go smoothly for her.

While most of the couples had waited a while into their marriage to get pregnant, that hadn't been the case for Emma and Tanner. They had married the previous October, and Emma was now six months pregnant with their honeymoon baby and thrilled about it.

Cece had known Josie Thompson casually since she had stopped by the bakery periodically. But it had only been as she'd seen her more frequently in the bookstore when Cece had been hanging out with Andy that they'd gotten to know each other better. They'd discovered that they shared a parental absence in their lives and also a love for stationery products. Josie and Hawk were scheduled to get married that next month, and Cece looked forward to her and Andy attending their wedding as a married couple.

Every person—whether they were a close friend or more of an acquaintance—was there to share in their happiness.

With a sigh, she leaned against Andy's shoulder. He looked at her, concern on his face. "Everything okay?"

"Everything is perfect." She smiled at him. "I love you so much. This day couldn't have gone any better."

His fingers drifted across her cheek. "I'm so glad. All I really cared about was that we were married by the end of the ceremony, but I'm glad everything else turned out like you wanted it to."

All of a sudden, the sound of people singing drew their attention. Looking over to the end of their table, Cece saw Gavin, Leah, Alessia, and Gio standing together, beaming smiles on their faces as they sang *Let Me Call You Sweetheart.* The lyrics had the word love in them, which Sarah had declared earlier was the only way to get the bridal couple to kiss.

Laughing, Andy got to his feet and held out his hand to Cece. She took it, allowing him to draw her up and into his arms, where they shared a lingering kiss to the applause and whistles from their guests.

Though Cece had been willing to leave New Hope Falls in hopes of protecting Andy, she was so glad she hadn't taken that path. If she had, she would have missed out on so much with these wonderful people and the man she could now call husband.

As she stood in Andy's embrace, Cece looked to the future, imagining how her friendships would continue to grow, and how, one day, she would raise a family with the man she loved in the town that had truly become a place to call home.

~*~ The End ~*~